Cast of Characters

Alexis Paphlagloss. A department store magnate who has recreated a Minoan palace on an island off the coast of California.

Ione Paphlagloss. His daughter. Young and beautiful, is she willing to marry for money?

Jennifer Paphlagloss. Alexis' second wife. She's in her forties but doesn't look it.

Marcus Bayard. Jennifer's son and Paphlagloss's stepson. He has only two interests in life: early American Indians—and his stepsister, Ione.

Dr. Arne Nielsen. One of the foremost experts in the world on Minoan culture. He's there to write his book.

Harvey C. Stoner. Another department store magnate, he wants to form a business alliance with Paphlagloss by marrying his son to his daughter.

Russell Stoner. Harvey's strapping son. He likes to play practical jokes.

Denis Glendon. An impoverished artist, he's there to paint frescoes.

Thomas W. Starr. Caretaker, boatsman and fisherman.

Anne Holden. The cook.

Della Winters. A maid. She was in love with the butler.

Carrie Winters. A maid, sister to Della. She disliked the butler.

Charles Danville. The butler. He's not around very long.

Felix Handleburger. The new butler. He's from England "with a haitch and a hay."

Prof. Theocritus Lucius Westborough. A small man nearing 70, he's an expert on Roman history as well as a superb amateur detective.

The police. Captain Albert Cranston, Investigator Gerald Brown and Constable Elmer Stebbins.

In the Theocritus Lucius Westborough canon:

The Fifth Tumbler, 1936
The Death Angel, 1936
Blind Drifts, 1937
The Purple Parrot, 1937
The Man from Tibet, 1938
The Whispering Ear, 1938
Murder Gone Minoan, 1939
(English title: *Clue to the Labyrinth*)
Dragon's Cave, 1940
Poison Jasmine, 1940
Green Shiver, 1941

MURDER GONE MINOAN

CLYDE B. CLASON

WITH AND INTRODUCTION BY
TOM & ENID SCHANTZ

THE RUE MORGUE PRESS
BOULDER / LYONS

Murder Gone Minoan
0-915230-60-7
was first published in 1939.

Printed by
Johnson Printing

PRINTED IN THE UNITED STATES OF AMERICA

About Clyde B. Clason

CLYDE B. CLASON'S career as a mystery writer took up only five of his 84 years, but in the short span between 1936 and 1941 he produced ten long and very complicated detective novels, all published by the prestigious Doubleday, Doran Crime Club, featuring the elderly historian Professor Theocritus Lucius Westborough.

Born in Denver in 1903, Clason spent many years in Chicago, the setting for several of his novels, including *The Man from Tibet*, before moving to York, Pennsylvania, where he died in 1987. During his early years in Chicago Clason worked as an advertising copywriter and a trade magazine editor, producing books on architecture, period furniture and one book on writing, *How To Write Stories that Sell*. For some reason, Clason stopped selling mysteries on the eve of World War II, although he published several other books, including *Ark of Venus* (1955), a science fiction novel, and *I am Lucifer* (1960), the confessions of the devil as told to Clason. He also produced several nonfiction works dealing with astronomy as well as *The Delights of the Slide Rule* (1964), his last published book-length work.

Why Clason left the crime fiction genre, never to return, remains a mystery today. Long after they went out of print his books remained popular with readers and have always fetched premium prices in the antiquarian book trade. And modern critics, though taking the occasional potshot at his sometimes florid prose, still commend him on his research and ability to construct convincing locked room puzzles.

Indeed, seven of Clason's ten Westborough mysteries feature locked rooms or impossible crimes. Along with John Dickson Carr and Clayton Rawson, Clason was a leading exponent of this very popular subgenre, with locked room mystery connoisseur Robert C.S. Adey referring to the Westborough canon as being among "the more memorable" entries in this narrow field. Adey had special praise for *The Man from Tibet*, calling it a "well-written. . . above average golden-age novel" that was "genuinely interesting, and well researched," and citing its "highly original and practical locked-room murder method."

Other contemporary critics also looked upon this short-lived series with approval. Howard Haycraft, the genre's first major historian, predicted that Clason was on the brink of becoming a mainstay of readers, while two-time Edgar-winning critic James Sandoe listed *The Man from Tibet* in his *Readers' Guide to Crime*, a 1946 compilation of required titles for libraries, noting that this, as well as other Westborough titles, appeared frequently on the lists submitted to him by other critics for inclusion in his guide. Modern critics like Bill Pronzini and Jon L. Breen have also offered kind retrospective reviews of Clason's work, although they disagreed on the merits of at least one of his books, with Pronzini praising *Blind Drifts* (1937) for its "particularly neat and satisfying variation on (the locked-room) theme," while Breen said "the plot is farfetched and overelaborate, and the killer stands out rather obviously." Both critics, however, were impressed with Clason's research in this book in describing the operation of a Colorado gold mine. Breen was far more enthusiastic about *The Man from Tibet*, listing it as one of the 25 best amateur detective books in Max Allan Collins' 2000 *History of Mystery*.

Research was obviously a passion with Clason, who certainly felt the need to provide his readers with an accurate portrait of Tibet, a country whose borders were closed to foreigners and whose religion, a form of Buddhism, was then little-known in this country. Purists might have objected to the amount of space Clason devoted to educating his readers but they can't fault the skill with which he works the fruits of his research into the narrative. Such scholarship is evident in other titles as well, including *Murder Gone Minoan* (1939), in which Clason recreates an ancient civilization on an island off the California coast, or *Green Shiver* (1941), his last mystery, in which the reader learns a great deal about Chinese jade.

Murder Gone Minoan also showcases the author's love of literary quotations. Westborough (and others) throw a bit from Shakespeare or Browning or Homer into their conversations whenever given the chance. Yet, these lines are far from mere window dressing and the reader would be well advised not to ignore this seemingly inconsequential banter. Very little of what Clason incorporates into his books is without motive. This was the age of "fair play" detection and Clason was a master of the form, planting clues and hints for the reader on practically every page.

Clason's narrative skills were not inconsiderable, although modern readers might wish that his characters could deliver their lines with more "he saids" or "she askeds" than with such Tom Swifty's as "he choked" or "he opined." On the other hand, it's somewhat refreshing to read a mystery in which ejaculations refer only to exclamations of speech.

Like other mystery writers of the day, Clason was not above inserting a little romance into his stories. In the crime novels of that era—Georgette Heyer's mysteries spring immediately to mind—such romantic entanglements were actually useful in helping the reader sort out potential murder suspects. If you could figure out which two young people would eventually find their star-crossed way to each other, you could automatically eliminate two suspects from your list. A wise reader of *Murder Gone Minoan* would do well to sort out such relationships. On the other hand, Westborough, like many other central characters of the period, seems if not asexual, at least beyond or above such temptations.

Unlike many other mystery novels of the time, Clason's books are remarkably free of racial prejudice, at least on the part of the ever-rational Westborough, who on more than one occasion gently rebukes his companions for expressing racist sentiments. In *The Man from Tibet* he even manages to find a kind word or two (their foreign policy notwithstanding) to say about the Japanese, who were at the time plundering most of their neighbors in a dress rehearsal for World War II. Clason recognized that anti-Japanese sentiment was rampant among most Americans of the late 1930s. Westborough's best friend, Lt. Mack, has little use for "Japs" and when the two visit a Chicago Japanese restaurant for lunch, Clason subtly mentions that the place is nearly empty. Westborough unfailingly treats the Tibetan characters with understanding and respect, going out of his way to explain to all the linguistic differences that account for their difficulties with the English language.

Too often modern critics excuse writers of the 1930s, like Agatha Christie or Dorothy L. Sayers, for fostering racial prejudice or anti-Semitic views, by jokingly dismissing complaints about such lapses as runaway political correctness. What these apologists forget is that while it may be acceptable and even necessary for an author to show that such views were commonplace at the time (as Clason does), the authorial expression of such views is never acceptable. Take for example, Bruce Hamilton's 1930 English mystery, *To Be Hanged* (much praised by those two great snobs of crime fiction, Jacques Barzun and Wendell Hertig Taylor) in which a very minor—and very disagreeable—character is offhandedly described in the narrative as a "little Jew." It is to Clason's great credit that he was able, in the words of Ruth Rendell, to fulfill "the duty of the artist in rising above the petty prejudices of the day."

Like other fair-play mysteries of the day, Clason's books tend to end very abruptly once the murderer is revealed. Yet, even some of his biggest fans, like Pronzini, suggest that his books could have been improved by some judicious editing to cut their length from 80,000 words to 65,000.

On the other hand, 80,000 or more words was the rule rather than the exception in the mysteries of Clason's era. It was not until World War II, when paper restrictions prompted publishers to use lighter paper and to cram more words on a page, that the length of a typical mystery was reduced to 60,000 words. This will fill 192 pages, the number needed to make up six 32-page signatures, a very economical size book to produce. This has remained the standard until quite recently, and it wasn't so long ago that Dodd, Mead cut—without explanation or editing to make sense—a major character from a Wendy Hornsby mystery just to ensure that the book did not exceed 192 pages.

Today, however, publishers are once again looking for bigger books, especially with "breakout" or bestselling authors, and a number of books in the crime fiction field have suffered from this verbal bloating. P.D. James, for example, started out writing tightly crafted gems, but all of her books after *An Unsuitable Job for a Woman* (1972) bog down in endless details about the contents of suitcases or in long pieces of melancholy introspection by her leading characters.

Clyde B. Clason, at least, stayed away from such pretentious drivel. Indeed, it's his asides into Tibetan culture, or Chinese jade, or the working of a gold mine, as well as his unobtrusive social commentary, that make his books as appealing to today's readers as they were to those of the pre-World War II era, even if his plots and characters are decidedly old-fashioned. Why he did not make the transition into the modern era will probably never be known, but we can't help but wonder if he was unable or unwilling to produce the shorter, more streamlined mysteries the Crime Club insisted upon after the country went to war. Whatever the reason, it's our loss, but he still left behind a remarkable body of work considering the brief portion of his life he devoted to the writing of mystery fiction.

Tom & Enid Schantz
Lyons, Colorado
Autumn 2003

CONTENTS

ACKNOWLEDGMENT *is gratefully made to Frank A. Nance, Coroner of Los Angeles County, and Captain R. A. Cook, Fairfax Sheriff's Substation, Hollywood, for their kind cooperation; to Elsdon C. Smith and P. C. B. for the help they have so willingly given me on this and the previous six Westborough stories; to Edwin F. Walker, research associate of the Southwest Museum, Los Angeles, for a great deal of information on extinct Southern California Indians, and to Herbert B. Copeland for many valuable suggestions.*

C. B. C.

MURDER GONE MINOAN

PART ONE: ADMISSIBLE IN EVIDENCE

Exhibit A. Letter from Denis Glendon to Fred Davidson —June 9

DEAR FRED:

What do you know about Minoan art? I thought not. Neither did I up to a few days ago, but now I do, and thereby hangs a tale of paint and plaster.

Both the said p. and p. are at present on the walls of the garage above which I live in true Bohemian fashion, sleeping on a studio couch and cooking what purport to be meals on a two-burner hot plate. As you know, my affairs have been going from bad to worse financially until now bankruptcy stares me merrily in the face—but enough of such doleful matters.

The garage was being replastered, and the smell of fresh mortar set my fingers itching to work at my old trade of fresco painting. (Jobs in that line have been few and far between, my boy.) On my assurance that the walls could always be plastered again if the picture didn't please him, Baker, my landlord, grudgingly said yes, and his wife selected the subject. That is, she asked me to copy her favorite chromolithograph, "An Afternoon in Venice," which looks just as you'd expect. However, both male and female Bakers were delighted with the blue monstrosity, and here's where Minoan art comes in. Baker, it seems, is an executive at the Los Angeles headquarters of Minos Stores, Inc.

Does that name mean anything to you? It would out here in the City of the Angels. The Minos stores (about a dozen strong, I think) are scattered up and down the Pacific coast and as far east as Kansas City, united under the determined slogan: "We will not be undersold." The controlling genius is a Greek by the name of Paphlagloss who was born in Crete. Is the connection clear? No? I'll have to go on and elucidate.

In the bronze age, somewhere around three thousand years ago, Crete was inhabited by a very superior race of human beings. The Greeks had a word for them, and so do modern archaeologists: several in fact, the most accepted of which is probably "Minoans." After King Minos, naturally. (Do you remember the story of Theseus and Ariadne?) Minos, authorities now believe, wasn't a personal name, but a royal title. Cretans of that prehistoric era would speak of their ruler as "*the* Minos" just as Egyptians called theirs "*the* Pharaoh." And the Minoans were more advanced in some ways than the historic Greeks, who came along a thousand years afterwards. They even knew about plumbing, including water closets, a discovery that no other ancient people had the wit to hit on. (Or sit on, if you must be vulgar.)

Enough of ribaldry. When it came to art these fellows were good. They mixed up front and profile eyes now and then, but, overlooking such details, they had what it takes. I've spent the past several days in the public library poring over reproductions of Cretan frescoes and reliefs, and it's good stuff by any standards!

Nobody knows where these prehistoric Cretans came from and nobody knows exactly what happened to them. They were suddenly blotted out as though the ocean had swallowed them—some people believe that the lost Cretan culture was the grain or so of reality behind the persistent Atlantis tradition. Ho hum! Stop yawning, Fred, will you? I'm coming to the point.

Paphlagloss, the Grand Panjandrum of the Minos stores, looks on those old fellows more or less as his own ancestors. Now and then he has a window display in one of his stores, just to show the gapers what sort of civilization they had back in those days. And he's built a home on an island near L.A. that's named and modeled after their most famous palace, Knossos. No, he isn't nuts, my boy. Anybody who knows the secret of making millions out of department stores is sane enough for my taste. And here's the point at last:

The original Knossos went in strong for frescoes, but Knossos Number Two hasn't as yet. Its builder has been waiting for a mural artist whom he can trust to convey the authentic Minoan spirit, which is where I come in. Provided that I'm willing to learn a few things about Cretan art, in order not to let him down too badly, Baker has agreed to drop a hint in the proper ears about my abilities. I'm working now on a series of sketches to show to the Minos, as his employees call him, if and when an interview can be arranged. Probably nothing will come of it, but at least it's another chance to stave off Old Man Bankruptcy.

Yours,
DENNY

Exhibit B. Entry in Journal of Ione Paphlagloss

June 9—I should be grateful to Jennifer for saving me from a fortune hunter, but "should be" and "am" are not always parts of the same verb, grammarians to the contrary. Part of me whispers to be glad it's over, but only part. It was sweet while it lasted, sweet, and something I shall never know again. Never!

I can't be myself, Ione, born in 1915 to Eleanor and Alexis Paphlagloss. I can't be allowed to forget that I am the heiress of the president, chairman of the board, principal owner and controlling genius of Minos Stores, Inc. Not because of fatherly affection—he's displayed mighty little of that—but because of some mental quirk that makes the claims of his only flesh-and-blood descendant seem more important to him than any other.

Poor, cheated, deluded Jennifer! He doesn't love her any more than he does me. If Alexis loves anyone, it's a lovely little lady of gold and ivory, who was worshipped as a goddess by the builders of gypsum palaces centuries before the Trojan War. But the Lady of the Golden Serpents cannot inherit—*quel dommage!* So Jennifer gets her pension, I practically everything else, and Marc nothing. And the only one of us who's really satisfied is Marc. Weedy, goggle-eyed Marc!

Funny, single-minded Marc! It would be rather startling for a stranger to wander in as I did last night and find him with half-a-dozen grinning skulls on his desk like a Hollywood Hamlet. Marc wouldn't soliloquize over poor Yorick though; he'd be too busy taking Yorick's skull measurements. It would be so easy to make him happy. Marc, not Yorick. And to make Jennifer happy at the same time, since his future is what she really cares about. Shall I? Is it worth while? I doubt it.

Exhibit C-1. Letter from Marc Bayard to Dr. Ernest Helm —June 11

DEAR DR. HELM:

I am happy to report that Site Number 3 is yielding a fruitful collection of artifacts, now being boxed and crated for shipment, and that Mr. Paphlagloss assures me that he will be only too happy to make the presentation of these valuable historical relics to the Garrick Museum. In accordance with your recent request, I am enclosing a description of the island for the museum's monthly bulletin.

Sincerely yours,
MARCUS A. BAYARD

Exhibit C-2. Supplement to Bayard's Letter of June 11

ISLAND OF THE SILVER GIRDLE

By Marcus A. Bayard

Isleta del Cinturon de Plata, to use the beautiful name of Sebastian Vizcaino, is one of the lesser members of the Channel Islands of California. Lying about twenty miles from the mainland, it may be reached in half-an-hour's speedboat run from the town of Ynez on the extreme northern coast of Los Angeles County.

Topography

The island is three miles from north to south and one and a quarter miles at the widest point from east to west, comprising about 2000 acres. In shape it may be likened to a roughly drawn figure 8, the indentation in the eastern or lee side forming the harbor above which the home of Mr. Paphlagloss (at present the only residence) is picturesquely located.

There is little level land on the island. The surface is a network of crisscrossing ridges, covered in patches by a thick chaparral. Numerous canyons descend to the sea, and the shoreline is marked by precipitous cliffs of varying heights. On the western or ocean side the continuous surging of the breakers has worn a large number of caves, in the conglomerate of which the island walls are formed.

History

The island is mentioned in the log of Cabrillo as the foggy islet (Islets de las Nieblas). Vizcaino rechristened it, bestowing the appellation the island retains today: Isleta del Cinturon de Plata (isle or islet of the silver girdle). This name, as well as the more prosaic one of Cabrillo, was undoubtedly suggested by the fog which (particularly during the early morning and late afternoon) appears from the sea like a broad belt of silver.

The title of the island has been traced to a Spanish grant of 1740, but the task of tracing it reveals little of excitement in its history. It appears to have had no other use than as a sheep and wild goat pasturage prior to its purchase by Alexis Paphlagloss in the summer of 1934. Mr. Paphlagloss has since built there his beautiful and unique home, Knossos.

Archaeology

At the time of this island's discovery by the Spanish, it was occupied by a now extinct tribe of Indians, but it is difficult to determine whether these were of the Chumash or Shoshonean races. The culture shows definite Chumash influence, but it is scarcely necessary to remind readers of this bulletin that Santa Catalina artifacts also exhibit the characteristics of Chumash civilization, perhaps even in its highest form. Yet Santa Catalina was certainly occupied by Shoshoneans.

Unfortunately, little documentary evidence exists to aid the archaeologist. Fray Pepe Romero, an eighteenth century chronicler, reveals that the primitive inhabitants persisted so stubbornly in their adherence to Chungichnish and the toloache cult that it was necessary to take "disciplinary action" against them. The good father describes with abhorrence the manner of preparing and drinking "the devil's brew." So detailed is his knowledge, that the writer believes the Island of the Silver Girdle was one of the centers of the cult which was once so widely practiced among these vanished races. As confirmation, he mentions the discovery of a valley near Site Number 3 in which the large flowering datura (*D. meteloides)* grows in profusion, and the unearthing of a few small but beautifully wrought mortars and pestles which may have been once used for pounding the roots of the plant.

Exhibit D. Letter from Arne Nielsen to Alexis Paphlagloss —June 12

DEAR SIR:

Your interest in Cretan prehistory is so well known that possibly you may have read my *Minoan Culture,* in which event I shall not be addressing you as a total stranger. If you have not read it, as is probably the case since one's ego nearly always leads one to overestimate the importance of one's achievements, please allow me to introduce my self. I am Arne Nielsen, Ph.D., professor of Greek History at Prescott University, University City, Pennsylvania, and author of a number of works of comparatively little merit, such as *A Short History of Greece* and *The Greece of Homeric Ages* (inflicted upon my luckless pupils), a monograph on the battle of Aegospotami, a biographical study of Alcibiades, and, of course, my *Minoan Culture.*

I am utilizing the summer holidays for a new work tentatively titled "The Derivation of the Asiatic Mother-Goddess from the Baetylic Cult of Neolithic Crete," in which I shall endeavor to prove that the Minoan snake goddess, Diktynna, is the common ancestress of such widely separated fertility deities as Aphrodite, Astarte, Cybele and Ishtar.

I have made a close examination of the chryselephantine figurine in the Boston Museum. You, I believe, possess the only other such figurine of the Cretan snake-goddess in existence. May I inquire in what manner it came into your possession and how you succeeded in bringing it from Greece? I ask these questions in no spirit of impertinence, but with a sincere desire to aid in the preservation of the very little that is known about the enigmatic but fascinating Minoan goddess. And if it is possible to trespass so far on your good nature, I should like permission to examine the statuette in person. I will gladly travel from Pennsylvania to California if you are willing to allow me this inestimable privilege.

Trusting that I may hear from you soon, I remain

Sincerely,
A. NIELSEN

Exhibit E. Letter from H.C. Stoner to .Alexis Paphlagloss —June 14

DEAR ALEXIS:

Surely wish to thank you for your kind invitation to visit Knossos, which I gladly accept. Deep-sea fishing has always appealed to me, and I'll welcome the chance for another crack at a marlin or tuna. May I bring my son Russell? The young fellow has just graduated from college and is temporarily at a loose end. I am planning, of course, on training him to eventually step into his father's shoes.

Speaking of business, have you given more thought to my proposition? I feel sure that it would be to the interests of both of us to consolidate our enterprises. The details, of course, have yet to be arranged, but I hope to have a concrete plan to submit to you when we arrive at Knossos. That should be on the first of July, so we'll be able to spend the Fourth with you.

Very truly yours,
HARVEY

Exhibit P. Letter from Alexis Paphlagloss to Harvey Stoner —June 17

DEAR H.C.:

Glad that you can come and hope that you will find the fishing all that I've claimed for it. By all means bring Russell. My daughter Ione and my stepson Marcus are approximately the same age, and the three can keep each other entertained. Ione will be pleased as the summer has been rather dull so far.

The details of the proposed merger remain, as you say, to be worked out. Naturally, I will not agree to any plan which would remove me from control of the Minos stores. Even though your chain is the larger of the two, the consolidation will be more to your advantage than to mine. However, I shall be glad to listen to any reasonable proposition.

Sincerely yours,
ALEXIS

Exhibit G. Letter from Alexis Paphlagloss to A. Nielsen —June 17

DEAR DR. NIELSEN:

Your *Minoan Culture* holds an honored place in the library of Knossos. (My island home, I must explain, and not the original Cretan palace.)

The chryselephantine figurine of the snake-goddess was discovered by my father, Stephanos Paphlagloss, in a cave in the mountains near Candia, where he was hiding to escape the Ottoman troops. My father, I claim with some pride, played a prominent part in the insurrection of 1889 and later became a member of the *Ethniké Hetairia,* a Greek secret society which aimed at the liberation of Crete and Macedonia from Turkish rule.

When I was no more than six years old, my mother was seized by Turkish soldiers. One of my most vivid memories is of her screams as they tortured her, vainly, I am proud to say, in an effort to make her divulge my father's hiding place. Three years later, when I had attained the ripe age of nine, my father risked imprisonment to see me. On that occasion he gave me the ivory figurine, explaining where he had found it. This was the last time, I might add, that I ever saw my father, who was killed in the general rebellion of 1897. But to return to the figurine:

This image, which measures only 7 inches high, was hidden in a natural niche at the back of a ledge in the cave in which my father was taking refuge. Swathed in linen like an Egyptian mummy, it fitted snugly within a hermetically sealed clay cylinder on the outside of which were incised several lines of writing in Linear Script B, like all Minoan script as yet undeciphered. The carving is of great beauty, and the goldsmith's work truly exquisite.

I could write a great deal more which might be of interest for your book, but I believe it would be to your advantage to see the figurine yourself. I suggest, Dr. Nielsen, that you stay with us the duration of your holidays. Really, I can think of no other place than the second Knossos so appropriate in which to write your book. I will not take no for an answer; it will be a pleasure to entertain so distinguished a scholar. Bring Mrs. Nielsen with you; there is plenty of room for her and your children.

Sincerely yours,
ALEXIS PAPHLAGLOSS

Exhibit H. Letter from Russell Stoner to Rosalie Evans —June 23

HELLO BEAUTIFUL!

Just when I was planning to get away from this grind and join you at the lake, the old boy throws his weight around and insists I got to go with him to California. A Greek named Paphlagloss out there owns some cut-rate stores the old boy would like to take over, and he thinks it would be good training for me to be on the spot when the deal goes through. Besides, the Greek has a daughter I'm supposed to be nice to.

No, gorgeous, I can't get away for a weekend; the old boy is making me sweat learning the ins and outs of this department-store racket. Business is business, honey.

But don't worry about this Greek baby who I have to kid along to keep Papa Paphlagloss happy. She's probably fat, greasy and sloppy. Besides I don't like Greeks. Even if she was good-looking, I wouldn't give her a tumble.

You know who's got her name on my ticket, keed.

RUSS

Exhibit I. Letter from Arne Nielsen to Alexis Paphlagloss —June 23

DEAR MR. PAPHLAGLOSS:

What can a lowly professor say? Your generous invitation completely overwhelms me, but I shall accept with alacrity lest your better judgment persuade you to rescind it. There is, however, no Mrs. Nielsen and consequently (although not always inevitably) no children. I shall arrive at Knossos on June 30 if that date is convenient.

As a slight return for your kindness—a very slight return, I acknowledge—may I be allowed to dedicate the work on the Baetylic cult to you? Trusting that this will not be displeasing, I remain

Sincerely,
A. NIELSEN

Exhibit J. Letter from Denis Glendon to Fred Davidson —June 29

DEAR FRED:

I drew my inspiration from a line of Plutarch: "In Crete it was the custom for the women as well as the men to see the games; and Ariadne, being present, was struck with the person of Theseus."

The games, if archaeologists have guessed right, were those of the bull ring. While I studied over the sentence, the whole vanished civilization sketched itself on my paper, and I saw those Cretan court beauties of a thousand years before Pericles.

They sit on terraced steps; they lean languidly against tapering pillars. Their flaring skirts are stiff as crinolines; their bodices lace audaciously below the universally bared breasts. Hair is flaunted in kiss curls across foreheads, in ringlets before the ears, in black wavy tresses over graceful shoulders. Women, pleasure-loving as Venetians, born to ease and fine linens! They laugh, talk, gesticulate among themselves, but she whose rank is highest of all—the Princess Ariadne—sits apart and sorrows secretly.

A stranger, an Achaian barbarian uncouthly named Theseus, is destined in a few moments to meet the Minotaur. She watches him as he stands in the oblong arena below the terraces. Unlike the copper-bronzed Cretans in loincloths and rolled girdles, he wears the short-sleeved *chiton* of classical Greece. He bears himself proudly among his foemen, but courage, even when coupled with the strength he has exhibited in the wrestling ring, will not suffice to save him from the Minotaur who, behind a grating of wooden bars, paws the ground and bellows like a thunderclap. The monster is no mythological beast-man, but a shaggy bull, larger by half again than any alive today, with horns two feet long, and Theseus is required to face him without weapons. It is a tradition of a thousand years and more that the sacred animal cannot be killed with the aid of metal.

Cretan athletes, men and women alike, trained from infancy and lithe-limbed as leopards, are able to dart swiftly aside from the bull's mad rushes, grasp his gigantic horns, vault gracefully over his bellowing head or somersault through the air above his broad back. But Theseus, though powerful, is untrained; these showy circus stunts are out of the question for him. Moreover, it is beneath the dignity of an Athenian prince to be chased by a bull in order to make a Cretan holiday. He folds his arms resignedly across his broad chest while wasp-waisted attendants prepare to loose the raging monster.

On the terrace Ariadne watches in agony. Is there nothing that can be done to halt this slaughter? Yes, one thing. It means breaking the tradition of a thousand years, but she hesitates scarcely an instant. She beckons to an officer with a plumed crest, who kneels before his princess. She snatches the long bronze sword from his girdle, throws it with both hands over the heads of the spectators and into the ring. There are cries of shame, of rage, of horror, but it is too late to undo the work of Ariadne's mad impulse. Theseus stoops, brandishes the sharp bronze weapon, and the bull charges!

Excuse the rhapsody, but I'm really steamed up about this thing. It's the best of a dozen scenes I've sketched in watercolors for this Greek department-store owner, Alexis Paphlagloss. I've used Venetian red and saffron yellow and sky blue—vivid primitive colors such as the Minoans loved—and I've copied their faults as well as their virtues. Who am I to correct the work of artists of thirty-five hundred years ago? Baker's made an appointment for me tomorrow morning with Paphlagloss. And I hope to hell that one or two of the things will catch his fancy. So wish me luck.

Yours,
DENNY

Exhibit K. Entry in Journal of Ione Paphlagloss

June 25—It seems that we are to have company. A professor of Greek history, who is writing a book on the Cretan goddess, will probably be only a minor nuisance. The major ones will be Harvey Stoner of Stoner Sterling Stores and his son Russell. The Lord of Knossos has given me a by no means veiled hint to treat the latter kindly. A sort of royal ukase, but what difference does it make? A bore, of course, but the fate of one born under the sign of the silver cocktail shaker, ah, woe is me!

Last night Alexis was all aglow because of some watercolors an artist submitted. They weren't bad, particularly one called "Theseus at Knossos." Alexis thinks they're marvelous. He's going to have this artist do a pair of them in fresco along the walls of our gloomy entrance passageway. He wants them right away, too—much to Jennifer's intense disgust, since fresco painting requires the walls to be replastered as the work goes on. Rather a mess for company to walk into, but what do I care? What do I care about anything that happens in this beastly pile of concrete and stucco which Alexis deludedly believes to be a home?

Exhibit L. Telegram to Theocritus Lucius Westborough —July 5

MR. T.L. WESTBOROUGH
HOTEL EQUABLE CHICAGO ILL
LOCAL POLICE HAVE RECOMMENDED YOU AS PRIVATE INVESTIGATOR TO UNDERTAKE HIGHLY CONFIDENTIAL MISSION STOP YOUR SERVICES URGENTLY NEEDED STOP PLEASE TAKE PLANE TO LOS ANGELES STOP SEE ME THURSDAY AT MINOS DEPARTMENT STORE THIS CITY STOP ALL EXPENSES PAID STOP NAME YOUR OWN FEE WHEN YOU HAVE HEARD PROPOSITION

ALEXIS PAPHLAGLOSS

PART TWO: A CASE FOR MR. WESTBOROUGH

(Thursday, July 7—Friday, July 8)

I

THEOCRITUS LUCIUS WESTBOROUGH, the author of *Trajan: His Life and Times,* of *Heliogabalus, Rome's Most Degenerate Emperor,* and noted among a select few for services to society of somewhat more startling interest, shook the hand of the man whose telegram had whisked him through the air from Chicago to Los Angeles as on a magic carpet. Alexis Paphlagloss, familiarly known to his hundreds of employees as "the Minos," wished his guest good morning and trusted he had had a pleasant journey.

"A very exhilarating one. My first major experience with air travel, I am chagrined to relate."

The historian seemed a trifle overawed by the richness of oak-paneled walls, luxurious divans, torcheres symmetrically doing guard duty and russet carpeting, the soft thick nap of which smothered footsteps as foundered ships are swallowed by the restless sea. In such a room—or in any other for that matter—frail, white-haired and undersized Westborough did not look impressive. His triangular face, though broad enough at the forehead, narrowed to a small pointed chin and his eyes, a very mild blue, peered nearsightedly behind gold-rimmed bifocals.

The Minos indicated a Spanish chair, thickly studded with ornate metal protuberances. "Shall we get down to business?"

"To brass tacks," the historian amended, ruefully eying those on which he was expected to sit. The joke—if it were worthy to be termed such—fell on ears utterly unresponsive. Westborough was constrained to wonder if the well-fed gentleman who occupied a carved walnut desk chair as a king a throne possessed a sense of humor. It did not matter. The portly Paphlagloss had many other laudable qualities, including the one most highly valued in the United States today. He knew how to make money.

"This," Paphlagloss said decisively, "is not a murder case." There was a hint of the predatory in the steel-gray brigand's mustache which flourished luxuriantly beneath his formidable nose. Contradictory to the nose and mustache, however, was the ruddy conviviality of the Greek's full-moon face. Contradictory again were the piercing black eyes of a Balkan bandit, and contradictory to all a cloak of cosmopolitan urbanity. Eleutherios Venizelos had also been born in Crete, Westborough reflected. An island which can produce such men as these is worth watching.

Aloud he said, "I am glad to know that it is not murder."

"You were recommended to me by an official of the Los Angeles police department, whom I consulted privately."

"Lieutenant Collins, perhaps? I met him in connection with the Launay affair."

"He spoke of you highly. I am hopeful that you will be able to bring about the return of my property."

"Such slight experience as I have had has been largely accident," Westborough demurred.

"Nevertheless, you have solved a number of perplexing mysteries."

"Say rather that I have unofficially assisted the police officers in charge of those cases," Westborough stipulated. The Minos shrugged. "It will be necessary for you to mingle unsuspected with my other guests. First, do you have any engagements which would prevent you from spending the next two weeks with me?"

"I can think of none."

"Good. Where's your luggage?"

"At the Biltmore."

The Minos issued terse instructions into a telephone. "My chauffeur will pick it up," he said, "and settle for your hotel bill. As soon as we have finished our talk, we will leave for Knossos. Your detective feats, I believe, are not known to a large number of people?"

"A very small circle, fortunately."

"Let's check on that before we go further. Are you personally acquainted with Harvey Stoner of Stoner Sterling Stores?"

"I have not the honor."

"Or Doctor Arne Nielsen of Prescott University?"

"Only by reputation. Our work, however, lies in adjacent fields."

"Very well, then, you will appear in your true character of the eminent Roman historian."

"Eminent is perhaps too laudatory a word," Westborough protested modestly.

"It is the right word," the Minos insisted. "I've checked with my book department on the sales of your *Heliogabalus.* Now I must bring you to Knossos in a way that will arouse no one's suspicions—very difficult to do in view of my recent loss."

"Loss?" Westborough repeated. "May I ask what is—"

"How's this?" Paphlagloss exclaimed crisply. "We are friends of long standing. Our friendship dates back to, to—let me see—to Washington during the war. I was a dollar-a-year man, and you were a—"

"A Christian slave," Westborough suggested facetiously.

Paphlagloss did not smile. "Well, you may say anything you please. My daughter was only three years old when we were in Washington, and I didn't marry my present wife until 1923. Naturally, I invite so old a friend to stay at my home when he happens to drop into my office. These precautions are necessary, I believe, since your mission will be delicate."

"What is my mission, may I ask?"

"To recover something which has been stolen from me by a guest or by a servant at Knossos. An article of unique and irreplaceable value."

"Dear me! Such an object would be—"

"A chryselephantine figurine of the Cretan snake-goddess."

II

The Minos rang for his secretary. "Please bring me the recent correspondence with Doctor Arne Nielsen. Also one of the photographs from my private file 'S.' " When the secretary had complied, he said to Westborough, "Before going any farther, I suggest you read the carbon copy of my letter to Doctor Nielsen."

"Dear me!" Westborough remarked upon conclusion of his reading. "This is most amazing! I thought there was only one such figurine in the world—the one in the Boston Museum."

"Here's the photo the Los Angeles Times ran in its Sunday rotogravure section a few months ago."

The Minoan snake-goddess had neither the rigid gloom of Egyptian images nor the cold perfection of Greek marbles, but was warmly and winsomely human. Studying the glossy print intently, Westborough saw that she wore a skirt of many flounces, sloping in a bell-shaped cone from her tightly girdled waist, and a bodice cut in the ne plus ultra of décolleté to expose her full naked breasts. A snake coiled about each of her extended forearms. The reptiles which, even in the photograph, twined and hissed with such sinuous realism were of gold, Paphlagloss said informatively. Her girdle was also gold and so was the hem of her skirt, but the rest was ivory, every line perfectly and exquisitely carved.

"Marvelous!" Westborough breathed in admiration. "What a high state of civilization they must have attained to do such wonderful work."

"This little ivory lady is my mascot," Paphlagloss declared earnestly. "I brought her with me from Crete nearly forty years ago. Years later—when I had time to study something besides business—I learned of her aristocratic lineage. We rose in the world together, so to speak. I'd give almost anything to get her back again."

"Perhaps," Westborough suggested gently, "it might be well if you related to me the circumstances of her disappearance."

"She was stolen on the evening of the Fourth while we were gathered on the terrace to watch the display of fireworks. Supposedly every member of the household—family, servants and guests—was on the terrace, but the flares of Greek fire and the bursts of brilliance from skyrockets and Roman candles alternated with periods of darkness. In the excitement and confusion it wouldn't be hard for one person to slip into the house unnoticed. A guest or a servant."

"How many servants do you maintain at Knossos?"

"Five. A butler, a cook, two maids and my caretaker. A skeleton staff, but it's difficult to get servants who are willing to maroon themselves on an island."

"And your guests?"

"At present four. Nielsen and Stoner, whom I've already mentioned, Mr. Stoner's son Russell and Denis Glendon, a young artist."

"And your family?"

"My daughter, my wife and my stepson."

"Your daughter, I believe you said, is not the child of the present Mrs. Paphlagloss?"

"That's correct. Ione's mother was Eleanor Staughton of the Santa Barbara Staughtons whom I married in 1914—the year after I established my first store. This very store at Sixth and Hill, but, needless to say, a good deal smaller. She was killed in 1920—fell from a horse—and I married my present wife three years later."

"May I ask the age of your stepson, Mr. Paphlagloss?"

"Same age as Ione—twenty-three. Boy's a bit of a problem. No head for business. Only thing he's interested in is Indian archaeology, and he can't make a living from that."

"Where was the snake-goddess habitually kept?" Westborough inquired.

"In a glass case in the room where Marc keeps his collection of relics. I've fixed up a shrine for her with authentic Minoan surroundings."

"Was this case locked?"

"Yes, ordinarily. No sense putting temptation in the way of a servant. But the goddess wasn't stolen from there. She was taken from Nielsen's room."

"Dear me! Will you explain the circumstances?"

"I turned over a key of the shrine to Nielsen, naturally, since he'd traveled all the way from Pennsylvania just to see my figurine. He had it in his room, taking detailed measurements, before joining us on the terrace, and when he went back there he found it gone."

"Indeed?"

"Nielsen's tremendously upset, naturally. Feels personally responsible." The mercurial Greek temperament emerged in the crisp staccato of the Minos' speech. "Don't know what to think myself. Can't think of any motive. Except for Nielsen—but that's absurd."

"Have you received offers for the purchase of your figurine?" Westborough asked.

"Only one. From the Metropolitan Museum."

"An organization beyond suspicion. You know of no private individual who might covet the Minoan lady?"

"Not to the extent of financing her theft."

"And it would be very difficult to dispose of such an objet d'art on the open market." Westborough pondered. "It is a perplexing problem! Have you conducted a search?"

"The matter was a little too delicate as far as my guests were concerned. With the servants, of course, I could be more direct."

"Yes, of course. Have any of your guests left the island since the theft?"

"Not to my knowledge. There's a slight possibility one borrowed a boat to make the journey at night. In fact, my daughter told me that she did hear the noise of a motor last night, but that was probably the boat Charles took."

"Charles?" Westborough repeated inquiringly.

"My butler. He departed unexpectedly, and left no more notice than a typewritten note to say that his sister's illness made it imperative for him to go to her, and he hoped I would excuse him."

"A little odd, was it not?"

"Yes, very."

"Do you suspect him of the theft?"

"No, I don't. He's been with me for ten years, and is loyal to the core. And yet," the Minos added slowly, "there was something damnably wrong about that note. Charles knows very well I know he hasn't any sister."

III

"May I ask," Westborough ventured to interpose just before they left the office, "if you took steps to discover the typewriter upon which your butler's note was written?"

"There's only one typewriter at Knossos—my stepson's."

"Is it readily accessible to others?"

"Accessible to anyone. Show you when we get out there." Paphlagloss halted en route to the door. "I'm going to give you the room next to Nielsen's."

"Any room you care to allot to me will be most satisfactory, I'm sure."

"A door connects the two rooms, and I carried the key away with me this morning. After dinner I'll see that Nielsen is detained downstairs while you . . ." He paused, leaving the sentence unfinished. "I don't exactly suspect him. The author of *Minoan Culture* should be above suspicion as a common thief. Still—well, I'd feel better if you searched his room, that's all."

Westborough bowed. He did not like the assignment, but he recognized its necessity. "May I express a hope," he said, "that Doctor Nielsen, a scholar for whose intellect I have great esteem, shall be fully vindicated?"

The Minos gave a perfunctory answer, and they left his private office to descend to the ground level. A uniformed chauffeur was waiting for them at the store's Sixth Street entrance. With exactly the proper grade of deference, he opened the door of a long black limousine.

"Mr. Westborough's luggage is in the trunk, sir."

"Good. To Knossos, Stephen."

The chauffeur respectfully touched the peak of his cap and climbed into his seat. How could he receive such an order so casually?

Westborough wondered. Knossos! The name held magic. It conjured pictures of a civilization which may have been the foundation of Plato's lost Atlantis, a civilization of stone oil lamps, fountains, parabolically curved runnels, plumbing fixtures most curiously modern, paved roads and arched bridges, chariots and swift war galleys. It made one think of a vast palace city of gypsum walls and painted pillars and glorious frescoes; a complex of courts and terraces, stately porticoes and colossal staircases, deep light wells and sunken treasure vaults; wings and chambers linked by an endless maze of stone-floored passages. It conveyed strange scenes of bull-leaping gymnastics—feats which were only half sport—and a vision of the forgotten lady of the lovely face, the Mother of Gods whose signs were the serpent and the dove. "The mighty city Cnossus, wherein ruled Minos, he who held converse with great Zeus."

The chauffeur guided the bulky limousine into the westbound traffic of Wilshire Boulevard, while the other Minos, he who held converse with modest Westborough, talked discreetly of baseball and deep-sea fishing. They passed Vermont and Western avenues, La Brea and Fairfax; they curved northward past Beverly Hills and into Santa Monica, and the Minos spoke dolefully of business and politics.

"The depression that's coming will make this one look like prosperity. When government spending is stopped, the whole lunatic financial setup will collapse like a house of cards. Wait and see! I've made my plans for the deluge, and the best advice I can give you is to do the same."

"Dear me!" Westborough exclaimed, reflecting that those most comfortably situated invariably hold the gloomiest views of the nation's future. The Minos bitterly criticized the country's banking system; Westborough, who knew very little of business and lacked the arguments to refute his host's pessimism, thoughtfully regarded the scenery.

Civilization had been left to the south with Santa Monica, and they were sandwiched now between hills and sea. The Pacific hurled its challenging waves against sandy stretches of beach, eddied in foamy swirls about the rock masses with the temerity to invade its blue domain. The mountains grudgingly moved back from the road a trifle, they passed beach houses gay with striped awnings, and halted finally in the tiny coast town of Ynez. Here they parked before the post office. The postmistress, Paphlagloss informed his guest, was likewise the wife of the township constable, who maintained his own office inside.

While Paphlagloss entered the premises on an errand of his own, Westborough, employing his time in conversation with Stephen, learned that the chauffeur slept at the village and garaged the car here. Transportation facilities appeared to be at a premium at Ynez, but Knossos itself was even more isolated. It did not, the chauffeur informed Westborough, even possess a telephone, since the cost of laying an ocean cable was prohibitive even to a millionaire. The island was just visible on the horizon, a tiny purple wafer sealing the line between sky and sea.

The Minos reappeared from the post office. Whether he had gone to see postmistress or township constable, the interview had resulted in a worried look on his previously jovial face. He led the way in silence to the pier where a trim-looking speedboat, with the ancient Cretan name of *Britomartis*, was waiting. Host and guest stepped into richly upholstered seats, host took the wheel, Stephen cast off the painter, and they were launched in a cascade of spray, roaring like a hundred sea lions.

Their craft rode the slight swell with ease, leaving in its wake a V of creamy foam. The purple dot toward which the Minos steered became noticeably larger, and at length it loomed before them as a full-fledged island. Fog veiled the lower contours, leaving only the tips of the mottled hills, ridge behind ridge, in the sharp and jagged outlines of cubistic art. The quicksilver mists rolled downward as they drew closer. When they reached a distance of a few hundred yards from shore, the haze would disappear altogether, the Minos prophesied.

"That is why they called it the Island of the Silver Girdle," he explained with the full force of his lungs. "There isn't really any fog on it now, and won't be until late this afternoon. Some scientific reason for the illusion, but nobody's been able to make it clear to me."

They cruised leisurely down the island's lee side, where the water was as placid as an inland lake and the coastline curved inward to form a natural harbor, in which the flotilla of the Minos rode proudly at anchor.

"The *Ariadne*," Paphlagloss explained, pointing to a speedboat that was the *Britomartis*' identical twin. "The launch is the *Diktynna*—a glass-bottomed boat." He shut off the power and glided skillfully to the side of the pier, protruding like a black tongue from the land. "We use the other launch, the *Velchanos*, for fishing."

"Your names," Westborough commented, "are authentically Eteocretan divinities, if I mistake not."

The Minos looped the painter about a post. "You're right. Diktynna the mother goddess, Velchanos her lover-son, Britomartis the sweet virgin. These few remnants are almost all that are preserved of the ancient language."

"A language already forgotten in Homer's day," Westborough added as he stepped onto the pier.

Stucco walls shone like clean white linen in the sunlight on the crest of the hill above their heads. Knossos was rectangular in shape with a flat roof and an upper terrace—the setback style of architecture that was old in the world at the time of the Trojan War, but new again by the turn of the twentieth century. They began the ascent of a long flight of stone steps. Westborough paused momentarily for breath; his wind, he conceded sadly, was no longer what it should be. At the top, a massive double door of cypress wood opened into a long square passageway. Tubular lamps glowed like white serpents from the ceiling above their heads. "Knossos has its own power plant," the host explained.

A short distance down the passageway they saw a young man and a girl, both in smocks. The man was smoothing the wet plaster walls with a trowel; the girl carefully stirred the various colors in an array of china dishes reposing on a trestle-supported table.

The Minos immediately strode forward. "Ione!" he exclaimed severely. "What are you doing here?"

"Mr. Glendon offered to give me a lesson in fresco painting."

"Is she in your way, Mr. Glendon?"

The plasterer relinquished his trowel. "On the contrary, sir, Miss Paphlagloss is a first-class assistant."

The Minos made belated introductions. "Mr. Westborough, this is my daughter Ione. And Mr. Glendon."

The clasp of the girl's brown hand was firm and cool and friendly. Taller than Westborough, she was as lithely slim as a Minoan bull-leaper. Her face, hands and throat had been tanned by the island sun to a gypsy brown, and her black silky hair curled into natural ringlets.

Glendon, whom Westborough estimated to be about twenty-six, was just under six feet, wiry and well proportioned. His hair was as black as the girl's, but crisp, and his sea-blue eyes sparkled with a merriment that could have descended only from an Irish ancestor. Both young people seemed very attractive, in fact, and the historian would have liked to linger in longer converse with them, but his host beckoned him to a door a few paces away.

It opened into one of the strangest rooms Westborough had ever seen.

IV

It was a room both long and narrow, constructed without windows. The indirect ceiling lighting, however, provided a plenitude of illumination. The floor was a checkerboard pattern of red and gray concrete, thick woolly rugs cushioning the cool stone. Shelves had been built along the light-tinted walls—obviously a temporary scaffolding to hold an array of cooking pots, water jars, mortars, pestles and numerous other implements of stone and bone and shell, some of which were surprisingly artistic in workmanship. The Minos pointed to a row of grinning skulls, reposing on a desk in one corner.

"Those are Marc's," he said. "Make the place look gruesome to a stranger, but he moved in bag and baggage with his Indian stuff."

Westborough bent to examine the portable typewriter which competed with the skulls for the surface of the desk. "You are sure, Mr. Paphlagloss, that it was this machine on which your butler's note was written?"

"Must have been," the Minos said decisively. "Only typewriter at Knossos. This way, please."

Westborough followed his host to the "shrine" at the far end of the room. The big glass case rested, he saw, some four feet above the floor level on a base of carved walnut panels. The reliefs were extremely interesting; they represented pillars with bulbous capitals, which tapered at the bottom and were flanked on either side by upright prongs. Westborough raised his eyes upward.

The shrine proper might be likened to a museum diorama. Its backdrop pictured the same type of columns as the carved panels, each pillar being flanked by the upright prongs. Against the blue of the painted sky fluttered painted doves, one of which had come to rest on the capital of the central column. The symbol Westborough recognized as one of remote antiquity, from a cult as far removed in time from the beginning of Christianity as the Roman Empire is distant from today. Objects pertaining to the vanished religion, which may have been that of sunken Atlantis, littered the sand flooring inside the case. They included an equal-limbed Greek cross of white marble, small urns and bowls, faïence representations in the round of flying fish, crabs, rocks, and a great many shells streaked in orange and brown, green and crimson. Crowning a mound of black velvet in the center of the shrine was a small stand with wire brackets, designed, obviously, for holding an object six or seven inches in height. But the stand was empty.

"The temple is desecrated, the shrine profaned," lamented a harsh voice from the doorway. "And through my own unspeakable carelessness."

Turning his head, Westborough saw a man a few inches taller than himself, gaunt, spare, with tawny hair shading to gray and a small gray goatee waggling comically on his broad flat chin. His pointed ears, his dense black eyebrows, arched closely together above the roots of his long thin nose, lent a puckish air to his countenance. His face was blisteringly rosy, sunburned as only a naturally fair skin can sunburn, and a pair of dark green goggles concealed eyes which, Westborough could not doubt, were keen and piercing.

"Doctor Nielsen!" Paphlagloss exclaimed. "I'd like you to meet an old friend of mine, Mr. Westborough, who's written on Trajan and Heliogabalus. You should have heard of him, since his field is similar to yours."

"Who has not heard of him?" Nielsen inquired as they shook hands. "This is indeed an honor."

"The honor," Westborough returned politely, "is entirely mine, but the pleasure of meeting so distinguished a scholar is mitigated by apprehension. Shall I be forgiven for my chapter on the Syrian sun-god?"

"Entirely," Nielsen said promptly. "Your conclusions agree for the most part with my own, but we must thresh the matter out before you leave Knossos."

Westborough bowed. "Most happy, I am sure. May I ask upon what foundation you base the assertion that—"

The Minos smiled with the indulgence men of affairs display to impractical scholars.

"Not now, please. My old friend, you have not yet seen the rest of Knossos."

Seeing Knossos was a matter of more than five minutes' duration, Westborough soon discovered. The entrance passageway led into an enormous court, paved with flagstones and open to the sky. A fountain sparkled like diamond dust in the afternoon sunshine. ("Of course they had fountains," the Minos maintained. "They were the greatest hydrostatic engineers of antiquity.") White pigeons, especially imported, Westborough suspected, to lend an authentic Minoan touch, drank in the fountain's cool basin.

Nielsen accompanied the two men inside. The place was as meandering, as confusing, as the original Cretan labyrinth. Room followed room, like the shifting lap dissolves of cinema creations. Westborough's impressions were kaleidoscopic. Concrete floors dotted with thick colorful rugs. Furniture of unbleached wood, ultramodern in design but blending unobtrusively with the painted pastel walls. Beamed ceilings. Windows overlooking the court; windows with enchanted sea vistas. Cream-colored Venetian blinds taped aristocratically with velvet ribbons. Long corridors, turning and turning. Stone benches draped with Navajo blankets. The universal indirect lighting. A broad staircase of marble-white limestone. Sunken baths in green serpentine and shining chromium.

("Questionably Minoan," Westborough censured.) Decorative friezes in unquestionably correct Minoan motifs: lilies and crocuses, double axes and 8-shaped shields, flying fish and dolphins, spiral nautiluses and writhing octopodes.

Knossos! A museum place, of course, not designed for modern living. But its beauty submerged one like the passage of a powerful breaker, leaving one stranded and gasping on the lone shore of vanished Atlantis. A mirage, not in space, but in time. Unbelievable, yet—in some weird way—existing, tangible, real.

Modernity, however, reasserted itself on the terrace. In the midst of potted plants, striped umbrellas, canopied swings and metal deck chairs, a woman glanced upward from a book, and Westborough looked into the face of Jennifer Paphlagloss.

Here, too, was beauty! The beauty of shimmering pale gold hair and violet-gray eyes, of a creamy skin carefully shaded from the sun, of hands like white flowers and a red mouth to speak with the silver of tinkling Christmas-tree bells.

"Any friend of my husband's is welcome at Knossos, Mr. Westborough. How fortunate that you found him at his office this morning."

"Exceedingly fortunate," Westborough agreed. The next instant, however, he was by no means so sure.

It was a trivial incident, yet it gave him his first glimpse of the undercurrents at Knossos. Baffling undercurrents in which he was destined to flounder, helpless as flotsam, for many terrible days! Their hostess lifted a perfumed cigarette to perfectly curved lips, Nielsen leaned forward to proffer a lighted match, and Paphlagloss strolled to the edge of the terrace. Ostensibly he had gone to regard the blue-green bay, but the hand lifted to his bandit mustache—Westborough saw in a single startled glimpse—was quivering with sudden, uncontrollable hatred.

V

But when Paphlagloss rejoined them his face was as roundly bland as ever. "Our guests might like some mint juleps," he hinted.

"Of course." She rose graciously to her feet. "They'll take a little time, though. Have you lunched, Mr. Westborough?"

He nodded smilingly. "Yes, we stopped at one of your famous drive-ins en route."

"Perhaps you would like to see something of the island while you are waiting?"

He caught the imploring look in the violet-gray eyes and said at once, "A stroll would be most pleasant."

"However, you mustn't go alone. It seems unbelievable, but one can easily get lost on this small bit of land."

Nielsen smiled wryly. "I can corroborate that from sad experience. But now I'm fairly well acquainted with the trails."

"No, Doctor Nielsen. We refuse to encourage you in shirking your work. I'll ask Ione."

Here was another of the Knossian undercurrents. The astonishingly beautiful Mrs. Paphlagloss, Westborough was almost certain, did not wish her stepdaughter to spend too much time in the company of the fresco painter, and neither, apparently, did the girl's father, who concurred at once in the suggestion. Westborough did not in the least enjoy being used as an instrument to break up the girl's afternoon, but he could think of nothing to do about the matter.

He met her a few minutes later at the fountain in the open courtyard. She had discarded her smock and was boyishly slim in russet slacks. A yellow silk scarf was knotted, gypsy-fashion, about her curling black hair. Knotted carelessly, but the effect was exactly right.

"I am sorry," Westborough said apologetically while they traversed a trail overlooking the sea, "to be making so much trouble for you."

Their eyes met: hers, dark and luminous; his, mild and blue and edged with multitudinous wrinkles. Her vividly red lips curved into a sudden smile. She sang softly:

> " *'But to be so kind*
> *To bear in mind,*
> *We were the victims of circumstances!'* "

Westborough was delighted. He was devoted to all the works of Messrs. Gilbert and Sullivan and recognized at once a kindred spirit. The white walls of the house sank shimmeringly out of sight behind an intervening ridge. "Your father's house," the little man said musingly, "is very beautiful."

"Poisonous place!" she retorted with quick intensity. "I hate it."

"Hate a house?" he questioned.

"Hate what it stands for."

"What does it stand for, may I ask?"

"Money. Capital M-O-N-E-Y. Oh, never mind."

Westborough could think of no adequate comment. Moreover, their trail led across a succession of ridges, each more steeply pitched in grade than the one before, and he needed all the breath he could muster for the continued climbing. Out of sight of Knossos and its harbor, the Island of Minos reverted quickly to primitive wilderness. Not an attractive wilderness by ordinary scenic standards. No verdurous glooms nor winding mossy ways, not even—as far as Westborough was able to discover—a single full-size tree. The brown dirt of the hills nourished only a scrubby dwarf forest, dull and dusty in the heat of the barren summer. But beauty was before them in the waters of the sparkling sea.

"Have you been out in a glass-bottomed boat?" she asked, pausing at a railing overlooking a deep and rocky pool. "You must let me take you in ours tomorrow morning."

"You are most kind, but I cannot allow you to inconvenience yourself furth—"

"Please!" she interrupted. "Early tomorrow."

The vehemence of her insistence puzzled him. It was plain, however, that she really wanted him to go with her, and he assented readily. Turning inland a slight distance, they crossed other ridges—there seemed to be almost no level land on the island—and came finally to a tent pitched beside a crisscross of trenches.

"Marc's field headquarters," the girl explained. "He sleeps here whenever he forgets to come home, which is entirely too often for Jennifer's peace of mind."

"Did he dig all these excavations by himself?" Westborough inquired.

"More than these. Marc hasn't any money for labor. This is Site Number 3, as he calls it. I don't see him working so he must be inside." She lifted the tent flap as she spoke. "Oh, Marco, company! Ugh! What a foul hole."

The accusation was not unjustified. The tent floor, Westborough saw, when his eyes had accustomed themselves to the curtailment of light, was an indescribable litter of neolithic debris. Marc Bayard—if this young man were he—was seated on the edge of a cot, devoting his attention to a long pointed stone, which had been propped to rest with the pointed end over the flame of an alcohol stove.

"Hello," he said, looking up at last.

"This is Mr. Westborough, Marco. Our new guest."

"Glad to know you, sir. Won't you both sit down?"

"Here?" Ione inquired—a not unnatural question. Marc hastily removed his alcohol stove from one camp chair and a bog of assorted molars from the other.

"Your Indian friends, Marco, seem to have lost a lot of teeth," she said, occupying one of the cleared chairs. "They couldn't have had very good ones."

"They had very good teeth," he answered indignantly. "Almost no cavities to speak of. Far better teeth than you'll find on people today. What brings you here besides the chance to insult my Indians?"

"Jennifer sent us to find you."

The young man seemed, Westborough fancied, a little disappointed. "Interrupting your lesson in fresco painting, I presume?" he asked.

"Definitely interrupting it."

"Too bad. Well, I was just about to mend an olla." He pointed to a heap of stone fragments. "Mind if I finish it before we go, Mr. Westborough?"

"He does mind," Ione said.

"On the contrary," Westborough differed, "I should very much like to witness the operation."

Removing his long slim stone from the flame, Marc dipped its hot pointed end into an abalone shell holding a black cake of solidified tar. "I like to work with their own implements," he explained. "Helps to understand their culture."

"He mends with that nasty pitch," Ione said informatively.

"Asphaltum," Marc corrected. "They gathered it on the ocean side of this island. It is still washed up there from the sea."

"And it's lovely for white shoes," Ione added plaintively.

"The Indians had a hundred-and-one uses for it. I've found one. It makes a fine cement. The islanders had the habit of breaking their household artifacts into pieces before burying them with the dead. Religion, probably. To break an article liberated its spirit so the owner could use it in the afterworld, or so we think."

"How he does go on," Ione giggled.

Marc, busy with his melted asphaltum and aboriginal soldering iron, said nothing more for some time. Westborough collated his impressions of the young man. Tall . . . at least six feet . . . but extremely thin. "Beanpole" was the word, was it not? A casual observer might assume that the youth's spare frame lacked stamina, but Westborough remembered the trenches in the greasy black soil outside—no weakling could have toiled so arduously under the broiling sun.

However, Bayard certainly did not look athletic. His peaked features and rimless nose glasses gave him far more of a scholar's appearance . . . undeniably nearsighted, poor fellow. Long bony fingers . . .

Marc removed the excess pitch with a scraper of thin shell. The stone fragments had been welded into a globular jar, a foot or so high.

"A Grecian purity of line!" Westborough exclaimed in admiration. "The maker possessed an inherent sense of form. No potter's wheel could turn out a better!"

"Carved from a block of stone by nearly naked savages," Bayard informed him. "With no other tools than stone picks and chisels."

"Remarkable!" Westborough breathed. "Will your repair work endure?"

"For museum purposes, yes."

"If you could only mend broken hearts as easily as you can broken pots!" Ione exclaimed.

Bayard smiled owlishly. "Then I'd mend my own. Shall we go back to the house?"

Westborough found the return walk most enjoyable. Bayard was a font of information on the island flora, and the little man's inquisitive mind caused him to put a great many questions. He learned that the very common bush with small round leaves was the scrub oak, *Quercus dumosa.* An oak? Impossible! One could never insult the noble oak family by allotting them this dwarfish by-blow. Yet here was the indisputable evidence of acorns, the acorns which, as Bayard pointed out, had formed the staple food supply of the aboriginal islanders.

The ubiquitous greasewood the historian easily recognized from its olive-green fronds, but there were many other shrubs he did not know. Sumacs, so called, which didn't look in the least like the eastern variety. Leathery-leaved California holly. Impenetrably spined buckthorns. Iron-hard manzanitas, as crooked as a Chicago politician. Pungent-smelling bay trees, and a sprawling purple-green plant blooming in fragrant white trumpets, eight to ten inches long.

"Can this possibly be related to the daturas of India?" Westborough inquired.

"Same genus," Bayard returned promptly. *"Datura meteloides.* The ten-angled corolla distinguishes it from the Asiatic species. It grows abundantly here, which leads me to believe that this island was one of the centers for the rites of the tolo—"

He broke off abruptly, his thin features twisting into an expression of profound distaste, as a brawny young man in slacks and polo shirt appeared at the top of the next ridge.

"Russell Stoner!"

The newcomer strode toward them with easy athletic grace, hatless, his fair hair blowing across his forehead, his shirt open at the throat to display a well-thewed neck tanned to the same golden bronze as his face. He was an inch or two taller than the six-foot Bayard and a great deal bulkier across chest and shoulders. A splendid animal! His hair was the color of corn silk, and his features, except for a small snub nose, were of classic regularity. Unfortunately, however, he was one of those annoying persons who believe that the purpose of a handshake is to inflict the maximum amount of punishment.

Westborough's frail hand suffered greatly in his powerful grip when they were introduced, and Bayard, vainly attempting to dodge the rite of greeting, was awarded an even worse fate. Young Stoner's ring was a disguised projector of an inky-black fluid. The joker shook with roaring laughter as Bayard disgustedly wiped the palm of his hand.

"Very very funny," Ione observed acidly. Bayard had turned his back to stroll toward a shrub flowering in greenish-white clusters. "Did you get that at the same place as your other playthings, Russ? The exploding matchbox and the squirt cigarette and the rubber-pointed pencil and the itch powder and the shooting coaster?"

Stoner nodded, his voice choked by guffaws. "He bit on 'em all, the sucker! How about it, pal? No hard feelings?"

"No hard feelings," Bayard answered gravely, divesting a branch of its glossy, pointed foliage. "This is the plant that bay rum comes from; smell these and see." He extended a handful of crumpled leaves. "But the odor's delicate. You'll have to breathe deeply."

Plunging his infantile-shaped nose into the herbage, Stoner sniffed with visible signs of olfactory pleasure. "That's swell!" he said.

"Deeper," Bayard instructed. "It takes a little time to get the full odor."

Stoner took several whiffs then jerked his head suddenly upward, clasping both hands to his forehead. His handsome face twitched with symptoms of acute internal agony.

"I've been poisoned!" he gasped.

"Fatally so," Bayard confirmed, dropping the leaves and strolling in the direction of the house. "Death follows invariably in twenty-four hours. Too bad, my friend, we've enjoyed having you with us."

The junior Stoner, contrary to his initial belief, was injured by his olfactory experiments only to the extent of a severe and persistent headache, but this sufficed to keep him moodily silent throughout the evening meal. Noting how consistently Bayard's three or four attempts at reconciliation were scowled down, Westborough quoted to himself the hair-trigger words of *The Rivals:*

" 'The quarrel is a very pretty quarrel as it stands; we should only spoil it by trying to explain it.' "

With the single exception of Ione, however, no one seemed to notice there was even a quarrel to be explained. Russell's father, a squat man of about fifty, with coarse gray hair, aggressively large features, a thick neck and a Napoleonic paunch, dominated the dinner conversation, holding it strictly within the channels of deep-sea fishing. But the epics of albacore, barracuda, sea bass, tuna and swordfish culminated finally in a bitter argument over the relative merits of live fish or kiting as lures for marlin.

The senior Stoner headed the live-fish advocates and his host, probably, Westborough reflected, because it was impossible for two men of such positive opinions to agree on any question, came out just as strongly for kiting. Bayard was stoutly in the Paphlagloss camp, but Ione appeared to take malicious pleasure in exploding her father's verbal torpedoes with skillfully directed countershots. Listening to the prolonged and acrimonious discussion, Westborough thought of Lilliput's Big- and Little-endians. Completely lost among the technicalities, he devoted his attention to the dinner wine.

It was a Greek wine, blackly purple in hue and sweet as love, a wine to be sipped slowly and rolled lovingly upon the palate, but their host, the historian noted, didn't drink it. After nearly forty years in the United States, Paphlagloss stubbornly retained a taste for a "retsina," which, his daughter informed them as the bait question came to an inconclusive end, tasted exactly like burning turpentine. Though Paphlagloss indignantly denied the allegation, none of his guests asked to sample the resinated beverage. Westborough, who had traveled in Greece, saw no reason to doubt the accuracy of the girl's description.

Coffee and a fiery Greek brandy were served alfresco. The salt air was pleasantly cool, the night like black velvet; a gibbous moon shone faintly to the south, and the broad terrace was dimly illuminated. It would not be difficult, Westborough mused, for a person to slip unobserved through the double doors into the upstairs hall, and return before his absence could be noted. But Paphlagloss was deep in discussion with Harvey Stoner. Westborough sipped his brandy and waited, before putting the theory to personal test.

Glendon drank his coffee hurriedly and excused himself; the voices of Marc and Russell were raised in angry dispute; Ione attempted to pacify them; the beautiful Mrs. Paphlagloss conversed animatedly with the uncomely Nielsen; the elder Stoner paced the concrete flooring like Napoleon, with a cigar. Paphlagloss left the department-store Bonaparte to saunter toward his wife's companion, and Westborough, recognizing the agreed signal, rose to his feet and slipped unobtrusively from the terrace.

He found the door between his own room and Nielsen's unlocked, as his host had promised. Feeling a little guilty, Westborough entered. He was not optimistic about results—quite the contrary. He was convinced that so distinguished a scholar as Arne Nielsen would not possibly stoop to steal, even had he coveted the priceless ivory snake-goddess. Westborough had consented to undertake the search largely because he hoped to vindicate his fellow historian of the ugly charge, but having given his word to his host, it did not matter for what purpose. The little man, who had learned from his friend, Lieutenant Mack of Chicago, the art of thoroughly combing a room without leaving telltale traces, set conscientiously about the uncongenial task.

He began with the writing desk. Since it was the most obvious place, it was one of the most likely to be utilized. At least, this was true theoretically. Actually it yielded nothing more compromising than a thick stack of handwritten yellow papers which, a perfunctory glance through them revealed, pertained exclusively to the Minoan Baetylic cult.

Using a flashlight like a midnight marauder, he rummaged through the dresser and the commode; he ransacked the bed covering and mattress; he raked through all the pockets of his fellow scholar's spare suits; he probed the cushions of the chairs and tested the folds of window curtains. At the end of an hour's exhaustive scrutiny he concluded that the room might be given a clean bill of health, and stepped back through the connecting door into his own chamber.

A man rose unexpectedly from a large chair.

"Good evening," he said equably. "Since my own room seemed to be occupied, I borrowed yours for the time being. I trust you will forgive me for watching you at work. You are most thorough in your methods, my dear Westborough."

VII

Westborough took a long deep breath. "In the words of Cicero," he said at length, " 'To obey necessity has always been regarded as the act of a wise man.' I consider that I owe you a full explanation of my conduct."

Nielsen arched puckish eyebrows. "Can you explain?"

"I can try. I was invited to Knossos in the character, shall we say, of a private detective?"

"You are not, then, Westborough the Roman historian?"

"Yes, the name is my own and so, also, are such crumbs of reputation as may attach to it. However, I have had some slight experience with police matters. Murder cases, to be exact; but Mr. Paphlagloss has rated my abilities in the sleuthing line far too highly."

"You were successful in solving these cases?"

"My associates were successful."

"I see. How many cases were there?"

"I believe six. Yes, that is correct. Three in Chicago, one in Wisconsin, one in Colorado and one in Hollywood. A most bewildering place, by the way. I was—for a very limited time—associated with Plutarch Pictures in the character of historical adviser. For a limited time, you will notice I stress. I was, in the quaint Hollywood patois, a total floparoo."

"I find you an amazing person, Professor Westborough. May I inquire how Mr. Paphlagloss learned of your sleuthing feats?"

" 'Feats' is much too strong a word. I believe that he consulted an official of the Los Angeles police department."

Nielsen frowningly stroked his goatee. "Then he does suspect me of stealing the chryselephantine goddess?"

"I fear that he does. *Did* you steal it, may I ask?"

"No."

"You are quite sure?"

"Yes, quite. I feel responsible for the theft, however. I was inexcusably careless in leaving the figurine in my room, unguarded, when I should have replaced it in the locked shrine."

"Please do not blame yourself too severely on that score," Westborough said consolingly. "After all, we are separated by many miles of watery belt from the area in which burglaries may be expected to occur. In your opinion, is the stolen goddess a genuine Minoan art object?"

"Decidedly."

"Would you be willing to place a monetary value on her?"

"Since only one other such figurine exists in the world, the monetary value might be anything. However, there's no market for Minoan antiques because the supply is nonexistent. The Greek government forbids their export."

"Yes, I know. There is, however, a manner in which a considerable sum might be realized. The little Minoan lady is Mr. Paphlagloss' greatest treasure. May not a goddess be held for ransom?"

Nielsen leaned forward in his chair. He was as ugly as Thersites, but his personality held an odd charm. "Your meaning is clear," he said slowly.

"You, Doctor Nielsen, through only a minor indiscretion, have been placed in an unfortunate position. Will you assist in apprehending the kidnapper?"

"With all my heart. What can I do?"

"For the present, I shall require no more than your answers to a few questions. Whom do you suspect of having stolen the figurine?"

"Obvious, isn't it? The butler who ran away."

"I do not believe it is quite so obvious. First, there is a rather puzzling time lag. Mr. Paphlagloss tells me that the goddess was stolen on the night of July fourth, but Charles doesn't decamp until the night of July sixth. To remain here for two full days, boldly taking the risk of exposure, and then to advertise his guilt by running away, is an illogical procedure. Moreover, the butler has been employed by Mr. Paphlagloss for ten years. During this period, surely, he must have had many other opportunities to pilfer the goddess if his intentions toward her had been dishonorable."

"Not so easy as you think. You are forgetting the locked shrine."

"I concede the lock—an extremely good Yale lock, by the way. And concede also the difficulty and danger of smashing the thick plate glass. The shrine, however, cannot antedate the house in age, and the house was not built prior to the purchase of the island, which, I believe, was in the summer of 1934. There remain a full six years in which Charles must have had innumerable chances to steal the ivory lady, if he had been so minded. By the way, did you ever notice him to manifest any undue interest when you removed the Minoan deity from her transparent prison?"

Nielsen shook his head. "I can't say that I did."

"How many times did you open the shrine?"

"Only twice. On the day after I arrived, and then again on the Fourth."

"In the afternoon or evening?"

"About four in the afternoon."

"You did not return the goddess to her case during dinner?"

"No. The thought didn't enter my head that she was not safe on my desk. I wanted to continue my examination of her after dinner. I did go up to my room for a while, but at nine o'clock or so someone interrupted to ask me to step on the terrace and look at the fireworks."

"May I ask who invited you to the terrace?"

"He was gone by the time I had opened my door. I believe the voice was that of our host."

"You did not lock your door when you left?"

"It never occurred to me to do so."

"Naturally not. Were you one of the early or late arrivals on the terrace?"

"It seemed that everyone else was there by the time I joined them."

"Servants, too?"

"Servants? Yes, I believe that they were all there."

"How long were you on the terrace?"

"An hour. Perhaps an hour and a half."

"Did you then return immediately to your room?"

"Yes."

"And found the goddess missing?"

"Yes."

"Concentrate, if you please, Doctor Nielsen. Can you recall any person leaving the terrace while the fireworks were exploding in their pyrotechnical splendor?"

"H'm . . . I'm not sure. There was a great deal of movement about the terrace, and it wouldn't take any longer time than two minutes to leave, visit my room, and return."

Westborough nodded. "Two minutes, exactly. I timed the operation."

"My impression is that it would be a more difficult feat for a servant than for a guest or a member of the family. The servants, as I recall, were in a rather compact group, and Charles was officiating as majordomo of ceremonies."

"Charles was fireworks majordomo? That is most interesting. In view of your statements, I am inclined to remove the servants en masse from the class of suspects. You also I will omit from that class, Doctor Nielsen. You have given me your word—the word of a scholar—and, furthermore, you may be eliminated on purely logical grounds. If you had planned to steal the Minoan goddess, you would scarcely have stolen her under conditions calculated to direct the maximum amount of suspicion toward yourself."

"I appreciate your consideration very much."

"It is not consideration at all, but reason. Mr. Paphlagloss also we may pass over. Although, as W.S. Gilbert might say, if a man can't steal his own property, then whose property can he steal?"

"Whose indeed?" Nielsen chuckled.

"There remain, then, six persons, one of whom is certainly guilty. Two women, three young men and one older man." Westborough paused before adding slowly, "Did it ever occur to you, Doctor Nielsen, that there exist certain, shall we say 'human strains' in this house?"

Nielsen nodded soberly. "Far too many of them."

"Miss Paphlagloss, for instance, obviously does not care a great deal for her stepmother. What is more strange, the dislike appears to extend to her own father. Perhaps she unconsciously resented his marrying for the second time. But—dear me!—when that event occurred she could not have been more than a child of eight."

"Is it necessary to be so Freudian?" Nielsen demanded.

"Perhaps not. But have you noticed the relations of which I speak?"

"Indeed, I have. And many others. Bayard and young Stoner—a most unpleasant cub with a fiendish addiction to practical jokes. I found rather a large array of tin bedbugs and rubber spiders in my own bed one night—but Bayard's been the particular butt. Matchboxes that explode. Cigarettes that squirt water. Cigarettes that stink up the house. Powder that makes you itch like the very devil. Luckily, Bayard is too far above that childish nonsense to take it seriously."

"Mr. Bayard, however," Westborough opined, "is not too far above it to retaliate in kind." He related the incident of the bay leaves, and Nielsen grunted in satisfaction.

"Bayard knows a lot of lore about the island plants. Brilliant young chap!"

"Extremely so," Westborough agreed.

"Glad he paid off young Stoner. Gives me more faith in the divinity that rough-hews our ends."

"A masterpiece of misquotation," Westborough acknowledged smilingly.

"Neat phrase of yours, too. Human strains. This place is haunted with them. Here's just one example. I went fishing with the senior Stoner and mine host one day. Stoner, probably operating on the theory that a college professor's limited intelligence makes it impossible for him to understand the ramifications of big business, talked to P. quite freely."

"Indeed?" Westborough queried, bending forward in interest. "Did you find evidence of still another human strain?"

"Rather. P. owns a chain of department stores on the coast. S owns a similar chain in the Midwest. Let us put our stores together, adding silver coin and gold. Ha! Not bad, if I do say it. But Agamemnon and Achilles can't agree on who's to sit in the Grand Panjandrum's chair. Achilles, the worthy ruler of Knossos, thinks he should. Stoner, Agamemnon, refuses: he has the most stores—control should remain in his hands. Our host sulks in his tent. Agamemnon prepares to yield Briseis. Stoner says, in effect, 'My dear and greatly esteemed colleague, Paphlagloss. You have a daughter. I have a son. Both are of marriageable age. Ergo, let them be married. Then it will not matter, really matter to me who rules our joint empire, so long as the ruler is one of the family.' P. was so pleased he even forgot that a nice-size bass had been nibbling about his bait, and the absentminded Professor Nielsen had to seize the rod of his shrewd and practical host to avert a fisherman's tragedy."

"Did you land the bass?" Westborough inquired.

"Yes. A mere fifty or sixty pounds. An infant as fish go here! So daughter Ione is to be thrown to the dogs, for it is almost impossible to consider young Stoner as greatly above that level. And there will be founded a department-store dynasty, with ruler Alexis I."

"Mr. Paphlagloss," Westborough cogitated, "appears to be decidedly more of a high-handed parent than the breed runs nowadays. And the characteristic, I might state, is not a racial one. Greeks, in general, are amiable, generous and easygoing. Can it be the power of money?"

"It can be and is," Nielsen said emphatically. "He rather fancies himself as a prehistoric autocrat. Look at this house, if you don't believe me. Complexes written all over it. Minoan culture belongs in the twentieth century—but B.C. and not A.D."

"I have had the same impression," Westborough confessed.

"And the island itself! Show me a man who buys an island, and I'll show you one with the soul of an absolute ruler."

"There is much in what you say," Westborough agreed.

"It's highly ungrateful to say it, though," Nielsen returned, a little shamefacedly. "In the first place, P. was kind enough to invite me here—an amazingly generous invitation to issue to a total stranger. And in the second place, he's been very decent over his stolen goddess."

"You are now," Westborough reminded gently, "talking off the record."

"Off the record, then—and in strict confidence—I am very sorry for Mrs. Paphlagloss."

Westborough's mild eyes widened inquiringly. "Why, may one ask?"

"Haven't you noticed it?"

"I have certainly noticed something."

"He hates her," Nielsen burst out. "She's beautiful, charming, gracious and attractive. But her husband hates her."

"Can it not be mere jealousy?" Westborough pondered.

"Jealousy, certainly. He's jealous of Stoner père, although Stoner hasn't said two words alone to his hostess; has almost rudely ignored her, in fact. And he's jealous of me." Nielsen laughed sardonically. "Jealous of a dry-as-dust Greek history professor with a face like mine! If this be reason, make the most of it."

Westborough chuckled. He was finding the distinguished scholar enjoyably stimulating. " 'The ruling passion, be what it will, the ruling passion conquers reason still,' " he quoted from Alexander Pope.

"Very apt!" Nielsen exclaimed admiringly. "And our host's ruling passion is simply to rule. His first marital experience ended disastrously, I gather. For second mate he was looking for a woman who would idolize him."

" 'He for God only, she for God in him.' "

"Exactly. And Jennifer—Mrs. Paphlagloss—married him for other reasons than adoration of his manly charms. He's never forgiven her."

"May I ask, Doctor Nielsen, how this bit of rather private history is known to you?"

"She told me so," Nielsen replied, a shade uncomfortably. "Told me her whole history one afternoon while her husband and Stoner were away on their daily fishing excursion."

"I see," Westborough said thoughtfully.

VIII

Mockingbirds, those nightingales of southern California, sang the night through, but did not trouble Westborough's slumber. The island's night air possessed, undeniably, a high soporific content.

However, he arose long before the rest of the household was astir and slipped out on the terrace. Normally, he had been told, the island was foggy in the early morning, but today the air was as limpid as hyalite, the sky a blue vista of infinity. Ten million coruscations rose and fell across the golden path that stretched over the ocean to the dim purple line of the eastern mainland.

"Hello," called a black-haired young man, seated leisurely in a metal chair. "Nice morning."

"An exceedingly nice morning," Westborough agreed, blinking because he had looked too long at the reflections in the shining waters.

"Cigarette?"

"No, thank you, Mr. Glendon. I rarely smoke anything but a pipe. And not that until later in the day."

"Smoking before breakfast's a bad habit to get into," Denis Glendon pronounced. He stretched slowly to his feet. "This air! Makes a fellow feel good."

"It does indeed," Westborough concurred. Glendon squinted at the sparkles in the blue-gray harbor. The older man ventured to continue the conversation.

"There's raw material for you, Mr. Glendon."

"Raw material, yes." The artist's voice conveyed the condescension of his profession toward a mere layman's viewpoint, and Westborough lapsed into a shy silence. Three gulls—white motes in the sunshine—

soared lazily above the water's surface. "Sea cats stalking their prey," Glendon mused. "Do you like the ocean, Mr. Westborough?"

"Very much."

"It's changeable as a woman. This morning—a golden strumpet. A Du Barry, dazzling and glamorous—but one looks and turns away. This afternoon, however, she'll put on a different garment—burnt-umber patches of kelp against a gray-green transparency. And tonight the demure wench will sing you lullabies—God, what nonsense!"

"Pray continue," Westborough pleaded. "I am enjoying it."

"Painting's my line," Glendon went on. "I don't know anything else. I've done one or two good things and others not so good, but enough fairly decent things to feel that the world might allow me a scanty living for working at my own trade . . . Oh, the devil!"

" *'Dulcia non ferimus: succo renovamur amaro,'* " Westborough quoted gently. "May I offer a free translation of Ovidius Naso? 'The sweet is not good for us; it is the bitter potion which restores our energy.' "

"Tripe!" Glendon exclaimed. "It isn't success that destroys the creative energies. It's the stink of failure."

"Who would have sung of Hector if Troy had triumphed?" Westborough added, a little severely. "You, Mr. Glendon, have now the opportunity to do a fine piece of work, and no man has the right to ask more than that of fortune."

"Yes, he has," Glendon differed. "He has the right to ask that he won't be tantalized by the daily sight of an infinitely desirable something that must remain, forever beyond his grasp."

"Dear, dear me!" Westborough exclaimed, making a furious show of polishing the lenses of his gold-rimmed bifocals. "You are in love with Miss Paphlagloss."

"With the moon?" Glendon demanded bitterly.

"She does not reciprocate your affections?"

"How could she? She's slated to marry that Stoner fellow."

"Is she in love with Mr. Stoner?"

"I suppose so. She wouldn't do it otherwise."

"Women," Westborough meditated, cloaking his thoughts in the rigid forms of logic, "are female beings who will not marry except for love. Miss Paphlagloss is a woman. Therefore, she is a female being who will not marry except for love." The reasoning, he saw at once, was founded upon a major premise by no means universal, but he refrained from pointing this out. A gull swooped in a sudden nose dive, emerging triumphantly from the spray in full possession of a piscatorial breakfast.

"He knew what he wanted," the painter commented. "Went after it and got it. Why isn't life that simple for the rest of us?"

"The difficulty is basically an arithmetical one," Westborough maintained. "It is called, I believe, the Law of Supply and Demand. When the number of fish is large in proportion to the number of gulls—"

"Then every gull gets his breakfast," Glendon interrupted.

"Exactly. And so all are satisfied. But if the number of fish is proportionally small, some gulls are inevitably cheated. A deplorable state of affairs, to be sure, but there isn't a great deal can be done about it. The condition is old—a great deal older than man. It probably arose with the first amoeba."

"Suppose that two gulls are after the same fish?" the artist asked reflectively.

"Another fundamental law goes into operation. The law Spencer named the Survival of the Fittest."

"But among *civilized* human beings?"

"Civilization," Westborough declared, "is a thin veneer over a very ancient structure. A rotting structure, some might say, but I will not be so cynical."

"So we're all jungle beasts at heart?"

"Do you doubt it?"

"No. It's true. And it probably explains—well, you take a group of people. Maroon them on an island like this where they can't get away from each other. Let them all want something, as people always do. And what happens?"

"What does happen?" Westborough asked.

"Strains! Tensions!" Glendon exploded vehemently. "Hatreds! The deadly hidden kind. Masked hatreds. You can't put your finger on them, but they're here. Intangible and invisible. And they may be dangerous."

"Dangerous?" Westborough repeated. He thought of the stolen goddess, the missing butler. "May I ask you to elucidate?"

"Forget it," Glendon retorted shamefacedly. "I'm talking tripe. What the devil's wrong with me this morning?"

"Is it the house," Westborough inquired gently, "which so stimulates your emotions?"

Vertical lines of puzzlement formed on the artist's forehead. "What's wrong with the house?" he demanded.

"Apparently nothing. And yet"—Westborough paused momentarily— "though I have been here not twenty-four hours, two people have already confessed to me their intense dislike of it."

"It's beautiful!" Glendon craned his neck to regard the white stucco wall at their backs. "Outside and in, it's lovely as a dream. But you're right. There's something definitely queer about it."

"Are you able to be more specific, Mr. Glendon?"

The artist shook his head lugubriously. "Just something I feel. The Irish in me, I suppose. My mother's people used to have an authentic banshee. You either believe in banshees or you don't, and if you don't, there's no use trying—no, wait a minute. There was one odd thing happened a day or so ago. It was in the morning, and I was just about through with my quota of plastering. Frescoes are done on fresh mortar, as you probably know."

"However, I was not aware that the painter was required to do the mason's work himself."

Glendon looked abashed. "I offered to do it," he said hesitantly. "I'm sure to get my mortar mixed right that way, and no danger of a clumsy workman smearing my work before it dries. Besides—well, I may as well confess the whole truth to you. Mr. Paphlagloss is paying me by the day for this job, a nice big sum! And it's the only real money I've sighted in a year. Do you understand?"

"Yes, decidedly. Please go on."

"Mr. Paphlagloss walked by me, said hello and went on. After he'd passed, I remembered there was something I had to ask him about before I started painting, so I hurried down the entrance passageway after him. Hurried, I say, because you have to work like the very devil after the plaster's ready. Paphlagloss had gone into a room—there's only one door between the front entrance and the place I was working, and it opens into a sort of private museum."

"I know the place," Westborough declared.

"Then you know it hasn't any doors except the one from the hall?"

"Yes."

"Or any windows at all?"

"I did notice that odd circumstance."

"Mr. Paphlagloss couldn't have gone into any other room, and when he was in that one, he couldn't leave it except by the hall where I was standing. That's the situation in a nutshell. Naturally, I expected to find him when I stepped inside."

"And didn't you?" Westborough queried.

Glendon raised troubled sea-blue eyes. "No. He wasn't there."

IX

It was a room both long and narrow, constructed, oddly enough, without windows. The indirect ceiling lighting, however, provided a plenitude of illumination. The floor was a checkerboard pattern of red and gray concrete, thick woolly rugs cushioning its cool stone bareness. Westborough's eyes traversed the light-tinted plaster walls. The surface was everywhere smooth and unbroken. No hidden door could possibly have been cut into those walls. Had Denis Glendon, from whom Westborough had excused himself a short time ago, been mistaken? Or had Alexis Paphlagloss succeeded in dematerializing into the fourth dimension?

The historian moved inquiringly toward the shelf on his right. The Indian objects did not bulk large enough to conceal any considerable portion of the wall. His eye fell upon some rather curious doughnut-shaped rings, about 4 inches in diameter and 2 1/2 inches in thickness. They had been carved from green serpentine and given a beautiful polish. He lifted one, experimentally, in his hand just as Marc Bayard entered.

"Good morning, sir."

Startled, Westborough nearly dropped the stone circlet. "Oh, good morning, Mr. Bayard. I was admiring these strange articles."

"The doughnuts?" Bayard's tall body stooped slightly as he walked across the room. "They are beauties, aren't they?"

"Remarkably accurate work for stone-age craftsmen. May I ask their purpose?"

"You may ask a dozen men and get a dozen answers. Experts don't agree, which is only another way of saying that no one really knows. Some will tell you they were made to be slipped over the women's root-digging sticks. But if so, why the extremely careful workmanship? And others say that they were sinkers for fishing nets. But we don't even know for certain that the Channel Islanders had fishing nets. My own belief is that the rings were sacred stones. Worshipped as gods, perhaps. Who knows?"

"Dear me, that is most interesting, Mr. Bayard. Have you mentioned this subject to Doctor Nielsen? It fits so beautifully into his study of the Minoan Baetylic cult."

"Yes, Nielsen and I have had some lengthy discussions." Bayard stretched his long thin neck to peer nearsightedly along the shelves. "Here's another type of charm stone. Looks like a porpoise, or maybe a whale. Obviously made to give power over the fish domain. And here's one like a pelican. Crude, but the likeness is there. He who carried this effigy about his neck took on the abilities of that masterly fisherman. These are simple animistic fetishes, but the doughnuts are more puzzling. So are these cigar-shaped spindles. One theory is they represent various harmful principles which must be overcome by the magic of the medicine man. Some say that the stones themselves were endowed with life—a mischievous life, hostile to man—and must be properly exorcised."

"A very strange concept."

"Isn't it, though?" Bayard agreed. "No, those aren't charm stones, Mr. Westborough. Those are common utilitarian stone pestles used by the tribal women in acorn grinding. Broken into two pieces when they were buried with their owners—but I told you the reason for that yesterday. Lift that big fellow and you'll see what muscles those women had to have."

Westborough lifted a tapered stone cylinder, approximately eighteen inches in length. It came apart in his grasp, the lower tip clattering noisily onto the shelf "Dear me," he exclaimed in dismay. "That was inexcusably careless of me."

"Careless of me," Bayard corrected. "Must have done a rotten job of mending, or it would have held together." He picked up another pestle from the shelf, whirled it about his head like a war club. "You see how solidly this holds."

"It is very strange," Westborough said, as if talking to himself. "Mr. Bayard, you are an expert mender of Indian artifacts."

"Good of you to say so."

"Merely a statement of fact. An expert, it has been my experience, seldom—if ever—performs a careless piece of workmanship. Ergo, some force has previously been employed to disrupt your pestle. But the clatter upon the concrete floor? Ah, the rugs, to be sure!"

"I don't understand what you're saying."

"I'm not altogether sure I understand, myself, but do you have a magnifying glass I might borrow?"

"A magnifying glass? Yes, there's one in the desk. Why?"

Westborough bent down to a crawling posture. "It would be interesting to see if we can find pitch on one of these rugs. Or asphaltum, to be more specific."

"Asphaltum on a rug?"

"Thank you for the glass. It will prove nothing, if we find the substance, I might add. 'He that toucheth pitch shall be defiled therewith,' and from what I have heard about your island shores it is extremely easy to be defiled. Particularly easy on the soles of one's feet. Dear me! It is really here. Three moderately large globules hidden in the nap of the rug. Pray examine them."

Bayard took the glass. "What made you know you'd find this?" he asked.

"I didn't know," Westborough confessed. "However, I had a theory which the presence of this substance would, to a slight extent, confirm. One rather gruesome, to be sure, but which might possibly exp—"

Ione strode through the open doorway, boyishly free in her slacks. "Sherlock the second!" she laughed. "Obviously, my dear Marco, you need only a plaid cap to be complete."

Bayard sheepishly restored the glass to his desk. "He's the Sherlock," he exclaimed, with a glance at Westborough.

"Shame on you, Marco, to cast the blame on the innocent stranger within our gates!" Her deep-toned laughter held an attractive resonance. "I was looking for you, Mr. Westborough, to remind you of your promise to go on a glass-bottomed boat ride. Or have you forgotten?"

"On the contrary," Westborough smiled, "I have been eagerly looking forward to the occasion."

"Will you come right now? Before breakfast?"

A younger man would have delivered an instant affirmative. Westborough merely looked puzzled.

"Oh, you won't starve," she continued hurriedly. "Marco can smuggle some rolls from the kitchen. And a thermos of coffee. Will you, Marco?"

"Of course." If she had asked her stepbrother to go to the ends of the earth, Westborough mused, he would probably have answered in just that tone. "Am I invited, too?"

She smiled indulgent consent. "Meet us on the pier. And don't let—you know—see us."

"I don't understand," said Westborough, while he was being hustled out the front door and down the long flight of steps.

"It's quite simple. If I don't show up for breakfast—and leave word that I've taken you for a glass-bottomed boat excursion—Russ may decide to go fishing. Then he won't be at the house when we come back."

"I am amazed at your duplicity. The plan is one worthy of Machiavelli."

"No, it's a very poor one. But the best I could think of on the spur of the moment. You don't mind being used?"

"On the contrary, I rather enjoy it. And if the junior Mr. Stoner is not at the house when we return?"

"Hurry, please, Alexis might try to stop us."

"But you have not answered my question."

Was any modern girl ever so self-conscious as to blush? But if the ruddy suffusion of her cheeks wasn't a blush, Westborough pondered, it was something very much resembling one.

"Russ is becoming a pest. And I want to learn something about fresco painting."

"The ambition to learn is very laudable," Westborough exclaimed, running down the stairs at an alarming gait for a man of his years. "You may be assured of my wholehearted cooperation."

"Thanks," she said, catching his arm in time to avert a potentially calamitous tumble. "I knew you were a good egg as soon as I saw you."

"An egg slightly on the soft-boiled side," Westborough qualified, his eyes twinkling. "Ah youth, my youth!"

They paused for a moment on the pier, beside the glass-bottomed *Diktynna*. "Marco should be here in a few minutes," she said absently. The historian glanced upward at the alabastrine walls on the hill above the tiny harbor.

" 'This castle hath a pleasant seat; the air —' "

" 'Nimbly and sweetly recommends itself unto our gentle senses,' " she finished promptly. "I memorized most of *Macbeth* at dramatic school. Those were the days before Alexis put his foot down, the days when I thought the stage needed me. *Quelle folie!*"

"I would say that you possessed all the prerequisites for a dramatic career," Westborough declared gallantly. Being excessively shy of personal remarks, he did not specify the curling tendrils of silky black hair, the husky charm of her voice, the fires smoldering beneath dark, luminous eyes, the fluent grace of every movement. But all of these qualities he noted.

Straight and lithe, she poised at the edge of the pier. "You're wrong! It's nice to be flattered, but compared to the other girls at school I was the ugly duckling in a crowd of swans. I can sing a little, though. If Alexis hadn't—"

Bayard ran breathlessly out on the pier, brandishing a paper bag in one hand and a thermos bottle in the other. "We'll have to get out in a hurry!" he exclaimed. "Your father's already looking for you."

Ione jumped in to take the wheel; Bayard deferentially assisted Westborough to step from the pier. The *Diktynna's* cabin contained eight very comfortable leather-cushioned chairs, arranged around a large rectangular pit floored by thick glass.

"Large kelp beds surround the island," Bayard explained in the manner of a professional cicerone, "like submarine gardens!"

Bayard weighed anchor; Ione started the gasoline motor; the launch sped rapidly from harbor. Westborough, resting his hands on the polished railing above the pit as he peered downward, was disappointed to see nothing but the opaque blue glass. Ione shut off the motor, allowing the *Diktynna* to glide of her own momentum, and her stepbrother closed the door, darkening the cabin. "Look now!" he directed.

The effect was miraculous. The murky panel lightened at once to a pale blue transparency. A mirror, Westborough mused, the magic mirror in which the shadows of the world had appeared to the Lady of Shalott . . . but these were shadows of the sea . . . of a world that had never been intended for man's vision . . . the primal ooze where life had its weird beginnings.

Amber trees waved rubbery fronds in the turquoise waters. "Kelp," Bayard called it, but the swaying, snaky plants seemed native to a fantastic Martian landscape. Soon other images entered the ken of the pale blue mirror. Shadows of the sea! A universe of sucker and tentacle, spine and scale, claw and carapace!

These flowerlike disks are sea anemones. Plant or animal? Let the zoologist classify. The bearded pasty-white cylinders are sea cucumbers; the bristling globes are sea urchins, peering shyly from rock crannies. Twisting curls dangle below a quivering purple-striped hemisphere! The thing is a jellyfish; life reduced to the basic stomach. An ocher starfish weaves sinuously across the white sand. A spider crab scuttles clumsily for a befriending boulder. A crayfish in chitinous armor brandishes fierce pincers.

Lordly vertebrates, the aristocrats of the underwater domain, swim gracefully into the mirror! Spotted rock bass, blue-eyed perch, a brilliant black-and-red sheepshead, a beautiful golden garibaldi. But other underwater denizens are not so harmless. Here squirms a savage eel, which can strike as swiftly as a rattlesnake. And here a hideous mass of groping tentacles sweeps the ocean floor, changing its color like a chameleon while the eye follows its writhing movements.

"An octopus!" Bayard called excitedly. "You're in luck. We don't often see these fellows here."

"Thank heaven, no!" Ione exclaimed, peeping into the cabin. She started the motor. The octopus vanished. But another drifting shadow took its place in the mirror's liquid blue field.

It floated up to them from the ocean's depth, an alien intruder covered with seaweed. It twisted and turned below the glass, and they saw—

Bayard gasped tensely, "It's got a *face!* My God!"

PART THREE: ON FILE AT THE SHERIFF'S OFFICE

(Statements made to Captain Albert Cranston, Bureau of Investigation, Sheriff's Department, Los Angeles County, in connection with the Charles Danville murder case. Taken in shorthand and transcribed for signatures of those questioned, by Investigator Ernest Miller on Friday, July 8, 1938, at island residence of Alexis Paphlagloss near Ynez, California, in presence of Captain Albert Cranston and Investigator Gerald Brown of the Bureau of Investigation, Sheriff's Department, and Elmer Stebbins, Township Constable at Ynez.)

A. Statement of Alexis Paphlagloss

CAPTAIN CRANSTON: It is my duty to warn you that anything you say here may be used against you.

PAPHLAGLOSS: I understand.

CAPTAIN CRANSTON: Well, Mr. Paphlagloss, have you viewed the body?

PAPHLAGLOSS *(shuddering)* : Yes.

CAPTAIN CRANSTON: Were you able to identify it?

PAPHLAGLOSS: There wasn't much left to identify.

INVESTIGATOR BROWN: Makes a fellow lose his appetite for fish!

CAPTAIN CRANSTON: Please don't interrupt, Brown.

INVESTIGATOR BROWN: Okay.

CAPTAIN CRANSTON: Have you examined the wrist watch, ring and billfold found on the person of the deceased?

PAPHLAGLOSS: Yes. They belonged to my former butler, Charles Danville.

CAPTAIN CRANSTON: Are you sure of the identity?

INVESTIGATOR BROWN: The wrist watch had the initials C.D. on the back. That's all anyone can be sure of.

CAPTAIN CRANSTON: I'll do the questioning, Brown. Well, Mr. Paphlagloss?

PAPHLAGLOSS: He's stated the facts accurately.

CAPTAIN CRANSTON: Please be more definite, Mr. Paphlagloss. Do you or do you not believe that the articles I've mentioned belonged to your butler, Charles Danville?

PAPHLAGLOSS: I think they were Charles'.

CAPTAIN CRANSTON: On Thursday morning, July 7, did you or

did you not report to Constable Stebbins that your butler had left your employ, under peculiar circumstances, during the night of July 6?

PAPHLAGLOSS: Yes. I wanted Stebbins to notify your office to look for his boat. Has it been found yet?

CAPTAIN CRANSTON: So far it hasn't turned up. When you talked to Constable Stebbins, did you suspect that Danville had met with foul play?

PAPHLAGLOSS: I didn't know what to think. His note said he'd gone to the mainland to visit his sick sister, but Charles had told me several times he had neither brothers nor sisters.

CAPTAIN CRANSTON: Was the signature to the note in his handwriting?

PAPHLAGLOSS: The signature was typewritten like the rest of the note.

INVESTIGATOR BROWN: The note was written on this typewriter here, Chief. I checked up on that detail first thing. And the machine was wiped clean of prints, worse luck!

CAPTAIN CRANSTON: Brown, please. Mr. Paphlagloss, will you describe the boat that was missing after the disappearance of your butler?

PAPHLAGLOSS: I've already described it to Constable Stebbins.

CAPTAIN CRANSTON: For the sake of this record.

PAPHLAGLOSS: It was a small rowboat with an outboard motor. Marc—my stepson—used it in transporting his Indian relics from his camp to the house, and he'd left it moored to the pier.

CAPTAIN CRANSTON: Did anyone at your house hear the noise of the motor during the night?

PAPHLAGLOSS: I didn't, but my daughter Ione said she did.

CAPTAIN CRANSTON: Was this rowboat capable of navigating the open sea?

PAPHLAGLOSS: Yes, except in rough weather. But it was only used around the coast of the island. Mostly by Marc.

CAPTAIN CRANSTON: Was your butler good at handling motorboats?

PAPHLAGLOSS: I never saw him handle one.

CAPTAIN CRANSTON: Was a valuable art object stolen from you two days before your butler's disappearance?

PAPHLAGLOSS (*starting*): How did you hear about that? I didn't tell Stebbins.

CAPTAIN CRANSTON: No, but you asked Captain Smithfield of the Los Angeles police department to recommend a private investigator.

He referred you to Lieutenant Collins who recommended Mr. T.L. Westborough, who is at present one of your guests. Is that correct?

PAPHLAGLOSS: Entirely correct.

CAPTAIN CRANSTON: Is Mr. Westborough's mission known to anyone besides yourself?

PAPHLAGLOSS: I hope not. I didn't tell anybody.

CAPTAIN CRANSTON: Not even a member of your immediate family?

PAPHLAGLOSS: No one.

CAPTAIN CRANSTON: Do you or did you believe that Danville had stolen the art object from you?

PAPHLAGLOSS: I don't believe it, and I never did believe it. Charles had been with me for ten years, and he was far more like a personal friend than a servant.

CAPTAIN CRANSTON: Was Danville on good terms with your other servants?

PAPHLAGLOSS: Charles was something of a martinet for discipline. The women may have thought he was a bit too strict.

CAPTAIN CRANSTON: How many servants do you have here?

PAPHLAGLOSS: Not many now. Three women in the house, and Tom Starr outside. But Tom is my caretaker and can't be called a servant. He keeps my boats in tune and supervises the house lighting system. A natural-born mechanic and a first-class fisherman!

CAPTAIN CRANSTON: Did Starr get along all right with your butler?

PAPHLAGLOSS: So far as I know. Their duties kept them apart. Charles stayed at the house, but Tom sleeps in a room over the boathouse.

CAPTAIN CRANSTON: Mr. Paphlagloss, please describe the anchor that was on the missing rowboat.

PAPHLAGLOSS: An iron cylinder packed with concrete. But you know what it looks like. It was the one that—that—

CAPTAIN CRANSTON: That was tied to the ankle of the deceased to hold the body below the surface of the sea?

PAPHLAGLOSS: Yes.

CAPTAIN CRANSTON: Who discovered the body?

PAPHLAGLOSS: My daughter, my stepson and Mr. Westborough. The young people were taking Mr. Westborough on a glass-bottomed boat excursion.

CAPTAIN CRANSTON: Did they report the circumstance at once to you?

PAPHLAGLOSS: Yes. Caught us just in time, too. Mr. Stoner, his son, Tom and myself were just about to leave on an all-day fishing trip.

CAPTAIN CRANSTON: What did you do on hearing the news?

PAPHLAGLOSS: Knossos doesn't have a telephone. Ione took Mr. Westborough to Ynez in the *Ariadne*. Tom, Marc, the two Stoners and I went to the spot where the body was submerged.

CONSTABLE STEBBINS: As soon as I'd telephoned you at headquarters, Captain, I set out to the island to make sure there wasn't no evidence disturbed. And I found that these fellows had moved the body.

PAPHLAGLOSS: What difference does that make? You can't do your detecting under the surface of the sea, you fool.

CONSTABLE STEBBINS: Who you calling a fool?

PAPHLAGLOSS: You.

CAPTAIN CRANSTON: Gentlemen, please. Mr. Paphlagloss, did you or did you not move the body?

PAPHLAGLOSS: Of course we moved it. Would you leave something that had once been human down there a minute longer than you could help?

CAPTAIN CRANSTON: Was it difficult to raise the body, Mr. Paphlagloss?

PAPHLAGLOSS: Not very. The rope had come unwound and was long enough so that he—it—floated within a few feet of the surface. We could touch it with our gaffs.

CAPTAIN CRANSTON: Did you have trouble in finding the spot?

PAPHLAGLOSS: No. Marc and Mr. Westborough had made a rough map, noting the shore landmarks, and Marc guided us right to it.

CAPTAIN CRANSTON: Is it very far from the house?

PAPHLAGLOSS: A mile or so. It isn't far from Marc's excavations on the northern tip of the island.

CAPTAIN CRANSTON: Who was operating the glass-bottomed boat at the time the body was discovered?

PAPHLAGLOSS: I never thought to ask. Either my daughter or my stepson.

CAPTAIN CRANSTON: Mr. Paphlagloss, can you think of anything else that would help us in the investigation of this crime?

PAPHLAGLOSS: Only that I'm willing to pay a reward of five thousand dollars for the discovery and conviction of Charles' murderer.

CAPTAIN CRANSTON: Have you read Mr. Miller's transcription?

PAPHLAGLOSS: Yes.

CAPTAIN CRANSTON: Do you find it an accurate record of our conversation?

PAPHLAGLOSS: Yes.

CAPTAIN CRANSTON: Then sign your name, please.

ALEXIS PAPHLAGLOSS
(Signed in the presence of Albert Cranston, Gerald Brown, Ernest Miller and Elmer Stebbins.)

B. Statement of Marcus Bayard

CAPTAIN CRANSTON: Do you understand that anything you say may be used against you?

BAYARD: Yes. Go on and get it over with.

CAPTAIN CRANSTON: Were you able to identify the body?

BAYARD *(shuddering)*: No one could identify it. But the wrist watch belonged to Charles.

CAPTAIN CRANSTON: Who first saw the submerged body?

BAYARD: A toss-up between myself and Mr. Westborough.

CAPTAIN CRANSTON: Were you operating the glass-bottomed boat?

BAYARD: No. Miss Paphlagloss was running it.

CAPTAIN CRANSTON: At her suggestion or yours?

BAYARD: What difference does it make?

CAPTAIN CRANSTON: Please tell us everything you did after discovery of the body.

BAYARD: Mr. Westborough and I made a map so we could find the spot again without trouble and then we went back to the house. Ione and Mr. Westborough ran over to Ynez to report to you while the rest of us went back there. Some of us went, I should say. Mother didn't go, naturally, and Glendon had to keep on working or spoil his fresco.

CAPTAIN CRANSTON: Who drew the body to the boat?

BAYARD: Stoner gaffed it first. Then I gaffed it. My hook caught in the clothing and the rotten stuff ripped away. I had to sink it deeper. Then Stoner and I pulled it into the boat. Rather a nasty business!

CAPTAIN CRANSTON: Which Stoner helped you?

BAYARD: The elder Stoner was too sick to be of any use. I don't blame him. The sight was enough to turn anyone's stomach. The only thing that saved me, I guess, was that I hadn't had any breakfast.

CAPTAIN CRANSTON: What did you do with the body after you'd drawn it into the boat?

BAYARD: Carried it to the pier and threw a tarp over it.

CAPTAIN CRANSTON: Did you examine the contents of the pockets?

BAYARD: No one wanted to handle it any more than he had to.

CAPTAIN CRANSTON: Did you place a guard to see that it wasn't touched?

BAYARD: No, but no one went near it. We were gathered at the other end of the pier talking until Constable Stebbins came. He was good and mad.

CONSTABLE STEBBINS: I had a right to be mad, young fellow. Moving the body!

BAYARD: I'm not responsible for that, Constable.

CONSTABLE STEBBINS: No, but I know who is responsible.

CAPTAIN CRANSTON: Bayard, I understand from your stepfather that you are excavating Indian relics.

BAYARD: Yes, I have a tent at the north end of the island. I call it my field headquarters.

CAPTAIN CRANSTON: Do you sleep at your camp?

BAYARD: Sometimes.

CAPTAIN CRANSTON: Did you sleep there last Wednesday night?

BAYARD: Yes, I believe I did.

CAPTAIN CRANSTON: Then, will you explain why your boat happened to be moored at the pier on that night?

BAYARD: I left it there and walked back over the hills after dinner. Mother didn't like me to use that small boat at night. It's pretty dark on this island, except at full moon, and it worried her. You know how mothers are. Mine is worse, if anything.

CAPTAIN CRANSTON: Please give me your opinion of Danville's character.

BAYARD: Best in the world! I owe him more than I could ever repay.

CAPTAIN CRANSTON: Tell me about it.

BAYARD: When Mr. Paphlagloss sent me away to a military school, I had a pretty tough time. I was always a weak sickly brat. I couldn't squawk at home about the hazings, but I could write to Charles in confidence, and he advised me almost like a second father. He's written me some masterly letters. Ione thought a lot of him, too. We were all fond of Charles. Even Mother.

CAPTAIN CRANSTON: Why do you say "even Mother"?

BAYARD: I don't know.

CAPTAIN CRANSTON: I understand from Mr. Paphlagloss that Danville didn't get along so well with the other help.

BAYARD: You must have misunderstood my stepfather. Everyone liked Charles.

CAPTAIN CRANSTON: Did Danville, to your knowledge, ever have an argument with one of your stepfather's guests?

BAYARD: Good lord, no! Charles wasn't the kind of servant who would forget his place. Besides, the guests are a pretty decent lot. You can't imagine a great scholar like Doctor Nielsen brawling with a butler. Or a big businessman like Harvey Stoner. And Russell Stoner—well, he's all right, too, I guess.

CAPTAIN CRANSTON: What about the artist fellow, Glendon?

BAYARD: He's very likeable.

CAPTAIN CRANSTON: Have you read the notes Mr. Miller has just transcribed?

BAYARD: Yes, they are an accurate record of the conversation. Do you want me to sign my name?

CAPTAIN CRANSTON: Please.

MARC BAYARD
(Signed in the presence of Albert Cranston, Gerald Brown, Ernest Miller and Elmer Stebbins.)

C. Statement of Ione Paphlagloss

CAPTAIN CRANSTON: Miss Paphlagloss, it is my duty to warn you that anything you say may be used against you. Investigator Miller is making a shorthand record of our conversation which I'm going to ask you to sign after he transcribes it.

MISS PAPHLAGLOSS: What a ghastly idea! Something like going on the radio, isn't it? You won't let them treat me too badly, will you, Constable?

CONSTABLE STEBBINS: I should say not, miss.

MISS PAPHLAGLOSS: If you do, I'll tell your wife.

CONSTABLE STEBBINS: Ha, ha!

CAPTAIN CRANSTON: Miss Paphlagloss, did you hear any unusual noise during last Wednesday night?

MISS PAPHLAGLOSS: What sort of noise? A motor? I heard that.

CAPTAIN CRANSTON: What time?

MISS PAPHLAGLOSS: I wasn't interested enough to get out of bed and look at the clock. However, it was long after midnight.

CAPTAIN CRANSTON: Didn't it strike you that there was something odd about taking a boat out at that time?

MISS PAPHLAGLOSS: Sorry, but I was too sleepy for anything to strike me. The noise seemed almost like a dream, and if it hadn't been for this morning, I'd have been ready to believe it was one.

CAPTAIN CRANSTON: Who suggested your excursion this morning?

MISS PAPHLAGLOSS: I invited Mr. Westborough. Marco rather crashed the party, but we were glad to have him.

CAPTAIN CRANSTON: Do you usually run the boat when your stepbrother rides with you?

MISS PAPHLAGLOSS: Yes, if I can get my hands on the wheel. Marc's so nearsighted!

CAPTAIN CRANSTON: Was it a shock to you to find. . . ?

MISS PAPHLAGLOSS: Wouldn't it be to you?

CAPTAIN CRANSTON: Yes, it would. You'd known him for a long time, hadn't you?

MISS PAPHLAGLOSS: Ever since I was a junior high school fledgling with dramatic ambitions. He and Marco were the only claque I could find, and poor old Marc wasn't very satisfactory. You should have seen him! Skinny as a rail, and big-horn-rimmed spectacles! They've gone out of fashion, thank heaven, and Marc's almost human now. Unless he happens to be talking about the Channel Island Indians. He's still very didactic on that subject.

CAPTAIN CRANSTON: I understand Mr. Bayard is doing excavation work at the north end of the island.

MISS PAPHLAGLOSS: Yes, he hopes it will land him on the staff of the Garrick Museum. Jennifer is sweetly furious. She's set her heart on having Alexis make him a big department-store magnate, but Marc isn't interested in business. He's one of the few in the world who really don't care about money.

CAPTAIN CRANSTON: Was Charles on good terms with your other servants?

MISS PAPHLAGLOSS: Cook and Della thought he was wonderful, but Carrie didn't like him. Don't ask me to explain that girl.

CAPTAIN CRANSTON: What about your father's guests?

MISS PAPHLAGLOSS: What about them?

CAPTAIN CRANSTON: Did any of them ever get into a fuss with Charles?

MISS PAPHLAGLOSS: Of course not! Guests don't row with servants, do they?

CAPTAIN CRANSTON: I've known them to—in Hollywood.

MISS PAPHLAGLOSS: Oh, Hollywood! Really, Captain Cranston, I'm enjoying our conversation, but do you mind telling me where it's leading to?

CAPTAIN CRANSTON: That will be all, thank you, Miss Paphlagloss.

CAPTAIN CRANSTON: Have you read over Mr. Miller's notes?

MISS PAPHLAGLOSS: Yes, and I ought to be shot for some of the things I've said. However, I can't deny my own words. Where do I sign?

CAPTAIN CRANSTON: Right here, please.

IONE PAPHLAGLOSS
(Signed in the presence of Albert Cranston, Gerald Brown, Ernest Miller and Elmer Stebbins.)

D. Statement of Jennifer Paphlagloss

MRS. PAPHLAGLOSS: Good afternoon, gentlemen. I hope this little room has been all right for your use?

CAPTAIN CRANSTON: Yes, thank you. It is my duty to warn you—

MRS. PAPHLAGLOSS: It seems so sparsely furnished. Are you sure you wouldn't like to have some more chairs?

CAPTAIN CRANSTON: No, thank you. It is my duty—

MRS. PAPHLAGLOSS: But then all the rooms in this house are skimpily furnished. My husband thinks because they didn't have a great variety of furniture in ancient Crete we should stint ourselves today. But I don't suppose you are interested in interior decoration, Captain Cranston?

CAPTAIN CRANSTON: I don't know a great deal about it, madam. It is my duty to—

MRS. PAPHLAGLOSS: Of course not. Why should you be? There are so many more manly subjects that you do know about! I have great admiration for gentlemen in your profession, Captain Cranston.

CAPTAIN CRANSTON: Anything you say may be used against you.

MRS. PAPHLAGLOSS: What would you gentlemen say—very confidentially—to some light refreshments? I have an old Southern recipe for mint juleps.

INVESTIGATOR BROWN: Did you say mint juleps?

CAPTAIN CRANSTON: Sorry, Mrs. Paphlagloss, but we don't drink while on duty. May I ask you a few questions, please?

MRS. PAPHLAGLOSS: Why, of course. That's what I'm here for, isn't it?

CAPTAIN CRANSTON: I hope so. Did you hear the noise of an outboard motor on Wednesday night?

MRS. PAPHLAGLOSS: I'm frightfully sorry, but I didn't. Nobody seems to have heard it but Ione. However, I am a very sound sleeper and so is Alexis. Ione, dear girl, sometimes has difficulty in falling asleep. And our three bedrooms are the only ones that face the ocean. Naturally, no one else would be able to hear it, do you think?

CAPTAIN CRANSTON: We'll have to try it and see. What sort of man was your butler in physical appearance?

MRS. PAPHLAGLOSS: Oh, he was about forty-five years old, not very tall, built rather slightly, but very distinguished. A dear old thing, really! We shall miss him frightfully.

CAPTAIN CRANSTON: How did he get along with your other servants?

MRS. PAPHLAGLOSS: He was just like a father to our two maids, Carrie and Della. Sweet girls; they're sisters and from the nicest family. And cook adored him. Simply adored him!

CAPTAIN CRANSTON: Then he had no enemies in this household?

MRS. PAPHLAGLOSS: Oh, my dear Captain, how could poor harmless Charles have an enemy anywhere? May I smoke? Or is that the proper thing to do while an investigation is in progress? Thank you. Do you have a match?

CAPTAIN CRANSTON: I'll light it for you.

MRS. PAPHLAGLOSS: Thank you so much..

CAPTAIN CRANSTON: Did Mr. Paphlagloss show you the note purporting to be written by your butler?

MRS. PAPHLAGLOSS: Yes. Who did write it?

CAPTAIN CRANSTON: If we knew that, Mrs. Paphlagloss, we'd know who killed him.

MRS. PAPHLAGLOSS: Killed, Captain Cranston? Was Charles *killed?*

CAPTAIN CRANSTON: We think so. The note isn't a suicide note, for one thing. It was written deliberately in the hope of making you and your husband believe that your butler had run away. And for another—well, no man can fracture his own skull by hitting himself from behind. This was cold-blooded murder.

MRS. PAPHLAGLOSS: How horrible! How unspeakably horrible!

CAPTAIN CRANSTON: Have you read the record of our conversation transcribed by Mr. Miller?

MRS. PAPHLAGLOSS: Yes. Hasn't he done lovely work?

CAPTAIN CRANSTON: You are ready to sign it as a true record?

MRS. PAPHLAGLOSS: May I borrow your fountain pen, Captain?

JENNIFER PAPHLAGLOSS
(Signed in the presence of Albert Cranston, Gerald Brown, Ernest Miller and Elmer Stebbins.)

E. Statement of Anna Holden

CAPTAIN CRANSTON: It is my duty to warn you that anything you say may be used against you. Your name is Anna Holden?

MRS. HOLDEN: That's the name that's the blame, I always say.

CAPTAIN CRANSTON: You are employed as cook by Mr. Paphlagloss?

MRS. HOLDEN: Yes indeedy. Been with him ever since my man died, which was three years come Labor Day.

CAPTAIN CRANSTON: What kind of employer do you find him?

MRS. HOLDEN: He pays good wages. There's them that wouldn't like to spend every summer buried on a lonesome island the way we do. But them that has to work shouldn't be choosy, I always say.

CAPTAIN CRANSTON: What's your opinion of the rest of the family?

MRS. HOLDEN: Mrs. Paphlagloss is sweet. Too sweet, maybe, sometimes. Mr. Bayard always has a good word for everyone, but he's that absentminded I'm afraid he'll walk over the cliff some night. And Miss Ione, she's funny. Singing like a bird some mornings, most beautiful voice you ever heard. And then again she'll be down in the dumps and you can't get her out of it for love or money. I like people that's always the same. Like Della, who helps me in the kitchen. You couldn't ask for a nicer, more sensible girl than what Della is. Carrie's her sister, but they're as different as day and night.

CAPTAIN CRANSTON: In what way are they different?

MRS. HOLDEN: Carrie likes to dress fancy. Tries to copy Miss Ione, but it ain't her style. Too squatty. Miss Ione's got a beautiful figure, even if it is on the skinny side. But we can't all be perfect, I always say. And the rouge and lipstick and mascara and eyeshadow that girl uses!

CAPTAIN CRANSTON: Miss Paphlagloss?

MRS. HOLDEN: Carrie. Must spend half her wages on them. But you can't make a silk purse from a sow's tail, I always say.

CAPTAIN CRANSTON: How did Carrie get along with Charles?

MRS. HOLDEN: Carrie's much too big for herself. "There ain't no butler going to order me around," I heard her say to him once, sassy as anything you please. But Della was different again. She thought Charles was wonderful. He'd 'a' been the last person to know it, but there wasn't nothing that girl wouldn't do for him.

CAPTAIN CRANSTON: Was Charles attracted to either of the girls?

MRS. HOLDEN: If he was, he kept it to himself. He was a great hand to keep things to himself. The poor man! Suffered something terrible. It was a crime against nature the things that man had to go through with.

CAPTAIN CRANSTON: Was he sick?

MRS. HOLDEN: He couldn't sleep. Insomila.

CAPTAIN CRANSTON: Do you mean insomnia?

MRS. HOLDEN: Maybe that is it. He'd sit up till two, three o'clock reading. A great hand to read, Charles was. I like a nice love story myself, if it ain't too trashy, but Charles always read Mr. Paphlagloss' books. There was one called *Candied* by a fellow named Volter and another by a fellow named Mountain. Only "mountain" ain't quite the way it's spelled. I couldn't make head nor tail of them myself. But let them that likes peaches, eat peaches, I always say.

CAPTAIN CRANSTON: Did Charles ever talk about his family?

MRS. HOLDEN: I don't think he had no family. Thought the world and all of Mr. Paphlagloss and the two young people. Mrs. P. too, of course. Maybe that's what made him so fussy about the house.

CAPTAIN CRANSTON: Was he fussy about the house?

MRS. HOLDEN: Do you know the last thing that man did just 'fore he went to sleep? He'd leave his room and walk around the house to see that all the doors and the downstairs windows was locked. "There ain't no burglars going to come in motorboats after us," I'd always tell him. But 'twasn't no use to try to stop him. Told me once he couldn't get to sleep until he'd had his nightly prowl. "Nightly prowl" was just what he said. Talked lovely, Charles did.

CAPTAIN CRANSTON: Did Charles ever get into an argument with one of your employer's guests?

MRS. HOLDEN: Charles never was no great hand to argue with anybody.

CAPTAIN CRANSTON: What's your opinion of the guests?

MRS. HOLDEN: If you ask me, I've cooked for people I've liked better than Mr. Stoner. Looks at you like you was dust under his feet. The old man, I mean. The son's right cheerful-like. Came into the kitchen once with a spider on the end of a string. Thought I'd die laughing at the tricks he made that fool thing do. Once he laid a cigar butt on top of my stove, and I yelled for him to take it away so it wouldn't hurt the enamel. Then he laughed and pretended to swallow it. I thought sure he was going to burn his throat, but it was a fake, too. Only it looked just like the real thing—lighted end, ash and all. He's a great hand for kidding, that Mr. Stoner.

CAPTAIN CRANSTON: What about Doctor Nielsen?

MRS. HOLDEN: I don't know much about him or that other little professor. The other one ain't been here long enough to get acquainted, and Professor Nielsen spends most of his time in his room, Carrie says. Makes her mad 'cause he's always there when she wants to clean.

CAPTAIN CRANSTON: How do you like Mr. Glendon?

MRS. HOLDEN: Don't he paint grand? Right on the wet plaster, too. I never heard tell of such a thing.

CAPTAIN CRANSTON: Have you read over the record of our conversation?

MRS. HOLDEN: Yes indeedy.

CAPTAIN CRANSTON: Will you sign your name to show that it's an accurate record of what you've told me?

MRS. HOLDEN: Fools' names, like their faces . . . I always say.

ANNA HOLDEN

(Signed in the presence of Albert Cranston, Gerald Brown, Ernest Miller and Elmer Stebbins.)

F. Statement of Della Winters

D. WINTERS: Mrs. Holden said you wanted to see me.

CAPTAIN CRANSTON: Yes. Come in, please, and close the door. Don't look so frightened, Miss Winters. We aren't any of us going to hurt you. You know, don't you, about the body found in the ocean?

D. WINTERS *(shuddering)* : Was it . . . ?

CAPTAIN CRANSTON: Yes, we believe it was.

D. WINTERS: My God!

CAPTAIN CRANSTON: It is my duty to warn you that anything you say may be used against you.

D. WINTERS: To think that he—to think that he's—

CAPTAIN CRANSTON: You were fond of him, weren't you?

D. WINTERS: Oh yes!

CAPTAIN CRANSTON: I'm sorry that I have to ask you these things.

But it's my duty to find out who killed him.

D. WINTERS: I'll do anything I can to help you.

CAPTAIN CRANSTON: You're a brave girl.

D. WINTERS: No, I'm a stupid girl.

CAPTAIN CRANSTON: Was he in love with you?

D. WINTERS: What's the use of fooling myself? No, he wasn't.

CAPTAIN CRANSTON: Was he in love with your sister?

D. WINTERS: With Carrie? Oh no! Never!

CAPTAIN CRANSTON: He and your sister didn't get along very well together, I understand.

D. WINTERS: Carrie was mean to him.

CAPTAIN CRANSTON: Did you know that Mr. Danville suffered from insomnia?

D. WINTERS: I knew he couldn't sleep. Sometimes I'd listen to his footsteps walking down the hall, and I wanted to get out of bed and put my arms around him—oh, what am I saying? What sort of girl am I?

CAPTAIN CRANSTON: Did you hear him walking on Wednesday night?

D. WINTERS: Yes. When he left his room and walked past my door, I woke up. He went down the stairs and out through the big paved court, and from there on I couldn't tell where he went. I couldn't hear him any longer. I waited and waited for him to come back, but he didn't come back. He never did come back!

CAPTAIN CRANSTON: Do you know what time it was when he walked past your door?

D. WINTERS: Not that night. It was usually about two-thirty. Sometimes two, and once in a while as late as three.

CAPTAIN CRANSTON: Did you hear the noise of an outboard motor that night?

D. WINTERS: No. I guess I must have fallen to sleep, finally.

CAPTAIN CRANSTON: Think very hard, Miss Winters, because a lot depends on your answer. While you were lying there, waiting for Mr. Danville to return, did you hear anyone else walking in the upstairs halls?

D. WINTERS: No one.

CAPTAIN CRANSTON: Do you have good hearing?

D. WINTERS: I suppose so. I don't know.

CAPTAIN CRANSTON: I'm going to test it. *(He walked across the room and whispered.)* What did I say?

D. WINTERS: You said: "If she hears this, she should be able to hear a person walking anywhere in the upper halls from her room." But I didn't hear anyone.

CAPTAIN CRANSTON: How long were you awake?

D. WINTERS: At least an hour.

CAPTAIN CRANSTON: Were you worried when Mr. Danville failed to return?

D. WINTERS: Yes. Yes, I was worried.

CAPTAIN CRANSTON: Then why didn't you get up and go downstairs to find out what had become of him?

D. WINTERS: At that time of night? What would he think of me?

CAPTAIN CRANSTON: You had never told him how you felt toward him?

D. WINTERS: No, never.

CAPTAIN CRANSTON: How did Mr. Danville get along with Mrs. Holden?

D. WINTERS: They were good friends.

CAPTAIN CRANSTON: Did Mr. Danville have an argument with anyone in the house? A guest? Or one of the family?

D. WINTERS: Oh no, no!

CAPTAIN CRANSTON: How much education have you had, Miss Winters?

D. WINTERS: I've been through high school.

CAPTAIN CRANSTON: Too bad you have to be doing this sort of work.

D. WINTERS: You have to take the kind of job you can get. I haven't minded—much.

CAPTAIN CRANSTON: You have read over the typewritten record of our conversation, Miss Winters?

D. WINTERS: Yes.

CAPTAIN CRANSTON: Will you sign it in order to show that you acknowledge it as a true record of what we said?

D. WINTERS: There's one or two—well, little personal things. Is it necessary for them to be included?

CAPTAIN CRANSTON: I'm sorry, Miss Winters. The record must include everything you said to me.

D. WINTERS: All right. I'll sign it.

DELLA WINTERS
(Signed in the presence of Albert Cranston, Gerald Brown, Ernest Miller and Elmer Stebbins.)

G. Statement of Carrie Winters

C. WINTERS: Which one of you is the sheriff?

CAPTAIN CRANSTON: The sheriff isn't here. I'm Captain Cranston of the Bureau of Investigation of his department. We'd like to have you answer a few questions.

C. WINTERS: All right. I get few enough chances to talk around here.

CAPTAIN CRANSTON: It's my duty to warn you that anything you say may be used against you. Mrs. Holden tells me that you didn't get along very well with Danville.

C. WINTERS: That old hag had better mind her own business.

CAPTAIN CRANSTON: Your sister Della told us the same thing.

C. WINTERS: Della's always a sap. Wouldn't keep us staying out here on this Godforsaken island if she wasn't a mushy sap about that sourpuss butler.

CAPTAIN CRANSTON: You are speaking of the dead, Miss Winters.

C. WINTERS: Well, he was a sourpuss.

CAPTAIN CRANSTON: Did he ever make improper advances to you?

C. WINTERS: My God, no! But I hated him.

CAPTAIN CRANSTON: Why did you hate him?

C. WINTERS: Bawled me out for the way I made the beds. Little things like that. Unimportant, maybe, but everything seems important when you're marooned in a place like this. What chance does a girl have here for any fun? So Godawful far away from things. I can't even get to the city on my day off. I couldn't stand it if it wasn't for Ione.

CAPTAIN CRANSTON: Do you always speak of her so familiarly?

C. WINTERS: I think of her that way. She's got style and class. More personality in her little finger than all the rest of her family put together. And now she's gone and fallen in love with—say, is that guy taking down what I've been saying?

CAPTAIN CRANSTON: Yes. I warned you that what you said could be used—

C. WINTERS: Oh, my God!

CAPTAIN CRANSTON: You were about to tell me something about Miss Paphlagloss.

C. WINTERS: I've said enough now to get me fired. Five times over! I'm through talking.

CAPTAIN CRANSTON: I've only got a few more questions to ask.

C. WINTERS: You won't get the answers. Not from me.

CAPTAIN CRANSTON: Did you hear the noise of an outboard motor on Wednesday night or early Thursday morning?

(C. Winters did not answer.)

CAPTAIN CRANSTON: Did you hear the butler walking in the hall at that time?

(C. Winters did not answer.)

CAPTAIN CRANSTON: You're behaving very foolishly. What harm can you do yourself by answering those two questions?

(C. Winters did not answer.)

CAPTAIN CRANSTON: You may go. But I'll expect you back later on to read and sign this record.

CAPTAIN CRANSTON: Have you read the typewritten record of our conversation?

C. WINTERS: Sure, I've read it. If I wasn't a lady, I'd sock you for the things you've made me say.

CAPTAIN CRANSTON: Are you willing to sign it as a true record of what you said to me?

C. WINTERS: No, I won't sign it. And you can't make me. Just try to make me put my name there!

(Miss Carrie Winters did not sign.)

H. Statement of Thomas W. Starr.
(Taken in boathouse at Knossos.)

STARR: Well, if it isn't old Elmer Stebbins! What can I do for you, Elmer?

CONSTABLE STEBBINS: Tom, Captain Cranston wants to ask you a few questions.

STARR: Always glad to oblige a pal of yours, Elmer. About this fellow drowning?

CAPTAIN CRANSTON: Call it murder, Starr. That's the proper name for it.

STARR: You don't say!

CAPTAIN CRANSTON: You understand, Starr, that anything you say can be used against you.

STARR: All right with me. Who was he?

CAPTAIN CRANSTON: We think it was the missing butler.

STARR: After looking at—what's laying under the tarpaulin—I'd kinda hate to have to deliver an opinion on that question. Yes sir, I sure would. Shucks, this is too bad! Danville used to ride over to the mainland with me now and then to order supplies. Right nice fellow.

CAPTAIN CRANSTON: Ever get into a quarrel with him?

STARR: What about?

CAPTAIN CRANSTON: Did he ever take a boat over to the mainland by himself?

STARR: He couldn't handle a craft none too well. I was sure surprised to learn he'd taken that rowboat out to run away in.

CAPTAIN CRANSTON: Would he have been able to reach the mainland in that?

STARR: I won't say yes. But on the other hand I won't say no.

CAPTAIN CRANSTON: Nice place you've got here, Starr.

STARR: A little snug, but it suits the missus and me. She's in San Berdoo with some relatives now.

CAPTAIN CRANSTON: You and your wife are the caretakers?

STARR: Guess you could call us that, Captain, and we wouldn't be much offended.

CAPTAIN CRANSTON: How long have you had this job, Starr?

STARR: How long has the big house been here? I came with the house, you might say.

CAPTAIN CRANSTON: You mean you were on the island before the house was built?

STARR: There wasn't no one on this island before the house was built, 'cept a few sheepherders. No, Captain, I was an islander, but not this island. Catalina was my stamping grounds. Owned a tuna clipper there.

CAPTAIN CRANSTON: Is that where you met Paphlagloss?

STARR: Yep, my best customer. One of the biggest men in L.A., and on the water he's just as common as an old shoe. His daughter's like him that way, but there's others staying here I could name who ain't.

CAPTAIN CRANSTON: Who, for instance?

STARR: Stoner, for instance.

CAPTAIN CRANSTON: The father or son?

STARR: Son's a smart-aleck kid, but he's young enough to grow out of it. It's his old man, I mean. To hear him talk, you'd think he knew everything there was to know about deep-sea fishing. Like to give me lessons, he would. Me, who's been fishing the channel since the year nineteen hundred and ten!

CAPTAIN CRANSTON: Does he know anything about deep-sea fishing?

STARR: What he knows, he got out of a book. I can tell you which book, too, though I never was one for reading. Not that I mind a fellow being ignorant. No one could be ignoranter than Doc Nielsen, but the doc has sense enough to know he don't know nothing, which makes it all right. Well, here I am gassing away like a couple of old women hanging clothes in their back yards. What was you going to ask me, Captain?

CAPTAIN CRANSTON: How did you happen to give up your tuna clipper?

STARR: Ever hear of a thing called the depression? It didn't do much to my trade—just practically ended it. I was poking around, trying to make a living and wondering who was going to take care of the missus and me in our old age, when along comes Mr. Paphlagloss. "I've bought an island north of here," he says, "and I'm building the biggest summer place you ever saw, Tom." "Glad to hear the banks left you two dollars to rub together," I says, knowing he'd lost a mint of money a few years back. And he says, "Won't seem right fishing without you, Tom. How'd you like to come work for me?" "Well, sir," I says, "don't see how I could be much worse off than I am working for myself." So here we are!

CAPTAIN CRANSTON: Is that a thirty-thirty rifle hanging on the wall?

STARR: That's just what it is, Captain.

CAPTAIN CRANSTON: Can't be much hunting here, is there?

STARR: Few wild goats. And once in a while I shoot a boar. Spelled B-O-A-R, you with the pencil.

CAPTAIN CRANSTON: I should think you'd be too busy in the summer to do any hunting.

STARR: That's right, Captain. I am.

CAPTAIN CRANSTON: Then why do you keep a rifle here?

STARR: Boss's orders. He says keep a rifle with me in the boat-house, and I do.

CAPTAIN CRANSTON: Sounds like he was afraid of pirates or something.

STARR: If he is, it ain't none of my business. But there's a dozen more like this up at the big house. Revolvers, too. The boss is a swell shot, and so is Miss Ione.

CAPTAIN CRANSTON: Well, the fellow we're interested in wasn't shot. He was hit over the head. And then he was taken out in a boat, the boat anchor tied around his ankle, and dumped into the ocean. All on last Wednesday night. You should've heard the noise of the outboard motor, Starr.

STARR: Think maybe I did.

CAPTAIN CRANSTON: Well, for the love of Mike! Why didn't you say so?

STARR: Waiting for you to ask me, Captain.

CAPTAIN CRANSTON: I'm asking you now.

STARR: It was this way. I ain't a light sleeper and then again I ain't a heavy one. Sort of 'twixt and 'tween. Well, I was laying here in my bed—the same bed you're setting on now—and I heard a noise. Galumph! Galumph! Galumph! Sounded like someone walking on the wooden pier. And I looked at my alarm clock—see, Captain, it's got a luminous dial—and the hands said just twenty-five minutes to three.

CAPTAIN CRANSTON: Did you get up to look out?

STARR: Sure did. But the moon had set and, lord bless you, it was dark as pitch. And by the time I got to the window, the noise had stopped. So I says to myself, "Tom, old lad, you've been having dreams. Go back to bed and have some more of 'em." So back I went. And then I heard the noise of the outboard.,

CAPTAIN CRANSTON: You knew which motor it was?

STARR: Sure I knew which it was. No two motors ever sounds just the same. And I think, "Here's some damn fool going to do some night fishing. I wonder if I ought to take one of the speedboats and try to find him and tell him he's taking a swell chance of being pulled overboard—a dinky little boat like that." And I think maybe I will. And then I think maybe it ain't none of my business. So I don't do nothing after all. And then the first thing I know here's the sun streaming in through the window, and it's morning. And I think maybe I dreamed the whole thing. But the boat ain't where Marc moored it. And it's his boat—leastwise no one ever uses it but him. And when he walks up to the house for breakfast, I yell for him to come down to the pier. Then he tells me he's been over at his camp all night and ain't never touched it. And the next thing we hear is that Charles is gone.

CAPTAIN CRANSTON: What do you think became of the boat, by the way?

STARR: Well, sir, there's two things you can do to an outboard motorboat you want to get rid of. One is to start the motor and shove her nose out to sea, but there ain't any guarantee that a wave won't turn her around and she won't come back at you. Then you can stove a hole in her bottom and sink her. And if you ask me, that's just what was done.

CAPTAIN CRANSTON: Is the water deep enough to sink her close to shore?

STARR: Bless you, the water's six to fifteen feet deep all along the coast of the island, 'cept at a few places. Take the glass-bottom and go cruising along the coast line, and you'll find her, all right. Here's a five-spot says you do.

CAPTAIN CRANSTON: We'll do that little thing, Starr, and thanks for the tip.

STARR: Always glad to oblige friends of Elmer's. Anything else I can do?

CAPTAIN CRANSTON: After Miller's transcribed his notes, you can sign your name to them.

CAPTAIN CRANSTON: Well, Starr, have you read over Miller's notes?

STARR: Bet your life. It made good reading.

CAPTAIN CRANSTON: Are you satisfied they are an accurate record of our conversation?

STARR: I'm satisfied. This the corner where you want me to put my John Henry?

THOMAS W. STARR
(Signed in the presence of Albert Cranston, Gerald Brown, Ernest Miller and Elmer Stebbins.)

I. Statement of Dr. Arne Nielsen

CAPTAIN CRANSTON: Do you understand, Doctor Nielsen, that anything you say may be used against you?

NIELSEN: I understand.

CAPTAIN CRANSTON: Are you a specialist or general practitioner?

NIELSEN: Neither.

CAPTAIN CRANSTON: What kind of a doctor are you?

NIELSEN: Philosophy.

CAPTAIN CRANSTON: My mistake. I supposed you were an M.D.

NIELSEN: Unfortunately, no. For my sins I am condemned to teach Greek history.

CAPTAIN CRANSTON: Do you teach at the University of Southern California, Doctor Nielsen?

NIELSEN: No. At a more or less obscure institution in Pennsylvania. Have you, by chance, heard of Prescott University?

CAPTAIN CRANSTON: Can't say I have.

INVESTIGATOR BROWN: What sort of football team does it have?

NIELSEN: A poor one, usually.

CAPTAIN CRANSTON: A long way from home, aren't you, Doctor?

NIELSEN: Admittedly.

CAPTAIN CRANSTON: Mind telling us what you're doing here?

NIELSEN: Not in the least. I came because I was invited.

CAPTAIN CRANSTON: Are you an old friend of Mr. Paphlagloss?

NIELSEN: We have a common interest in Minoan culture.

INVESTIGATOR BROWN: He means they raise fish.

NIELSEN: No, Officer. Your zeal is commendable, but your conclusions erroneous. Not minnow culture, but Minoan. M-I-N-O-A-N.

INVESTIGATOR BROWN: What does it mean?

NIELSEN: It pertains to a vanished race, with a surprisingly high degree of civilization, who inhabited the lands of the Aegean Sea some centuries before the Trojan War.

INVESTIGATOR BROWN: When was that?

NIELSEN: There is weighty evidence for believing that Knossos, the principal seat of Minoan civilization, fell circa 1400 B.C.

INVESTIGATOR BROWN: Then they're all dead?

NIELSEN: I believe so.

INVESTIGATOR BROWN: Then why bother about 'em?

NIELSEN: I have sometimes asked myself the same question.

CAPTAIN CRANSTON: Doctor Nielsen is a scholar, Brown, and scholars go for such things. Right, Doctor?

NIELSEN: Quite accurately stated. Reviewing my words of a few moments ago, I feel that I was unnecessarily terse. Will you pardon my rudeness?

CAPTAIN CRANSTON: Forget it.

NIELSEN: At least allow me to answer your question more fully. I was invited to Knossos to work upon my book, "The Derivation of the Asiatic Mother Goddess from the Baetylic Cult of Neolithic Crete."

INVESTIGATOR BROWN: Whew! Try to figure out that mess, Chief!

CAPTAIN CRANSTON: It sounds like deep stuff.

NIELSEN: The title, I must confess, is formidable. However, the subject matter is not. The etiological myths of such deities as Aphrodite, Artemis, Astarte, Cybele and, to a certain extent, Ishtar, bear unmistakable internal evidence of a common origin.

CAPTAIN CRANSTON: We'll take your word for it.

NIELSEN: It is my purpose to show these and similar goddesses were the direct descendants of the Cretan snake-goddess Diktynna. And that Diktynna herself derived, or, better, was evolved over a period of perhaps two thousand years, from the aniconic baetylic worship of a stone-age culture.

INVESTIGATOR MILLER: My shorthand isn't good enough for some of those words. How do you spell aniconic?

NIELSEN: A-N-I-C-O-N-I-C. Having no images; literally, "without icons."

INVESTIGATOR MILLER: And baetylic?

NIELSEN: B-A-E-T-Y-L-I-C. From the Greek baitylos. Pertaining to the worship of a sacred stone. My theory is that man's first gods were stones. Meteors generally; objects blazing a fiery trail from the heavens and hence, supposedly, imbued with the divine powers of their origin.

CAPTAIN CRANSTON: This is all very interesting, Doctor Nielsen.

INVESTIGATOR BROWN: Like fun it is!

CAPTAIN CRANSTON: But I'm afraid we must confine ourselves to more practical matters. How well were you acquainted with the deceased?

NIELSEN: As well as one usually knows a butler when one is a house guest.

CAPTAIN CRANSTON: What sort of personality did he have?

NIELSEN: Quiet and unobtrusive, most pleasant in manner.

CAPTAIN CRANSTON: To your knowledge, did any of your fellow guests have any trouble with Danville?

NIELSEN: To my knowledge, no. My imagination boggles, may I add, at the conception of such a situation.

CAPTAIN CRANSTON: By the way, what's your opinion of your fellow guests?

NIELSEN: Since I'm speaking for public record, I should prefer to keep my opinions to myself. However, there is one highly intelligent man staying here; to wit, Mr. Westborough. He has written two books that I have read with admiration. I refer you to *Trajan: His Life and Times* and *Heliogabalus, Rome's Most Degenerate Emperor.*

CAPTAIN CRANSTON: Don't get much of a chance to read. Will you tell me what you did on Wednesday night? All of you?

NIELSEN: We played bridge. Mr. Paphlagloss and myself against Mr. Stoner and Mrs. Paphlagloss. Mr. Bayard said he was returning to his field camp. I don't know what became of the younger Stoner, Glendon and Miss Paphlagloss.

CAPTAIN CRANSTON: When did you see the butler last?

NIELSEN: Some time just before midnight. Mrs. Paphlagloss rang for him to put away the bridge things. I was heartily thankful to see that game end.

CAPTAIN CRANSTON: Did you lose money?

NIELSEN: I did. Eighty-seven odd dollars! No doubt an insignificant amount to such men as Paphlagloss and Stoner, but considerable to me.

CAPTAIN CRANSTON: So it can be pretty expensive to be the guest of a man like Paphlagloss?

NIELSEN: In the week I have been here it has already cost me more than a stay at one of the finest resort hotels. But what can one do? A hundred dollars isn't much more than a cigarette paper to these people.

CAPTAIN CRANSTON: What did you do after the bridge game ended?

NIELSEN: I went to bed.

CAPTAIN CRANSTON: Did you hear the noise of an outboard motor during the night?

NIELSEN: No.

CAPTAIN CRANSTON: Or the sound of someone walking in the hall?

NIELSEN: No, I heard nothing.

CAPTAIN CRANSTON: You are a sound sleeper?

NIELSEN: Usually I am.

CAPTAIN CRANSTON: When Miller has transcribed these notes, will you read them and affix your signature to show that they represent an accurate record of our conversation?

NIELSEN: With pleasure.

CAPTAIN CRANSTON: Have you read Miller's notes?

NIELSEN: I have enjoyed that privilege.

CAPTAIN CRANSTON: Did you find his recording of our conversation accurate?

NIELSEN: No. It was necessary for me to correct the spelling of the proper names, Astarte, Cybele and Diktynna. On the whole, however, a fair transcript.

CAPTAIN CRANSTON: Will you sign it?

NIELSEN: Yes, certainly.

ARNE NIELSEN, PH.D.
(Signed in the presence of Albert Cranston, Gerald Brown, Ernest Miller and Elmer Stebbins.)

J. Statement of Harvey C. Stoner

CAPTAIN CRANSTON: It is my duty to warn you that anything you say may be used against you.

H. STONER: Do you know that I'm the head of Stoner Sterling Stores? It's unthinkable that a man of my position could descend to such a crime as the murder of a butler.

CAPTAIN CRANSTON: Nobody said you had.

H. STONER: Now that I am here, I will agree to answer such questions as you may ask me. But I will not submit to gratuitous insults.

CAPTAIN CRANSTON: The insults, Mr. Stoner, are in your own imagination. When did you last see the butler?

H. STONER: The night he disappeared.

CAPTAIN CRANSTON: At what time?

H. STONER: Shortly before midnight. Mrs. Paphlagloss rang for him when we finished our bridge game.

CAPTAIN CRANSTON: Who had been playing bridge?

H. STONER: The usual foursome. Mrs. Paphlagloss and I against Paphlagloss and Nielsen.

CAPTAIN CRANSTON: Who came out ahead?

H. STONER: We did. Mrs. Paphlagloss is far superior to her husband. And Nielsen is poor.

INVESTIGATOR BROWN: He'll be poor, all right, when you guys get through with him.

H. STONER: I beg your pardon?

CAPTAIN CRANSTON: I'm sorry to say that Brown mistakenly thinks he's funny. We were talking about your bridge game, Mr. Stoner. What were the others doing while you played bridge?

H. STONER: My son and Miss Paphlagloss were on a speedboat ride.

CAPTAIN CRANSTON: Did you go to bed after the bridge game broke up?

H. STONER: Yes. We all did.

CAPTAIN CRANSTON: Were your son and Miss Paphlagloss back by that time?

H. STONER: Yes. They entered the living room shortly before we stopped playing. We all went upstairs together.

CAPTAIN CRANSTON: Leaving the butler below?

H. STONER: He was in the living room when we left.

CAPTAIN CRANSTON: Where were Bayard and Glendon?

H. STONER: I hadn't seen either of them since dinner time.

CAPTAIN CRANSTON: Do you and your son occupy separate bedrooms?

H. STONER: Yes.

CAPTAIN CRANSTON: Did you leave your room for any reason whatsoever?

H. STONER: No.

CAPTAIN CRANSTON: Did you hear the noise of an outboard motor?

H. STONER: No.

CAPTAIN CRANSTON: Or the sound of someone walking?

H. STONER: No. Wait a minute. I believe I did hear that kind of noise.

CAPTAIN CRANSTON: At what time?

H. STONER: I don't know. I was half asleep, and the sound didn't seem worth bothering about.

CAPTAIN CRANSTON: What kind of sound was it?

H. STONER: The kind you mentioned. The noise of someone walking.

CAPTAIN CRANSTON: Near or far?

H. STONER: It sounded rather far.

CAPTAIN CRANSTON: Would you say the walker had on shoes?

H. STONER: Yes, absolutely. It would be impossible otherwise to hear him.

CAPTAIN CRANSTON: Why do you say that?

H. STONER: Because of these floors. Concrete, with very thick rugs scattered about. Send one of your men to walk down the hall in his stocking feet and see if you can hear him in this room.

CAPTAIN CRANSTON: That's a good suggestion, Mr. Stoner. We'll follow it. Now do you mind telling me your opinion of the man who was killed?

H. STONER: One butler is like another to me. This one was skinnier than most and probably shorter. As a servant, he seemed efficient enough.

CAPTAIN CRANSTON: That's all you know about him?

H. STONER: That's all.

CAPTAIN CRANSTON: Do you believe your host, Mr. Paphlagloss, is capable of committing murder?

H. STONER: I refuse to answer that question.

CAPTAIN CRANSTON: Have you read the typewritten record of our conversation?

H. STONER: Yes. It's accurate enough. I'll sign it.

H.C. STONER
(Signed in the presence of
Albert Cranston, Gerald
Brown, Ernest Miller and
Elmer Stebbins.)

K. Statement of Russell Stoner

CAPTAIN CRANSTON: It is my duty to warn you that anything

you say may be used against you.

R. STONER: All right, Pop, now that's off your chest.

INVESTIGATOR BROWN: Wise guy, huh?

R. STONER: Stop pushing me around.

CAPTAIN CRANSTON: That'll do, Brown.

R. STONER: Good thing for him you made him lay off me, Pop.

INVESTIGATOR BROWN: Yeah?

R. STONER: I've licked bigger guys than you.

INVESTIGATOR BROWN: Izzat so? Well, here's one you're not going to—

CAPTAIN CRANSTON: Once and for all, Brown, will you let me handle this young man? Maybe he could lick you. He looks husky enough. Play football, son?

R. STONER: Played guard three years. And earned my letter in track.

CAPTAIN CRANSTON: What did you go out for?

R. STONER: Shot-put. Forty-nine feet, two inches, on my best day.

CAPTAIN CRANSTON: That's not so bad.

R. STONER: What do you mean "not so bad"? The world's record is only fifty-seven feet, one inch.

INVESTIGATOR BROWN: Only, huh? This guy sure hates himself.

R. STONER: I've done better than thirty feet with my left hand.

CAPTAIN CRANSTON: Using the official sixteen-pound shot?

R. STONER: What else would I be using?

CAPTAIN CRANSTON: It would be easy to kill a man with one of those weights, wouldn't it?

R. STONER: Hope to tell you.

CAPTAIN CRANSTON: Strangely enough, a man was killed here two days ago.

R. STONER: Well, what of it?

CAPTAIN CRANSTON: He was struck on the back of the head by some object like your sixteen-pound shot.

R. STONER: Don't look at me, Pop. I didn't do it.

CAPTAIN CRANSTON: What did you do Wednesday night?

R. STONER: Ione and I had been out for a speedboat ride. She was going to show me the flying fish at night, and that's just what we saw. Flying fish. Anybody got any cracks to make about it? No? Good thing.

CAPTAIN CRANSTON: When did you get back to the house?

R. STONER: Just before midnight. Ione and I went into the living room and watched 'em total the bridge score. Doc Nielsen had been nicked for eighty-seven bucks, and he was sorer than a boiled owl, but trying not to show it. Paphlagloss offered to pay the whole thing, but

Nielsen wouldn't let him. Old goat whiskers isn't a half-bad sport.

CAPTAIN CRANSTON: Was the butler there?

R. STONER: He came into the room to put away the card things. That was the last I saw of him.

CAPTAIN CRANSTON: Were you in your room all night?

R. STONER: That has all the earmarks of a dirty crack, Pop.

CAPTAIN CRANSTON: It's a plain question, Stoner. It calls for a plain answer. If I were you, I'd give one.

R. STONER: I hit the hay, and that's the last thing I knew till morning.

CAPTAIN CRANSTON: Sure you didn't hear any kind of noise during the night?

R. STONER: No. I was dead to the world.

CAPTAIN CRANSTON: Will you give me your opinion of the deceased?

R. STONER: Had plenty of nerve, if you ask me. I pulled the shooting-coaster gag on him, and he never turned a hair.

CAPTAIN CRANSTON: What do you mean by the shooting coaster gag?

R. STONER: Know what a coaster is, Pop?

CAPTAIN CRANSTON: Yes. Would you just as soon address me as Captain Cranston?

R. STONER: Well, Cap, this coaster looks just like the ordinary kind, see? You slip it under a glass, and nobody can tell the difference. Until the glass is lifted.

CAPTAIN CRANSTON: Then what happens?

R. STONER: It makes a noise like a revolver shot. Well, I slipped one of those under a glass the butler was getting ready to lift, and it goes bang right in his face. Does he jump? Not that boy. He picks up coaster, glass and all, and carries 'em into the kitchen just like nothing had happened. Never says a word about it, either.

INVESTIGATOR BROWN: Bet you felt like two cents.

R. STONER: Mind your own business.

CAPTAIN CRANSTON: Have you read over the notes?

R. STONER: Sure, Cap. Want me to roll 'em up and play a piccolo?

CAPTAIN CRANSTON: I want you to sign your name in the lower right-hand corner to show that you acknowledged them as an accurate record of our conversation.

R. STONER: Well, here goes nothing.

RUSSELL STONER

(Signed in the presence of Albert Cranston, Gerald Brown, Ernest Miller and Elmer Stebbins.)

L. Statement of Denis Glendon

CAPTAIN CRANSTON: It is my duty to warn you that anything you say may be used against you.

GLENDON: Quite all right, Officer. There isn't much I can say.

CAPTAIN CRANSTON: You're an artist by profession, I hear.

GLENDON: Mr. Paphlagloss shares the prevailing delusion. I was invited to Knossos to paint frescoes.

INVESTIGATOR BROWN: This bird's a fake, Chief. He can't paint worth two cents.

GLENDON: So I have been told. However, I find your bald and unsolicited remarks offensive. Please be good enough to step outside when the present interview ends.

INVESTIGATOR BROWN: You mean you want to fight?

GLENDON: It would be a pleasure.

CAPTAIN CRANSTON: None of that now. You'll go to jail, Glendon, if you assault an officer in the performance of his duty.

GLENDON: Is it his duty to insult my painting? This oaf obviously knows nothing about art.

INVESTIGATOR BROWN: I do, too. I know enough to know when you draw a guy's head in profile, you've got to draw his eyes profile, too. And half the time you don't.

GLENDON: Listen carefully, my friend, and I'll endeavor to make the reason for that clear. Mr. Paphlagloss wants—and I'm trying to give him—faces and figures painted the way they painted them thirty-five hundred years ago. Not the way they paint today, but the way they painted then. Naturally, the human race has learned a few tricks in the meantime.

INVESTIGATOR BROWN: And look at his women! Nothing on over their breasts! It's indecent, that's what it is!

GLENDON: The only indecency is in your own mind. Moreover, I refuse to take the responsibility for Minoan fashions.

CAPTAIN CRANSTON: You're no art critic, Brown. Keep quiet and let Mr. Glendon do the talking. Well, Glendon, who recommended you for this job?

GLENDON: One of the executives of the Minos Stores. A Mr. Baker.

CAPTAIN CRANSTON: An old friend of yours?

GLENDON: A friend in need. I lived in the room above his garage.

CAPTAIN CRANSTON: Did you know any of your fellow guests before you came here?

GLENDON: No.

CAPTAIN CRANSTON: Or any of the servants?

GLENDON: I do now. The cook is always trotting in with a cup of tea—usually just when the mortar is beginning to dry when every minute's like fine gold. But I don't like to hurt her feelings.

CAPTAIN CRANSTON: How did you become so friendly with her?

GLENDON: Tin boxes.

CAPTAIN CRANSTON: Tin boxes?

GLENDON: I asked her to give me all the tin boxes that cookies and so on come in. In my sort of work and in this damp climate you can't have too many moistureproof containers.

CAPTAIN CRANSTON: What do you use them for?

GLENDON: I mix my colors dry. As soon as I've got a tone prepared, I put it away in a separate box with a label telling what colors and what proportions were used, so I can duplicate the shade at any time.

CAPTAIN CRANSTON: There seems to be a lot to this fresco painting.

GLENDON: There is.

CAPTAIN CRANSTON: Was the butler a special friend of yours? Like the cook?

GLENDON: I rarely saw him except during meals.

CAPTAIN CRANSTON: When was the last time you saw him?

GLENDON: I believe at dinnertime Wednesday night.

CAPTAIN CRANSTON: Not after dinner?

GLENDON: I don't believe so.

CAPTAIN CRANSTON: What did you do after dinner?

GLENDON: Bayard asked me to walk down to his camp. He wanted to show me some stuff he'd just excavated.

CAPTAIN CRANSTON: Is Bayard a particular friend of yours?

GLENDON: He's one of the two persons at Knossos who's treated me like a human being.

CAPTAIN CRANSTON: The other being Mrs. Holden?

GLENDON: She, too. But I didn't mean Mrs. Holden.

CAPTAIN CRANSTON: How long did you stay with Bayard?

GLENDON: Two hours or so. He lent me his only flashlight to walk back to the house. I didn't want to take it but he insisted.

CAPTAIN CRANSTON: How far is Bayard's camp from the house?

GLENDON: Mile and a quarter or mile and a half. There's a well-marked trail, and I could have found my way easily in the dark. But Bayard couldn't.

CAPTAIN CRANSTON: I should think it would be a lot easier for him than for you.

GLENDON: He'd absentmindedly worn his reading glasses instead of his distance glasses. Without the latter he can't see well, even in the daytime.

CAPTAIN CRANSTON: Was it dark when you walked over to Bayard's camp?

GLENDON: Yes.

CAPTAIN CRANSTON: Then why didn't he notice his mistake when you started?

GLENDON: Probably because it was dark. I walked ahead with the flashlight and he followed me. I was never more than two or three feet in advance of him.

CAPTAIN CRANSTON: What time was it when you got back?

GLENDON: Eleven or eleven-thirty. I'm not sure.

CAPTAIN CRANSTON: Who let you into the house?

GLENDON: The butler.

CAPTAIN CRANSTON: You told us you didn't see him after dinner.

GLENDON: I was wrong. I forgot about this time.

CAPTAIN CRANSTON: Have you forgotten any other times?

GLENDON: No.

CAPTAIN CRANSTON: What did you do after he'd let you in?

GLENDON: Went up to my room.

CAPTAIN CRANSTON: Did you go near the living room?

GLENDON: Near enough to hear the sound of voices.

CAPTAIN CRANSTON: Why didn't you join the others?

GLENDON: And lose money I don't have trying to play bridge with them? No, thank you. I went to bed.

CAPTAIN CRANSTON: Hear any noises during the night?

GLENDON: None whatsoever.

CAPTAIN CRANSTON: Have you read the notes, Glendon?

GLENDON: Yes.

CAPTAIN CRANSTON: Are they an accurate record of our conversation?

GLENDON: As nearly as I can remember.

CAPTAIN CRANSTON: Then will you sign your name?

GLENDON: Glad to.

DENIS GLENDON

(Signed in the presence of Albert Cranston, Gerald Brown, Ernest Miller and Elmer Stebbins.)

M. Statement of Theocritus Lucius Westborough

WESTBOROUGH: Good afternoon, gentlemen.

CAPTAIN CRANSTON: Sit down, Mr. Westborough, and let's get all our cards on the table. Paphlagloss told me who you were, and we've a mutual friend in Collins of the L.A. police department.

WESTBOROUGH: Dear me, yes! How is Lieutenant Collins?

CAPTAIN CRANSTON: Fine, the last I heard. Westborough, I'm not exactly young, and I've been in police work all my life. But this case has got me out on a limb. It's the weirdest, craziest, stupidest, most senseless murder I've ever run up against. It's stark, raving loony.

WESTBOROUGH: I am inclined to agree with you.

CAPTAIN CRANSTON: The murderer has to be someone staying on this island. That point stands out like a sore thumb. I've taken statements from everybody here. Family, servants, guests. Twelve statements all together. There couldn't be an outsider. One of these twelve people killed Charles Danville. But which one? I don't know, and I've a hunch this case will never be solved from the outside. Its roots are too deep for that. Deep! I can't even imagine how deep underground they may grow. That's why I want your help.

WESTBOROUGH: In what respect do you believe that I shall be able to aid you?

CAPTAIN CRANSTON: You're one of these people. You can stay here without any of them suspecting. You can watch them without any of them realizing he's being watched. I can't break this case open, but you can. Will you?

WESTBOROUGH: Dear me!

CAPTAIN CRANSTON: I'm offering you a job. It's a hard job; probably a dangerous one. It won't pay anything to speak of.

WESTBOROUGH: That matters very little.

CAPTAIN CRANSTON: I can't even promise you any help. It would spoil the plan to quarter one of my men on the island. Stebbins at Ynez will have to be your nearest source of assistance. And there's no telephone to call him.

WESTBOROUGH: You make your proposal, Captain Cranston, sound singularly unattractive.

CAPTAIN CRANSTON: I was afraid you wouldn't agree to it.

WESTBOROUGH: On the contrary, I'm delighted to accept it. The problem interests me.

CAPTAIN CRANSTON: Good! I suggest that, first of all, you read the statements Miller has just transcribed. Then we can have a talk about them.

WESTBOROUGH: I shall be most happy.

CAPTAIN CRANSTON: Well, have you read the statements?

WESTBOROUGH: Indeed, yes. I found them very interesting.

CAPTAIN CRANSTON: Do you see any motive for this crime?

WESTBOROUGH: As yet, none.

CAPTAIN CRANSTON: The victim is a butler, a harmless inoffensive servant.

WESTBOROUGH: Also a man of a very amiable personality, it would appear.

CAPTAIN CRANSTON: That stands out through practically every statement. Paphlagloss, Mrs. Paphlagloss, Miss Paphlagloss and Bayard can't say enough in his favor. His fellow servants had no quarrel with him. One of them was in love with him.

WESTBOROUGH: Another, however, apparently disliked him.

CAPTAIN CRANSTON: That girl! But there's no reason for her to hit him over the head with—whatever he was hit with.

WESTBOROUGH: No adequate reason as yet, certainly. However, I notice that some very interesting questions have been brought up in these statements. First, the one mentioned by Mrs. Paphlagloss. Can the noise of a motorboat be heard from the back bedrooms?

INVESTIGATOR BROWN: Just checked up on that. It can.

WESTBOROUGH: Apparently there are some very sound sleepers at Knossos.

CAPTAIN CRANSTON: Something queer about that!

WESTBOROUGH: Dear, dear, the salty air is extremely soporific! However, there are at least four persons of varying degrees of wakefulness. Miss Della Winters, Miss Paphlagloss, Mr. Starr and Mr. H.C. Stoner. The latter, incidentally, makes a very good point about the floors.

CAPTAIN CRANSTON: He was right, too. We've found that if you're inside a room with the door closed, it's impossible to hear a person walking in his stocking feet.

WESTBOROUGH: That may, perhaps, be significant. Now can we make any eliminations in the number of suspects? Miss Paphlagloss, certainly. She could have scarcely suggested the glass-bottomed boat expedition had she been aware of what we might find.

CAPTAIN CRANSTON: Sounds reasonable. And we can let Bayard out, too.

WESTBOROUGH: I am sorry to disagree, but I do not see how Mr. Bayard can be eliminated.

CAPTAIN CRANSTON: He wasn't in the house, but up at his camp. Glendon said he couldn't have walked from his camp in the dark without his right glasses.

WESTBOROUGH: But are we sure—can we be sure on Mr. Glendon's word alone—that Mr. Bayard *didn't* have his right glasses?

CAPTAIN CRANSTON: I see what you mean. So there are still eleven suspects?

WESTBOROUGH: Yes, on logical grounds, the number must remain at eleven. However, a pattern is beginning to emerge from my mind. Or should I say the nebulous ghost of a pattern?

CAPTAIN CRANSTON: What sort of a pattern?

WESTBOROUGH: First, Mrs. Holden brings out the fact that the deceased was in the habit of making a nightly tour of the house at a very late hour. Miss Della Winters not only confirms that, but adds the further information that she heard his footsteps in the hall outside her door.

CAPTAIN CRANSTON: Someone's footsteps.

WESTBOROUGH: Exactly. Someone's footsteps. The elder Mr. Stoner also heard footsteps—the footsteps of a shod person. We do not know at what time. But Mr. Starr heard the noise of a person walking on the pier at twenty-five minutes to three. Immediately after that the outboard motorboat departed.

CAPTAIN CRANSTON: But who killed him? And why?

WESTBOROUGH: I regret deeply I am not able to answer either of those two perplexing questions. I believe, however, that I do know how he was killed. And probably where.

CAPTAIN CRANSTON: You know *where* he was killed?

WESTBOROUGH: We are seated now in the very room.

PART FOUR: MAZE WITHOUT A PLAN

(Saturday, July 9—Sunday, July 10

I

THE JURORS, solemn as a row of nine Athenian owls, sat in their box overlooking the county inquest room in the Hall of Justice and listened with varying degrees of attentiveness to a lengthy opinion concerning whether the deceased, tentatively identified as Charles Danville, had met his death by drowning or as a result of concussion and hemorrhage of the brain caused by a blow from a blunt instrument.

("The well-known blunt instrument," Westborough mused irrelevantly, his eyes fixed on a green-shaded lamp. "But what possible paraphrase is there for it?")

"Concussions and hemorrhage of the brain do not necessarily rule out death by drowning," the county autopsy surgeon asserted. "Possibly he was already dead when his body entered the water. On the other hand, it is possible that he was still alive at that time, in which case the immediate cause of death would be drowning. In the latter event one might say, since the deceased, Mr. Paphlagloss has assured us, knew how to swim, that unconsciousness was one of a chain of circumstances which resulted in death—unconsciousness of the fact that he was in the water and should be swimming."

Two jurors scratched their ears, two the sides of their noses, two crossed and recrossed their legs, one fidgeted with a mechanical pencil, another gazed meditatively downward at his shoes and the last wiped his forehead with a handkerchief.

"In your opinion, Doctor Martin," inquired the deputy coroner from the bench, "was the brain injury sufficiently severe to cause death?"

"To cause death eventually," the county autopsy surgeon qualified. "Yes, indeed, I have no doubts on that score. The blow had been delivered from behind with a force great enough to open the parietal-frontal suture. The post-mortem examination shows a skull fracture on the right side, just above the ear . . ." He described in bewildering technical detail the lines of the fracture and the part of the brain affected.

"What sort of object would cause such a fracture?" questioned the deputy coroner.

"A blunt instrument."

("There it goes again," thought Westborough. Immediately ashamed of his facetiousness, the little historian lowered his gaze to the checkerboard linoleum. "A man has been killed," he pondered reproachfully. "Dear me!")

The deputy district attorney picked two fragments of rough stone from a table and held them together to form a long and very slender cone.

"Could this broken club, if whole, have caused such a fracture, Doctor Martin?"

"Yes, provided that it was applied with sufficient force to the area involved in this particular case."

"Thank you, Doctor Martin," said the deputy coroner while the stone fragments were being handed around the jury. "Captain Cranston, please." The captain mounted to the witness stand. "Do you solemnly swear and affirm that the testimony you are about to give before this inquisition now pending shall be the truth, the whole truth and nothing but the truth, so help you God?"

"So help me God," the officer repeated in a firm deep voice. He stated his name and occupation. "Captain Albert Cranston, Bureau of Investigation, Sheriff's Department, County of Los Angeles. On Friday morning, July 8, I received a telephone message from Constable Elmer Stebbins of Ynez to the effect that the body of an unidentified man had been found in the water along the coast of the island owned by Mr. Alexis Paphlagloss. I proceeded immediately to the island, taking with me Investigators Brown and Miller of my bureau. When we drew near the island, we saw Constable Stebbins on the pier standing beside a body covered by a tarpaulin."

"Was it the body which you have just viewed in the adjacent room?"

"It was. We had a hard time identifying it as Danville's."

(" 'Nothing of him that doth fade,' " Westborough quoted under his breath, " 'but doth suffer a sea-change into something rich and strange . . .' ")

After he had rapidly summarized his investigations, Captain Cranston pointed to the stone fragments, which had been returned to the table. "This thing," he said, "is an Indian war club dug up on the island."

("Pestle," Bayard corrected in a whisper. "The Channel Islanders were a peaceful people prior to the advent of the Spaniards.")

"The Indians broke it when they buried it, and Mr. Bayard dug up the pieces and mended it—the way the Indians used to mend things—with hot pitch. So it was in one piece when he put it on the shelf where we found it, in a sort of Indian museum." Cranston leaned confidentially toward the jury. "But now I'm going to show you some photographs which were taken by Mr. Brown under my direction. This one shows the position of the shelf in the room. And this one's a closeup of the shelf with the club lying there just as we found it—in two pieces."

The jury meticulously studied the photographs; head after head bobbed in confirmation. "I know Mr. Bayard did a good job of mending," Cranston went on, "because I've handled others of these war clubs—"

("Pestles," Bayard hissed.)

"—that he mended this way. You can swing 'em around your head and they won't come apart. But this one wouldn't stand handling. Mr. Westborough told me that when he'd barely lifted it from the shelf it fell apart. Do you know why it came to pieces?" he asked rhetorically. "Because it had been broken after Mr. Bayard had mended it. The pieces were pressed together so it would appear the same as before, but the cold pitch didn't stick like the hot pitch would've done. And how was it broken?" He paused, but the jury supplied no answer. "It was broken, gentlemen, against the skull of the deceased, Charles Danville. And where? Gentlemen, in the Indian museum room where it had been lying on a shelf. Several gobs of pitch were found in the nap of a rug in that room, and those gobs of pitch must have come from this club. That fact ought to prove, gentlemen, that the deceased was slugged in the Indian museum room—inside the house."

The Minos sat rigidly in one of the comfortably upholstered chairs supplied by the county and directed a hostile stare toward the head of the Sheriff's Investigation Bureau. Westborough glanced quickly back to the witness.

"He was either stunned or killed outright by the blow," Cranston continued. "Then the person who hit him picked up the body—Danville was a small, slight fellow, remember—and carried it out of the house and down the stairs to a small boat moored at the pier. He started the outboard motor, steered the boat north along the coast of the island until he'd gone a mile or so away from the house, removed the boat's anchor, tied it around the ankle of the deceased and dumped him—alive or dead—into the ocean. And the body would've been there yet if three people hadn't happened along in a glass-bottomed boat,"

Concluding on this note of climax, the broad-shouldered officer strode vigorously from the stand. Witness followed witness in the manner of a cinema montage. Investigator Brown declared he had tested the "war club" for latent fingerprints, but the impressions, he took pains to inform the jury, could not be developed on rough unpolished stone surfaces. Marc Bayard declared that he had mended the tapering stone in the manner described by Captain Cranston and that, to his knowledge, it had remained in one piece until Mr. Westborough had lifted it from the shelf. Bayard also explained carefully that the object was not a "war club" but a pestle used for the peaceful purpose of grinding acorn meal. (The next morning every newspaper in Los Angeles would refer to it as an Indian war club.) Westborough confirmed that the pestle had broken in his hands when he had lifted it in Mr. Bayard's presence . . . . Witnesses were at length exhausted, and the jurors trooped into the jury room to begin the sometimes argumentative process known as "arriving at a verdict."

"I've got to get out of here!" Paphlagloss exclaimed, springing abruptly to his feet. "Need fresh air." He waved aside offers to accompany him and hurried down the aisle. A small wizened man rose from the section allotted to the general public, brushed past fellow spectators in his row and followed the Cretan with an air of determination.

"I do believe that individual is planning to speak to Mr. Paphlagloss," Westborough pondered. "Do you know who he is, Mr. Bayard?"

Bayard's high narrow head revolved on his thin neck. "No, never saw him before. Looks rather seedy, doesn't he?"

"A little on the seedy side," Westborough assented, "but his clothes are undeniably garments of gentility. Dear me! What do you suppose he wants?"

But both men had now passed through the double doors into the corridor, and Bayard's mind had strayed to some inner world of his own—doubtless a world inhabited solely by Channel Island Indians. The historian regarded the black hands of the wall clock as they solemnly measured the interval required for nine men to reach agreement when and in what manner and by whom the body herein lying dead came to its death.

" 'I'll tell you who Time ambles withal, who Time trots withal, who Time gallops withal, and who he stands still withal. . . !' " Westborough sighed to himself. Time was ambling now, a slow pace that barely exceeded a snail's progress, yet minute by minute crawled over the line separating the now from the hereafter, and still Paphlagloss did not return to his seat.

The jurors filed back to their box, faces glowing with the satisfaction of men whose duty has been done. The sporadic whispering in the room died away. Conscious that all eyes were regarding his least movement, the foreman cleared his throat with a loud, "Hem! Hem!" and read aloud:

"VERDICT OF CORONER'S JURY

"State of California, County of Los Angeles,

"In the Matter of the Inquisition upon the Body of Charles Danville, Deceased, before Edward N. Chase, Coroner.

"We, the jurors summoned to appear before the Coroner of Los Angeles County at the Hall of Justice, City of Los Angeles, on the ninth day of July, A.D. 1938, to inquire into the cause of death of Charles Danville, having been duly sworn according to law, and having made such inquisition and hearing the testimony adduced, upon our oaths, each and all do say that we find that the deceased was named Charles Danville, a male, single, a native of California, aged about 45 years, and that he came to his death on the seventh day of July, A.D. 1938, between 2 and 3 A.M., at the Island of the Silver Girdle, Los Angeles County, California, and that this death was caused by drowning or by brain injuries received as the result of a blow from a blunt instrument delivered at the hands of a person or persons unknown.

"All of which we duly certify by this inquisition in writing, by us signed this ninth day of July, 1938 . . ."

In a comparatively quiet corridor of the always busy Hall of Justice, Alexis Paphlagloss removed a thick Greek cigarette from its individual glass container. A seedily dressed man held a lighted match to the big white tube—a man whose small wizened face was oddly reminiscent of a spider monkey's.

"Andleburger, sir. With a haitch and a hay, if Hi may say so. Hi'll give satisfaction, sir. Hi swear Hi will."

Paphlagloss trod underfoot the expensive cigarette from which he had not derived more than three puffs. "All right," he exclaimed tersely. "You're hired."

II

Below the blue and yellow frieze of partridges in the dining room at Knossos, candles glowed in silver candelabra. The flames were soft, yet the reflections glinting from the facets of expensive crystal goblets were of iridescent hardness. The new butler, looking more simian than ever despite his white linen coat, served the dessert plates and retired toward the kitchen with a self-conscious shuffle.

"Scarcely an improvement over poor Charles." The unsullied blonde head of Jennifer Paphlagloss rose like a yellow stamen of a flower from petals of pastel blue gossamer. Her voice, however, was brittle. The brittle tone a goblet yields when tapped lightly with the tines of a fork. "If it were not for the difficulties one has in persuading servants to stay in this lonely place, I should never tolerate such a creature as this Handlebar."

"Handleburger." Ione, a brilliant tropic blossom in her flaming red dinner gown, laughed warmly and mischievously. "With a haitch and a hay."

"My dear"—Jennifer's sweetness somehow conveyed the sharpened pitch of an overtaut violin string—"he might overhear us. Even servants have feelings, we must remember."

The momentary flush appearing on the girl's tanned cheeks reminded Westborough of the quick intense heat of burning cellophane.

"Hi'll try to give satisfaction."

The three young men laughed as Elizabethan courtiers at a bon mot of their idolized princess, and Jennifer's shoulders shrugged slightly.

"What an amusing person you are, dear!"

Paphlagloss sipped dourly at the resinated wine which—to all but him—had the unpalatable taste of turpentine. "Handleburger showed me excellent references. I hired him and I insist," he stated in the cold tone of one issuing a royal ukase, "that he be given a fair trial."

The gruff voice of Harvey Stoner cut into the conversation. "I don't wonder that you have so many unsolved mysteries out here! Those sheriff's police! Bustling around yesterday as if their jobs depended on getting statements from us, and today perfectly content to drop the whole matter!"

It is always a disastrous mistake to criticize, even by implication, any California institution in the presence of a Californian. Paphlagloss' brigand mustache bristled almost instantly.

"What makes you think they have dropped it, H.C.?" he asked.

"Should be fairly obvious," Stoner grumbled. "There's not a man of theirs on the island now."

"Not even that rube constable," young Stoner added.

"Stebbins is a friend of mine," Bayard began hotly, but stopped at a warning glance from his beautiful mother. The mother, ageless as Iolanthe, who looked younger than her grown son, rose graciously to her feet.

"Shall we have our coffee in the living room tonight?"

"I'll have mine on the terrace, please," Ione answered.

"Darling," said Jennifer coaxingly, "the fog makes the terrace a little chilly tonight."

"I'd prefer to have my coffee there," Ione insisted.

"So would I," chorused young Stoner, Bayard and Glendon.

"Very well," Jennifer smiled and issued instructions to the shuffling Handleburger. The courtiers followed their princess to the terrace. They were an oddly dissimilar trio of young men, Westborough reflected while sampling the excellent benedictine his host proffered. Russell Stoner who lived in the body, Bayard who lived in the brain, and Glendon who lived in the beauty which his sensitive fingers transferred to wall and paper.

"Shall we play bridge?" inquired their hostess.

"May I?" Westborough asked, catching the imploring glance Arne Nielsen directed toward him.

"Why, yes," Jennifer concurred. "We should love to have you, Mr. Westborough. But that makes five of us!"

"Count me out," Nielsen said hastily. "I have been a drone too long in your charming home. It is really time that I settled down to do some serious work. I hope you'll excuse me." He walked from the living room in the manner of an escaping prisoner.

The deal fell to Paphlagloss, who was matched with Westborough against Harvey Stoner and Mrs. Paphlagloss. "We ordinarily play for five cents a point," the Minos informed his partner.

"Quite all right, I am sure," Westborough murmured, feeling a little sorry for the luckless Nielsen. Later on he felt even sorrier. At five cents a point one can manage to lose in the course of an evening's play a rather large sum. Moreover, the historian, who could play very well when he gave his mind to it, sensed a disturbing lack of attentiveness in his partner. Several times Paphlagloss made leads grossly unjustified by the bidding; once he was even so careless as to throw away a good trump on a trick that was already theirs, losing as a result the game and rubber. A man with the shrewd business brain which Alexis Paphlagloss undeniably possessed should have been an excellent bridge player. But the blunt facts were that a twelve-year-old would have done much better.

Westborough and Paphlagloss were down better than two thousand points, Stoner announced after he had totaled the scores.

"Fifty dollars apiece!" Westborough exclaimed in pretended dismay. "Dear me! I wonder if you are right in your addition? If you don't mind . . ."

He reached for the bridge score and, when he was sure he was not observed, turned back the upper sheet and wrote on the blank score underneath: "Must see you tonight alone. Please meet me in Indian room as soon as you are able to come." Abstracting the lower sheet as deftly as he could manage it, he returned the pad to Harvey Stoner.

"I beg your pardon, Mr. Stoner. Your arithmetic is impeccable." As he reached for his billfold to pay his share of their joint loss, he contrived to pass the note into the hands of his host. Paphlagloss read it and crumpled it into his pocket in one swift movement; then nodded curtly.

"Another day another dollar," Stoner exclaimed yawning. "I'm getting sleepy! If you'll excuse me, I think I'll go to bed."

"It does seem rather silly to sit up for the young people," Jennifer smiled sweetly. "Let's all go upstairs."

Westborough remained in his bedroom only long enough to exchange his shoes for soft-soled bedroom slippers which would make no noise on the cement floors of Knossos. Then he descended the stairs and walked down the east passageway, past the brilliant colors of Glendon's frescoes to the room in which Alexis Paphlagloss was waiting for him.

"Speak softly," Paphlagloss directed, closing the door. "I trust you and you trust me, but there's scarcely an other person here we can trust."

"I wonder," Westborough said slowly, "if I can trust you, Mr. Paphlagloss." He saw that the eyes of the Minos were smouldering jet flames, but continued nevertheless. "You deliberately allowed Mr. Stoner to win at bridge. I believe that I have a moderate financial interest in your reason."

Paphlagloss broke the tension with a forced laugh. "Smart of you to figure that out. Shall I explain?"

"Pray do."

"Stoner is here to negotiate a merger between his stores and mine. I have no more reason for trusting his altruism than he has for trusting to mine. It's devil take the hindmost in business."

"I know very little about business," Westborough said.

"If Stoner underestimates my intelligence, I will have a psychological advantage over him which may be worth a great deal in dollars and cents."

"That," Westborough declared, "I can understand."

"And if he believes me to be a poor bridge player, he probably will underestimate my intelligence."

"I see. That is very clever of you, Mr. Paphlagloss, but isn't the plan a bit ruthless on Doctor Nielsen's pocketbook?"

"I'll see that he is reimbursed in full for all bridge losses before he leaves," the Minos answered a shade testily. "Is this your only reason for waiting to see me tonight?"

"No," Westborough replied slowly. "I wonder if I might borrow the key to that glass case?"

"Why do you want it?" Paphlagloss demanded.

"The thought occurred to me that perhaps the little figurine might be hidden somewhere within her own shrine."

"It isn't," the other returned curtly.

"But may I be allowed to satisfy my own curiosity?" Westborough smiled.

The Minos hesitated. "The truth is I'm not sure myself just where the key is," he answered at length. "It's been mislaid."

"That is most unfortunate."

"As soon as it turns up, I'll let you have it. But there's nothing in there to see. You may take my word for that."

Westborough walked across to the shrine and rested a hand upon its carved wooden panels. "A most interesting piece of furniture," he observed, his fingers idly tracing that ancient curious symbol of a column flanked by the sacral horns.

"I'm glad you like it."

"Has it been here long, may I ask?"

"Since last winter. Why?"

Westborough took a long and deep breath. He was in for it now, and he knew it. Nevertheless, the question had to be put.

"Mr. Paphlagloss, what is the secret of this room?"

"I don't understand you," the Minos said. But he was breathing excitedly in quick short puffs.

"I believe you do," Westborough said mildly. "Why is your caretaker required to keep a rifle in readiness at the bathhouse? What is it that you fear, Mr. Paphlagloss?"

The Minos slowly tapped the end of a long Greek cigarette against its glass container. "One man has been killed here, Westborough. It would appear to be dangerous to try to learn too much."

III

Westborough, who was addicted to early rising, had just completed his Sunday morning toilet in his chrome and green serpentine bathroom when Arne Nielsen knocked on their communal door. "Good morning," Nielsen said, stepping across the threshold. "Hope I don't disturb you."

"Not in the least," Westborough said cordially. "It is always most enjoyable to hold converse with you, Doctor Nielsen."

"Mutual," Nielsen returned succinctly. "However, I came to thank you for taking my place at the bridge table last night."

"The pleasure was mine."

"With Paphlagloss as a partner?" Nielsen laughed sardonically. "I'll admit I don't know much about the game, but it seems to me our host has an undoubted genius for doing the wrong thing."

"His playing is a little erratic," Westborough conceded. "He decided against revealing the reason on the grounds that the motives of Alexis Paphlagloss were his own business."

"Did you lose much?"

"Not a large sum, thank you."

"Highly embarrassing for me to play bridge now," Nielsen faltered self-consciously. "The blunt facts are that the last match stripped my cash down to twenty dollars. Oh well, I still own a return ticket to Pennsylvania, which is some consolation."

"If I may offer pecuniary assistance . . ."

"No." The monosyllable was short and vigorous. "Thank you, but I didn't drop in for that." Nielsen stared awkwardly for a moment at the buff and black octopus frieze adorning the walls of Westborough's bedroom. "Ha!" he exclaimed, changing the subject in evident relief. "Typical Minoan marine motif! Did you ever see the Octopus Vase from Gournia?"

"No, I never did. However, I saw a living-representative of the species in these very waters only last Friday. It was just before . . ."

Arne Nielsen, however, was not interested in octopodes of any later date than 1400 B.C. "Marvelous thing!" he exclaimed, meditatively stroking his pointed beard. "Reaches straight out at you. You can see every separate sucker on every tentacle."

"It sounds a trifle on the gruesome side," Westborough ventured.

"Do you like your pictures pretty-pretty?" Nielsen demanded witheringly.

"Not exactly. Still . . ."

"They gazed into the sea, and they painted with fidelity what they saw. That, my dear sir, is art.'"

"If realism be art's ultimate goal," Westborough qualified, a little rebelliously. "My own personal belief, however, is that the soul has some importance."

"Soul!" Nielsen exploded, looking not unlike an irritable troll of his ancestral northland. "The word has become meaningless."

Westborough was unoffended. "It is difficult to find words for such an abstraction, but I am beginning to sense the quality in Mr. Glendon's Minoan fresco. I do not know how to explain it—it is not a matter of technique, nor is it, exactly, a matter of composition—but perhaps if we examined the painting itself?"

"Soul!" Nielsen spluttered as they went out the door. "Soul, my dear sir! Soul!"

The two scholars encountered Denis Glendon circling the fountain in the open courtyard. "Foggy this morning," the artist greeted them.

"Extremely foggy," Westborough agreed.

"Moderately foggy," Nielsen corrected. Glendon wheeled abruptly.

"Why are we all so damned formal?"

"Are we, my dear sir? I cannot say I have noticed it."

"A man was killed here only three days ago. Murdered! And we talk of everything under the sun except that."

"Doctor Nielsen and I were talking of your beautiful mural," Westborough said gently. "We walked down here purposely to look at it."

The artist's jangled emotions were soothed immediately by the twin declarations. "Glad you like it, gentlemen," he said gratefully. "It's beginning to shape well, I think."

"Extremely well," Westborough agreed.

"Fairly well," Nielsen qualified tersely.

Glendon accompanied them to the wall where the partially finished fresco loomed brilliantly in its predominating reds and blues and yellows.

"Westborough is hopeful of exhibiting a soul," Nielsen rumbled splenetically. The painter, flushing uncomfortably, broke into a rapid flow of professional chatter.

"I've adopted the technique of the period. Flat tones—two dimensions—no chiaroscuro. Everything sacrificed to movement and color. And drama! The panel is only a stage setting, in a way. You know my theme? The arena at Knossos where Theseus is about to meet the Minotaur?"

Westborough nodded. "Yes, a striking concept, and you have well conveyed the impression of the crowded terraces. Those many tiny heads must have been exceedingly difficult to portray."

"I used a Minoan shortcut," Glendon informed them. "A wash of red under the men's heads; ivory white under the women."

" 'Dear dead women, with such hair, too,' " Westborough broke in, unable to repress the Browning line while gazing at the array of frills and furbelows, the elaborate curled and ringleted headdresses.

Greece had been an insignificant realm of barbarians when this gay court had flourished! The puffed sleeves, tight waists and flaring bells of skirts bore not the slightest resemblance to the austere drapes and folds of Hellenic costume. No, these women belonged, flounces and all, to the eighteenth-century Paris, where fribbles had been the glass of fashion and the mold of form. Watteau could have caught the lilt of saucy face and vivacious gesture, the cadence of large roguish eye and pert tipturned nose, and, momentarily, it almost seemed as if Watteau had painted them. But one aspect of style remained incontrovertibly Minoan. Not even in the rakehell century of the three Louis were women's breasts flaunted nakedly in public.

Westborough remarked, "Your ladies are a trifle seductive, perhaps, by today's standards."

"One of the sheriff's men told me they were indecent," Glendon said, his laugh tinged minutely with bitterness. Nielsen grinned sardonically.

"Shame, my dear sir, had not yet been born."

The Cretan princess, depicted in the act of hurling a huge bronze sword to the weaponless Theseus in the arena, was like Ione Paphlagloss in face and feature, Westborough could not help but note. He ventured a mild protest.

"But you have given your Ariadne black hair, Mr. Glendon."

"She had black hair," Glendon insisted.

"Dear me, but I thought that—"

"No blondes among the Minoans. Isn't that right, Doctor Nielsen?"

Nielsen nodded in confirmation. "Correct. Archaeologists are in accord—if archaeologists may ever be said to be in accord—that they were definitely a brunette race."

"I bow to superior wisdom," Westborough yielded. "Horace is verified; the worthy Homer has nodded again."

"Did Homer call Ariadne a blonde?" Glendon asked.

"He was so indiscreet. Let me see if I can recall the passage. Ah, to be sure! Book Eighteen of the Iliad: 'And Phaedra and Procris I saw, and fair-haired Ariadne, daughter of the baleful Minos, whom Theseus bore from Crete to the hill of sacred Athens, yet gat no joy of her . . .' Also in the *Odyssey* we have another reference: 'The glorious lame god did devise a dancing floor'—*choros* was the Greek, was it not, Doctor Nielsen? 'like that which in broad Knossos Daidalos wrought for Ariadne of the fair tresses.' Dear me, my memory is beginning to falter."

"Your memory is prodigious," Nielsen exclaimed.

"How do you do it?" Glendon questioned admiringly.

Westborough's eyes twinkled behind his gold-rimmed bifocals. "The result of a misspent youth. 'Myself when young did eagerly frequent Doctor and Saint, and heard great argument . . . but evermore—' "

The shriveled Handleburger appeared suddenly in the passageway to address them in whining cockneyese.

"Mr. Paphlagloss wishes you to come to the terrace, gentlemen. 'E wishes to see heveryone in the 'ouse, hif Hi mye sye so."

"What for?" Glendon demanded.

" 'E did not tell me, sir," Handleburger answered, moving quickly out of the range of further questions. The three men went upstairs at once. They found Jennifer Paphlagloss, lovely and cool as "dawn the rosy-fingered," attempting to cope with a barrage of questions from her son and the two Stoners. The servants, except Handleburger, were there, but Paphlagloss and his daughter were absent.

"Some whim of my husband's," Mrs. Paphlagloss was saying. "It can't be anything serious."

Harvey Stoner paced the terrace, hands clasped Napoleonically behind his ample back. "Whims haven't any place in business," he grumbled.

The portly figure of the Minos appeared suddenly in the doorway. The master of Knossos scrutinized the group without speaking and then turned to the butler who had followed him onto the terrace.

"Where is my daughter?"

"Hi notified 'er, sir. Miss Hione said she would come 'ere."

"Very well, take your place." While Handleburger joined the other servants, Paphlagloss removed one of his Greek cigarettes from its glass tube and placed it in a long jade holder. "The Levantine touch," Nielsen whispered.

"Considering that Crete was under Ottoman rule for some three centuries, it is not surprising that Turkish pomp should be in our host's blood," Westborough returned in an undertone.

"Remember what I said about the complexes of island owners? We're in for a practical demonstration, unless I'm vastly mistaken."

"Why all this mumbo jumbo?" Stoner demanded irately.

"What mumbo jumbo, H.C.?"

"Ordering us out here as if you were an Oriental potentate! What's the meaning of it?"

"As soon as my daughter comes you'll all know the answer," Paphlagloss replied enigmatically.

"Do I hear my cue?" Ione called. A red knitted cap perched jauntily on her black curls, the sort of silly little cap that only one girl in a thousand can wear without looking silly. Paphlagloss greeted his tardy daughter with a scowl.

"Please be seated. I have an announcement to make."

"You are an Oriental potentate, Alexis."

"You are speaking to your father," Jennifer chided gently.

"I hope I am," the girl returned with a light laugh. "It wouldn't be very nice to think—but let's skip it."

Paphlagloss said coldly, "Nobody but you thinks that is funny, Ione. Please sit down." He removed the cigarette from its jade holder and trampled it underfoot. "Some of you," he began oratorically, "are my family, some are my guests and the rest are in my employ. A man has been killed here, a man who worked for me, and I believe I know why. Perhaps one or two of you can guess the reason also." The Greek's eyes shifted at this point, Westborough fancied, from Starr's lobster-red countenance to Bayard's thin pinched features, but the pauses were so momentary it was impossible to be sure. "If so," the Minos continued, "those persons will oblige me by remaining silent. No matter what the provocation, they will remain silent."

"But that is hardly cooperative with the sheriff's office," Westborough ventured to remonstrate.

"The sheriff's office may pursue the course of action it thinks best. At Knossos I am the law."

"Incipient paranoia," Nielsen whispered. "Delusions of persecution and the rest of it. He's headed straight for an asylum."

"Did you say something, Doctor Nielsen?"

The troll-like face of the Minoan authority wrinkled in a saturnine grimace. "I did. I asked what steps the law of Knossos proposes to take."

"Every boat on the island has been run into the boathouse and is now securely under lock and key. None of them may be taken out from now on without my permission. For the present, none of you may leave the island."

"Unlawful!" the senior Stoner sputtered. "Illegal detention!"

The Minos smiled equably. "I'm not frightened by names, H.C. You and your son came to Knossos to spend three weeks with me. Until that period ends you can't complain that I've changed your life in any respect whatsoever."

"He's got you there, pal," grinned young Stoner.

"But I have important affairs! I can't afford to be out of touch with my office. Alexis, I'll sue you for every dollar this costs me, if it's the last thing I ever do."

"You won't be any more out of touch with your office than you were before, H.C.," the Minos declared in a conciliatory tone.

"What about my mail?" Stoner bristled.

"Tom will make a daily trip over to the mainland and bring it, as usual. He'll take care of any letters you have to post."

"Well, if I can get my mail," assented the mollified magnate.

"Are there any further objections?" Paphlagloss inquired. "If so, I'd appreciate hearing about them."

The servants began to mutter discontentedly. "The boss is paying you wages, ain't he?" Starr addressed them. "Them wages ain't going to be cut. It's up to you to be good sports and do like he wants." The grumbling soon died away, except on the part of one maid, Carrie. She, however, as Westborough had already noted, was a difficult person to satisfy under any conditions.

"As an American citizen," Nielsen said abstractedly, "I rather resent curtailment of my personal liberties. In fact, I'm reminded with more patriotic fervor than I knew I possessed of such incidents as the Boston Tea Party."

"My most important ancestors were Irish," Glendon added. "The principle's the same, however."

Paphlagloss held up a pudgy hand. "One at a time, please. Do you object to staying here under my conditions, Doctor Nielsen?"

"Under any conditions," Nielsen returned bluntly. As if realizing the ungraciousness of this he added, "I haven't any desire to be disagreeable, and still less of a desire to display ingratitude for your hospitality. The plain facts, however, are that you've managed to keep me so confoundedly busy I haven't had the chance to get any writing done."

"Do you work best during the day or during the evening, Doctor?"

"The evening," Nielsen flung back instantly.

"Very well." The fencing was superb, Westborough reflected. "We'll take care your evenings are no longer disturbed, Doctor. Glendon, you were engaged to paint two frescoes, and so far you haven't completed even the first. You assured me that the engagement meant a great deal to you, and I certainly should dislike to lose your services. However, I'll be fair. If you really want to leave now, Tom will run you to Ynez within the next hour."

Glendon gulped quickly. "I'll stay," he said in a low voice.

"Do you mind remaining, Russell?"

"I'll say I don't!" the blond athlete exclaimed, with a glance toward Ione. "I like the scenery here."

"And you Mr. Westborough?" Paphlagloss purred like a huge sleek cat.

"I should like very much to stay."

The Minos bowed suavely. "My friends, my family, employees, it is a relief to know that we are now in substantial agreement, so life at Knossos may go on as before." His voice roughened noticeably. "But only apparently as before. There will be a major difference inwardly—a psychological atmosphere of constraints, tensions, mutual suspicions." Slowly and with deliberate precision he inserted another bulky Greek cigarette into his long jade holder. "I apologize for the unpleasantness; unfortunately it is necessary. One of you," he rasped harshly, "is a murderer, and before the week is out I intend to know which."

IV

"We are all virtually prisoners," Westborough wrote on the ornate embossed and expensive stationery of Knossos. "Nevertheless, Mr. Paphlagloss has exerted himself to be the perfect host. To placate the ruffled feelings of the elder Mr. Stoner, a boar hunt has been announced as the main event on the Sunday program.

"As you know, the descendants of once harmless domestic porkers raised by early Spanish colonists are today wild savage brutes, weighing up to four hundred pounds, I believe, and equipped with murderous razor-sharp tusks at least six inches long. Eternal enmity has been sworn between Mr. Paphlagloss and these scattered members of the porcine tribe, and today our host called upon his guests to aid in the holy war of extermination.

"Unlike the 'boar sticking' of India, this hunt is being conducted on foot. There are no horses on the island and even if there were, I doubt very much if mounts could be utilized over the rugged, broken and brush-covered terrain the boar frequents. Stalking an animal of such ferocity over ground so unfavorable is certainly far from a sinecure, yet many Nimrods heeded the dangerous call. To be exact, Mr. Stoner and his son, Doctor Nielsen and Miss Paphlagloss, the latter striding away in a boyish shooting jacket like Atalanta at the Calydonian hunt. Pray pardon the classical simile; it is not so apt as it first seemed, since the younger Mr. Stoner must be cast in the heroic role of Meleager. Mr. Glendon refused to leave his work, and Mr. Bayard's eyesight is too poor for him to shoot accurately.

"As for the remaining dwellers at Knossos, the hostess engages in no form of exercise beyond an occasional ocean dip, and your correspondent, too aged and too decrepit for such a strenuous sport, sensed an invaluable opportunity to indulge undisturbed in his letter writing. By the way, I should greatly appreciate your kindness in posting the enclosed two missives via air mail, and your further kindness in ignoring, for the present at least, such hints as you may receive from the addresses. With conditions in the present state of flux, to act too precipitously would be a very grave error, I believe.

"I was very sorry to hear that yesterday afternoon's search of the submarine gardens failed so signally to disclose the whereabouts of the missing rowboat. Yet another mystery is added to the many which at present overwhelm us. Nevertheless, though groping in darkness, I believe I discern a faintly luminous glow to mark the cavern's end. I believe that I have stumbled upon the motive which you found so puzzling on the day you conducted your admirable investigations. Thinking, as it were, on paper, I might say:

"Alexis Paphlagloss entrusted a secret (as yet unknown) to the deceased Danville. Mr. Paphlagloss, I believe, knows why his butler was killed and so do others under the roof of Knossos, whose identity I may surmise. But nothing is clearly defined as yet.

"Pray pardon the meagerness of this report. As soon as I am able to secure data worthy of your attention, I will write again."

Westborough concluded with the very conventional "very truly yours," scrawled his signature in cramped handwriting below the meaningless phrase, folded the letter and placed it with two already sealed and addressed missives into a single large envelope, which he sealed and addressed to his publisher in New York City. Neither the publisher's name nor address was false; nevertheless, he was not intended to receive the epistle.

Walking down to the pier, Westborough found Tom Starr standing guard over the boathouse. "Good morning, Mr. Starr. Were you planning on making a trip to the mainland today?"

"Well, I might be," the other returned cannily. "And then again I might not be."

Starr's visage had been conditioned not only by time but by wind and sun and salt air, but his weatherworn skin, which should have been gloriously tanned, had succeeded in achieving only a lobster scarlet. His small gray eyes squinted through narrow slits, from which radiated pencils of tiny wrinkles and a handlebar mustache drooped despondently over cracked lips. His costume never changed. No matter what the day or what the hour, Star wore his blue shirt and faded dungarees, with a neat yachting cap jauntily atop his salt-and-pepper hair.

"What's on your mind?" he questioned.

"Might I trouble you to post a letter for me at Ynez?"

"Well, I might," Starr answered warily, "and then again I might not."

He scrutinized carefully the name and address. "To my publisher," Westborough said mendaciously. "I am explaining to him my reasons for not completing my next book sooner."

He did not add that the return card in the upper lefthand corner bore the citation "Theocritus X." Westborough, instead of the customary "Theocritus L." Nor did he mention that the "X" was a code signal worked out between him and Captain Cranston and Constable Stebbins. The constable's wife, the postmistress at Ynez, had been instructed by her husband what to do with a letter from Knossos bearing the return card "Theocritus X."

Starr, however, pocketed the bulky document without so much as a glance at the name in the upper left corner. Only the recipient of a letter (and, sometimes, postal employees) ever reads a name in that position, the historian cogitated.

"All that weight for a few explanations?" Starr asked in genial camaraderie.

"The explanations are very weighty ones," Westborough returned smilingly. "At least they are to me. Whether or not they will carry weight with him is, of course, a different matter. Probably not, I fear. Publishers are at times difficult."

"Well, I guess it's okay."

"May I ask, Mr. Starr, if you have been officially appointed postal inspector at Knossos?" Westborough took the liberty of inquiring.

"Well, I'm not saying I have," Starr drawled, "and then, again, I'm not saying I haven't."

It being impossible to converse satisfactorily with a person of such protean answers, the little man returned to the house, where he found his hostess on the terrace, book in hand, basking in the effulgence of a sun which had just put to rout the last vestige of fog.

"May I join you?" he asked.

She smiled archly, allowing the book to fall unheeded to the red concrete flooring. Jennifer Paphlagloss, Westborough was unkind enough to opine, was one of those women who smile archly whenever a male approaches, whether said male be seventy or seventeen.

"Why, of course. We have seen far too little of each other during your stay at Knossos, Mr. Westborough. Do be seated, and we'll have a nice cozy chat."

Westborough, occupying the chair she indicated, wondered tremulously what he—a man approaching seventy, narrow-shouldered, flat-chested and scrawny-necked, a man whose hair was white and scanty and whose eyes peeked owlishly from gold-rimmed bifocals—could say to interest so charming, so attractive a woman. Yet he must not only interest her, he must also succeed in diverting the conversation into intimate channels, where, instinct told him, she would be loath to proceed. He sighed dolefully. Compared to such a task, Hercules had had rather an easy thing in the Augean stables.

"You sigh as if you are sad, Mr. Westborough."

"I am sad," he owned. Taking a long breath, he plunged headlong into the oily waters of gallantry. "I am sad because I am at the same time the most fortunate and the most luckless of men."

"Intuition tells me that you are about to pay me a compliment." Her laughter rang like the tinkling of silver chimes. "If so—well, candidly, I do not dislike compliments."

"You are sure you will not be offended?"

"Not in the least."

"So be it. I shall explain the paradox. I am fortunate to be in the presence of one of the most rarely beautiful women I have encountered in the past decade." (That much was true, he consoled himself, eying the shimmer of sunlight in the fine-spun gold she wore for hair.) "I am sad, alas, because I am not thirty years younger."

"You do very well, for any age, Mr. Westborough."

"Though dimmed by the mist of the years, my eyes are yet capable of appreciating feminine pulchritude. But I shall say no more, remembering the wise words of Cicero that age may have nothing to do with sumptuous banquets."

"You are a quaint old-fashioned gentleman," she smiled softly.

"And who," thought Westborough, "suspects a quaint old-fashioned gentleman of ulterior motives? No one—unless he shows them. And if he shows them, we may fail. 'But screw your courage to the sticking-place, and we'll not fail.' "

Aloud, he said: "I am dazzled from looking too long at the light. Shall we talk of other matters?"

"Cabbages or kings?"

"I know little of cabbages and even less of kings. Shall we make our topic your husband's hobbies?"

"Yes, Alexis does have strange hobbies."

How quickly her curving lips sobered! Would she follow his lead or not? From her indifferent manner one could tell nothing.

"A Cretan palace, a Cretan goddess and a Cretan shrine. The latter interests me particularly since I am, on a humble scale it is true, an antiquarian myself. Has it been here very long?"

"Only since last winter. Alexis built it himself."

It was the opening for which he had been fervently praying to all the household divinities of Knossos!

"Your husband is very talented, but surely he did not carve the panels and paint the background?"

"No, those were done at Los Angeles, but Alexis brought them out here and put up the shrine himself. Silly thing, isn't it?"

"It is perhaps a trifle outré," he granted. "Did your husband—"

"He likes to play with tools. Fishing is another of his hobbies, and, of course, hunting. But hunting is dangerous here. Did you ever shoot a wild boar, Mr. Westborough?"

"Once, a great many years ago. But tell me—"

"I had an experience, too. Right on this island, two years ago. Alexis had invited me to go hunting with him and I was stupid enough to assent! What a horrible day! Creeping and crawling—yes, literally crawling—through the thickest, most impenetrable brush. My clothes were cut to ribbons in no time at all. We should have had dogs to stalk with—small dogs are best, they say—but my husband doesn't like dogs and won't have any on this island. What do you suppose is wrong with a man who doesn't like dogs, Mr. Westborough?"

"Prejudices are sometimes difficult to explain. But I should like to know if—"

"There I was with my clothes literally in tatters, my face a sight and my mouth dry as an old shoe from all that walking through the awful dirt and dust. We hadn't seen a boar, and after four hours of it I didn't care. I would have been perfectly content if all the wild pigs on the island had decided then and there to run straight into the ocean and drown themselves, like the herd of Gadarene swine in the Bible—but that was just the time one of them would pick to come crashing down from the side of the hill. A perfect monster! It looked as big as a house to me, and it ran as fast as an express train. Those awful tusks! My heart was in my mouth. Alexis fired and wounded him, but not fatally. Then . . ."

The narrative didn't by any means lack excitement, but it was apparently interminable. Westborough groaned inwardly at the vexing chance which had snatched away from him the thread that seemed secure in his grasp. "Just when I was about to learn," he lamented to himself, while the boar charged and was wounded, charged and was missed, charged and was hit, charged and dropped in his tracks, a gallant blood-flecked foe, failing by only a few feet of his goal.

"I've never hunted since," she concluded.

"Dear me, no!" Westborough exclaimed sympathetically. "After that harrowing experience, I should think not. But tell me some more about the shrine." It was risky to broach it, but he felt that he must accept the risk. "Did your husband do all the work of assembly by himself?"

"Did he?" It was evident she wasn't very greatly interested. "I can't really remember—no, of course he didn't. Marc helped him and—"

"Hello!" called Ione, who had just come onto the terrace and was still in her hunting clothes. "Is Russ back here yet?"

Westborough hastily swallowed his disappointment. He had played and lost, but perhaps he had not lost permanently.

"Why no, dear," Jennifer answered, with the special smile she seemed to hold in reserve for her stepdaughter. "We haven't seen him. Is the hunt finished so soon?"

"The hunt," the girl returned, "was a fizzle and a washout—at least as far as I'm concerned. I'm going to find Russ. Why don't you come with me, Mr. Westborough? The walk will do you good."

Westborough, fortunately, was sensitive to vocal inflections. "Why, I believe I shall," he replied at once. "Will you be so kind as to excuse me, Mrs. Paphlagloss?"

"Deserted without compunction," she laughed, retrieving her book. "I'll never believe another thing you say, never."

"Come along," Ione urged, taking his arm and propelling him forcefully into the upstairs hall. The historian pointed ruefully to his immaculately white shoes.

"May I change?" he pleaded. "A stroll over the island's hills will be sure to ruin—"

"No," she flamed. "I'll buy you a new pair of shoes—a dozen new pairs. But please don't stop now. There isn't time."

V

"Crabbed age and youth cannot live together," the greatest mind of all ages once observed profoundly. Certainly, Westborough reflected, trudging doggedly and a little breathlessly behind the Lincoln-green jacket of his tireless companion, they cannot walk together. Particularly not when youth is in a hurry. And youth is always in a hurry. Impatience is its besetting characteristic; when one learns the virtues of patience he has lost those of youth, since the two, unfortunately, are mutually exclusive. This interesting trend of thought so absorbed Westborough's attention that he failed to see an encroaching manzanita until one of its crooked branches had rudely snatched away his spectacles.

"Dear me!" he gasped in surprise. "Was this done with malice-afore-thought?"

Turning her head, his companion saw the glasses neatly reposing on the shrub's dark red fingers and reacted as might be expected. Now the methods of expressing mirth are many—the nervous titter, the self-conscious giggle, the dry chuckle, the mean snicker or the vulgar guffaw. Ione's merriment, however, bubbled from the inner depths of her being as naturally as the mockingbird's song, and, since laughter is a universal language, it banished completely the reserve normally existing between a girl of twenty-three and a man approaching seventy.

"You poor dear!" she exclaimed, when laughter would allow her words. "I've walked you way too fast."

"Not—in the—least," Westborough gasped untruthfully. "Pleasure—I'm sure."

"We'll go slowly until you catch your breath."

"But you're in a hurry," Westborough objected. His breathing was more natural now, his heart and lungs no longer labored. "Isn't someone in trouble?"

"Not yet." He noted the quick proud toss of her head. "Maybe never. Probably I'm just being silly."

"I don't believe that of you."

"Yes, you'd understand," she flung back over her shoulder. "I felt you would, and that's why I asked you. Mr. Glendon would have come, of course, but you can't ask a fresco painter to spoil his work."

"Not without a powerful reason, certainly," Westborough agreed. "Pray tell me about the hunt."

"Russ and I became separated from the others. Even if this island isn't much bigger than a pocket handkerchief, you can get lost on it. Finally, we broke out of the brush and found ourselves on the cliff overlooking the strip of beach near Marc's camp. We hadn't had a sight of a boar, and Russ was wild to kill something. So he potted a gull that was skimming along the beach way below us. Hit it squarely! Russ knows how to shoot; I'll give him that much credit. But I was furious!"

"Gulls are not game birds?"

"No. They're scavenger birds and protected at all times. But it isn't just that. Maybe I can't explain it, but it isn't my idea of sport to shoot a bird just because it happens to make a good target."

"Nor mine," said Westborough.

"A boar's different. It weighs more than you do and can run three times as fast. It's got tusks to rip with and a devilish disposition, so you meet on more or less equal terms, if you know what I mean."

The historian nodded. "Gilbert once observed that deerstalking would be a very fine sport, if only the deer had guns."

She laughed. "I wish I'd known that for Russ, but even so, I didn't do such a bad job of telling him off. Then I ran away to give him plenty of time to think it over. I expected to find him waiting for me at the house, with a humble and contrite heart, but he wasn't. So that's why we must hurry now."

"Will you pardon my obtuseness. I fail to see the connection."

"It's perfectly clear to me," she answered, smiling indulgently. "Russ isn't the type to be crazy over his own company. If he didn't chase up to the house after me, he might decide to drop in at Marco's camp." She quickened her pace as she spoke. "They don't like each other, at any time, and Russ will be in an especially ugly mood today. Russ is built like Tarzan, and Marc—just imagine, yourself, what's likely to happen if they fight."

Westborough, dolefully considering the probable results of a physical encounter between the herculean Russell and the beanpole Marc, was thankful that the latter's camp was no farther away than over the next ridge.

And he was equally grateful that Bayard, his countenance unmarked by any tussle, was in a camp chair before his tent, staring raptly at an ellipsoidal stone, a little smaller than an ostrich egg.

"Have you seen Russ?" Ione called.

"I'm thankful to say no. Here's something much more pleasant." Bayard's face shone with almost supernal ecstasy as he displayed the object of his contemplation. "Discovered today in Trench 5 at a distance of six feet, seven inches, from the surface. Isn't it a beauty?"

"That?" Ione winked slyly at Westborough. "I wouldn't leave home for it, whatever it is."

The oval stone, Westborough noted, was encrusted with a calcareous deposit reminding him of the fused exterior of a fallen meteor. "A sacred stone?" he queried.

"No, a mano for seed grinding," Bayard returned. "One of the first of all artifacts. Any idea how old this is?"

"I could not even hazard a guess, but it does appear to be of great antiquity."

"It's so old, it will decompose if it isn't handled with the greatest care. The stone itself will disintegrate—imagine it!" Laying his hat on the ground, Bayard cradled the Indian grinding stone gently within the crown. "This is the most important thing I've ever found! A relic of the First Culture people, Mol Mol 'ique, the Ancient, Ancient Ones! They'd faded out of the picture probably several centuries before Christ. Who were they? What killed them? We don't know—we know almost nothing about them."

"And who cares?" laughed Ione, reaching in the pocket of her jacket for a pack of cigarettes.

"I do, for one," Bayard said, a little nettled. He cupped a flame for her with both hands. "The topic's fascinating."

"But it doesn't matter, Marco darling! Nothing really matters, except having a good time."

"So you are a hedonist?" Westborough smiled. He was amazed at the sudden warmth of her response.

"Do you know a better philosophy?"

"You do, my dear, I believe." Their eyes met and clashed—his, weak, faded, wrinkled; hers, glowing luminously with the splendid strength of her healthy young body.

"You are wrong," she said coolly. "Selfishness is the first law of nature. I believe in being frankly selfish."

"So does a jellyfish!" Bayard broke in fractiously. "We've gone a little up the scale since—oh, hello, Stoner! Glad to see you."

But he was not glad to see Russell Stoner and the antipathy was entirely mutual.

" 'Lo, Marc," Stoner said shortly. "Been looking for you, Ione. Just came from the house. I tried to follow you, but got lost in—"

"Did you leave your rifle at the house?" she interrupted chillingly.

"Yes. Why? You know, Ione, I'm sorry for—"

"I suggest, Mr. Stoner, that you return for your rifle and attempt to eliminate another kind of boar from the island. Or is that sport too dangerous for a gull-killer?"

Only the young can be so studiedly cruel, Westborough reflected. Russell Stoner's immature face was woefully miserable.

"Oh, I'm still in the doghouse, am I?" he muttered.

"Permanently."

Obviously the young man's overcharged emotions could be relieved only through the tested medium of physical action. He picked up a stone and hurled it over the bluff. Even as it fell, the thrower's broad square-tipped fingers groped for another missile.

"No!" Bayard yelled furiously. "Put it down, you fool!"

It was the very worst time to employ the offensive epithet. Stoner, poising the heavy ellipsoid on the palm of his right hand, smirked self-consciously and drew back his arm for the throw.

"For God's sake!" Bayard screeched. "Don't—"

He darted forward a fraction of a second too late. With the skill and strength of a trained athlete, Russell Stoner had cast the ancient mano far out over the still more ancient sea. Into the hyacinthine waters, Bayard's irreplaceable treasure sank as calmly as a soul entering Nirvana.

VI

"There are men created to destroy," Westborough pondered when he should have been getting ready for dinner. "The confirmed practical joker is invariably a sadist, I believe. Frequently a bully. 'O, it is excellent to have a giant's strength; but it is tyrannous to use it like a giant.' (Is there any problem of psychology on which Shakespeare's wisdom has not been shed?) Shooting the gull was an act of wanton brutality. But the other! True, he afterwards displayed a rudimentary remorse. Equally true, he did not know the unique value of the article to poor Bayard. But if he had known, would it have made any essential difference? Would he not have . . ." A knock on the connecting door interrupted the flow of thought.

"Yes, Doctor Nielsen, do come in," Westborough called aloud. "I understand that you enjoyed only moderate success at the Calydonian hunt."

Nielsen chuckled sardonically. "Moderate, my dear fellow, is euphemistic for no success at all. The only boar I saw was a two-legged one y-clept Harvey Stoner. For a period approaching seven hours I endured his condescending wisdom." He vented a tremendous sigh. "Why do I do these things?"

"Why, indeed?" Westborough chided. "And the manuscript on the Baetylic cult as yet only half written!"

"Half written? You flatter me. It goes slowly, my dear sir, slowly. In the atmosphere of this house the organ I jokingly designate as a brain refuses, for some inexplicable reason, to function." His voice sank to a sober whisper. "Will you please oblige me by stepping into my room for a few minutes?"

"Why, whatever is the matter?" Westborough exclaimed as he crossed the threshold. Nielsen pointed gloomily to a sheaf of yellow paper covered with his thin spidery writing.

"Someone's stolen a whole page of my manuscript. 'From him that hath not shall be taken away even that which he hath.' "

"Dear me! Are you sure you have not mislaid it?"

"Yes. All this may look like a muddle to others"—Nielsen indicated the jumble of notes littering his writing desk—"but it is of crystalline clarity to me. The instant I returned to my room, I received the distinct impression that my papers had been rifled. Nothing obvious, mind you, but I'm sensitive to minute changes in the position of my personal belongings. My own words being my greatest treasure, I examined the font of their wisdom. Pages twenty-two and twenty-four were intact, but page twenty-three"—he sighed—"has entered the limbo of the lost. Vanished, disappeared, melted as the shifting creations of a dream. Does it make sense to you?"

"No," Westborough replied slowly, "it does not."

"I am robbed of a priceless article which was not mine. I am robbed of my purse's vile trash through the medium of the card table. Now I am robbed even of the barren fruits of my toil. This house," he concluded his jeremiad, "is driving me to the verge of lunacy."

"I am sure," Westborough ventured gently, "that the page is somewhere among your notes. Who here would want to steal such a thing?"

"Who, ah who? I shall go mad in attempting to reason the unreasonable. It wasn't H.C. Stoner; it couldn't have been Paphlagloss. My worthy host and his esteemed rival were with me up to the very minute I reentered my room. Beyond this point, however, logic breaks down. Logic I scorn thee, intuition thou art equally valueless. Fortunately, the waxen tablets of memory are not yet an expunged slate. What the moving finger has writ, may be wrote again. I write by rote. A rite by rote. Ha, very good! Westborough, if you will excuse me, I shall devote the remaining few minutes before dinner to literary endeavors."

The evening meal could scarcely be termed a success, despite prodigious efforts of the hostess to brighten the conversation. Nielsen frowned down all morsels of small talk tossed in his direction; his gloom deepened with every succeeding course; it was obvious that his attempt to reconstruct the missing page of his manuscript had not as yet been successful. Paphlagloss and the elder Stoner, who had evidently enjoyed too much of each other's uninterrupted society during the boar hunt, were ripe for argument, and a slight spark on the inconsequential topic of old-age pensions sufficed to start a fusillade of explosions. Ione refused all overtures of the younger Stoner to effect a reconciliation; Glendon sat in solemn silence; and Marc Bayard was more moody than Westborough had ever seen him. Even the purple-black Greek wine seemed to have turned mysteriously sour.

The meal, however, dragged its way at last to a dispirited ending. The Minos, who apparently overlooked nothing, took steps to counteract his daughter's coldness to Russell Stoner with a mandate that the two young people join their fathers at the bridge table. Westborough, thus released from his duty to act as Nielsen's substitute, gravitated by training and inclination into the library.

The room was empty except for Marc Bayard, who was taking notes from a very large book on a very small slip of paper. Westborough paused, reluctant to disturb the man whom he knew had been made to suffer so keenly, and was turning to depart unseen when Bayard closed the book with a decisive bang, crumpled the paper, tossed it into the library wastebasket and jumped to his feet.

"I beg your pardon," the historian apologized, acting as if he had that instant entered the room. "Do I interrupt your studies?"

Bayard laughed mirthlessly. "My studies. What are they worth to anybody?"

"A very great deal to the advancement of human knowledge," Westborough answered.

"Are they?" Bayard demanded bitterly. "I doubt it. And if they are, what am I worth? Because he happens to be feeling peevish, an oaf throws my greatest find into the ocean. And what do I do about it? Nothing. Nothing at all."

"There was not a great deal you could do, Mr. Bayard."

"I could have knocked him down, couldn't I?"

Westborough was silent. Seldom had he been so sorry for anyone as for this unhappy young man.

"Or tried to knock him down," Bayard amended.

"Would that act have restored your archaeological treasure?"

"It would have restored my self-respect."

"There is no reason why your self-respect should be missing, Mr. Bayard."

"No? What do you suppose Ione thinks of me?"

"She is sure that you followed the dignified and reasonable course." Westborough, however, was expressing his own viewpoint. He did not actually know Miss Paphlagloss' present opinion of her stepbrother.

"Ione despises me, and I despise myself!" Picking up his book from the table, Bayard restored it to the shelf. "I'm going up to the camp. Good night."

"Dear, dear, dear me!" Westborough clucked helplessly, eying the drooping shoulders and sagging back as they retreated from the room. "The poor fellow! So unnecessary, too. If there were only something I could say to him!"

But there was, he knew very well, nothing. There are crises—and this was one—which the soul must face with his own strength or be damned eternally. A diabolical thought insinuated itself into his own mind. He thought of the slip of paper which poor Bayard had crumpled into the wastebasket.

Like Lancelot Gobbo, Westborough was torn between his conscience and the fiend. The fiend, unfortunately, succeeded in getting the better of the brief encounter, and the elderly historian reached regretfully into the wastebasket. He smoothed out the paper. Written in pencil were a scant seven words:

"Dry root, scrape, steep in hot wat—"

The last word trailed away, as if it had already served its purpose in the writer's mind, so that there was no necessity of completing it. Westborough went to the shelf for the book Bayard had been reading. It was a weighty volume, written by A. L. Kroeber, under the imposing title: "Smithsonian Institution, Bureau of American Ethnology, Bulletin 78, *Handbook of the Indians of California.*"

"Handbook," Westborough reflected, "might perhaps be a trifle inappropriate title for a scholarly tome of 995 pages." He turned to the lengthy general index, the compiling of which must of itself have represented a feat of no mean magnitude. "Roktso, Roquechoh, Round Valley . . . " The word "root" was conspicuously absent, and Westborough closed the book in a sudden fit of revulsion at all forms of snoopery. He selected Arne Nielsen's *Minoan Culture* from the library shelves, and, for want of any better occupation, went up to his room and read himself to sleep.

From the depths of dreamless slumber, he was aroused by a light rap upon his doorway. Slowly he struggled to consciousness. The sound was repeated; he was not then dreaming. He yawned and stretched out his hand to turn on the night lamp.

"Doctor Nielsen!" The voice was masculine, softly pitched but carrying overtones of tremendous excitement. Westborough ran to the door without bothering to hunt his dressing gown and slippers. "Doctor Nielsen!" the voice called again, and Westborough flung the door open.

"Oh, I beg your pardon. I thought this was Doctor Nielsen's room. I'm sorry I—"

"One minute, please," Westborough directed a trifle sharply. "Do you mind telling me why you want Doctor Nielsen at this hour of the night?"

"Because I've stumbled on a thing right down his alley." Marc Bayard's sandy hair was ruffled; his clothing was soiled and disorderly. "You won't believe it, but it's there. A Minoan altar! With blood smeared on it! *Blood!*"

VII

The small bedside lamp cast the eerily pink glow of a conjurer's flame. Beyond the three in its charmed circle, Westborough mused, night's hideous spawn stretched slithering tentacles. He shivered, thinking of elemental beings to be propitiated by weird shadowy rituals, but the act of shivering restored the twentieth century.

He was, he reminded himself, on an island under the jurisdiction of Los Angeles County, and he shivered merely because the island's nights were cool, and he had as yet draped nothing over his pajamas. Neither was Arne Nielsen wearing anything over the old-fashioned white nightshirt from which his bony shanks protruded.

"Ridiculous!" Nielsen exclaimed. His voice, as if to counteract his sartorial deficiencies, was more exactingly professional than ever. "A Minoan altar! My dear young friend, you are suffering from the delusions of somnambulism."

"I'd like to think that." Bayard's pinched face showed haggard in the night lamp's rosy effulgence. "But I don't walk in my sleep. The thing was put up on the beach, just below my camp. An altar made of flat stones, about the diameter of my body. They'd been stacked to form a pillar as high as my shoulders."

"A pile of stones, my dear sir, can represent other objects than a Minoan altar. The simplest, of course, being merely a pile of stones."

"I know." How weary, how tired Marc Bayard's voice sounded. "I'm probably crazy. But two straight sticks had been driven vertically into the sand, one on either side of the column. It looked like the carving on the panels of the shrine downstairs."

"The pillar between the horns?" Westborough questioned.

Bayard nodded soberly. "Yes. The effect was like that. Crude, of course. A child's representation."

"Pillar? Horns?" Nielsen's eyes flamed with quick interest. "Ha! Ancient aniconic symbol. Dates back long before Rome. Before Greece and Persia. Even before the Assyrian wolf. The Philistines got it from Crete, and the Hebrews got it from them. Read your Bible. I Kings II, 28. 'And Joab fled unto the tent of the lord and caught hold on the horns of the altar.' "

"Those were sacrificial horns, I believe," Westborough proffered. "Projections to which could be tied the victim to be immolated."

Bayard shuddered. "I saw blood smeared on the stones. Blood! It had dried there. And there was something on top of the column."

"What?" Nielsen asked.

"I don't know. I—I couldn't look. Just a vague dark shape." Sinking on the edge of the bed, he plunged his face into his hands. "It was horrible."

"Interesting. Ha! Very interesting, indeed!" Nielsen had strayed into the distant world of the prophet and seer. "Old concept, sacrifice— Give a part to the gods in order to bribe them into letting you keep the rest. One of the fundamental ideas of religious history."

"Homer describes the method of his day in a wealth of detail," Westborough contributed. His voice sounded so weakly in his ears, he wondered why he spoke at all.

"Homer!" snorted Nielsen. "My dear fellow, he was virtually a contemporary. The concept is older than Homer. Far, far older! The tradition of sacrifice originally came from Crete. Diodorus Siculus is my authority for it. The oracle of Apollo at Delos was also of Cretan origin. Perhaps all the Greek mysteries. What were these in their essence but methods of evoking Kore from her shadowy domain in Hades? And what was Kore but the chthonian manifestation of the Cretan mother goddess?"

"Let us dress and immediately go down to the beach," Westborough suggested.

Nielsen emerged with a start from his trance. "Dress? Ha! Good idea. Examine it ourselves while the half-world sleeps."

"And tear it down," Westborough urged. "It must be destroyed before—"

"Destroyed, certainly," Nielsen interrupted brusquely.

"A religious atavism—altar to the ancient pagan love goddess. Offends all that we consider decent today."

"What does it mean?" Bayard inquired.

"Mean?" Nielsen snapped. "A possible meaning is that the world's gone mad." He returned to his own room for his shirt and trousers. "That condition, however, has long since ceased to surprise me," he added from the doorway.

" '*Furor in cursu est,*' " murmured Westborough, who was now well on the road to normalcy. Dressing hastily, he joined his two companions. Softly as three conspirators they stepped along the deserted halls, descended the broad staircase, tiptoed across the flagging of the central court and emerged at last from a side entrance into the open air.

Darkness hovered over them like a great black bowl. Only the strongest of stellar rays could penetrate the fog blanket which nightly draped the Island of Minos, and the gibbous moon had sunk low in the west. They kept closely together, marching in single file, across the successive series of hogbacks—Bayard in advance, Westborough following, Nielsen last.

Night's myriad noises sounded lonesomely, as their feet padded along the soft dirt of the trail. Twigs crackled beneath their weight, leaves rustled, insects hummed in shrill cacophony, a whippoorwill's eerie call traveled faintly from the distance.

Nielsen cleared his throat. "Harumph! My young friend," he called to Bayard, "the matter is decidedly not my business. However, what made you choose this ungodly time to consort with nature?"

"I couldn't sleep," Bayard answered. "I've been walking around the island for hours." The explanation was a little too pat, thought Westborough, and very much too trite. As if conscious of its inadequacy, Bayard broke into a torrent of speech. "It's not far now. A little valley on the other side of the next ridge leads down to the beach. But there's no trail to speak of, so be careful where you step."

Nielsen, who had not sufficiently heeded the admonition, measured his length on the ground soon after they had entered the valley. "Dear me!" Westborough cried, turning back in alarm at the crash. "Did you hurt yourself in that stumble?"

"I didn't stumble," Nielsen denied angrily. While they assisted him to his feet he voiced his protests in a vocabulary of remarkable fluency. "Something reached out and grabbed my ankle. A horrible slimy hand."

"It could not be a hand," Westborough argued. He made the contention, however, for the sake of common sense. Privately, he was convinced that anything could happen on the Island of Minos. Even the sudden appearance of Caliban would not greatly have startled him.

"Oh, couldn't it?" Nielsen muttered, brushing his clothing as men do after a fall. "I distinctly felt its grip. What's more, it snatched my confounded flashlight."

"Your flashlight is here, Doctor Nielsen," Westborough informed him, stooping to the ground. "Still lighted; the glass not even cracked." He twirled the metal cylinder in his hand; its beam came to rest on a tangle of sickly green leaves and giant white morning-glory blooms. "And that shrub, I believe, is what tripped you." He pushed the foliage with his foot as he spoke. "Dear me! Most certainly that is what tripped you. You can see how it has been uprooted by your fall."

"It felt like a hand," Nielsen said sheepishly. "However, I dare say you're right. My apologies for making a fool of myself."

"Dear me, you could not help it, Doctor Nielsen." Though Bayard laughed, and even Nielsen chuckled, Westborough, ordinarily one of the most considerate of men, remained unconscious of the rudeness of his words. Fragments were jostling through his brain, fragments obstinately refusing to adjust themselves into a pattern. "Oh dear," he exclaimed in vexation. "I have dropped my fountain pen—possibly when I stooped for Doctor Nielsen's flashlight. I wonder where it can be? No, gentlemen, please go on, I pray you. I will find it in a minute."

The instant he was sure that they were no longer watching him, he dropped to his knees beside the shrub. The heavily sweet fragrance of the trumpet-shaped blooms was exotic, faintly repulsive. Doubtless, the night intensified the scent. The flashlight Westborough had retained traveled over the purplish stems . . . . He sprang abruptly to his feet. "Dear me! Dear, dear me. Can it be possible?"

It could be possible, he answered himself, since the condition existed. The plant was rootless, and the root had not been jerked from the stalk by the weight of the falling Nielsen, but cut from it with a sharp knife. The purplish-bronze stem showed the traces of the cutting instrument quite plainly.

He hurried to rejoin his companions, overtaking them just as they stepped onto the beach. "Fountain pen recovered?" asked Nielsen.

Westborough nodded. "Fortunately, yes. Dear me, is that the mysterious altar?"

"It would appear so," Nielsen answered. "Do you mind returning my flashlight? Thanks. Yes, it looks just as Bayard described it."

It did, indeed, Westborough conceded—the flattish beach boulders piled in a shaky tower, the vertical saplings, divested of branches and driven into the sand, which flanked the neck-high stone column. As if by tacit accord, the three men halted at a distance of about ten feet from the altar.

"The ancient symbol of divinity," Nielsen said in an awed whisper. "She dwelt on the mountain tops and in the green depths of the sea, centuries before the Hellenic deities were born, and the pillar was her aniconic emblem. We don't know why. A phallus, perhaps, since she was primarily the goddess of fertility, in herself the quintessence of all the reproductive energies. We know how Astarte was worshiped. And Cybele."

"Yes," Westborough shuddered, his mind conjuring the vision of the lewd and horrible rites of humanity's obscene childhood. Astarte, who had demanded the universal prostitution of her female worshipers! The bloodthirsty Cybele, who had claimed her priests' manhood!

"Sometimes the column was supposed to be transmogrified into the goddess herself," Nielsen continued. "We may imagine the rites. Music or prayers or incantations—whatever they were; if the worshipers succeeded in their aim, the goddess settled on the pillar in tangible form. Not in her own form, whatever that was, but in the shape of a dove. The sacred doves of Aphrodite and Astarte are—"

"God!" Bayard ejaculated, jumping three feet backward. "It's got a *beak!*"

"What has a beak?" Nielsen demanded, taking a firm hold of the young man's arm.

"The thing I told you about. The thing that's on top of the altar."

Nielsen's flashlight slowly traversed the column. "He's right. It has a beak. Feathers as well. But it isn't a dove. It's—"

"A gull," Westborough finished. "Moreover, a very dead one. Unless I err greatly, this is the hapless bird shot some hours ago by Mr. Russell Stoner."

PART FIVE: THE CRETAN GODDESS

(Monday, July 11—Tuesday, July 12)

I

DATURA, Westborough discovered, visiting the library shortly after breakfast on Monday morning, was not listed in the general index of Kroeber's *Handbook of the Indians of California.* He did, however, find the word in the classified subject index, under the heading, "Religious Culture: jimsonweed (toloache, datura) cult . . ." Twenty-five page references followed, but Westborough had not had time to consult even the first when Marc Bayard entered.

The historian allowed the book to drop carelessly on the floor beside his armchair, hoping very much that it was not the particular volume which Bayard had come to consult. The hope was not well founded. Bayard, after a brief nod of recognition, went directly to the shelf from which the bulky work had been removed, blinked nearsightedly as if mistrusting his eyes, then turned his attention to the library table.

"That's funny!"

"Strange or comical?" Westborough queried.

Bayard laughed self-consciously. "I was reading a book last night, and it's disappeared. Rather dull subject, too—that is, dull for anyone here but me."

Westborough reached to the floor. "Is this it, by any chance?"'

"Why, ye-es. Yes, that's it. Where did you find it?"

"On the table," Westborough falsified.

"I thought I'd put it back on the shelf."

"Evidently, however, you did not. My attention was drawn to the title because of your interesting lectures on the aboriginal culture of this island. However, pray take it. I would not dream of depriving you of the work."

"Thanks," Bayard said, tucking the volume under his arm. "Find anything in it that interested you?"

"I didn't have the opportunity to do more than scan a few pages. One aspect of the subject interests me very much, but I was unable to find anything on it. Do you remember the shrub you pointed out to me on the afternoon of my arrival? Dear me, that is not very definite, I fear, as you were kind enough to name a great many. This one had very large blossoms—like huge white trumpets, edged with violet."

"Oh, that!" Opening the drawer of the library table, Bayard uncovered a number of the big Greek cigarettes encased in their individual glass tubes. "Do you care for a smoke, sir?"

"No, thank you. I didn't know, Mr. Bayard, you favored this exotic brand."

"Oh, now and then," Bayard replied, fidgeting with the glass container. "I'm the only one in the family besides Mr. Paphlagloss who likes them. Mother and Ione simply can't stand the things."

"May I ask the name of that particular flower?" Westborough persisted.

"It has a number of names." Absentmindedly, Bayard placed the glass tube in the pocket of his green sport shirt. "Jimson weed, for one, but that's wrong. The true jimson weed is a different species. Some people call it thorn apple. Because of its fruit, you know, which is a prickly sphere about an inch in diameter. The Aztecs called it *coatlxoxouhqui*—don't ask me to spell it! But in California the common Indian term is toloache."

"None of these, however, is the appellation you gave me the other day," Westborough demurred.

Bayard nervously extinguished his cigarette. "The scientific name is

Datura meteloides," he informed the historian in a strained voice.

"Dear me, yes! How stupid of me to forget! The designation, meteloides, would imply, I believe, that the plant was very similar in properties to the *Datura metel* described by Linnaeus?"

"I'm not enough of a botanist to know."

Bayard was, as Westborough was well aware, an excellent botanist, but there are times when it is just as well to take a person's asseverations at face value.

"Metel, a nut," the little man murmured cheerfully, reaching into his coat pocket. "I see you have a pipe, Mr. Bayard. Can I inveigle you into accepting some of my tobacco? My own blend, I might add. I have a tobacconist in Chicago who does not do too badly."

"Yes, thanks," said Bayard, taking the pouch. When he had returned it, Westborough carefully took his own pipe, amber-stemmed with a bowl carved to resemble a human skull. He had found it some years before in a little shop in a side street in Rome, and, despite its grotesque shape, was singularly attached to it. Applying the flame, he took a tentative puff, and, satisfied that the stem was clear of all obstructions and that the bowl was not packed too tightly, relaxed at once into the pipesmoker's blissful content.

Bayard wasted three matches before he succeeded in inducing his own pipe to draw properly.

"We were talking of the datura shrub, I believe," Westborough observed, returning his pouch to his pocket. "Did you not tell me it was employed by the primitive inhabitants of this island in religious ceremonies?"

"I may have said something about it," Bayard admitted.

"The subject holds great interest for me. Would you mind enlightening me further?"

"I don't know much about it myself." Bayard had the grace to look uncomfortable as he said this. "But they had a god named Chungichnish, who dwelt in the sky and was rather more like Jehovah than the usual Indian spirit god—a universal deity who saw everything and kept a set of celestial books to record the infractions of his laws. Incidentally, Chungichnish was believed to have created the human race out of earth. Striking similarity, isn't it, to the Hebrew teachings?"

"Very striking," Westborough agreed. "Was this—er, Chungichnish—what a tongue-twister of a name!—a deity to be dreaded and propitiated?"

Bayard's pipe had gone out again, and he used a fourth match to relight it. "We don't know much about their religious rites," he said.

"You must remember that the old Indian ceremonies were stopped when the Spaniards introduced Christianity, and the friars, unluckily, kept spotty records."

"Something, however, must have been preserved of the datura cult," Westborough asserted, his mind returning to the twenty-five references in Mr. Kroeber's comprehensive "handbook."

"Well, yes, a little." Bayard's pastel blue eyes fixedly regarded the four matches in the ash tray before him. "The purpose of the main ceremony was to initiate adolescent boys into manhood."

"The young Indians were made to swallow the seeds of the datura?"

"No." Bayard's teeth clenched firmly upon the mouthpiece of his pipe. "Not the seeds."

"The root, perhaps?"

Bayard's pipe clattered to the library floor. "Dear me," Westborough exclaimed, helping to stamp out the sparks scattered over the carpet. "You have bitten off the mouthpiece."

"Ten-dollar pipe, too," the young man proclaimed, ruefully inspecting the damage. "Oh well! How did you happen to know about the roots?"

"Merely a guess. My actual knowledge is nil upon this most interesting subject. What took place after the root was consumed?"

Bayard waved his hands vaguely. "Oh, a lot of hooting and hollering, I suppose. You know what Indian ceremonies are like." He twirled the broken pipestem in his hands. "Tell me what you think of last night's business?"

"It was very strange." Westborough lowered his voice. "Perhaps it would be just as well to close the door, Mr. Bayard. You remember that we agreed last night the secret should be confined to the three of us."

"Yes," Bayard assented, pulling the door shut as directed. "God, it was gruesome! That altar smeared with the bird's blood and that horrible dead gull! Suppose Mother had happened to find it? Or Ione?"

"That danger is now obviated, however. The stones have been cast into the sea, and our feathered friend given respectable burial."

"Next time," Bayard said solemnly, "it may not be a bird."

Westborough knocked the dottle from his pipe. He could not trust himself to speak calmly.

"I can't get the idea of sacrifice out of my mind," the other continued. He laughed a little hysterically. "Sounds crazy, doesn't it?"

"It does not sound any too sensible."

"Well, the altar was crazy! And so was the murder! There simply wasn't any motive for killing poor harmless Charles."

"Dear me!" Westborough exclaimed. "When you assisted your stepfather to build his shrine was—"

"How did you know that?" Bayard broke in quickly.

"Your mother so informed me."

"She shouldn't have said—"

"Was the deceased butler also a member of the construction crew?"

"Yes. But that had nothing to do with his death. It couldn't have."

"You are sure of it, Mr. Bayard?"

"I was never more sure of anything in my life. Charles was killed by a madman. The madman who built that senseless altar."

"It was meant to be a pillar, I believe," Westborough corrected softly. "Or perhaps simply a crude image, as a cone represented Astarte at Byblus."

"Imagine a worshiper of Astarte in the twentieth century!"

"Perhaps of a more ancient divinity than Astarte," Westborough suggested, strolling absently toward the library window. "The archaic lady of Crete, the goddess of the Beautiful and the Terrible, who could be evoked from the underworld in the form of a snake or summoned from the heavens as a dove."

"A dove!" Bayard ejaculated. "That was mentioned in Doctor Nielsen's manuscript. So were the pillars and horns—all on the page stolen from his room yesterday afternoon. Stolen for what reason? What do we dare guess?"

Westborough peered out upon the concrete walk below the window. "Doves were sacrificed to Aphrodite at the celebrated shrine of Paphos," he said finally. "Sacrificed also, I believe, to Astarte throughout Syria centuries before the birth of Christ. And Astarte and Aphrodite, as Doctor Nielsen justifiably contends, are only later modifications of the Cretan mother goddess. Yet, I must remind you, a dove and a gull are not identical. The former is of the family Columbidae, the latter of the web-footed Laridae."

"Quibbling!" Bayard exclaimed hotly. "A madman, if he found a dead gull, wouldn't trouble over zoological classifications."

"Yet this madman is surprisingly sane," Westborough opined.

"Sane enough to fool us all," Bayard acknowledged. "That's the terrible part of it. He's one of us. Sleeping in the same house, on the same floor, eating at the same table. Going fishing and hunting with us; taking an ordinary part in our conversations." The young man's voice sank to a tremulous whisper. "And all the while that crazed brain of his goes on plotting. Plotting God knows what horrible obscenities."

A man on the walk below entered Westborough's line of vision, a man who was slinking along the side of the wall, pausing from time to time to glance furtively behind him. The historian sprang rapidly away from the window.

"Please excuse me," he requested, racing for the library door. "I have just recalled an important matter which must be attended to immediately."

II

Behind, stucco walls gleamed like the prehistoric palace of the legendary sea king; ahead, the trail forked into two branches. That on the right was the familiar path to Marc Bayard's camp, but that on the left plunged boldly into the interior of the island. Savage boars frequented the brush forest, Westborough had been told, but freshly made footprints showed in the brown crumbly soil of the left fork, and he followed them, conscious that the sinister force which haunted the halls of Knossos had revealed yet another of its surprising manifestations.

The man he now tracked, the man who had disappeared from sight in the chaparral behind the house, was not, could not have been, on the island at the time the murder was committed. He was the new butler, Handleburger! The imbroglio seemingly had more tentacles than a squid.

It was possible, of course, that the wizened little cockney was merely taking a casual stroll. But that had not been his demeanor when spied from the library window. No, he had skulked closely to the wall in the stealthy manner of one anxious to avoid observation. . . . Westborough futilely endeavored to hasten his progress.

The horizon showed hazily, an indeterminate blending of blue-gray sea and gray-blue sky. Despite its greasewood and dwarfish oaks, its holly and Ceanothus, the island was for the most part as dustily drab as any of the Grecian isles. Yet bird life was abundant. A crested partridge rose unexpectedly from a covert of dried grass, hummingbirds whirred like emerald, ruby and amethyst gyroscopes, a horned lark caroled unseen and a glossy raven croaked a harsh note of warning.

The trail dipped into a sandy wash, where prickly pears bloomed in satiny flower and cholla spread in spiny menace; the wash deepened into a dry-bottomed canyon; the canyon became a gorge, with precipitous sides draped by fantastic green festoons of snake cactus. What horribly weird forms these xerophytes were enabled to assume! Should he not heed the raven's warning? Should he not return to the house for aid? But what aid? Whom at Knossos did he dare trust? He was alone, cut off from all forms of assistance. Captain Cranston had stated the point unequivocally. Because the job threatened to be dangerous, was it therefore to be shirked?

Some men are brave because they are unimaginative, others because they are too proud to yield to fear's icy touch, but Westborough's courage was of a third order. He would not turn back simply because he was condemned to live with himself for all the remaining days of his life. Dust settled in a thick layer over his brown-and-white sport oxfords; they were expensive shoes, but he did not greatly care what happened to them. How odd even to be thinking of footgear at such a time! He tried to center all of his attention on the mystery that enveloped Knossos, but instead found himself recalling inconsequential details of his past life. A rather pointless life, on the whole, he concluded. The trail was a winding brown ribbon beneath his feet; the sky had shrunk to a weaving blue strip above his head . . . Without warning, the gorge opened suddenly into the sea.

On the lee side the waters were calm as those of an inland lake, but here, on the weather side of the island, they boomed like the diapason of an almighty organ. Along a thread of beach, stilt-legged sandpipers coolly dared the advance of the white-frothed breakers. Turning his eyes from the sea, Westborough glimpsed a man's form silhouetted on the cliffs above his head. Quickly, he sprawled on the sand and lay motionless.

The black speck on the rim of the sea wall did not interrupt its plodding movement. Concluding finally that he had not been observed, the historian rose to his feet. The cliffs, he saw, were broken here into a series of terraces. A line of footprints across the sand indicated the method of ascent—a difficult trail but, obviously, not an impossible one.

Doubtless the terrace levels were the remains of former beaches. Either the island had risen or the sea had sunk—but who can fathom earth's titanic mysteries? The ancient beaches formed a series of gigantic steps which, fortunately, were broken at the back, permitting men of merely mortal size to scramble breathlessly from level to level.

Gulls fluttered lazily away at his approach; their guano lay in spotty crusts upon the ledges. He climbed higher, passing a colony of web-footed cormorants with a twinge of envy. The black hook-bills reclined so peacefully on their seaweed nests. Only to rest! But the sweet luxury was not for him; he should never overtake his quarry if he did not hurry. Onward and upward, though his hands were bleeding from the scraggly edges of rock, though leg muscles ached and heart had become a racing engine, though lungs gasped in torment for the air denied them.

A bald eagle swooped threateningly near to his head. He crouched tightly against the rocks, fearful for the moment that he had climbed too close to its eyrie. The huge bird was admirably equipped for warfare. He had no wish to argue the question of trespass with that fiercely curved beak and those formidably sharp talons. To his relief, however, the white-headed monster took on altitude and was soon a soaring speck above the sea. A magnificent creature! Only a financial tycoon could be so lordly disdainful of its lowly prey.

Using his last atom of reserve strength, he forced himself to the top. The man he trailed had become a tiny ant, just barely visible; in a few instants he would be completely lost. Westborough attempted to run. He could manage only a scant dozen steps before collapsing ignominiously on a patch of mesembryanthemum. The stiff three-edged leaves rendered the plant far from an easeful couch, but one who fights in agony for the mere right to breathe is oblivious to all minor physical discomforts.

When his heart had quieted its pile-driver pounding against his chest, he rose shakily to his feet. The object of his pursuit was out of sight, naturally. Worse! Even his footprints had vanished, for footprints could not show on the cliff rock. The historian managed a sorrowful smile. Decidedly, he was a very poor man of action.

Nevertheless he continued his advance, picking his way carefully across the conglomerate of which the cliffs were composed. The island, he now realized, was in reality a mountain, one of the scattered crests of a great range which, millions of years ago, had raised itself from the sea's bottom. He looked shudderingly downward. The beach had narrowed to the vanishing point, and the ocean now hurled its massive waves directly against the cliff walls. Before the relentless surging, continued over a period of countless years, the solid rock had melted as cheese under the attacks of a nibbling mouse. The cliff face was perforated with hundreds of wounds. Most of these were tiny crevices, but other openings, particularly those closest to sea level, appeared to be caverns of very respectable dimensions. Heaven alone knew how far into the rocks some of them might extend!

The crags sank gradually as he progressed; their sides no longer loomed so precipitously but sloped brokenly downward. Indeed, one possessed of sufficient daring might be able now to descend, perhaps, even to the ocean. A crumpled white blob of cloth showed a short distance below his head, and Westborough halted abruptly.

He removed his glasses; he cleansed them of salty moisture; he polished them vigorously; he looked again. No, he had not been mistaken. It was a large handkerchief, he saw. A lucky accident had restored him to the trail taken by the man he sought. But such a path! A mere zigzagging fissure in the rocks!

Where one man led, however, another might follow—even though that other were nearly seventy and had spent most of his life in sedentary pursuits. The historian scrambled downward. He reached the handkerchief, left it where it was and continued his descent. The fissure terminated abruptly at a ledge behind which the entrance of a cave yawned blackly. The ledge extended beyond the cave opening and was wide enough for a man to stand on comfortably. A litter of broken abalone shells revealed that it had once served as the threshold of some aboriginal cliff dweller. Westborough paused momentarily, then stiffened swiftly against the rocky wall. Above and beyond the ever-present murmur of the sea, he could detect the rumble of human voices.

One was whining in quality; the other, harsh and peremptory. The historian strained his ears, the painful stages of his journey forgotten. The whiny tones, he was almost certain, belonged to Handleburger, even though, oddly, the cockney speech was not present. But the harsh voice he could not recognize.

The conversation was rather cryptic in character.

"I was in the clear till you showed up." It was the other voice, chilled and menacing. "Now you'll jim the deal with your stinking limey act."

"Oh, it stinks, does it?" the other whined.

"Like a week-old fish," was the acid retort. "This crowd is too smart for fifth-rate vaudeville."

"I came here for my cut, my fine-feathered friend, and don't forget it."

"What cut? What good are you? If you were a boxer, we might do a deal."

"How're ya going to get grease? Or use it after you get it?"

"I'm not going to shoot it." The cold voice paused, deliberately pointing the next remark. "I'm going to make him open it."

"*Him?*" the other repeated incredulously.

"That's what I said. M-m-m! Maybe I can use you."

"What do I get out of it?"

"Twenty."

"Twenty!" the whiner all but shrieked. "Fifty."

"Don't be more a yap than you can help. I've done the work."

"Who tipped you off to the locker?"

"Thirty, then."

"Forty."

"Done for thirty-five."

"Okay, pal."

"Oke. Now get this, before we go any further. There's a little old guy with googs who—"

A sudden gust of wind snatched Westborough's panama from his head, and, to his utmost horror, wafted it directly in front of the cave where it could not help but be in full view of those within. The problem of whether or not to retrieve it so occupied his attention during the next few seconds that he lost the conversation completely. While he was still hesitating, unable to make up his mind whether to reach for it or not, a second puff of wind settled the matter by whisking the chapeau from the ledge.

Though it was quite a good panama and was, moreover, the only hat he had brought with him to Knossos, Westborough did not essay to follow its descent into the spumescent sea but remained where he was, clinging like a caryatid to the vertical wall behind him. The discussion, however, had terminated. Though he listened intently, nearly losing his balance in the effort to catch what might be said within the cave, he could hear nothing except the omnipresent boom of the surf. The sudden cessation of dialogue, he realized distressfully, could be interpreted in only one manner. His hat, as it rested momentarily on the ledge, had been seen by those within the cave.

Westborough was egotistical enough to fancy that he had recognized his own description in the last phrase he had overheard. If the little old guy with googs (could they possibly be spectacles?) were so indiscreet as to blunder into his adversaries' lair, it was not difficult to predict the outcome. The calculation sent icy shivers coursing his spine, for Westborough's courage, it had been admitted, was not of the unimaginative order. Death, he well knew, was waiting for him, waiting inside the black hole the sea had carved.

Nevertheless he made no attempt to scramble up the fissure and cut across the island to safety. For one thing, he didn't believe he would be able to outrun his pursuers, and, secondly—the thought came to him in a flash—the rabbit is at a serious psychological disadvantage in its flight from the greyhound. A rabbit who turned upon its pursuer might . . .

Westborough, the frail, elderly scholar who only yesterday had counseled the doctrine of nonresistance for Marc Bayard, stepped boldly into the entrance of the cave.

Heavens, how dark it was! Until his eyes had become accustomed to the lack of light, he could see almost nothing beyond the immediate circle of the opening. But, though vision had been rendered temporarily inutile, he was in full possession of a larynx and vocal chords.

"Good morning," he called in a voice determinedly cheerful. "My hat just this minute blew over the cliff. Have you gentlemen by any chance seen it?"

He waited expectantly for a growl of recognition, for a torrent of threats, for a discussion of his personal shortcomings and those of his ancestors back to the *nth* generation; in fact, for almost any product of human speech. The one thing he had not expected, however, was the continuation of the silence, and the silence (if the absence of human sounds might be referred to in that category) persisted unbroken.

"Dear me," Westborough observed, a trifle set back. "I thought sure I heard someone talking. Very indistinct, of course. There is someone here, isn't there?"

His prattle elicited no response whatsoever, and he stopped it hastily. The power to penetrate the gloom had now been conferred on his eyes, and he saw that the cave was not at all of large extent; in fact, a mere dent in the cliff's face. It was strange, it was remarkable, it was almost unbelievable, but, as nearly as he could tell, he was the grotto's only occupant.

A few matches sufficed to confirm the incredible truth. There wasn't a hidey hole in the cavern. There was no other outlet by which a person might escape from it. He had heard voices coming from this place, yet there was no one here. In heaven's name, how was the weird conjurer's trick worked?

He sat on a loose boulder to cogitate on the puzzle. It was a boulder near the entrance, for he was, admittedly, a trifle unnerved by the bizarre experience. His ears had proved false as dicers' oaths. They had conveyed to him sounds which, reason told him, could have no physical existence.

Nothing was to be gained, however, by remaining longer in the cryptic cavern. He began the wearisome ascent of the trail—it was no more than a series of disjointed footholds—down which he had slipped and slithered to the ledge. Below his feet, the sea boiled milky white about the rocks; a slight misstep would send him hurtling into that witches' maelstrom.

However, he reached the top without mishap and paused for an instant to consider a course of action. The thought of the long arduous descent of the giant terraces to the ocean level was not a comforting one, but the thorny shrubs of the chaparral hemmed closely the rocky bluffs in an apparently impenetrable wall of underbrush. He set his face resolutely toward the cliff path and was rewarded by the sight of a man walking a short distance ahead. Unless his eyes were made the fools of the other senses, the vanished butler had amazingly rematerialized.

Overtaking his quarry was now not at all difficult, since Handleburger was sauntering at the snaillike pace of a lover composing "woful ballad made to his mistress' eyebrow." Indeed, when Westborough came up to him, he had halted altogether and was attentively regarding the narrow bright magenta petals dotting the juicy green carpet of mesembryanthemum.

"Good morning, sir. A streynge plant, hif Hi mye sye so."

"*Mesembryanthemum aequilaterale,* the noonflower or fig marigold," Westborough said mechanically. Could this pleasant-mannered servant be the man whose "limey act" had only recently been libeled as fifth-rate vaudeville? Or had there been such a man at all? With all the sternness he could master, the historian demanded, "Why are you not at the house?"

"Mr. Paphlagloss gyve me permission, sir, to hexplore the hisland. Hi was always a great 'and for a bit of a walk, sir, begging your pardon."

"Have you visited any of the caves this morning?"

"Cyves? No sir. Hi've been 'ere, sir."

The cockney whine was blandly innocent. The wrinkled simian face apparently held no guile. And yet, and yet—Westborough sighed aloud.

"Dear me, it is most confusing. May I ask you to accompany me to the house?"

"To the 'ouse, sir?"

"And walk ahead of me, if you please," Westborough directed. He had no wish to be pushed over the cliffs; the drop to the jagged rocks along the rugged shoreline was not enticing.

The descent of the beach terraces was easier than he had anticipated. Handleburger was helpful in the matter—yes, exceedingly helpful, Westborough conceded reluctantly. Had he misjudged the new butler? It is easy to mistake one voice for another. But the phrase "limey act" stuck obstinately in his craw. There simply wasn't another person on the island to whom the offensive term might be applied.

Though it was perhaps unfair to withhold such information from Handleburger's employer, Westborough decided, for the present at least, not to reveal his discovery. The fact must not be overlooked that it had been the Minos himself who had hired the enigmatic cockney.

They walked along the gorge of the snake cactus, the butler in advance, Westborough following closely. The deep cleft was as weirdly strange as a gully on Mars. In response to a slight breeze, the dangling tendrils swayed like writhing green pythons; they were horrible to behold, but they saved his life. If his interest in the curious ophidian forms had not impelled a chance glance toward the canyon's brink, he would not have glimpsed the mammoth boulder that an unseen hand was pushing down on him.

Shrieking a warning, he leaped aside from the crushing impact. A very near thing! The boulder bit deeply into the ground a scant foot away.

"Gord, hit's murder, sir!" shrieked Handleburger. They were fellow human beings, trapped in the same primitive ambush, and Westborough's mistrust of his companion momentarily vanished. The boulder had fallen between them. Who was to say for whom it had been intended? Raising his head, the historian looked upward.

The big stone might have been a meteor from the sky for all trace perceivable of the person who had rolled it. He saw, however, that the forces of erosion had scarred the gorge's sandy sides. One might mount the indentations like the rungs of a ladder—a perilous climb, but no more dangerous than to remain at the bottom, helpless as a sheep in the slaughterhouse. He had no illusions that the invisible assassin would abandon his hideous objective. The topography was far too advantageous for him.

Taking care not to clutch the spiny cactus tendrils, Westborough began the nightmarish ascension. His adrenals spurted fresh energy into his jaded body, and he climbed as mechanically, almost as effortlessly, as a chimpanzee. Afterwards, when he looked down the giddy distance traveled in that panic-driven splurge, he did not see how the feat had been possible. Momentarily, he expected the onrush of another crashing boulder, but none came. When at last he reached the top, Handleburger following him closely, he found that their assailant had melted into the chaparral like a dream phantom. Pursuit being impossible through the tangled growth, Westborough turned his attention to the canyon's brim.

He spied the declivity in which the ponderous rock had lain, perhaps for centuries, until rolled to the edge by the one who sought his death. Very shortly he discovered also why the abortive attempt at murder had not been followed through to successful conclusion. Ammunition had been exhausted. The one boulder had been a freak of erosion; no others like it were near at hand. To a whimsy of nature he owed his life . . . but curved shards of glass glittered in the sunshine.

When he was sure that Handleburger was looking in the other direction, Westborough hurriedly bent to pick up the largest fragment. He held it appraisingly between his thumb and forefinger. The radius of curvature, he meditated, was that of a small glass tube. Perhaps a tube which had once held a bulky Greek cigarette!

III

Denis Glendon's sable brush passed gently as a breeze over the fresh plaster. All day the artist had awaited this hour of fleeting enchantment, when the lime had begun to act on his colors but the mortar was not yet too dry. In these rare minutes every lightest touch seemed to enter the wall of its own accord, to model itself into the forms of the last Minoan ladies to take seats about the terraced arena. He completed the panel in an ecstasy of creation.

Dumpy Mrs. Holden waddled into the passageway while he was cleaning his brushes. Although the tin cookie box she brought with her was too large to be of any service to him, Glendon accepted it with profuse thanks. He set the big tin on the trestle table, already loaded to the groaning point with his paraphernalia, and removed his smock.

"And you stopping work so early!" she scolded.

"C'est fini, ma viedle! There's a companion panel to do on the other wall, but this one's done, ended, terminated. With the help of God and a long-handled paintbrush."

"That's blasphemy," Mrs. Holden informed him severely. She relented in her censorship, however, long enough to admire the completed fresco. "My, but you do paint beautiful! Them that has talents shouldn't hide 'em under a bushel basket, I always say."

To an artist, even a cook's praise rings sweetly in the ears, and Glendon was smiling to himself when he left her in the courtyard to go upstairs. In the spacious and incredibly beautiful room which had been allotted to him, he stripped to the skin, throwing his discarded clothing helter-skelter around the room. He was late already for his appointment, and their minutes together were precious—more precious to him than rubies or gold. He jerked on his bathing trunks, hurriedly pulled a sweat shirt over his naked chest, fastened his sandals and raced downstairs. While his feet pounded a tattoo on the trail across the hogbacks, he had a frightful foreboding. She might not be able to make it.

They allowed her so little time to herself, the people of her father's court. He stopped the absurd fancy with a forced laugh. His cursed romanticism! But he knew that he would never be able to think of Knossos as a mere house. Always to him it must be a palace, miraculously restored—a palace of semi-legendary Crete where the Minos had exacted his terrible tribute from Athens. Where the proud princess Ariadne had tossed away her heart to the ingrate Theseus.

The beach where they had arranged to meet was so little visited that a path to it had not yet been worn. Leaving the trail as he had been instructed, Glendon descended an unkempt valley where white trumpets of tropical dimensions were floundering from the rank foliage of sprawling weeds. He gave the big blossoms only a glance, his mind centered exclusively on his terrible obsession. Suppose she didn't come. Suppose—

But she was there.

She stretched with catlike languor on the sand, her robe thrown aside to display her superbly brown back. He had seen her in shorts, in slacks, in afternoon frocks and filmy dinner gowns, but he had never before seen her in a bathing suit. It was of white silk and molded like a glove to her supple contours. He could paint her like this, he mused.

Paint her against the background of mottled green-brown hills, with a foreground of little waves lapping at the calcimine glare in which he sat. He could seize all of her—even the tiny tendril which had escaped from beneath her bathing cap to curl in a black wisp across her cheek. He could snare her graceful body, make it forever his on imperishable wall or canvas. That was the power of his craft. But when he had completed the painting what should it be called. Pride? Insolence?

Sitting on the ground beside her, he removed his shirt. There were things he wanted to say to her—splendid things, glorious things—but he used instead the meanest commonplace.

"I'm sorry I'm late."

Her smile was inscrutable. "I'm not surprised. Artists are devilishly unreliable."

"Not always," he differed. "Here's one who—"

"Did you finish the fresco?" she interrupted.

"Yes, it's done." He added, hesitantly, "I want you to look at it when we get back to the house. Right away, before we change. Will you?"

She nodded. "You know I'm interested in your work."

"Only my work?" he asked.

"Yes, your work," she said firmly. Locking his hands beneath his head, he lay flat on his back. The afternoon sun beat warmly on his uncovered chest; he was conscious that she was critically regarding his skin's ivory pallor.

"I haven't been in yet this season."

"The fact's self-evident," he said bitterly to himself. "Why be fool enough to apologize for it?"

"Don't you like to swim?"

The casual question augmented his ire. "Damn it all!" he thought savagely. "I've been living twenty miles from the ocean, and there are people to whom carfare means the difference between eating and not eating. But you wouldn't know about them. And why the devil should you?"

Aloud he said, "Yes, I like to swim."

She smiled amusedly. "You paint better than you talk, Denis Glendon."

"I dare say I'm only an oaf," he muttered.

She laid her brown hand upon his pallid arm. The touch excited but did not comfort him. "You're in a bad temper, my friend." .

"Ione," he began. It was the first time since he had stopped using the formal Miss Paphlagloss that he had called her anything but "you." "I didn't mean—"

She sprang lithely to her feet. "A little exercise is what you need. Come on, I'll race you to the rock!"

The water enfolded their bodies like cool green jade.

She swam with face submerged, smoothly, effortlessly as a seal. His crawl was a fumbling awkward thing compared to her swift progress! He splashed after her as best he could, humiliated that his strongest strokes had no appreciable effect in cutting down her early lead. Her proficiency seemed to widen the gulf between them—the chasm already deeper and wider than the Grand Canyon.

When he clambered up the rocky slope of the tiny islet, she was basking as leisurely as a silk-clad Lorelei, globules of salty water clinging to her golden brown skin.

"You win!" he exclaimed, grinning over his defeat.

But victory meant little to her. Her cool indifference was her most baffling quality. Indifference in one so superbly, vitally alive! Resting an elbow on the wet pitted surface of the big rock, she pillowed her cheek in the palm of her hand. Her skin, he saw, was a nearly perfect thing. There wasn't a blemish to mar its firm smooth texture.

She said, "Now we're really alone, Denis. Cut off from all the world."

"Yes," he answered huskily, turning away to seek calm in the tranquil sea. He didn't dare say more. Not just then, not to her.

But he thought, "If you take a beggar from his garret, house him in a palace, give him a princess for a confidante, you can't expect him not to—"

"Suppose we had only fifteen minutes to live!" Her rich deep voice was like a lullaby. "Fifteen minutes to fritter away on this rock, and then eternal oblivion. What would you do?"

"God!" he murmured. "Stop it, Ione. I'm only—"

Her eyes were enigmatic slits glowing through half-closed lids. He traced on his mind the fine dark curve of her eyebrows. He could paint her face from memory—every line, every shadow. The memory was his, ineffaceably, and it was all he would ever have of her.

She smiled tantalizingly. "Well, Denis, what would you do?"

"Stop it! Hell, I'm trying. You're engaged to Stoner, and—"

"Not yet," she broke in quickly.

"You will be."

"But if we have only fifteen minutes to live?"

"Fifteen lifetimes!" he ejaculated. "Ione, if I kiss you, I'll never forget you. Never! And—"

"Kiss me if you can," she jeered.

His hands gripped her shoulders. She twisted, protean as an eel, in his grasp. He held her head, prisoning her cheeks between his palms . . . Suddenly the sharp quick struggle was over. Her arms came together behind his neck; her lips pressed his. They were cool and salty from the sea.

They created in him an unquenchable thirst. He held her lithe body in his arms, her body that had the supple strength of a coiled spring. Her eyes were closed, her lips smiling. Calmly as a sleeping baby, she rested her head in the circle of his forearm.

"Denis," she whispered. "Denis dear." Her fingers brushed through his hair, and the tingling thrilled his whole being.

"Ione! Sweet! Darling!"

Her finger tips softly stroked his cheek; the sensation was unique, incomparable. "Your funny scratchy face," she murmured. "It's you! I love it." Gently as butterfly wings, her lips caressed his eyelids.

"I love you!" he said hoarsely.

"I know, dear. I know you do."

"What's to become of us?" he cried in sudden dismay. Her arms tightened spasmodically about his neck.

"Don't think of it now! Love me, darling. Just love me!"

Standing on the wet slope of the rock, they clung like the two halves of one shell, their bodies volitionless instruments for biology's magnetism. She kissed him; her lips were no longer cool and salty, but hot as searing flame. His fingers pressed deeply into her flesh; he crushed her to him with all his strength. They couldn't get close enough together, he thought; there was no way in which they could get close enough. Suddenly she wriggled from the tense circle of his arms. She dived from the shivering ecstasy of their refuge into the still green sea.

"Ione!" he called in his despair. He plunged after her; he might as well have been embracing a mermaid. In the water she was unapproachable, swimming like a naiad forever beyond his reach. He plowed dejectedly for shore. When his feet touched bottom he found that the sun had settled appreciably nearer to the horizon, plunging their little beach in shadow.

She had begun to towel herself, and he went through the same rite grimly and in silence. Words were unnecessary between them. He knew, only too well, what she was going to say. He said it first. He had to say it, though his throat felt as if invisible fingers were constricting his windpipe.

"So it's Russell Stoner after all?"

The big gaily colored beach towel hid her face as she answered.

"It has to be, Denis. Alexis would turn me out, bag and baggage, if I didn't marry Russ."

Some women, his mind whispered to him, would follow their men anywhere, endure any hardship, so long as two who loved might not be separated. He shook off the disloyal thoughts. It wasn't Ione's fault she hadn't been born a fool.

The towel seesawed briskly over the rippling contours of her golden back.

"I'm selfish! Cold-bloodedly selfish, perhaps, but not a hypocrite."

"No," he agreed gloomily. "You're not a hypocrite."

"For better or worse, I'm a realist. Suppose I were foolish enough to marry you, Denis, do you know what would happen? We'd both starve."

"There are worse things than starving," he contended wearily. "To paint poorly when you've learned how to paint well."

"Yes, for you," she answered.

He was silent. Words couldn't bridge the chasm that yawned between their two worlds.

"When we were on the rock," she continued, "we were living in a dream. Both of us. Now we're back to reality. I hate saying these things. But it wouldn't work out. It just wouldn't. You know it wouldn't."

"Please!" he said. "Don't ask me to justify you." He pulled the sweat shirt over his head, fastened the buckles of his sandals. "You can't ask a man to help twist a knife into his own heart."

"You hate me, don't you?"

He whipped the answer disjointedly through the gates of his teeth. "I think—nothing—you could say—or do—could ever make me—hate you."

"Oh, my dear!" she cried compassionately. "Why does it have to end this way?"

He found his cigarettes half-buried in the sand. He offered her the pack, but it might not have existed for all the attention she paid to it. "Thank God for tobacco," he thought. "Thank God for the few things that don't change."

"If I could make it up to you, I would. I can't! All I can do is to say I'm sorry. And that's poor consolation, isn't it?"

"You needn't apologize." The words weren't his own, but those of a distant, omniscient stranger. "It isn't your fault; it isn't mine. It's just the way things are. I've known all along this couldn't have any other ending."

"Shall we go back?" she asked in a flat tired voice.

The big white trumpets had crumpled like tissue paper in the afternoon heat, he noted indifferently. They emerged from the valley in silence; they took the trail which wound as sinuously as a monstrous brown serpent toward the glittering stucco walls of Knossos. The palace in which dwelt his unattainable princess! They opened the cypress door—how odd a Minoan guardsman with pluming crest and oxhide shield did not appear to challenge them as they entered. They stopped in the paved court where doves flickered white wings over the basin of the fountain. The jet splashed with mechanical regularity; dully, he remembered that its waters drained into a concealed reservoir and were pumped over and over again. Nothing was wasted in the mansion of Minos, nothing thrown wantonly away. Nothing except a man's love!

"Thank you for a very pleasant afternoon, Ione," he called as he started for the stairs.

"No, Denis," she demurred. "Have you forgotten?"

"Forgotten what?" he asked curtly.

"I was to be the first to see it. The finished fresco."

"You can't be the first. Your cook's already had the doubtful pleasure." He wondered how one who suffered as he did could speak so calmly. "But if you want to see the thing, come on."

She turned on the lights which flooded the white ceiling of the passageway. He noted, without thinking, that the big tin box Mrs. Holden had brought him was not where he had put it, but had been moved to the edge of the trestle table.

"Well, there it is," he said roughly. He didn't look at it again himself; he was watching her fine sharp profile. Her eyes were intent on the reds and blues and saffrons, the brown and terra cotta and umber, which blended into the background for his painted men and women. Her lips curved into a pleased smile. "Denis, you've done it! Congratulations."

Yes, he told himself caustically, he had done it. He had created a thing of loveliness, unsullied and unblemished, and once that had been enough. Now—

"It's really marvelous! Even better than your sketch."

He couldn't help but be gratified, though pride counseled stiffly that her words were less than the wind ruffling the harbor's silken smoothness. "The colors will alter a little when they dry," he said professionally.

She didn't answer. In the luminous wells of her glowing eyes he read all of her swift sure instinct for beauty. It was the quality which had drawn them together—the one quality they enjoyed in common. As suddenly as it had appeared, the rapture faded from her face.

"That's odd, Denis! The little shrine. Where did you get your idea for the pillar and—"

"Did you two have a nice swim?" asked Mrs. Paphlagloss, stepping from the door of the Indian museum room. She was wearing a dusty pink chiffon gown which made her pale gold fragility as exquisite as peach bloom porcelain.

"Very nice," Ione assented brusquely. "Is it time to dress for dinner?"

"Yes, dear, a little past time. Most of them are upstairs now. Do be careful, child. You'll spoil Mr. Glendon's lovely painting if you happen to brush against it before it dries. Isn't that right, Mr. Glendon?"

He bowed, as impoverished painters do bow to the wives of rich patrons, and her perfectly formed mouth smiled acknowledgment of the tribute.

"It is lovely, Mr. Glendon," she confirmed graciously. "Simply charming." She leaned forward to achieve a better view, her small hands fluttering on the table like pinkish white moths. "May I be the first to congratulate you? But I suppose this brash daughter of mine has already—"

"Look out!" Ione shrieked as the table top tilted beneath the unequally balanced weight. "You'll tip it into his—"

"Oh, I'm so sorry!" Jennifer wailed contritely. She removed her hands; the table top sank back on the supporting trestles, dislodging the tin container which Mrs. Holden had brought that afternoon. The big box clattered noisily to the floor. "Can you ever forgive me for such clumsiness?" she asked in dismay. "Oh, I do hope I haven't broken anything."

Glendon, whose heart had knocked at the roof of his mouth during the whole of that terrifying second, contrived a wan smile.

"Not the slightest harm done, Mrs. Paphlagloss. The table didn't touch the paint, luckily, and that box is empty."

"Oh, but it isn't!" she contradicted, stooping to lift it before he could perform the task for her. "It's much too heavy."

"It must be empty," he insisted.

"Why, Mr. Glendon! Whatever do you keep in this Pandora's box? One of my good pillowslips? Shame on you, sir! And what's this tucked away inside?"

The question need never have been asked; the answer was self-evident. The object wrapped within the pillowcase was a winsomely carved lady, seven inches high—a lady whose ivory forearms were entwined with tiny golden serpents.

IV

Jennifer said frostily, "Really, Mr. Glendon, I think you should explain this."

The artist turned despairingly from the cream-white countenance to the gypsy-brown one. "I haven't an idea in the world how it got in here," he informed both faces despondently. "The last time I saw this thing it was under lock and key in its glass case."

"I'm sorry, Mr. Glendon, but that isn't satisfactory. I insist upon knowing how and why my husband's valuable property happens to be in your box."

"My box!" Glendon exclaimed heatedly. "I never saw it until this afternoon. Ask your cook if she didn't bring it to me just before I left for the beach."

Jennifer formed her lips into a cool smile. "You are rather naive, Mr. Glendon. Or perhaps you think it is we who are naive. If so, you're mistaken. Alexis will not overlook the theft of his choicest treasure. You may rest assured of that."

Ione snatched the figurine from the table and rewrapped it in the pillowcase. "I'll handle this," she said crisply. "Run on, Denis, and get ready for dinner."

The artist's voice was a compendium of wretchedness. "I guess it's up to me to see this thing through."

"But not in bathing trunks," she retorted, giving him a brief protective glance. "Run along, you cluck, and dress. We can thresh it out later." As he stumbled dejectedly down the passageway, she said fiercely to her stepmother, "You and I are going to have a talk. Upstairs, where we won't be overheard."

"You speak so angrily," Jennifer murmured.

"Just now I'm in no mood for syrup. Your room or mine?"

The perfect lips of her stepmother curved into a smiling mask—the mask she had worn so long it had now become an essential part of her. "My room, if you please."

Upstairs, Ione flung herself on a chaise longue, her brown legs contrasting vividly with its silver-gray cushions. "Your damp bathing suit will ruin the upholstery," Jennifer complained.

"Then you'll get another chair," Ione retorted, helping herself to one of Jennifer's perfumed cigarettes. "You always do everything you want, don't you? What do you want this time?"

The second Mrs. Paphlagloss raised thin and delicately arched brows. "I don't understand."

"Bunk!" Ione muttered, blowing a cloud of smoke toward the molding of the pearl-white ceiling. "Don't be a hypocrite. Denis Glendon didn't steal the snake-goddess, and we both know it."

"Gracious, child, how impetuous you are!"

"I'll put it in Alexis' room," Ione declared, patting the linen-wrapped figurine. "He can find it there without compromising anybody. Only you and Denis and I know about the tin box. Will you promise me you won't tell Alexis?"

Jennifer seated herself at her dressing table. "Now let us not decide too hastily," she demurred. "I'm not so convinced of Mr. Glendon's innocence as you seem to be. You must remember, dear, I've lived longer in the world than you."

"Nineteen years longer, to be exact," Ione said unkindly.

"I'm not quite sure my conscience will allow me to shield a thief," Jennifer faltered

"Bunk!" Ione exclaimed. "What's your price?"

"Price?" Jennifer repeated. "I don't understand you today."

"All right," Ione answered. "Put it your own way then." She tossed her lighted cigarette disgustedly into the fireplace. "Ugh! What foul weeds you smoke!"

Jennifer, however, was not troubled by insults. She picked up a file from the table and began absently to work on her already perfect nails. "Why are you so warm in defending a man who may be a thief?"

"He's not a thief! You know that as well as I do."

"Are you in love with him?"

"What if I am?" Ione demanded defiantly. She wouldn't lie—not to Jennifer.

"I knew it!" her stepmother exclaimed elatedly. "You fell in love with him two days after he came here." She abandoned the file to dust her small straight nose with the barest possible minimum of powder. "You didn't conceal it very well, dear. You're such a—"

"Shameless hussy," Ione supplied curtly. Her glance strayed from Jennifer's pale gold hair to the creamy skin of her throat, where wrinkles make their first appearance. There wasn't the slightest trace of a wrinkle, however; Jennifer took great pains to preserve her exquisite complexion. Her own skin, Ione reflected, was ivory (where untouched by the sun) but Jennifer's was cream. Ivory is a warm white and cream a cool one, and that would always be the essential difference between them.

"Not shameless, dear, of course not. Probably the others didn't even notice your sudden interest in fresco painting, your cunning little plans to maneuver Russell out of your way. Tell me what you told Mr. Glendon this afternoon."

Ione remained silent.

"Did you promise to marry him?" Jennifer persisted.

Lying with her dark head against a cushion, Ione gazed at the frieze of conventionalized lilies and long-tube crocuses, in blues and buffs against a cloudy salmon-pink background. Alexis had ordered the decorative scheme, as he had ordered that of every room in the house. Alexis ruled Knossos. He ruled Jennifer. He ruled everybody. No one could contend with Alexis—neither she nor Jennifer. He was born to rule as the sparks fly upward.

She replied very slowly, "I told Denis that it was hopeless. I'm going to marry Russ."

"And God," she thought, "how I'll hate it!"

Jennifer turned her patrician head to look sweet thoughts. "May I congratulate you?"

"Congratulate Alexis," Ione returned brusquely. "He ordered it."

"You can't have it all," she thought. "If you choose one thing, you have to give up something else. Always. It's a universal law."

"Your father dislikes you," Jennifer informed her dulcetly.

"He doesn't care much for either of us," Ione retorted, but Jennifer ignored that.

"He dislikes you—not for anything you can help—but because of your poor mother."

"I know," Ione said tonelessly. "One of the Santa Barbara Staughtons. 'Aughty! Married Alexis for his money—he's had bad luck that way, don't you think?—and then looked down on him because he was a Greek. Well, damn it, he is one! He tried to lay down the law about riding a certain horse; she slashed him across the face with her riding crop and ran for the stables. Thrown and killed that very afternoon! And I'm her daughter. It's unforgivable."

"It's not your fault, dear," Jennifer cooed.

"So you said before. Let's get back to Denis Glendon. Promise me you won't tell Alexis where we found the snake-goddess, and you can name your own terms."

Jennifer raised artless violet-gray eyes. "I don't like to think of your marrying Russell Stoner. He's so far beneath you."

"What's Russ got to do with this?"

"But you have already discarded Mr. Glendon for—well, might I say a sordid financial reason?"

Ione winced from the deft thrust. The charge was true, and because it was true it hurt and would go on hurting, but Jennifer shouldn't know that—ever. She smiled amiably.

"Said the pot to the kettle! Come to the point, Jennifer, please!"

"Very well, Ione." Jennifer's voice was quietly tense. "I want you to marry Marc."

"What?" Ione exclaimed, for once in her self-confident life taken completely aback. "Marry Marco? Why, I can't!"

"Because of your father?" Jennifer asked coolly. "Please don't worry over Alexis."

"You're not being a bit clever, you know," Ione said with a forced laugh. "I was to be—there's a good Norse word—handsel to bind his bargain with the Stoner interests. One doesn't like one's handsel to walk out on one before the contract can be sealed and delivered. Now does one?"

"The argument, dear, applied in the case of Mr. Glendon, and it was very farsighted of you to see it."

"And you think it wouldn't apply to Marco?" Ione demanded incredulously.

"Your father—I'm going to speak with your own charming frankness—cannot disinherit his entire family. He may storm, he may rage, he may make terrific scenes, but if we all three stand together, in the end he'll give way to us."

"So that's what you're gambling on!"

"It isn't a gamble, Ione. I believe I know him more intimately than you do."

"I see. You are being clever. Very, very clever!" Irrelevantly Ione wondered why she was breathing so heavily. "But suppose I won't swim in your kind of pool?"

"Such a metaphor!" Jennifer scolded. "Let's not be unpleasant. You will be very happy with Marc."

"You think so?"

"He simply worships you! And you two always got along so beautifully together. From the time you were little kiddies."

"Kiddies," Ione thought, "does give away her generation." She asked aloud, "Marco doesn't know about your little plan, I presume?"

"No. The secret must remain between us."

"Must?" Ione repeated.

Jennifer had the grace to flush—even Jennifer. "Marc wouldn't understand, I'm afraid. He's so—so unworldly."

"Just like his mother," Ione observed sarcastically. "Please tell me—if it's possible for you to speak straight about anything—when you want the bomb to explode."

"Since you insist on making me put it so bluntly, I want you to announce your engagement tonight. Before dinner would be nicest, I believe."

"Nicest for what?" Ione demanded. "Not Alexis' digestion! And suppose I don't—"

"But I am sure you will," Jennifer cut in sweetly. "The consequences—such an unpleasant word, but I must use it—would otherwise be rather disagreeable for poor Mr. Glendon."

"Enter the iron hand!" Ione exclaimed. "Well, I was getting a bit tired of the velvet glove. Your case isn't such a perfect one, Jennifer. Suppose Denis and I were to tell you to go right ahead and do your damnedest?"

"Mr. Glendon would be the principal sufferer, I fear. Even you can't deny that the snake-goddess was found in his possession."

"We both know how it got there," Ione declared angrily.

"But to refute facts, child, one needs more than unprovable opinions. Particularly when the case is to be tried before an unsympathetic judge."

Ione sprang, lithe-limbed, to her feet. "I'll hate you for this as long as I live."

"I'm sorry you feel that way. I've always loved you like my own daughter."

"You smiling, sugary devil! Did you take a stone club and knock Charles on the head?"

Jennifer whitened beneath her makeup. "How can you say such a horrible, horrible thing?" she asked in a tense frightened voice.

"I consider you quite capable of it. Good-by!"

V

Jaded by his strenuous exercise of the morning, Westborough went to his room immediately after luncheon for a nap. He slept a great deal longer than he had anticipated, so that it was nearly dinnertime when he finally emerged from retirement. Passing the paved courtyard, he spied Denis Glendon listlessly circuiting the fountain. Glendon's shoulders were hunched, his head bowed far forward; every line of his drooping body suggested a profound dejection.

Westborough immediately joined the artist in his circular promenade. "May I offer my congratulations, Mr. Glendon?"

"Congratulations for what?" Glendon asked in a voice sufficiently gloomy to entice Cerberus from the Stygian caves.

"The completion of the Ariadne fresco. The work is singularly well executed, the conception truly magnificent."

Glendon, however, was in no mood for compliments. "Thanks," he said shortly. "Glad you like it."

Since it was normal for that wayward clan who live by the brush and the pen to respond favorably to words of praise as for flowers to open to the sun, Westborough sensed immediately that a lamentable event had occurred. Perhaps it was nothing more serious than the usual quarrel between a young man and a young woman, but on the other hand, one could never predict accurately into what one might blunder at Knossos. Curiosity sang its siren song, and the elderly historian was shamefully vanquished.

"I am sorry to be meddlesome," he began apologetically, "but may I inquire the cause of your distress?"

Glendon wheeled savagely. "Is it so obvious?"

" 'Your face, my thane, is as a book,' " Westborough produced from his literary storage bin. "Perhaps I may be able to offer assistance."

"No one can help me," Glendon said drearily. "I'm sunk."

"Truly, a dismal participle! But allow me to cite a sometimes inaccurate maxim. Perhaps two heads would be better than one."

"Couldn't be worse, anyhow," Glendon conceded dolefully. "Mine can't seem to figure out how it got there. I mean the snake-goddess."

"The snake-goddess!" Westborough repeated in excitement. "You have seen the snake-goddess?"

"Mrs. Paphlagloss thinks I've stolen the damn thing," the artist returned despondently. "I can't blame her. It did look that way."

"Where did you find the figurine?" Westborough asked eagerly. Glendon, by way of answer, took his arm and propelled him down the passageway.

"In there," the artist said, pointing to the table which held his painting materials. "Wrapped up in a pillowcase inside that box."

Westborough asked a number of pertinent questions.

"What time was it when Mrs. Holden brought the box to you?" he inquired at length.

"Three-thirty."

"You are very prompt in your reply," the historian observed, making a note in his pocket memo book. "May I ask if you are sure of the exact hour?"

Glendon smiled wryly. "I ought to be sure. That was when I was due to meet Miss Paphlagloss. The work had taken longer than I figured, and I was way behind schedule."

"Do you believe the figurine was inside the box when Mrs. Holden brought it in?" Westborough continued to interrogate.

"I didn't look."

"Perhaps, however, you lifted the container?" Westborough suggested.

"Yes, come to think of it. It felt like an empty box."

"Dear me! Now we are beginning to get places, as the saying goes. Immediately after you had deposited the box on the table, you quitted your painting, did you not? Was Mrs. Holden with you then?"

"Yes. We walked as far as the court together, and then I went on upstairs."

Westborough nodded in satisfaction. "The point is significant, but we must not lean too heavily on it. The argument might be advanced that you could return to the passageway after Mrs. Holden's departure. Who was the next person you encountered?"

"Miss Paphlagloss."

"Here?"

"No, at the beach." Glendon added hesitantly, "I was twenty-five minutes late for our appointment."

"During those twenty-five minutes you went to your room, changed into your bathing trunks and walked very nearly a mile to the beach?"

"Ran most of the way," Glendon corrected.

"Dear me! Even so, it does not seem like an excessive amount of time to allow, and yet we must not be unduly optimistic. A loophole in your alibi undoubtedly exists. True 'tis not so deep as a well, nor so wide as a churchdoor . . . ." His voice trailed meditatively away. "I suggest, Mr. Glendon," he said at length, "that you do not worry. Truth crushed to earth will rise again. *Magna est veritas!*" He opened the engraved hunting case of his old-fashioned gold watch. "Goodness, how late it has grown! Shall we join our fellow guests in an aperitif?"

Glendon squared his shoulders. "Might as well get it over with," he muttered.

"You do not mind facing them?"

"I want to hear the worst. I'll be damned if I take it lying down!"

"That," Westborough cried delightedly, "is what may be termed the proper spirit. Lead on, my valiant friend."

They sauntered into the living room—actors making an entrance upon a crowded stage. Virtually the entire cast was present. Mrs. Paphlagloss, serenely functioning as the perfect hostess, pressed a martini upon Westborough and a manhattan upon Glendon. Her cordiality to the artist was as disconcerting as it was unexpected. One does not usually behave so agreeably to a person whom one intends shortly to decapitate, Westborough reflected, as he peered about the living room in search of the other witness to the surprising episode. But Miss Paphlagloss alone was absent.

What a pity! He particularly wanted to engage her in a confidential chat. Now, he was almost certain, there wouldn't be time for it before dinner. Also, it looked as if Mr. Paphlagloss were getting ready to make an announcement. He was twirling his brigand's mustache as if in preparation, and his rubicund face shone like a jack-o'-lantern.

"You all may be interested to know," the Minos proclaimed, in a voice loud enough to be heard above the din of seven persons on their second cocktail, "that my Minoan figurine has been recovered."

In the ensuing buzz of questions Westborough looked toward his hostess. Her smile was cryptic; it conveyed some other meaning, he believed, than that of a dutiful wife dutifully rejoicing over a husband's fortune.

"I found her in my room tonight," Paphlagloss explained, economically proffering one answer to several inquiries. "How she got there, I don't know." He paused briefly. "Nor shall I take the slightest steps to find out."

"Hear, hear!" cried Dr. Nielsen, who was fast acquiring an unprofessorial tipsiness. "Let's drink to the oldest woman in the world. A toast to the Cretan goddess!"

Glasses were raised immediately. It was the beatific Hour of the Third Cocktail when nonsense passes for high wisdom. In the middle of the hubbub Ione entered.

Russell Stoner, Glendon and Westborough converged toward the girl from three different parts of the room.

She dodged them as neatly as a back carrying the ball sometimes manages to elude the opposition tacklers to stand, slim and straight, beside Marc Bayard. Against her deeply tanned skin, her dinner gown seemed to glow with the lambent fire of rubies. Had the selection been deliberate, Westborough mused, she could not have chosen a color more certain to obliterate the dainty pink in which her stepmother had previously appeared so charming.

"Well, Marco, shall we speak our little piece?"

"I'll speak it," Bayard answered. His manner was self-conscious, his voice shy, but his face was the face of a man who has found the high god's nectar. "Ione has done me the honor of agreeing to become my wife. I don't understand how it all happened. She's much too good for me, but that goes without saying. Anyway"—he glanced about the room as if uncertain which of those on whom his eyes rested were friends and which foes—"that's how it is. We're going to be married as soon as it can be arranged."

In the confusion that followed Westborough noticed four things very distinctly.

Harvey Stoner looked at his host. Paphlagloss looked at his daughter. The Minos hurled his fragile crystal glass at the stone fireplace. And his lady smiled.

VI

In a kitchen that was a twentieth-century miracle of gleaming enamel and spotless chrome, Westborough conferred privately on Tuesday morning with a lady who peeled potatoes. "I wonder," he began hesitantly, "if you have an empty tin box of moderately large size I might borrow for my fishing tackle?"

He had brought no fishing tackle of any description to Knossos, but had hopes that the falsehood might pass undetected.

"Now if you'd only come to me yesterday afternoon!" Mrs. Holden exclaimed, dropping a flayed tuber into the aluminum pan on her ample lap. "I had a box that'd been just right then."

"Dear me," Westborough said mildly, and waited for her to continue.

"I gave it to Mr. Glendon for his paint. First come, first served, I always say."

"Quite rightly, too. But perhaps Mr. Glendon is not using it."

Mrs. Holden dexterously girdled a potato. "Maybe not," she conceded. "Though he did seem right pleased when I took it to him. He asked me to save him all the tin boxes that mints and so on come in. The one yesterday was a cookie box and bigger than the others I'd given him, but I carried it in anyway. Never can tell till you try whether you're right or wrong, I always say."

"No indeed," Westborough concurred. "Was it early or late in the afternoon when you brought it to him?"

"Latish. Past three, going on four. Mr. Glendon was just washing up his brushes."

"He does not, however, usually stop work at such an early hour," Westborough observed.

Mrs. Holden hushed her voice in the immemorial manner of a gossip who has found an interested listener. "He was so set on rushing away that, if you ask me, he had a date. And it wasn't with no man, neither." She whispered sepulchrally, "I seen him look at Miss Ione once. Well, a cat can look at a queen, I always say."

"Ah, youth!" Westborough murmured, assuming a sage expression. "The grace of being new is to love. As the gloss to the fruit, it gives life a luster, which when gone returns no more."

"Now ain't that a pretty thought of yours!"

"The thought is La Rochefoucauld's," Westborough disclaimed. "Had you looked inside the box to make certain it was empty before you carried it to Mr. Glendon?"

"I certainly had. Mr. Bayard was here, fiddling around with my electric range, and I gave him the last cookie."

"Mr. Bayard was using your range? I did not know that cookery was one of his accomplishments."

"It ain't. Leastwise, he ain't never done none of it 'round here before." She lowered her voice confidentially. "Do you know what he was cooking?"

Westborough said, "I should like very much to know."

"Just some dirty old weeds. Ever hear the beat of that?"

"Greens may be an excellent dish," the historian opined.

"But 'tweren't greens he was cooking. 'Twas nasty old roots."

"Roots? Dear me!"

"And do you know how he fixed 'em? First thing he did was to put 'em in the oven in an open pan. Not even a smidgin of water in it. Then he set the temperature indicator and left 'em for about six hours. When he come back, you should've seen the shriveled up old things."

"I should have liked very much to have seen them."

"They was dry as bones. 'Well, Mr. Bayard,' I says to him, 'you may be the cook here, but don't ask me to eat the results of your cooking,' I says. 'I left the oven alone just like you told me to, knowing full well what was going to happen, and now what have you got to show for it? Just a dirty pan that I got to scour. Maybe next time you'll listen to advice,' I says. But he just laughed and carted his shriveled up mummies away in a paper sack. You can't make *him* mad."

Westborough, however, by no means shared the cook's conviction. " 'When found, make a note of,' " he murmured to himself upon leaving the kitchen. "Captain Cuttle's sage advice is recommended in this instance." He reached into a coat pocket for his small memo book. "Six hours, let me see." Counting upon his fingers, he wrote: "Monday, July 11. Mr. Bayard puts roots into oven at approximately 9:30 A.M. Removes desiccated product just before 3:30. Datura roots? For what purpose were dehydrating experiments conducted? Investigate."

He wandered through the house in search of his hostess, whom he found at last in her favorite spot on the terrace, basking as contentedly as an Angora kitten in a swing with a huge blue canopy. The swing was large enough for two, and he at once accepted her graciously worded invitation. Concealed from the world as by a striped marquee, he peered abstractedly at the plants in a window box on the rail at the edge of the terrace. It was extremely difficult to begin this interview, which was bound to be fully as unpleasant as it was necessary. He regarded the leaves of a dusty miller and reflected that the silvery shrub was not undeserving of its picturesque name. These dilatory tactics, however, were merely postponing the inevitable showdown between them. Resolutely, he turned from the dusty miller to the rose-and-cream countenance of his hostess.

"Mr. Glendon yesterday related to me a most interesting story concerning the finding of the Minoan goddess."

"Indeed?" Her cool violet-gray orbs flickered indifferently away. "I shouldn't think he would care to discuss that with anyone."

"It is just as well that he did mention it. Otherwise, you might have occasion to believe the poor young man a thief."

"I do believe him to be one." She tilted her small straight nose superciliously. "Only Ione's pleading kept me from reporting the matter to Alexis. I am not sure, however, that I have made the right decision."

"I shall prove it to you," Westborough said, speaking a great deal more straightforwardly than was his wont. "It was utterly impossible for Mr. Glendon to have placed the figurine in the tin box where you found it."

"Can you prove that?"

"Yes indeed." He uttered a silent prayer that feminine intuition might fail to pierce the one vulnerable spot in the unlucky Glendon's alibi. "That particular box, Mrs. Paphlagloss, was in your kitchen until just before three-thirty. Your son himself consumed the last cookie it contained, after which Mrs. Holden carried the box to Mr. Glendon, who laid it on his table. He did not open it while she was there, and, as she walked from the passageway with him, he could not have opened it afterwards. Leaving Mrs. Holden in the courtyard, Mr. Glendon went to his room, donned his bathing trunks and ran to a beach situated a good distance from the house. He joined Miss Paphlagloss at five minutes to four and remained in her company until the box was jarred from the table. Hence, you may see how utterly impossible it is that he could have placed the goddess inside."

To his great relief, she found the array of facts overwhelming. "Then who did put it there?"

"Who, indeed?" Westborough inquired. "Let us consider three facts. One. The box was moved from the place Mr. Glendon had deposited it. It was moved to the edge of the table where it might be more easily upset in a pretended accident. Two. A certain person was in a room opening from the passageway when the two young people arrived. Was that a coincidence? Or was she waiting for them, knowing with her shrewd understanding of human nature that an artist will not fail to display his work at the earliest opportunity to a loved woman? The latter alternative seems to me the most probable. Three. The woman who waited in the Indian room was the same woman who tilted the table, dislodging the box so that the goddess might be discovered. Do not these three together render it logically inevitable that she must possess advance knowledge of the container's contents?"

"You are accusing me, Mr. Westborough?"

"I regret the necessity very deeply. More deeply than I can ever say. But I am accusing you of stealing the Minoan goddess from Doctor Nielsen's room."

She glanced downward at the tips of her small white sandals. "Do you intend to acquaint my husband with your alarming theories?"

"I regret that you find them alarming."

"Please!" She held up a soft rosy palm. "Let's not fence any more, Mr. Westborough. I concede that you are more clever than I. Please tell me what you want from me."

"Merely to see justice done."

"Justice!" she repeated. "Mr. Glendon has never been accused of the theft. He never will be accused of it. Where is the injustice?"

"It was not," Westborough answered softly, "Mr. Glendon of whom I was thinking."

"No?" she breathed.

"Miss Paphlagloss surprisingly announces her engagement to your son last night; the charge against Mr. Glendon is immediately hushed. You will pardon me if I insist upon seeing a connection between these two events?"

She flashed him a dazzling smile. "Doubtless I am very stupid. But I fail, even yet, to see the injustice you mention."

"Browning once observed that it is an awkward thing to play with souls. You"—Westborough added sternly—"have played with that of your stepdaughter in a cruel and inhuman fashion."

"Supposing your belief is true—mind you, I do not in the least admit it is true—what actual harm has been done to the girl?"

"Harm!" Westborough echoed indignantly. "You would play upon her affections. You would seek to know her stops. You would pluck out the heart of her mystery, and you ask what harm you've done. Dear me! Dear, dear me."

"Let us not be so Shakespearean," she pleaded. "You think that my daughter is in love with Mr. Glendon?"

"She would scarcely have agreed to sacrifice herself if she were not."

"Sacrifice? After all, Marc is not such a horrible ogre."

"The word sacrifice was used advisedly." Westborough knew that he must be firm or lose the day. "She does not love your son, except in a sisterly way."

"But Ione doesn't love Mr. Glendon. If you don't believe I'm telling you the truth about it, ask either of them. She informed him, only yesterday afternoon while they were at the beach, that she was going to marry Russell Stoner."

"But she cannot be in love with him!" Westborough exclaimed, feeling like one who has gone into battle for a nonexistent cause.

"No. She was being forced to marry Russell to please Alexis. Now she is willing to marry Marc to please me." Her bell-like voice sank to a mere rustle. "It is an awkward thing to play with souls, as you have just told me. But I wonder if even you know just how awkward it is? Which of the three would you select for her, Mr. Westborough?"

"I don't know," Westborough confessed faintly. "If I could only be sure she were in love with Mr. Glendon!"

"Even if she were, where would it lead to? Ione herself had the good sense to see it would never work out. He hasn't a dime, and she has nothing except what Alexis gives her. Alexis rules us all—rules by the terrible power of his money. And Alexis would never permit the match."

"You think that he will permit this one?" Westborough inquired.

She nodded ebulliently. "Alexis has treated me like a dog, almost from the first year we were married, and he's behaved abominably toward Ione. He doesn't love me; he doesn't love her; but in some curious way I don't quite know how to explain, he needs one or the other of us. On the few occasions when we've stood together—there weren't many of them, I'll admit—he's been forced to give in. And he will this time, too."

Footsteps sounded on the stone flooring behind them—the ponderous footsteps of two middle-aged fleshy men. Knowing that he and his companion could not be seen while they were in the canopied swing, Westborough started to rise. He halted at an imploring look from Mrs. Paphlagloss, whose face had grown whiter than fresh linen.

"I'm telling you once and for all, Alexis, that I cannot allow you the controlling voice unless our families are allied by marriage. I refuse even to consider it. Either talk your daughter into breaking her crazy engagement, or meet my terms. Which is it to be?"

"My daughter's engagement will be broken," the Minos answered harshly. "You may count on that, H.C."

VII

The dilemma, Westborough pondered, after he had left his hostess to go in search of her son, was one worthy of the subtleties employed by medieval dialecticians. If he revealed to Miss Paphlagloss how she had been duped, he forced her directly into the caveman arms of Russell Stoner. He shrank from the responsibility of that. On the other hand, if he did not tell her, she would undoubtedly stand by her promise to marry Marc Bayard. That course, all things considered, might not be so bad for her as marriage with the intellectually immature Stoner, but it did not seem just that the intrigante should receive the full rewards of her unprincipled intrigue. Moreover, one or two circumstances about Bayard himself were very puzzling. Westborough found the Indian excavator star-gathering on the wharf.

"She's wonderful!" the stringy and thick-spectacled young man exclaimed, gazing deeply into the blue spun glass that passed for water. "I've loved her all my life, of course, but I've never dreamed until yesterday that she—"

Yes, the situation was an extremely delicate one, Westborough reflected. One could not rudely sweep away such matchless happiness as this, merely to allow two department-store magnates the fulfillment of their dynastic ambitions. The historian decided—wisely, he hoped—that he would confine their conversation for the present to other matters.

"Might I be permitted to borrow that interesting book you carried away with you yesterday morning?"

"It's up at my camp," Bayard mumbled dreamily. "I can't go after it now. Ione's meeting me in a few minutes. Isn't she marvelous?"

"The most marvelous young woman in the world," Westborough agreed, his eyes twinkling. But Bayard, he saw at once, accepted the hyperbole as a mere statement of fact.

"Dear me, I should not think of inconveniencing you. But perhaps you will be able to give me some more information on the subject we were discussing yesterday; to wit, the datura cult."

Bayard glanced up from the water, momentarily startled. "All right," he agreed at length. "What do you want to know about it?"

"First of all, how was the plant prepared?"

"The ritual varied slightly among different tribes. The usual thing seems to have been to dig up the roots and dry them in the sun."

"To dry the roots in the sun," Westborough repeated. "Pray go on."

"After full apologies had been rendered to the all-powerful toloache for disturbing its rest, the dried roots were scraped into a tamyush—the toloache mortar—and pounded with a stone pestle by the chief shaman to the accompaniment of a sacred chant. Then the powder was sifted into hot water and allowed to stand until the drinking, which was done after dark in a ceremonial enclosure. The candidates for initiation were young boys, and the rite marked their admission into the state of manhood."

"The potion had the usual narcotic effect of the Asiatic daturas, I presume?" Westborough conjectured.

"Yes, I suppose," Bayard returned cautiously. "They dreamed dreams and saw visions. Sometimes a drinker of toloache became clairvoyant, or at least the Indians believed so. He was able to inform his fellow tribesmen where their lost articles were hidden . . ." The young man's voice faded away. "That's about all I can tell you from memory."

"It is a very great deal," Westborough said.

"Kroeber goes into the question thoroughly," Bayard continued in the helpful manner of one scholar to another. "Also there's a peach of a paper by a man named Safford on the various daturas of Asia and America, published in one of the annual reports of the Smithsonian Institution. If you're interested, you can look it up at the L.A. public library."

Westborough made a note of the author's name. "Thank you," he said, "the subject does interest me intensely. Now do you mind answering a personal question, Mr. Bayard? Yesterday, you were reluctant to talk at all on the datura cult, but today you cheerfully give me all the information at your disposal. May I ask what has occurred to cause your change of attitude?"

Bayard laughed self-consciously, dangling his long legs over the pier. "Yesterday," he returned, "I wasn't myself."

"You did not seem at all yourself, if you will pardon my bluntness. But when Miss Paphlagloss—"

"Yes," Bayard interrupted hastily. His pallid blue eyes focused on a white cluster of barnacles, which could be seen through the transparent water, clinging to the side of a post. "Do you think," he added finally, "that a fellow should be held responsible for every mad thought that enters his brain?"

"I do not," Westborough replied.

"A man's thoughts are his private business, aren't they? If he told them—if any man did—he would sound to others like a monster."

"Very likely," the elder man concurred.

"I was going to do something. But I didn't do it, and I don't intend to do it now."

"Therefore," Westborough interposed gently, "let us say no more about it. The infinitives 'to plan' and 'to perform' belong in an entirely different category."

"Thanks," Bayard said, flicking a splinter off the pier. "You're a good sort, Mr. Westborough."

"Dear me," the other murmured, fully as abashed now as Bayard had previously been. "That is extremely kind of you, Mr. Bayard."

"Make it Marc, please. We're going to be friends."

"Very well, Mr. Bay—Marc, we are going to be friends. Very good friends, I hope."

"I have a feeling you won't let me down if I tell you a secret."

"I shall do my best not to let you own," Westborough said.

"It's a horrible secret. The identity of our madman."

"What! You know that!"

Bayard nodded gravely. "I think so. I learned one thing this morning and when I put something else with it, the pieces fitted. It's—it's unbelievable! But you can't be too sure about such a terrible thing. That's why I haven't said anything."

"Please tell me everything you have learned," Westborough pleaded. "You have no idea how important it is, Marc." But Bayard demurred.

"Not now. There's Ione coming, and besides I want to thresh it out in my own mind before I decide anything."

"When?" Westborough asked quickly. "And where?"

"Tonight," Bayard said in a terse whisper. "But late. Meet me at the camp after they've all gone to bed. And please don't tell a soul about this. No one at all. If we keep it quiet, it will be a good deal safer for both of us."

VIII

Westborough wrote on the embossed stationery of Knossos:

". . . Mr. Bayard, however, will say nothing further until tonight. I cannot help but wonder if his suspicions are the same as mine. What I suspect is so monstrous that I will not set it down. I would not dare even to entertain it were it not for one highly significant circumstance. However, I will say nothing of that at present, knowing that it might not strike you as significant and not wishing to prejudice your mind until a definite confirmation can be secured.

"A few days more should serve to clarify the matter, I believe, and in the meantime I do not anticipate any immediate danger to the others. As far as I personally am concerned, you may rest assured that I will not be so stupid again as to walk along the bottom of a narrow canyon. In fact, so prudent have I become, I shall not leave the house unless it becomes urgently necessary.

"Here is a line of inquiry on which one of your young men with a taste for a little 'book larning' might work. I should deeply appreciate an abstract of a paper on the daturas of both hemispheres, which was written by William E. Safford and published in one of the annual reports of the Board of Regents of the Smithsonian Institution. The volume may be obtained at the excellent Los Angeles Public Library. I am sorry I can tell you neither the correct title of the paper nor the year in which it was published, but doubtless the librarian, even without this information, will be able to find it.

"This particular thread, I warn you in advance, is so tenuous it may well snap in our grasp. The chances are excellent that it leads only into a blind alley. Yet I have the feeling, unreasoning and unreasonable, that it is a true clue from the labyrinth. Labyrinth, dear me! Though I used this word of ancient Crete without particular thought, the metaphor is an astonishingly apt one. The second Knossos has its Minos and its Pasiphae; it has its Ariadne and several contenders for the role of Theseus. Does it have also its Minotaur? If what I suspect is true, it does—a horrible and inhuman monster."

Signing his name, Westborough addressed an envelope to Barry Foster, a young Chicago attorney who was one of his intimate friends. Mr. Foster would have puzzled considerably over the communication, but that did not matter because he would never receive it. The return card bore the name Theocritus X. Westborough instead of the true Theocritus L.

Sealing the missive, Westborough went down to the securely padlocked boathouse in search of a postman. He was fortunate enough to find the normally elusive Tom Starr, but there his good fortune ended. Starr pushed back the yachting cap on his grizzled head, fingered the grizzled stubble on his chin and allowed that maybe he might run over to the mainland tomorrow morning. He couldn't exactly say that he would. But on the other hand, he wouldn't exactly say that he couldn't.

"Then I shall have to wait," Westborough said, pocketing his letter along with his disappointment. "Would there be a chance that you might change your mind about this afternoon?"

"Nary a chance," Starr maintained, reaching into the pocket of his faded blue shirt for a sack of tobacco and cigarette papers. "The boss says that I got to take a party fishing right after lunch. Himself and the two Stoners. Give me that letter again tomorrow morning, and I'll try to do better by you."

Westborough thanked him and returned to the house. Marc Bayard was much on his mind, but Marc, after a stormy interview with his stepfather of which Westborough learned indirectly, absented himself from Knossos for the entire afternoon. He was not there for cocktails; he did not even join them for dinner. Westborough knitted his brows a little apprehensively at the vacant chair next to him. Even young men in love must eat.

"Where is Marc tonight?" he asked in an undertone of his right-hand neighbor, but Ione was looking across the table at Denis Glendon and didn't answer. Shamefacedly the little historian lowered his eyes to his plate. He had intercepted a glance which had not been meant for him—a glance like liquid fire.

He plunged his fork into the baked sea bass Handleburger had just served. They were, he mused, a strangely assorted company. Paphlagloss, at the head of his table, was conducting an animated conversation with the senior Stoner on his right and the junior Stoner on his left—a conversation concerned entirely with the big tuna "H.C." had caught that afternoon. (He had caught a cold along with his fish, Westborough observed, noting the Chicago magnate's incipient sniffles.) From the corner of his eye, Westborough studied the three of them: the Minos, whose round ruddy face should by all rules have been jovial and rarely was; Harvey Stoner, squat, broad-shouldered, Napoleonic—his bulbous nose displaying absolutely no kinship to the tiny button that adorned the sunburned countenance of his tall brawny son; Russell Stoner, eating heartily, drinking deeply, laughing loudly, sandwiching, somehow, between the food and the wine and the guffaws an occasional attempt to snatch the attention of Ione, who almost never spoke to him.

Westborough turned his gaze to the opposite side of the table. To Nielsen, goat-bearded, puckish, grinning as mischievously as Thersites at the camp of Agamemnon. To the crisp-haired Glendon, sitting with unnatural rigidity in his chair, his sensitive mouth drooping, his once merry eyes like dreary blue pools. To Jennifer Paphlagloss, at the foot of the table, golden-haired and gracious as ever, but in some imperceptible manner subdued—as a moth whose dusty wings have been singed by flame. Passing rapidly by the empty chair which Marc should have occupied, Westborough turned again to Ione, dark and proud as the lady to whom Shakespeare had penned immortal sonnets. Again he essayed his question, but he saw that she was listening to the opinions of the blond young athlete on her right. In the end it was the Minos, turning momentarily away from "H.C.'s" tuna, who succeeded in broaching the subject:

"Where's Marc tonight, Ione?"

"At his camp," she replied shortly.

"Gracious!" Mrs. Paphlagloss exclaimed. "The poor boy will get hungry. When did you leave him, dear?"

But Ione ignored the question as if it had not been spoken. The constraint which had always been present between the two women had lately grown into an almost palpable substance, Westborough mused. Suddenly he decided that he must have an interview with his host's daughter. "Will you speak to me in private at the earliest possible occasion?" he contrived to whisper.

She was looking straight ahead, her finely chiseled profile toward him, her eyes lost in reverie of some secret world in which only she could enter. He did not know whether she had heard the question or not, but a lull had descended on the table, and he did not dare to repeat it. However, while coffee was being poured in the living room, he learned that she had heard.

"Mr. Westborough is going to take me to look at the moon," she informed the entire assembly.

Russell Stoner laughed coarsely and others were soon laughing with him, but Westborough was not in the least offended. Indeed, he found the merriment of his late table companions rather more flattering than otherwise. They stopped upstairs, while she went to her room for a wrap. It was of velvet—the rich deep red of Dubonnet wine—and she flung it carelessly across her bare shoulders as they strolled onto the terrace.

The moon was full and well up in the sky, rippling through gossamer mists in pearly luster over the tranquil harbor. Far to the southeast the lights of the metropolis could be discerned close to the horizon, glowing very faintly, like a spiral nebula innumerable parsecs distant.

"I should like to ask you some questions," he began a little reluctantly. "The matter is none of my business, naturally. Somehow the things I want to know never are my business. Unfortunately, I seem to have become a professional meddler during the last few years. If I annoy you, please do not hesitate to say so."

Behind them, the walls of Knossos gleamed luminously in the moonlight. Millenniums were swept away as they stood there! He had the fancy that they were standing, princess and elderly counselor, on a terrace of legendary Crete. " 'Fair Ariadne, daughter of the baleful Minos,' " he murmured softly, shamed the next instant at having voiced the absurd thought aloud. "A line of Homer," he added explanatorily. She smiled and threw back her wrap. How tightly the long folds of her dinner gown clung to her supple body! Abruptly the twentieth century was again upon them.

"You don't annoy me, Mr. Westborough. I like you, and so does poor old Marco."

"Neither of those adjectives is exactly suitable to your fiancé," he ventured to remonstrate.

She laughed, warmly and richly. "I've always thought of him in that way."

"Does one marry a man whom one thinks of 'in that way'?" he was emboldened to continue.

She cupped her firm round chin in her right palm. "Really, Mr. Westborough, you are becoming horribly personal."

"It isn't my desire to give offense. Dear me, no, the last thing in the world I want to do is to give offense. But I have already had occasion to secure the viewpoint of the other corners of the triangle. Or should I say, in this instance, the quadrilateral?"

"Please tell me what you mean," she commanded. Her lips were slightly parted, her eyes glowed lustrously in the mellow moonlight flooding the terrace.

"It was a gallant and generous act, my dear," he said softly, "but the sacrifice, if such it be, is no longer necessary. I have had a few words on the subject this morning with a person who shall be nameless. You may rest assured that no accusation will ever be made against Mr. Glendon."

Her fingers dug with quick intensity into the fabric of his sleeve.

"You're priceless! I can't even begin to guess how you learned it."

"That is of no importance," he broke in hastily. "What does matter is that you are free again."

"Free!" she repeated bitterly. "When I was born a prisoner? When I don't know any other life?"

"Dear me," he clucked, shaking his head regretfully. "Unfortunately the geometrical figure is not a quadrilateral but a pentagon. I was so thoughtless as to overlook Mr. Russell Stoner. Now I know that he cannot be overlooked."

She shivered and drew the wrap closely to her slim body. "Why do things have to be in such a perfect devil of a mess?"

His mild eyes peered distressfully through his gold-rimmed spectacles. "The question, I should conjecture, has been propounded rather frequently during the four thousand years of recorded history. However, I am unable to recall a single instance where it was answered satisfactorily."

"You are very wise!" she exclaimed.

He shrugged deprecatorily. "My wisdom is confined to a single fact. I have lived long enough to learn that most of my fellow creatures—and myself, as well—must of necessity be a little foolish."

"What would you advise me to do?"

"I dare not advise you, my dear. The situation is too delicate. As delicate," he added thoughtfully, "as the ripples of a Chopin nocturne."

"Take poor old Marco." He noted but proffered no further comment on the two adjectives he had previously labeled as unsuitable. "I can't hurt him. Only this afternoon he offered to release me from our engagement."

Westborough's eyes blinked rapidly. This was news indeed! "Did Marc give his reasons?" he inquired aloud.

"I read between the lines. I'm rather good at that with him—we've had lots of practice. He suspected that Jennifer was back of my sudden change of heart. He wanted to know—asked me point-blank—if she had been putting on the pressure."

"Did you answer that question?"

"Not truthfully."

"You have a kind heart, my dear!" She smiled, a little wistfully, he fancied, at the old-fashioned phrase.

"Don't go making a plaster image of me! I'm basically selfish, I think, and I know I have a naturally vile disposition. But when people are decent to me, I have to meet them halfway. I can't help it; that's how I'm made. And that's why I don't know what to do about Marc. He's genuinely in love with me. I don't know what he'd do if I broke our engagement now."

"May I ask, by the way, why he didn't come home with you?"

"He wanted to be alone, he told me. Said he had a problem he wanted to thresh out by himself."

Westborough leaned anxiously toward her. "That is most interesting! You will pardon my curiosity, but did he give you an inkling of what that problem was?"

"He said it had nothing to do with me, so I didn't press it."

"Naturally not," he agreed, concealing his disappointment. It did not really matter anyhow, he reflected. He would know everything Marc knew in a very few hours at the most.

Perhaps he should go to the young man now. Yes, that would be better. It did not seem right to leave him isolated in that lonely spot. But that had been Marc's own wish, he remembered. Marc had been most emphatic that their appointment was not to be until the household slept. And what harm could possibly come to him?

"Dear me, it has grown quite chilly!" he observed aloud. "My ancient bones are a little uncomfortable. Shall we join the others downstairs?"

Mechanically starting to accompany him, she wavered precipitantly.

"Do you mind if I look at the moon a while longer?"

"I don't like to leave you alone," he demurred. "Though I realize," he added shyly, "that I am scarcely the right company."

"You're a dear," she rejoined, patting his arm, "but I'd rather be alone just now."

He bowed a good night and left her on the terrace. She would not be alone long, he believed. As soon as he had reached the head of the stairs, the prediction was confirmed. Two men in light-colored summer coats were swaggering up from the landing just below him. One was a blond and dolichocephalic Nordic, the other a dark and brachycephalic Mediterranean, but despite racial differences they walked arm in arm like boon comrades.

"Where's Ione?" demanded one of them bluntly.

"She wishes to commune with solitude," Westborough replied pointedly. However, Stoner *fils* was impervious to hints. "Thanks," he answered, and sprinted for the terrace.

Paphlagloss caught the historian amiably by the arm. "Do you mind coming to my study for a few minutes?"

Before replying, Westborough opened the hunting case of his thick gold watch. The time, he noted, was exactly ten-fifteen.

IX

The cozy little room wasn't in the least Cretan. It had paneled walls and hunting prints, leather-seated chairs and a brick fireplace where everything was in readiness for lighting. Stooping, the Minos applied the flame.

"July, southern California and wood fires don't seem to go together, do they?" he exclaimed genially. "Yet we do need our open fireplaces."

"Particularly when the fog sweeps in from the sea," Westborough qualified.

"Yes, the fog is bad at times." Paphlagloss lifted a tray containing a decanter and two glasses from a cabinet. "How about a spot of whisky to go with the fire?"

"An excellent idea!" Westborough said approvingly.

"Pardon me. I should have remembered that brandy is your favorite drink."

"I do not in the least wish to trouble you," Westborough protested.

The Minos laughed and gestured toward the interior of the well-stocked cabinet. "Brandy, scotch, Irish, rye, bourbon. Soda's in there"—he pointed to a miniature electric refrigerator—"if you want it."

"Yes, I should like soda." Westborough watched the yellow flames lick tentatively the bark of a log so huge it could not possibly have been grown on the island. "Dear me, but you are fortunate. This room is the quintessence of comfort."

"This is my retreat," Paphlagloss informed his guest, producing a siphon and a tray of ice cubes from his tiny refrigerator. "When I want to escape, I come here."

"Escape?" Westborough repeated. "From what do you, the master of an island kingdom, find it necessary to escape?"

Paphlagloss jabbed his thumb on the handle of the siphon, causing it to squirt viciously into the brandy. "From my family," he said shortly. "My wife and daughter."

"A most astonishing person," thought Westborough. "I really cannot make him out at all."

The Minos lifted his glass. "Your health!" he proposed. "And congratulations on your success."

"But I did not succeed," Westborough objected mildly.

The Minos halted his glass before it reached his lips. "You didn't put the snake-goddess in my room last night?"

"I am sorry, but I didn't."

"I thought you were merely being discreet."

"I regret that I have failed most lamentably."

"I wonder if you have failed," the Minos conjectured, sipping slowly at his highball.

"I assure you that I have."

"Do you know who did put the goddess there?"

"No." The negative, Westborough pondered, was literally true. He did not know definitely.

"Well, well. At any rate, your mission is now at an end. Do you want to undertake a fresh one?"

"To find the murderer of your former butler?" Westborough inquired.

"I'd be grateful for any aid you can give on that, of course." By the light of the open fire Paphlagloss' ruddy countenance looked a little haggard. "This, however, is a more personal problem."

"You interest me. Pray continue."

"Can you break up my daughter's engagement to my stepson?" the Minos asked bluntly.

"I am not a professional smasher of engagements," Westborough answered, endeavoring to conceal his distaste. "I really should not have the slightest idea how to go about the matter."

"Before you refuse, let me make it clear to you what this thing means.

If Stoner and I merge our interests, we'll have one of the largest retail businesses in the United States. The man who heads the combine will be one of the country's biggest men."

"You and Mr. Stoner cannot agree, however, on whom that man is to be?" Westborough speculated.

"That's the situation in a nutshell! I won't give in to him. He won't give in to me—except on one condition. Do you know what it means to scheme and fight for something all your life? To have it just within your grasp and then to see it all swept away because of a girl's silly whim?"

"I know very little about business," Westborough said meekly. "I do not understand, however, why your daughter's marriage is indispensable."

"In the event of my death, her interests would naturally be in the care of her husband."

"Or in the care of her prospective father-in-law?"

Paphlagloss nodded. "That's why he's willing to meet my terms."

Westborough wondered if it might not be a little risky to be the head that wore such a crown.

"May I speak frankly?" he asked. "Your daughter, my dear sir, is not a pawn to be moved on a financial chessboard. She is a human personality with hopes, dreams, wishes and aspirations."

Paphlagloss jabbed the poker savagely at the burning log. "I don't know what's got into her," he grumbled. "Up to yesterday she had a clear grasp of the situation and didn't complain of her own part in it. Now I can't make her listen to reason."

The log he was poking rolled to the back of the grate but refused to burn better in its new position. "Lead her, but do not drive her," Westborough suggested.

"Lead her!" Paphlagloss echoed contemptuously. "How? I don't even understand her. If it had been Glendon she'd picked, I wouldn't have been surprised. There's a romantic glamor about these arty down-and-outers. But Marc?" The Minos shook his head in perplexity. "She can't be in love with Marc. I know that, but she swears that nothing can stop her from marrying him." He turned his attention again to the obstinate log.

"Perhaps if she were left to her own devices," Westborough hazarded.

"There isn't time for that! Stoner needs me now, but in a few weeks he may find fresh capital. This whole thing's got to be settled right away."

"Settled in what manner?" Westborough inquired.

The Minos laid down the poker and returned melancholically to his glass.

"I thought you might have some suggestions."

"I am sorry, but I have none."

"Neither have I. I've never met a business problem yet that was too big for me, but my own daughter has me at my wit's end." He sighed gloomily. "Oh, well! You mentioned chess a little while ago. Do you play?"

"After a fashion."

"Good! Let's have a game now."

"Isn't it too late?" Westborough remonstrated, his thoughts on a lonely young man whom he must visit that night.

"Too late? Why, the evening has just started!" Paphlagloss reached for the bell cord. "I'll have Handleburger bring up the board and men."

The battle which followed was of titanic proportions. All of the historian's mental resources were marshaled in the effort to avert defeat, and he won, finally, only because his host neglected the importance of one apparently insignificant pawn in a coup five moves ahead. But even when the tide turned definitely in Westborough's favor, it did not turn rapidly, and it was not until over two hours had elapsed that their game was finally over.

The hour, Westborough noticed, when he had called a good night to his host and entered the solitude of his own room, was twelve forty-five. "Dear me!" he exclaimed. "I had no idea that it had grown so late." He yawned sleepily. Having consumed three moderately stiff brandy-and-sodas during the course of the evening, the covers beneath his sea-green spread looked most inviting. Far less alluring was the prospect of the dreary, perhaps dangerous, walk over the hogbacks to Bayard's camp, but to that lonely jaunt he had no alternative. He knocked lightly on the connecting door to his fellow scholar's room and called softly, "Doctor Nielsen!" Hearing only the savant's labored and heavy breathing, however, Westborough decided against waking him and turned his attention to his shoes.

They were the only presentable pair he had at Knossos, and if he didn't change them, the night's walk would leave them as disreputable as the brown-and-white sport oxfords he now took from beneath his bed. That rakish footgear had been almost new when he had first arrived, but the island trails had quickly reduced both shoes to a deplorable condition. Dear me, there was even a small triangular rent in the right sole, which had been made on yesterday's strenuous excursion. Fortunately, however, it did not go entirely through the leather.

He carried the shoes in his hand while he opened the door into the dim hall. Knossos was as deserted as a museum after nightfall and ten times as shadowy. How still it was! Westborough's stockinged feet made absolutely no noise as he stepped from one to another of the rugs, scattered like fluffy oases over the desert of concrete flooring. He turned into a short hall which led, he had previously discovered, to an outer staircase descending directly to the open court on the first floor. The place was a labyrinth—almost as labyrinthine in architecture as the ruins of the original Cretan palace. Tonight its halls seemed haunted. He stepped with relief onto the flagstones of the great courtyard. Yes, haunted by specters which should have been laid a thousand years ago.

It did not matter about noise now; the side entrance was only a few paces away. He seated himself on a bench by the fountain to put on his shoes. The moon was a pale nimbus, almost directly overhead. Its light permitted him to see that a man was entering the courtyard through the very passage he must himself traverse. A youth garbed in the scanty trunks of ancient Crete!

Westborough shivered in spite of himself. There was something uncanny about the sudden appearance, at this hour and in this place, of a bronze-bodied slim-waisted phantom who might have stepped to miraculous life from Glendon's mural. But the Minoan youth brushed a strand of lank hair from his forehead, and the muscles of his bare arm swelled buoyantly in the moonlight. He walked toward the fountain and his thick-soled sandals clumped noisily against the stone paving. He drew closer, and it was possible to see the water glistening in translucent drops on his herculean chest. This could be no mere figment of a disordered brain. The illusion was too perfect.

Westborough called politely, "Good evening. Have you been enjoying a midnight swim, Mr. Stoner?"

"Naw, picking daisies," the other answered, with the broad sarcasm which sometimes passes for wit among the very young. To this gem of repartee he added, grinning a clumsy apology, "Don't do anything I wouldn't do, Pop," and strode on.

One who hasn't learned the meaning of courtesy at the age of twenty-four probably never will learn it, Westborough reflected, completing the lacing of his shoes. Moreover, it seemed something of a pity that a body as magnificent as a Greek god's had to be bestowed on such a boorish personality.

It was also rather a pity, the historian pondered while unbarring the side entrance, that he himself had been seen in the act of clandestinely leaving the house. It added one more hazard to the scales already piled so high against him. Dear me, he would be fortunate if he survived! And yet, paradoxically, he did not want the harrowing experience to end too soon. Even a frail and elderly scholar may taste the exhilaration of living dangerously.

He had remembered to bring a flashlight. Without it, he could never have hoped to find his way to Bayard's camp, familiar though the trail had now become. The fog which gave the island its nightly bath was too thick for stars to be visible, and even the brilliant full moon shone as "through a glass, darkly." The moisture condensed on the lenses of his bifocals, necessitating occasional stops for cleansing. He breathed deeply of the water-soaked vapor. It was brisk and invigorating. It had the brackish tang of the sea.

How easy it was to walk in the enchanting cool of the night! Ridges up which he had puffed laboriously during the broiling day were surmounted now as swiftly as obstacles confronting a fairy-tale prince. He started downward to the intervening valley, beyond which lay Bayard's camp. Suddenly he halted, resting the beam of his flashlight on a depression in the trail. Stooping to the ground, he examined it more closely. It was the print of a man's right shoe.

It had been made by a man walking hurriedly in the direction opposite that to which he was now traveling. Yes, haste was clearly indicated, since one who hurries must necessarily rest his weight on the fore part of his feet. He studied the print carefully. In the moist brown dirt the details were very well defined. Nearly as well defined, in fact, as in a plaster impression. The shoe had had a small three-cornered rent in its sole. Dear me! Could it be possible? Standing with heels very nearly off the ground, Westborough left the print of his own right shoe beside the other. The two were as identical as only things turned out by the same mold can be. The strange shoe was unmistakably his own!

The rent had been made during that distressing trip across the island yesterday morning. Yes, he was sure that the triangular hole had not been in the shoe before. But he had not been this near to Bayard's camp since Miss Paphlagloss had led him there on the afternoon Russell Stoner had thrown the ancient Indian mano into the ocean. Sunday afternoon! The full significance of the reasoning flashed instantaneously across his consciousness. He shuddered involuntarily. It was rather like meeting one's own ghost!

No ghost, however, had worn these sport oxfords, but a flesh-and-blood human being. For what purpose? Westborough hastened his pace to the fullest extent of his sprinting ability. He could think of only one reason for such unauthorized borrowing, and the imagining was an accusing finger boring icily into his brain! He was to blame! If he had not been so stupidly blind as to allow himself to be lured into that chess game with Alexis Paphlagloss, he might have prevented this. At least he could have done his best to prevent it. But perhaps it was not, even yet, too late.

The tent loomed suddenly, a dark hump on the ridge. "Marc!" he shouted, straining his lungs to their utmost.

"Marc! Marc!" The echoes were hurled back into his face. Only the nocturnal silence answered. He stumbled through the fog. He lifted the canvas entrance. The beam of his light swept the interior of the tent in a single frantic gesture. Marc wasn't there!

To his relief, everything seemed to be normal. The cot was littered with Indian relics. Obviously, it had not been slept in for some time. He looked among the debris for Kroeber's *Handbook,* which Marc had said he'd brought here, but he could not find it. Among the objects on the floor of the tent, however, he spied a small stone mortar. A few drops of liquid clung to the hollow interior. What weird brew had it once contained? And contained how long ago?

His light, circling the tent, was reflected from a small transparent cylinder. A glass tube, the size and shape of those which held the big Greek cigarettes.

"Look in the trenches!"

Horror seized him in its frosty grasp. The suggestion did not seem to be his own. The command came as sharply, as swiftly as if an unknown power had established telepathic communication. And yet it must be his own mind which was thinking. He lurched unsteadily from the tent . . . .

He found Bayard crumpled at the bottom of one of his own excavations.

Westborough leaped into the pit, thrust his hand anxiously inside the young man's blue pullover sweater. Even before he leaped, however, he knew what he would discover.

Marc Bayard was dead! Marc, with his shy friendliness, his eager thirst for knowledge. Marc who had loved a woman unselfishly and who had never done a really bad turn to anyone.

Heartsick, Westborough veered away. His light focused on a pile of stones at the young man's foot. They had been heaped into a rough pillar, a foot or so high, flanked on either side by a twig pushed vertically into the greasy black earth.

He looked upon the ancient symbol of Minoan Crete. And he loathed it!

PART SIX: SEVEN WITHOUT ALIBIS

(Portions of statements made to Captain Albert Cranston, Bureau of Investigation, Sheriff's Department, Los Angeles County, in connection with the Marcus Bayard murder case. Taken in shorthand and transcribed for signatures of those questioned by Investigator Ernest Miller on Wednesday morning, July 13, at the island residence of Alexis Paphlagloss near Ynez, California, in presence of Captain Albert Cranston and Investigator Gerald Brown of the Bureau of Investigation, Sheriff's Department, and Elmer Stebbins, Township Constable at Ynez.)

A. Statement of Alexis Paphlagloss

PAPHLAGLOSS: Well, gentlemen, I scarcely expected to see you again under such sad circumstances. Poor Marc! He was like a real son to me. I can't get over his tragic death.

CAPTAIN CRANSTON: For the sake of the record, Mr. Paphlagloss, please tell us everything that happened last night.

PAPHLAGLOSS: Shortly before two o'clock in the morning I was awakened by a knock on my bedroom door. I went to see who it was and found Mr. Westborough standing in the hall in a greatly agitated state. He told me he had just discovered Marc's body. That was the first I learned of the murder.

CAPTAIN CRANSTON: Did you go to view the body?

PAPHLAGLOSS: No. Westborough and I talked the thing over and decided that no one should go up there again until after your men got here. We didn't want the trail to be confused.

CAPTAIN CRANSTON: That was the right move.

PAPHLAGLOSS: Were you able to find anything?

CAPTAIN CRANSTON: Yes, several things—some of them important. After Mr. Westborough had brought you the news, did you rouse anyone else in your household?

PAPHLAGLOSS: Only Tom Starr. He took the *Ariadne* over to Ynez to report to Stebbins—but you know all that. Neither Westborough nor I could stand the thought of going back to bed, so we sat up in the living room until you came at five-thirty.

CAPTAIN CRANSTON: Was there anyone else up besides you and Westborough?

PAPHLAGLOSS: Only Starr. He brought Stebbins back with him about three-thirty or so, and they went outside to stand guard over the trail in case anyone else should try to sneak up there. But no one did.

CAPTAIN CRANSTON: Do you know how your stepson was killed?

PAPHLAGLOSS: No. Westborough was very indefinite about the whole thing.

CAPTAIN CRANSTON: He was hit on the back of the head with a heavy piece of stone.

PAPHLAGLOSS: Eh? Good God! That's just the way Charles was killed!

CAPTAIN CRANSTON: Yes, the same brutal technique, but it isn't surprising. A criminal usually repeats himself; each of his crimes will conform to his own individual pattern. We call it the "modus operandi."

PAPHLAGLOSS: Do you think the same person killed both Charles and Marc?

CAPTAIN CRANSTON: I feel sure of it.

PAPHLAGLOSS: What else have you learned?

CAPTAIN CRANSTON: The marks in the soil on the floor point to the conclusion that your stepson was killed inside his tent. The murderer, as we dope it out, stole up in the darkness and made a noise to lure Bayard out of the tent. While Bayard was away, the murderer sneaked inside and picked up the first heavy stone he could lay his hands on. It wasn't hard to find; the tent is full of Indian relics that would serve. When Bayard returned, he was slugged from behind. The blow was delivered with terrific force. He must have died very shortly afterward.

PAPHLAGLOSS: Good God, how horrible! Did you say you found Marc's body in the tent?

CAPTAIN CRANSTON: No. What I said was that we thought Bayard was killed in it. The body was dragged outside and flung into one of the trenches a short distance away.

PAPHLAGLOSS: Like the body of a slaughtered animal!

CAPTAIN CRANSTON: It was the worst mistake the murderer made.

PAPHLAGLOSS: Why do you say that?

CAPTAIN CRANSTON: The murderer couldn't know that when the body was thrown into the trench its weight would fall on your stepson's wrist watch, breaking the crystal and stopping the hands.

PAPHLAGLOSS: At what time?

CAPTAIN CRANSTON: Immediately after the murder was committed.

PAPHLAGLOSS: Yes, but when was that?

CAPTAIN CRANSTON: I'd prefer not to go into it just now, Mr. Paphlagloss. Do you mind telling me your own movements during the day?

PAPHLAGLOSS: Beginning when?

CAPTAIN CRANSTON: Yesterday afternoon will do.

PAPHLAGLOSS: Yesterday afternoon we went fishing in the Velchanos. Myself and the two Stoners and Starr. We hadn't been out very long before H.C.'s s bait went down the gullet of a 170-pound tuna. H.C. fought that six-foot monster for three hours before he could bring him close enough to gaff. Maybe you think there wasn't some excitement on the launch! And, to add to everything else, by the time we'd finally got the gaffs into him, Stoner fell overboard. But his son threw him a rope and hauled him back over the side before you could say Jack Robinson. Russell has the strength of Hercules!

CAPTAIN CRANSTON: And big feet, too, I suppose?

PAPHLAGLOSS: Wears a size eleven, he said. H.C. and I both wear eights. But the younger generation, in general, has bigger feet than its parents. My statisticians once worked out some very interesting charts, using data from the shoe departments of the Minos Stores.

CAPTAIN CRANSTON: Who else in your present household has big feet?

PAPHLAGLOSS: I don't know that anyone does.

CAPTAIN CRANSTON: What time did the fishing party return to the house?

PAPHLAGLOSS: In time to get ready for dinner.

CAPTAIN CRANSTON: Were you all at the dinner table?

PAPHLAGLOSS: Everyone except poor Marc.

CAPTAIN CRANSTON: Who knew your stepson's whereabouts?

PAPHLAGLOSS: Everyone. Ione told us while we were eating.

CAPTAIN CRANSTON: Of her own accord?

PAPHLAGLOSS: No, I asked her.

CAPTAIN CRANSTON: What were her words?

PAPHLAGLOSS: Just that Marc was at his camp. She was very curt with me, but I am accustomed to her rudeness. Manners seem to have gone out of fashion in the younger set. My own opinion, Captain, is that we're living in a degenerate age.

CAPTAIN CRANSTON: Did anyone show any unusual interest in your daughter's reply?

PAPHLAGLOSS: Mrs. Paphlagloss was upset, but that's nothing out of the ordinary. Come to think of it, Westborough seemed to be greatly concerned, too.

CAPTAIN CRANSTON: Anyone else?

PAPHLAGLOSS: No.

CAPTAIN CRANSTON: What did you all do after dinner?

PAPHLAGLOSS: Nothing special. Westborough asked Ione to go

out on the terrace, or she asked him. Glendon excused himself shortly after that, and so did Nielsen. H.C. was worn out from his battle with the tuna and was catching a cold, so he went on up about ten o'clock. Jennifer went out to order him a hot toddy ten minutes or so later, and she didn't come back to the living room again. That left Russell and me alone, so we went upstairs to look for my daughter. We met Westborough at the head of the stairs. Russell went on to the terrace, but Westborough and I played chess the rest of the evening.

CAPTAIN CRANSTON: How late?

PAPHLAGLOSS: I didn't look at the time. I went to bed immediately after Westborough left me, but he sneaked up to Marc's camp on some mysterious errand of his own. He was very vague about it all. I hope you can get more out of him than I could.

CAPTAIN CRANSTON: Who do you suspect of killing your stepson?

PAPHLAGLOSS: I don't suspect anyone. This whole business is like a ghastly nightmare!

CAPTAIN CRANSTON: Are you willing to answer some personal questions?

PAPHLAGLOSS: Any that will help you clear up the case.

CAPTAIN CRANSTON: Please tell us about your daughter's engagement to your stepson. It was very sudden, wasn't it?"

PAPHLAGLOSS: It was totally unexpected.

CAPTAIN CRANSTON: Did you approve of it?

PAPHLAGLOSS: Does that matter now?

CAPTAIN CRANSTON: It may matter.

PAPHLAGLOSS: No, I didn't. It interfered with certain plans I had made for Ione.

CAPTAIN CRANSTON: Is it not a fact that you asked one of your guests to undertake the mission of breaking up your daughter's engagement?

PAPHLAGLOSS: He told you that?

CAPTAIN CRANSTON: Answer the question, please.

PAPHLAGLOSS: Yes, I did ask him. He refused.

CAPTAIN CRANSTON: To what lengths were you willing to go to smash the engagement?

PAPHLAGLOSS: I don't believe I can be compelled to answer that question.

CAPTAIN CRANSTON: Ordinarily, what were the relations between your stepson and yourself?

PAPHLAGLOSS: Extreme friendly. I can't remember that Marc

and I ever had a serious argument before this thing came up.

CAPTAIN CRANSTON: Did you have a dispute with him yesterday?

PAPHLAGLOSS: I had a heart-to-heart talk with him before lunch. I told him Ione didn't love him, but had been influenced by Mrs. Paphlagloss into making the decision. I was hopeful that I had sown a seed in his mind, but just before dinner my charming dutiful daughter assured me that they were still engaged. Ever since she was a child Ione has taken a perverse delight in provoking me. I told her that this time she had gone too far.

CAPTAIN CRANSTON: How is your estate to be divided?

PAPHLAGLOSS: Will my answer be treated in confidence?

CAPTAIN CRANSTON: In so far as possible.

PAPHLAGLOSS: My last will provides that the bulk of it is to go to Ione. Jennifer gets only as much as my attorneys say I have to give her, and Marc was to receive nothing. Why should he? He wasn't my own flesh and blood. He had no claim on me.

CAPTAIN CRANSTON: You said, however, Mr. Paphlagloss, that he had been like a son to you.

PAPHLAGLOSS: He had been. And in return I was willing to help him fit himself for any career he cared to pick. But a man must stand on his own feet. Marc knew that.

CAPTAIN CRANSTON: Does the figure I'm drawing mean anything to you?

PAPHLAGLOSS: It looks like the pillar and horns.

CAPTAIN CRANSTON: What's that?

PAPHLAGLOSS: A Minoan symbol. Doctor Nielsen can tell you more about that than I can. He's probably the foremost authority in the United States on the ancient Cretan civilization.

CAPTAIN CRANSTON: Why did you have the doodad carved on the panels of your, what-you-may-call-it?

PAPHLAGLOSS: I suppose you mean the shrine. The pillar and horns made a more logical decoration for the panels than anything else, the symbol being one of the important emblems of the Minoan religion.

CAPTAIN CRANSTON: What were the beliefs of that religion?

PAPHLAGLOSS: They believed in a nature goddess. There isn't a great deal more than that known.

CAPTAIN CRANSTON: Did they believe in blood sacrifices?

PAPHLAGLOSS: How did we get on this topic?

CAPTAIN CRANSTON: You didn't answer my question.

PAPHLAGLOSS: I don't think any accounts of Minoan ceremonies have been preserved. But Doctor Nielsen knows more about that than I do.

CAPTAIN CRANSTON: Do you see the object on the table?

PAPHLAGLOSS: The round stone ball?

CAPTAIN CRANSTON: Yes. What is it?

PAPHLAGLOSS: I don't know, but I've seen others like it among Marc's Indian things.

CAPTAIN CRANSTON: Please examine the ball closely.

PAPHLAGLOSS: Why, there's blood on it!

CAPTAIN CRANSTON: Don't touch it, please.

PAPHLAGLOSS: IS it Marc's blood?

B. Statement of Jennifer Paphlagloss

MRS. PAPHLAGLOSS: You wanted to see me?

CAPTAIN CRANSTON: Madam, this is good of you. We won't keep you any longer than we can help.

MRS. PAPHLAGLOSS: Marc! My son! His death is a judgment on me. What I did was wrong, and so he had to be punished. Marc, I killed you! Your own mother killed you!

CAPTAIN CRANSTON *(to Miller):* Be sure to get down in your notes that Mrs. Paphlagloss was in a hysterical condition at the time she made the admission.

MRS. PAPHLAGLOSS: I never loved anyone else in my whole life but my boy! I never had a thought that wasn't for him. My Marc!

CAPTAIN CRANSTON: All of us sympathize with you. He was a fine boy. You can be proud of him.

MRS. PAPHLAGLOSS: Yes, I can be proud of him.

CAPTAIN CRANSTON: Come, come now! Brace up! You're too brave a woman to cry.

MRS. PAPHLAGLOSS: He—he's dead! Why can't I die, too? What do I have to live for now?

CAPTAIN CRANSTON: Are you too upset, madam, to answer just a few questions? Can you remember what you all did after dinner?

MRS. PAPHLAGLOSS: Mr. Stoner went to bed early with a bad cold. After he'd gone I went out to order a hot toddy for him. That's all I can remember.

CAPTAIN CRANSTON; Did you return to the living room?

MRS. PAPHLAGLOSS: No, I didn't. I had a headache, so I went up to my room and took two aspirins. Perhaps three. I can't remember.

CAPTAIN CRANSTON: Then did you go to sleep?

MRS. PAPHLAGLOSS: Yes, very soon. And while I was sleeping Marc was killed. No, it's too horrible! This can't be real!

CAPTAIN CRANSTON: Do you recognize the symbol I'm drawing?

MRS. PAPHLAGLOSS: Yes. I've seen it somewhere, but I can't remember.

CAPTAIN CRANSTON: Do you know the meaning of the symbol?

MRS. PAPHLAGLOSS: Does it have a meaning? I wouldn't know.

CAPTAIN CRANSTON: Do you see the round stone ball on the table?

MRS. PAPHLAGLOSS: The Indian football?

CAPTAIN CRANSTON: Is that what it is?

MRS. PAPHLAGLOSS: Yes, Marc told me. My boy had a brilliant mind. I learned so much from him.

CAPTAIN CRANSTON: Did he ever tell you about the datura cult?

MRS. PAPHLAGLOSS: Datura? The name means nothing.

CAPTAIN CRANSTON: Perhaps he referred to it as toloache?

MRS. PAPHLAGLOSS: No, that doesn't mean anything to me either. Why did this happen to him? Why?

C. Statement of Ione Paphlagloss

MISS PAPHLAGLOSS: Yes, my engagement to Marc was rather sudden. I can't see that the fact concerns you, however.

CAPTAIN CRANSTON: There is no occasion for taking that tone with us.

MISS PAPHLAGLOSS: What tone do you expect me to take when you put me on the grill within a few hours of Marc's death?

CAPTAIN CRANSTON: I understand that the engagement had been broken before his death.

MISS PAPHLAGLOSS: You have been misinformed.

CAPTAIN CRANSTON: Were you the last person to see Mr. Bayard alive?

MISS PAPHLAGLOSS: No.

CAPTAIN CRANSTON: Who saw him after you?

MISS PAPHLAGLOSS: His murderer, I suppose.

CAPTAIN CRANSTON: We're not your enemies, Miss Paphlagloss.

MISS PAPHLAGLOSS: I've been pretty tart, I guess. I'm sorry.

CAPTAIN CRANSTON: That's all right. We understand you're not yourself today.

MISS PAPHLAGLOSS: Yes, I am upset. Who wouldn't be?

CAPTAIN CRANSTON: Please tell us what you and Mr. Bayard did yesterday.

MISS PAPHLAGLOSS: Nothing important. In the morning I met him on the pier, and we started out for a walk, but Alexis caught us. He hauled Marc away and put him on the carpet. Marc wouldn't tell me what Alexis said to him, but I gathered it was something pretty bad. After lunch we walked over to the other side of the island where we wouldn't be disturbed and had a long confidential talk. He offered to release me from our engagement but I wouldn't accept.

CAPTAIN CRANSTON: What kind of mood was he in?

MISS PAPHLAGLOSS: Low. His inferiority complex was out full blast. Here-am-I-less-than-the-worms-of-the-dust. That sort of thing. I tried to snap him out of it but he wouldn't snap.

CAPTAIN CRANSTON: Can you recall anything he said to you that might have bearing on his death?

MISS PAPHLAGLOSS: Only one thing. When he went to his camp he said he had a problem to thresh out and wanted to be alone.

CAPTAIN CRANSTON: Did he tell you what that problem was?

MISS PAPHLAGLOSS: All he said about it was that it had nothing to do with me.

CAPTAIN CRANSTON: Did you walk over to his camp with him?

MISS PAPHLAGLOSS: No. I left him on the trail, half a mile or so away.

CAPTAIN CRANSTON: At what time?

MISS PAPHLAGLOSS: About five-thirty in the afternoon.

CAPTAIN CRANSTON: Did you see him again after that?

MISS PAPHLAGLOSS: No.

CAPTAIN CRANSTON: What happened after Mr. Westborough left the terrace?

Miss PAPHLAGLOSS: I was alone for a minute or two, and then Russ Stoner found me. He'd been mad ever since I'd announced my engagement to Marc, but he wasn't mad then. Quite the opposite, in fact.

CAPTAIN CRANSTON: He made love to you?

MISS PAPHLAGLOSS: That's one name for it. He said he was crazy over me and begged me to break off with Marc. I answered I wasn't having any, thank you. We argued for a long time.

CAPTAIN CRANSTON: How long?

MISS PAPHLAGLOSS: Until nearly eleven-thirty. Russ wanted me to take a swim with him, but I said I was too tired. So we both went to our rooms.

CAPTAIN CRANSTON: Did you go to bed?

MISS PAPHLAGLOSS: No. After twenty minutes or so, I went back to the terrace.

CAPTAIN CRANSTON: How long did you stay there this time?

MISS PAPHLAGLOSS: Until nearly two o'clock.

CAPTAIN CRANSTON: Alone?

MISS PAPHLAGLOSS: No. Mr. Glendon was there.

CAPTAIN CRANSTON: All of the time?

MISS PAPHLAGLOSS: Yes.

CAPTAIN CRANSTON: You met him by appointment?

MISS PAPHLAGLOSS: He was there.

CAPTAIN CRANSTON: What did you talk about until 2 A.M.?

MISS PAPHLAGLOSS: Nothing that had anything to do with Marc.

CAPTAIN CRANSTON: Do you recognize this thing I'm drawing?

MISS PAPHLAGLOSS: Yes, I do.

CAPTAIN CRANSTON: Please tell me where you've seen it.

MISS PAPHLAGLOSS: On the shrine where Alexis keeps his ivory goddess. Also, on Mr. Glendon's fresco. The completed one.

CAPTAIN CRANSTON: Do you know what thorn apple is?

MISS PAPHLAGLOSS: A weed with white blossoms like enormous morning-glories. There's lots of it on the island.

CAPTAIN CRANSTON: Do you know it by any other name?

MISS PAPHLAGLOSS: Marc used to call it datura.

CAPTAIN CRANSTON: Did he tell you anything about the Indian datura cult?

MISS PAPHLAGLOSS: If he did, I don't remember what it was.

CAPTAIN CRANSTON: Do you recognize the stone ball on the table?

MISS PAPHLAGLOSS: It's something Indian, I suppose. Where did it come from?

CAPTAIN CRANSTON: We found it in your fiancé's tent. Someone had kicked it underneath the cot after finishing with it.

MISS PAPHLAGLOSS: Do you mean that it was used to—to . . . ?

CAPTAIN CRANSTON: Yes.

D. Statement of Denis Glendon

GLENDON: Look here! I don't know what you're trying to prove by this line of questioning, but it isn't going to get you anywhere. I liked Bayard very much. He was one of the few real friends I had on this damn island.

CAPTAIN CRANSTON: Were you surprised at their sudden engagement?

GLENDON: Yes, I was surprised.

CAPTAIN CRANSTON: Because of the engagement?

GLENDON: Because it was sudden. Your own word, Captain Cranston.

CAPTAIN CRANSTON: Are you in love with Miss Paphlagloss?

GLENDON: I'm a paid employee, hired to do a job. As such, I don't bother with things that are none of my business.

CAPTAIN CRANSTON: That isn't an answer to the question.

GLENDON: It's the only answer you'll get from me.

CAPTAIN CRANSTON: Glendon, this is a murder case. A man's been killed by one of you people staying in this house. I've got the right to lock you up as a suspect, and unless you change your tone, that's just what I'm likely to do. Now forget this fool chivalry of yours and talk turkey. You were on the terrace with Miss Paphlagloss from midnight until two o'clock.

GLENDON: I was on the terrace those two hours, but not with Miss Paphlagloss.

CAPTAIN CRANSTON: You persist in that statement?

GLENDON: I'll go over my whole evening with you, if you like. After dinner I went to my room to work on some sketches. I've told you what they were—bits of detail that have to be thoroughly fixed in my own mind before I can risk putting them on the wet plaster. I was in my room until twenty minutes past eleven, when I went on the terrace to smoke a cigarette.

CAPTAIN CRANSTON: And found Miss Paphlagloss talking to the younger Stoner? And went back to your room before they saw you? That isn't the part of your evening that's in question, Glendon. What happened the second time you went out on the terrace?

GLENDON: I've told you.

CAPTAIN CRANSTON: You expect me to believe that you sat there, alone, in the dark, for two hours?

GLENDON: I don't expect you to believe anything, but it's true.

CAPTAIN CRANSTON: Do you know what you're doing, young man? You're deliberately destroying Miss Paphlagloss' alibi.

GLENDON: Good God in heaven! You don't mean to tell me there's a soul here idiotic enough to dream she had anything to do with this thing?

CAPTAIN CRANSTON: Why not?

GLENDON: Leaving everything else out of it and getting down to your own plane, she couldn't hit a man hard enough to kill him. No woman could do that.

CAPTAIN CRANSTON: It depends a lot on the thickness of the man's skull. Also, on the woman's strength. Miss Paphlagloss is a very athletic girl.

GLENDON: Just because a woman shoots and fishes and swims it doesn't mean she is muscled like a gorilla.

CAPTAIN CRANSTON: And it doesn't take a gorilla to kill a man by hitting him over the head with a heavy stone ball. We know she had a motive.

GLENDON: Motive be hanged! He loved her and she loved him.

CAPTAIN CRANSTON: You think so?

GLENDON: I know so. Her father was furious with her over this engagement. Why would she risk being disinherited if she didn't love him?

CAPTAIN CRANSTON: We think maybe you can tell us that.

GLENDON: I don't know anything about it.

CAPTAIN CRANSTON: For the last time, did you see Miss Paphlagloss on the terrace from twelve to two?

GLENDON: For the last time, no.

CAPTAIN CRANSTON: You young fool! She's given you an alibi as well as herself.

GLENDON: I'm not taking it from her, thank you. And she doesn't need one.

CAPTAIN CRANSTON: Do you recognize this sketch?

GLENDON: I ought to. It's my own watercolor.

CAPTAIN CRANSTON: When was it made?

GLENDON: I don't remember the exact day.

CAPTAIN CRANSTON: Before or after you came here?

GLENDON: Oh, before. It was one of those I submitted to Mr. Paphlagloss. The original idea for the Ariadne mural downstairs.

CAPTAIN CRANSTON: Where did you get this thingamajig?

GLENDON: The temple by those women?

CAPTAIN CRANSTON: The pillar inside the temple. And the two hinkies on either side of the pillar.

GLENDON: I copied the whole thing from a reproduction of a Cretan miniature fresco I found in a book at the public library.

CAPTAIN CRANSTON: Do you know what it means?

GLENDON: I didn't know it meant anything. It's just a bit of decorative detail, as far as I'm concerned.

CAPTAIN CRANSTON: Have you seen the same design anywhere else since you came here?

GLENDON: Yes. On the carved panels holding up the chamber Mr. Paphlagloss built for his Cretan goddess.

CAPTAIN CRANSTON: Nowhere else on the island?

GLENDON: Where else would I see it?

CAPTAIN CRANSTON: I'm wondering that myself.

E. Statement of Arne Nielsen

NIELSEN: My dear sir! The longer I live the more I am convinced that the type of mind the world most needs is invariably the type it kills. I might refer to Moseley as the classic example of the contention.

CAPTAIN CRANSTON: Let's stick to Bayard, Doctor Nielsen.

NIELSEN: He should have had a brilliant future. He was only twenty-three! Twenty-three and the world before him!

CAPTAIN CRANSTON: Did his death surprise you?

NIELSEN: Yes and no. I was shocked and horrified that the victim was my poor young friend, but I was not surprised to learn that there had been a victim.

CAPTAIN CRANSTON: Can you explain that remark?

NIELSEN: There was a full moon last night.

CAPTAIN CRANSTON: What of that?

NIELSEN: Astarte was once worshiped as the moon-goddess throughout the Near East. Cybele required the blood of her votaries. And what are Astarte and Cybele?

CAPTAIN CRANSTON: I'll bite. What are they?

NIELSEN: Later forms of the Lady of Crete, that ancient, ancient divinity whose image Mr. Paphlagloss preserves in his curious shrine.

CAPTAIN CRANSTON: Is this meant to be a hint?

NIELSEN: Say, rather, a bit of specialized information.

CAPTAIN CRANSTON: We may want some more specialized information later on. For the present, however, I think we'll confine ourselves to the regular routine. Did you remain in the living room with the others after dinner last night?

NIELSEN: No, Glendon and I excused ourselves at nine-thirty. He went to his room and I went to mine.

CAPTAIN CRANSTON: Wasn't that an unusual thing for you to do?

NIELSEN: It's what I've been doing every evening since last Sunday.

CAPTAIN CRANSTON: No more bridge games, eh?

NIELSEN: No, thank goodness, I have been released from that particular form of mental torture. Evenings I now devote to my book, which, in consequence, is beginning to get itself written.

CAPTAIN CRANSTON: Did you remain in your room writing the whole evening?

NIELSEN: Yes.

CAPTAIN CRANSTON: Did anybody drop in to see you at any time?

NIELSEN: No. My friends show a respect for my working hours which, I confess, isn't always merited.

CAPTAIN CRANSTON: How are we to know you actually were in your room?

NIELSEN: I can only give you my word for it.

CAPTAIN CRANSTON: What time did you stop working?

NIELSEN: Shortly before midnight.

CAPTAIN CRANSTON: Did you go to sleep right away?

NIELSEN: Yes, I was very tired.

CAPTAIN CRANSTON: Do you recognize the round ball on the table?

NIELSEN: It looks like an Indian football.

CAPTAIN CRANSTON: Football?

NIELSEN: Teams from different Indian villages used to play a game comparable to football. Each side staged a rally before the game and if the home team won, there was a victory celebration afterward. Very collegiate! It all goes to show there's nothing really new under the sun.

CAPTAIN CRANSTON: How could a heavy stone ball like this be kicked by barefooted Indians?

NIELSEN: It wasn't kicked. It was lifted and thrown by the toes, Bayard told me. He was well up on his subject; we used to have some interesting discussions. Some of his information, by the way, is going to find a place in my book. Did you know the Canalino believed that certain stones were endowed with life?

CAPTAIN CRANSTON: No.

NIELSEN: A life inimical to man. The stones had to be subdued by the shaman in a midnight session, since there was no telling what harm they'd work if left to their own devices. Interesting, isn't it?

CAPTAIN CRANSTON: If you go in for that sort of thing.

NIELSEN: The quaint belief fits very well into my own theories of the Baetylic cult. Man's first gods were stones. Some were worshiped because of real or fancied resemblances to men or animals. "Images not made with hands." Others must have been meteors dramatically blazing through the sky. If a meteor isn't suggestive of divine origin, what is?

Then, in historic times, we have the image of Diana of Ephesus, supposedly placed there by Jove himself. "Great is Diana of the Ephesians!" Before the rise of Mohammed, a black stone was the god of Mecca. Another black stone reposed in the temple of the Great Mother at Rome. I could cite further instances . . .

CAPTAIN CRANSTON: Some other time. Do you know a thing that looks like this? A pillar standing in a pair of horns?

NIELSEN: Certainly. It's an ancient Minoan and Mycenaean symbol.

CAPTAIN CRANSTON: What does it mean?

NIELSEN: The pillar or the horns?

CAPTAIN CRANSTON: Both.

NIELSEN: The sacral horns merely indicate divinity. Perhaps they were symbolic of the bull, which we know was worshiped in ancient Crete as the male principle of fertility. Or perhaps they were suggested by the horns of the new moon. Anyway, you can think of them as a sort of shorthand sign, if you like. Draw them at the foot of a man, and you point out he's meant for a god. Put them at the foot of a pillar, and you show that a god dwells there.

CAPTAIN CRANSTON: In the pillar?

NIELSEN: The pillar *was* the god. Or goddess, in this instance, since the chief Minoan deity was certainly feminine. The baetylic pillar was the goddess, and yet no more the actual goddess than the image of Zeus, say, was the actual Olympian deity. Do you follow me?

CAPTAIN CRANSTON: No.

NIELSEN: It's a difficult point to comprehend.

CAPTAIN CRANSTON: Someone had left a rough model of this pillar-horns thing at poor Bayard's feet.

NIELSEN: Again?

CAPTAIN CRANSTON: Why do you say "again"?

NIELSEN: Bayard, Westborough and myself found such a rough pillar altar last Sunday night on a beach not far from Bayard's camp. We tore it down!

CAPTAIN CRANSTON: Shouldn't have done that without telling me.

NIELSEN: I'm sorry. It was too nerve-racking to find that a goddess forgotten for thirty-three centuries now has a worshiper.

CAPTAIN CRANSTON: The book you're writing covers this sort of thing, doesn't it?

NIELSEN: I'm attempting to cover it.

CAPTAIN CRANSTON: Has anyone else read your manuscript?

NIELSEN: Not with my permission.

CAPTAIN CRANSTON: Without it?

NIELSEN: A page was stolen from my room. A single handwritten page. It dealt with the matters we've just been discussing.

CAPTAIN CRANSTON: The pillar and horns?

NIELSEN: Yes.

CAPTAIN CRANSTON: What do you make of it all?

NIELSEN: At the risk of being considered as a candidate for an asylum, I'll tell you. We'll have to start, however, with that point you couldn't follow. The baetylic pillar, which is no more the actual goddess than a statue of Aphrodite is Aphrodite. Now is it clear?

CAPTAIN CRANSTON: You mean that the pillar's the same as a statue of the goddess?

NIELSEN: Not quite that, either. The aniconic form of the deity, we'll call it, and that will have to do because the idea can't be expressed in simpler language. After a certain ritual, however, the pillar actually becomes the goddess. The ancients used to symbolize the happening very picturesquely by a dove settling on the capital as a sign that the goddess had come down from the heavens. And something else happens, Sir Arthur Evans thinks. Not only the column becomes divine, but the worshiper whose rites brought it about becomes divine also. God enters into him, and he becomes as God, but I suppose this is all gibberish to you?

CAPTAIN CRANSTON: Not quite. How was the trick worked?

NIELSEN: Very, very little is known. But my own opinion is through sacrifice. Diodorus wrote that honors paid to the gods, sacrifices, and initiation into the mysteries were Cretan discoveries. Modern archaeologists have proved him right. Among the ruins of the ancient Cretan palaces have been found altars with drains attached, drains that could serve no other purpose than to carry away the blood of the sacrifice.

CAPTAIN CRANSTON: Was it a human sacrifice?

NIELSEN: Evans thinks that the victims were small animals. But ancient Crete is not today. A goddess forgotten for thirty-three centuries could only be worshiped by a madman today, and a lunatic, my dear Captain, might well resort to human sacrifice.

F. Statement of Harvey C. Stoner

H. STOKER: He was the type of young man I can't understand. No interest at all in sports or business. Unsound views on politics. Mooning around half the time as if he wasn't in the same room with the rest of us. Didn't seem to be quite all there.

CAPTAIN CRANSTON: Were you surprised when the engagement was announced?

H. STOKER: I was. I certainly was. Couldn't understand how a live wire like Ione could be attracted to such a stick as Marc. I still don't understand it.

CAPTAIN CRANSTON: The engagement was a severe blow to your son, wasn't it?

H. STOKER: I protest against that question. I will not answer it.

CAPTAIN CRANSTON: Let's put it in another way. You and Mr. Paphlagloss, I have been given to understand, were anxious to bring about the union of your two families. Is that true?

H. STOKER: We thought it would be a good thing all around if our families were united. However, the last word was rather up to Ione, wasn't it? This being the twentieth century?

CAPTAIN CRANSTON: Is your son in love with Miss Paphlagloss?

H. STOKER: I refuse to answer that question.

CAPTAIN CRANSTON: Mr. Paphlagloss told me that you had good luck fishing yesterday afternoon.

H. STOKER: A 170-pound tuna. Six feet of fighting fish! We battled for three hours, and it took everything I had to land him.

CAPTAIN CRANSTON: Not everybody could have landed him.

H. STONER: I almost didn't. Just when I'd brought him up to the boat, I messed things up by falling overboard. But Starr and Alexis had their gaffs in my catch by that time, so no harm was done.

CAPTAIN CRANSTON: How about yourself?

H. STONER: Oh, Russ pulled me out right away.

CAPTAIN CRANSTON: Any ill effects from the ducking?

H. STONER: Not now. I started sneezing after dinner, but I went to bed at ten o'clock. Mrs. Paphlagloss ordered a hot toddy for me, and I woke up this morning feeling like a million.

CAPTAIN CRANSTON: Did Mrs. Paphlagloss bring the toddy to you herself?

H. STONER: No, the butler brought it.

CAPTAIN CRANSTON: What time?

H. STONER: About ten-thirty. I don't know what was in it, but it certainly packed a wallop. I was dead to the world until seven o'clock this morning.

CAPTAIN CRANSTON: Do you recognize the stone ball on the table?

H. STONER: Is it from Marc's Indian stuff?

CAPTAIN CRANSTON: Yes. We found it in his tent.

H. STONER: He'd have done better if he'd put his mind on his stepfather's business. That young man had a priceless opportunity before him, but he didn't have sense enough to recognize it.

CAPTAIN CRANSTON: Do you recognize the design I'm drawing?

STONER: No. What is it?

CAPTAIN CRANSTON: You will find it on the panels forming the lower portion of your host's shrine.

H. STONER: Alexis would be better off if he didn't go in for this sort of folderol. It doesn't do him any good.

CAPTAIN CRANSTON: Don't you believe in hobbies?

H. STONER: As a plain, blunt businessman, I'll stick to golf, fishing and bridge, with a little shooting during the season. No objection, of course, if a fellow wants to read a book now and then . . .

G. Statement of Russell Stoner

R. STONER: Sure, I played practical jokes on Marc. He was the sort you can't help but play jokes on.

CAPTAIN CRANSTON: Did he ever play any on you?

R. STONER: He pulled a dirty trick on me. Asked me to smell some leaves that gave me one swell headache. It didn't leave me until the next morning.

CAPTAIN CRANSTON: Did you get mad over that?

R. STONER: Naw!

CAPTAIN CRANSTON: You and Bayard had a little trouble last Sunday, I understand.

R. STONER: If you want to call it trouble. I was up at his camp, throwing rocks into the ocean just for something to do, and I happened to pick up an old Indian thing before he could yell to me. Just a rock that looked like all the others. How was I to know he thought it was worth a million dollars?

CAPTAIN CRANSTON: What happened then?

R. STONER: You'd think I'd robbed a bank and shot six cops with a tommy gun, the way Marc took on. I told him I was sorry. Fellow can't say any more than that, can he?

CAPTAIN CRANSTON: Did he accept your apology?

R. STONER: He was still sore. So I asked him if he wanted to make something of it, but he didn't. Then Ione said we were behaving like a pair of fools, and we both shut up. But she didn't think much of Marc for the way he backed down. No woman would.

CAPTAIN CRANSTON: You think a lot of Miss Paphlagloss, don't you?

R. STONER: She's one swell kid. I'd marry her in a minute if she'd have me. But there isn't much a fellow can do about that, is there?

CAPTAIN CRANSTON: How did you feel when she said she was going to marry Bayard?

R. STONER: How would you feel? I told her I wished her luck and I hoped she'd be happy. Fellow can't take it any better than that, can he?

CAPTAIN CRANSTON: A big husky like you shouldn't have quit so easily.

R. STONER: I didn't quit. Had it out with her last night on the terrace, but no dice. So I pulled the brother act again and went down and had a good long swim. I was in the water over an hour.

CAPTAIN CRANSTON: Alone?

R. STONER: Yes.

CAPTAIN CRANSTON: What time did you leave the terrace?

R. STONER: About half-past eleven.

CAPTAIN CRANSTON: Did you see anyone on your way down to the beach?

R. STONER: Beach? I didn't go to any beach. I went down and dove off the pier.

CAPTAIN CRANSTON: Well, wherever you went did you see anyone?

R. STONER: Not on the way down, but I saw Mr. Westborough when I was going up to my room. He was in the court, on a bench by the fountain, and here's a damn funny thing. He was putting on his shoes. I got the idea he'd been pulling a sneak from the house, but it wasn't my business so I didn't sing out. But here's my advice to you, Cap. That old guy ought to be watched.

CAPTAIN CRANSTON: Thanks for the tip.

R. STONER: Don't mind keeping an eye on him myself, if you say the word. Always thought I had the stuff for a detective if I didn't have to go into Dad's business. I'd like a chance to show what I can do.

CAPTAIN CRANSTON: Well, that's fine. Just now I don't know how we're going to use you, but something may turn up. Ever see a thing like this drawing of mine before?

R. STONER: Nope, what is it?

CAPTAIN CRANSTON: What does it look like?

R. STONER: Looks like a pile of stones with a stick on either side of it. What does it mean?

CAPTAIN CRANSTON: If we knew that, young man, the problem

would be solved. We'd know who killed the butler and who killed Bayard and why. But we don't know.

R. STONER: Maybe I can find out for you.

CAPTAIN CRANSTON: Do you recognize the round stone ball on the table?

R. STONER: It's just about the diameter of a sixteen-pound shot. Only the shot isn't stone.

CAPTAIN CRANSTON: If you threw that at a fellow's bead from close range, you'd probably kill him, wouldn't you?

R. STONER: How would I know?

CAPTAIN CRANSTON: What size shoes do you wear, Stoner?

H. Statement of Tom Starr

STARR: Being an early riser, so to speak, and having had a busy day, I was in bed by nine-thirty last night.

CAPTAIN CRANSTON: Did you sleep well?

STARR: Slept like a log, brother. Like a log. First thing I knew was when the boss pounded on the door at two o'clock or so to tell me to run the *Ariadne* over to Ynez and tell Stebbins here that Marc'd been killed. Poor Marc! I was sure sorry to hear about it. He was a nice fellow.

CAPTAIN CRANSTON: Did you like him as well as you do Miss Paphlagloss?

STARR: In a different way, so to speak. I was right surprised to hear them two had decided to get hitched. Yes, sir, right surprised.

CAPTAIN CRANSTON: What was surprising about it?

STARR: There's game fish like marlin and tuna that are fighters all the way through, and there's fish like rock bass that you just haul in. People are divided pretty much the same way, so to speak. Now you take a fellow that's the rock bass kind, and you marry him to a girl who belongs to the marlin and tuna class, and it ain't going to work out. I'm telling you, brother, it ain't going to work out.

CAPTAIN CRANSTON: Not even if they are fond of each other?

STARR: Don't make no difference how fond they are of each other. It ain't going to work out.

I. Statement of Anna Holden

MRS. HOLDEN: Well, sir, after the dinner dishes had all been put away, we decided to have a little bridge game, just among ourselves.

Della and me against Felix and Carrie. They beat us by fifteen hundred, but if you don't get the cards today, you'll get 'em tomorrow, I always say.

CAPTAIN CRANSTON: How long did your bridge game last?

MRS. HOLDEN: Well, sir, it lasted a good long time. No, maybe not so long. Let's see, it was after ten o'clock when we started. So it couldn't have lasted more'n two hours. Not much more'n two hours 'cause by twelve-thirty we was all sitting down to supper.

CAPTAIN CRANSTON: Supper?

MRS. HOLDEN: Mr. Paphlagloss ain't the man to begrudge an occasional can of beer to them that works hard for him. And Della, she made some sandwiches—liverwurst on rye. There's nothing like liverwurst with beer, I always say.

CAPTAIN CRANSTON: Did any of you leave the kitchen while the bridge game was going on?

MRS. HOLDEN: Only Felix. Once to carry up Mr. Stoner's hot toddy, and once when Mr. Paphlagloss rang for him. He wasn't gone long either time.

CAPTAIN CRANSTON: That will be all, Mrs. Holden. But tell this Felix of yours I want to see him.

MRS. HOLDEN: He ain't mine, sir.

J. Statement of Felix Handleburger

HANDLEBURGER: 'Andleburger's the nyme, sir. With a haitch and a hay.

CAPTAIN CRANSTON: English, huh?

HANDLEBURGER: Hi ham, sir.

CAPTAIN CRANSTON: How long have you been working here?

HANDLEBURGER: Since Saturday night, sir.

CAPTAIN CRANSTON: Who recommended you to Mr. Paphlagloss?

HANDLEBURGER: Hi took the liberty of recommending myself, sir.

CAPTAIN CRANSTON: Where did you meet Mr. Paphlagloss?

HANDLEBURGER: The hinquest, sir. Hi'm a great 'and for hattending those sad hevents. Heducytional, hif Hi mye sye so.

CAPTAIN CRANSTON: You had references, didn't you?

HANDLEBURGER: Mr. Paphlagloss 'as my letters now, sir. Very fine ones, hif Hi mye sye so. Hive always given satisfaction, sir.

CAPTAIN CRANSTON: Can you give me any local references?

HANDLEBURGER: No sir. Hi've just arrived from New York, sir.

CAPTAIN CRANSTON: Then give me the names of the people you've worked for in New York.

HANDLEBURGER: Hi can't, sir. Hi didn't work there.

CAPTAIN CRANSTON: Well, where did you work?

HANDLEBURGER: Hengland, sir.

CAPTAIN CRANSTON: All your references are English ones?

HANDLEBURGER: They hare, sir.

CAPTAIN CRANSTON: You mean to tell me you came directly from England to Los Angeles?

HANDLEBURGER: Because of the cinema, sir. Hi've halways wanted to hact. Hi thought Hi might be ible to secure bit parts.

CAPTAIN CRANSTON: Tell me what you did last night from ten o'clock on.

HANDLEBURGER: Hi plyed bridge with my fellow servants, sir, hin the kitchen.

CAPTAIN CRANSTON: Did you leave the kitchen at any time?

HANDLEBURGER: Twice, sir. Mrs. Paphlagloss hasked me to tyke a 'ot toddy to the room of Mr. 'Arvey Stoner, which Hi did, being gone not more than five minutes.

CAPTAIN CRANSTON: What was the second time?

HANDLEBURGER: Mr. Paphlagloss rang for me, sir. 'E hasked me to bring the board and chessmen from downstairs to 'is study, which Hi did.

CAPTAIN CRANSTON: What time was it then?

HANDLEBURGER: Between 'arf-past ten and heleven, sir.

CAPTAIN CRANSTON: How long were you gone from the kitchen?

HANDLEBURGER: Not hover ten minutes, sir.

K. Statement of T.L. Westborough

WESTBOROUGH: I've taken the liberty of making a time-table of the movements of the occupants of Knossos last night. You may find it interesting.

CAPTAIN CRANSTON: H'm. I see you've put your name at the head of the column.

WESTBOROUGH: Not in egotism but merely because my own movements are the most familiar to me. It is rather surprising, is it not, when the normal vagueness of human memories is taken into consideration, that there are no important contradictions?

CAPTAIN CRANSTON: I can't agree that there are no contradictions. What about Glendon and Miss Paphlagloss? One of them is certainly lying.

WESTBOROUGH: Yes, to shield the other. My belief is that the prevaricator is Mr. Glendon. Obviously, he does not wish it to become known that Miss Paphlagloss, who was an engaged woman, spent two hours alone with him after midnight. He is certainly enough of an idealist to reason in that manner.

CAPTAIN CRANSTON: You think Glendon's an idealist?

WESTBOROUGH: One who speaks so bitterly of life is very nearly always an idealist.

CAPTAIN CRANSTON: H'm, here's something else. If Glendon or Miss Paphlagloss was on the terrace until two o'clock, wouldn't they have heard you and Paphlagloss going down to the boathouse to wake Starr?

WESTBOROUGH: Perhaps not. The house is very large.

CAPTAIN CRANSTON: Did you meet either of them in the halls?

WESTBOROUGH: No.

CAPTAIN CRANSTON: You've left one very important fellow out of your timetable. The murderer.

WESTBOROUGH: Truly a deplorable omission. Let us rectify it at once.

CAPTAIN CRANSTON: Well, let's see. It would take at least fifteen minutes to walk from the house to Bayard's camp.

WESTBOROUGH: Twenty, more nearly.

CAPTAIN CRANSTON: And at least another twenty to kill Bayard, drag the body to the ditch and build the altar.

WESTBOROUGH: That does not seem like an unreasonable estimate.

CAPTAIN CRANSTON: So we've got an hour altogether to account for. "Murderer: must leave house by eleven-thirty and cannot be back in it before twelve-thirty." There's your timetable completed! Do you check with me?

WESTBOROUGH: Perfectly.

CAPTAIN CRANSTON: Now, let's see how we stand for alibis. Westborough, yes; he was with Paphlagloss during the time. Paphlagloss, yes; he was with Westborough. Mrs. Paphlagloss, no.

WESTBOROUGH: Surely you do not suspect a mother of killing her own son?

CAPTAIN CRANSTON: I've seen worse things than that happen. Miss Paphlagloss, yes by her own admission, no by Glendon's; we'll compromise and put a no with a question mark after it. Glendon, ditto.

Nielsen, no. Harvey Stoner, no. Russell Stoner, no. Tom Starr, no. Servants other than Handleburger, yes; unless they're all three lying. Handleburger? Well, the last time he left the kitchen was before eleven, and he wasn't gone for more than ten minutes.

WESTBOROUGH: During which ten minutes he was in Mr. Paphlagloss' study twice.

CAPTAIN CRANSTON: Handleburger, yes. Now let's count the no's. H'm, seven of them. Seven without alibis! Written on this sheet of paper is the name of the murderer. What are you going to do about it?

WESTBOROUGH: Dear me, it's hardly within my province to say. I have bungled most deplorably so far.

CAPTAIN CRANSTON: I know the circumstances, and I don't blame you. I probably would have acted just the same way. The man with the strongest motive for killing Bayard was Paphlagloss. You were right to watch him.

WESTBOROUGH: To no avail, however. Dear me! That unfortunate young man's blood weighs heavily on my conscience.

CAPTAIN CRANSTON: I know how you feel about it. Well, it's too late to do anything for Marc Bayard. But his murderer's going to be headed for the state's new lethal gas chamber, and headed for it pronto, I promise.

WESTBOROUGH: You may count upon my utmost assistance. May I ask, by the way, what you learned about shoes?

CAPTAIN CRANSTON: Glad you brought that point up. It was a smart dodge to borrow your other shoes so he wouldn't leave his own footprints. Well, the only person on the island whose feet are too big to wear your oxfords, Westborough, is Russell Stoner. He's certainly qualified for the police profession with regard to feet.

WESTBOROUGH: Provided only that the stock jokes are true, Captain. Your own feet, I might cite in rebuttal, are not a great deal larger than mine.

CAPTAIN CRANSTON: Two or three other things I ought to talk over with you while we've got the chance. We've got no fingerprints yet and probably won't have. Cagey devil to always use unpolished stone for his killings! Impressions can't be developed on that rough surface. And I had something else . . . Oh yes, the book. We didn't find it.

WESTBOROUGH: Mr. Bayard assured me yesterday morning that he had carried it to his camp.

CAPTAIN CRANSTON: It was probably pitched into the ocean. However, we can look it up at the public library. Along with the paper you named in the letter you didn't get to post yesterday.

WESTBOROUGH: I should appreciate the information very much.

CAPTAIN CRANSTON: You believe that this angle is the one thing we need to break the case?

WESTBOROUGH: I am very nearly certain it will prove one of the leading factors. Unfortunately, there are still some rather large lacunae in my reasoning. I am unable to say at the present juncture just how toloache is to be linked to the problem as a whole.

CAPTAIN CRANSTON: I could take action now on the basis of what you've already given me.

WESTBOROUGH: Pray do not. It is much too soon. There is still a probability that my conjectures are erroneous.

CAPTAIN CRANSTON: I wonder if they are.

WESTBOROUGH: If we act without evidence, the injury may be irreparable.

CAPTAIN CRANSTON: We'll wait. I can post men on the island to keep you in sight.

WESTBOROUGH: Dear me! That course, I fear, might have the undesirable effect of freezing the situation in the present status. We must give rope, Captain Cranston. A very great deal of it.

CAPTAIN CRANSTON: Your point has some sense, I'll admit. But I can't leave you here alone.

WESTBOROUGH: Pray do not consider my safety

CAPTAIN CRANSTON: They got Bayard; they very nearly got you. The next time they try, your luck may be out.

WESTBOROUGH: Personal danger is greatly preferable to the risk of doing a monstrous and terrible injustice.

CAPTAIN CRANSTON: M-m-m. Well, the coroner has scheduled the inquest for four o'clock this afternoon, so things can't possibly come to a head before tonight.

WESTBOROUGH: You will give me tonight alone?

CAPTAIN CRANSTON: I'll stretch a point and give you tomorrow, too. But I don't dare give you any more time than that.

WESTBOROUGH: Your trust renders me deeply grateful.

CAPTAIN CRANSTON: You may not be so grateful later on. H'm. Well, remember, it's your own funeral.

WESTBOROUGH: Let us hope it will not come to that.

L. Movements of Occupants of Knossos on the Night of Bayard's Murder

WESTBOROUGH: At ten-fifteen meets Russell Stoner and Paphlagloss on the landing. Goes immediately to P's study on the second floor. Stays with P. until twelve forty-five when he goes to his own room. Learns then Nielsen is in the room next door, sleeping. Meets Russell Stoner in the court at twelve fifty-five. Returns to Knossos shortly before two and wakes Paphlagloss to report murder. Alibi: YES.

PAPHLAGLOSS: In living room after dinner. Remains there with Russell Stoner after Glendon, Nielsen, H. Stoner and Mrs. Paphlagloss have left. Paphlagloss and R. Stoner go up stairs together, meeting Westborough at ten-fifteen. P. and W. play chess until twelve forty-five. After W. has left, P. goes to own room and remains there until awakened by W., returning shortly before two. Alibi: YES.

MRS. PAPHLAGLOSS: In living room until ten-ten when she goes into kitchen to order hot toddy for H. Stoner. From kitchen she goes upstairs to her own room, takes aspirin and falls asleep very shortly. Remains sleeping until morning. Alibi: NO.

IONE PAPHLAGLOSS: On terrace with Westborough until ten-thirteen. Joined by Russell Stoner at ten-sixteen. He stays with her until nearly eleven-thirty, when she goes to her room and remains there for twenty minutes. At eleven-fifty she returns to the terrace, and stays there until nearly two with Denis Glendon. But Glendon denies her presence on the terrace. Alibi: NO??

GLENDON: Goes to his own room at nine-thirty and remains there until twenty minutes past eleven when he goes to the terrace to enjoy a cigarette. Seeing Miss Paphlagloss and R. Stoner, he leaves immediately, without notifying them of his presence, and returns to his own room where he remains until midnight. At midnight he returns to the terrace and remains there until nearly two. Denies that Miss Paphlagloss was on the terrace for any portion of the latter two hours. Alibi: NO??

NIELSEN: Goes to his room at nine-thirty and works at his book until shortly before midnight when he goes to bed. Falls asleep almost immediately. Is sleeping at twelve forty-five, Westborough ascertains. Alibi: NO.

H. STONER: Goes to bed at ten o'clock. Is visited by butler with hot lemon toddy at ten-thirty. Sleeps until 7 A.M. Alibi: NO.

R. STONER: On terrace with Miss Paphlagloss until eleven-thirty, then returns to his own room and changes into trunks for his swim. Says that he is in the water over an hour. Was seen by Westborough in court at twelve fifty-five. Alibi: NO.

STARR: Goes to bed at nine-thirty in his own room above the boathouse and sleeps until roused by Mr. Paphlagloss at two o'clock to make trip to Ynez. Alibi: NO.

SERVANTS *(except Handleburger)* : In kitchen from ten o'clock until at least twelve-thirty. Alibi: YES.

HANDLEBURGER: In kitchen with other servants, except when delivering Mr. Stoner's hot toddy at ten-thirty (gone five minutes) and when bringing the chessboard and men to Mr. Paphlagloss' study some time between half-past ten and eleven (gone ten minutes). Alibi: YES.

MURDERER: Must leave house by eleven-thirty. Cannot return to house before twelve-thirty. The hands of Bayard's watch stopped at the hour of eleven fifty-five.

PART SEVEN: CLUE TO THE LABYRINTH

(Thursday, July 14)

I

ONE OF CAPTAIN CRANSTON'S MEN had contrived to slip the paper unobtrusively into Westborough's hand during the crush from the inquest room late on Wednesday afternoon. It had been hidden secretly between his pillow and pillowslip all of that night, but now, at a very early hour on Thursday morning, he consigned it to the flames.

It was dangerous to leave it in his room, dangerous even to carry it about on his person, and besides there was no need. The information had long since been transferred to Westborough's photographic memory. A great deal of highly condensed information concerning plants of the genus Datura.*

To employ the open hearth in his host's paneled study was undeniably risky, but his own quarters contained no fireplace. Moreover, at 6:30 A.M. the household was not astir. Or was it? As he left his room, he had received the distinct impression that unseen eyes were following him. An overwrought imagination, most probably. Dear me, it was little wonder that his imagination should be overwrought! While the paper flared brilliantly, he turned his attention to his host's liquor cabinet. It was kept locked, luckily. One less spot to guard!

Undoubtedly, the attempt would be made during dinner. Yes, that was the perfect time. There would then exist a valuable and unique opportunity. Should he issue a warning? He vetoed the thought almost

*NOTE: The fact apparently withheld from the reader is not one peculiar to this case but a matter of public information. C. B. C.

immediately. Until definite confirmation was forthcoming, it would be most unwise to take any other person into his confidence. He might be wrong! His reasoning was no more than a thin crust on which he walked over a molten lava of uncertainty.

The paper had been reduced to a black flaky ash, but Westborough's gaze was caught by a framed map hanging on the wall behind the door. A map of the island with the various trails clearly defined. Marc's work, probably; it bore the earmarks of that unfortunate young man's thorough draftsmanship. What a pity he had not known of its existence earlier!

Tracing his route of last Monday, Westborough soon discovered that he had wandered by an unnecessarily roundabout way to the eastern side. Here was a shortcut to the south of the house which would have spared him the perilous jaunt through the gorge of snake cactus, the arduous ascent of the giant terraces. His pencil poised at a spot along the ragged coast line. This, he concluded, from recognizable contours, must be the site of the enigmatic cave in which he had heard the voices of nonexistent men. It had been awarded a name by the conscientious draftsman, a long Spanish name. Straining his eyes, he succeeded in reading the extremely fine India-ink lettering. *La Cueva de los Dos Pisos.*

Although Westborough's Spanish was a trifle rusty, he was sure he did not mistake the meaning. The word "pisos" propelled him from the study in a fast undignified scamper, sent him scurrying down the hall toward the stairs. A door swished behind him, and he turned his head. All the doors were closed, as doors should be at this early morning hour. Odd how the illusion persisted that he was being watched! He must sweep his brain of such fusty cobwebbery. He had only today to knit together all of the raveled ends—a gigantic task only a clear mind could accomplish. Luck—a very great deal of it—was also needed, but luck, he believed, is compounded largely of alertness, persistence and action.

The night fog had not yet been dissipated. The sun's disk shone red-orange, an enormous Persian moon, and the small-leaved chaparral shrubs dripped with moisture. They brushed clammily against his clothing like dank fingers seeking to stay his progress. He heard a rustle of branches behind him, a sound which he was sure his own advance had not caused, but he could see nothing. Everything to the rear was swallowed by the opaque formless mists; even the huge rectangular bulk of Knossos had become as tenuous as a castle of clouds. Like a magic wall, the fog unrolled before him.

Presently, he heard the rhythmic pulse of the sea. It boomed louder and louder against his eardrums, the deep voice of Titans who carved such curious caverns as the one he sought. The fog was like time itself.

Behind, lay the past—misty, obfuscated; before, the future—veiled, uncertain. Only the present—the now in which he walked—was sharply delineated. But he had found the fissure which led to the grotto's lip. Scrambling down the slope, he reached the ledge on which he had stood during the previous visit.

The cave was open before him, but he did not enter. He found—what he had failed to notice the other day—that the descent could be continued from the far side of the ledge. The rocks were slippery with sea slime, but clinging as best he could, he slithered downward. The spray beat saltily into his face, the waves roared unbridled pandemonium.

Reaching the sea level, he saw the water churning in a milky frenzy before a second black opening. Marc's map had told truthfully that this cavity should be here—the basement, as it were, of the chamber above. *La Cueva de los Dos Pisos*! In English the name meant, "The cave of the two levels."

Doubtless, the two stories were connected. The vent between them could not be large enough to admit a man's passage, else, he was positive, he would not have overlooked it in his frantic search of the upper cavern. But a comparatively small hole, which the flickering match flames had failed to reveal to him, would suffice to transmit a voice. The weird disappearance was now readily explained. The men he had heard talking had been, all the time, on the lower level.

Why, he wondered, had they chosen this strange and inconvenient meeting place? The secret, perhaps, lay in the grotto itself. The tide was advancing, but would not reach high water for several hours. Westborough removed his shoes and his socks. He rolled his trousers high on his thin pipestem legs and began to splash through the wavelets to the entrance. His bare feet trod painfully on the cave's pebbly bottom.

He struck a match. Wind and water had done their work well! The chamber was a great deal larger than the one above; indeed, it appeared large enough for Polyphemus to have imprisoned Odysseus and his unlucky mariners. Only with the aid of an electric torch could it be thoroughly explored. He scratched more matches. Fortunately, a thorough exploration would not be necessary. He saw a sizable depression in the wet gravel. A flat-bottomed rowboat might once have been dragged there, the very boat which had been used to transport the body of the hapless Charles. The marine hearse, however, had now been removed to another hiding place.

Always too late! The most brilliant, the most ruthless adversary with whom he had ever contended had again outmaneuvered him. Tonight, though no herald would cry the challenge, he must meet that puissant opponent in the lists for the final joust. But the odds, he realized, were still very much against him. Unless . . .

Splashing from the cave, he sat down on the rocks where he had left his shoes to dry his feet with his handkerchief. "If I were a small boat," he thought, "where would I go to hide myself?" He pulled on a sock and laced a shoe. Preoccupied in meditation, he failed to note, when he rolled down his trousers, that he had left his other foot entirely bare. "On the lee side of the island, I believe, and not too far from the house. Near the house? Ah!"

A large stone rolled noisily into the ocean only a few feet away. Startled, he sprang to his feet. No one was in sight, of course. No one ever was. It was disconcerting to be followed by the Invisible Man. Dangerous, also.

Commencing to scramble upward, he realized that he had stupidly neglected to put on his right shoe. With a wry smile he sat down again to rectify the error. Was there not, he pondered, a saying about dying with one's boots on? He would be given little opportunity to choose if better-aimed stones followed the first. Would it not be wiser to retreat at once into the shelter of the lower cavern? However, there was no repetition of the incident, and he began to wonder if the stone had been deliberately thrown.

If thrown, he mused, hurriedly knotting his shoelace, it had been by an unskilled hand. The hand of which he was thinking was by no means unpracticed in the matter of providing a lethal contact between stones and human skulls. Perhaps the boulder had been dislodged inadvertently, dislodged by a person overanxious to reach the concealment of the ledge above.

He found no one on the ledge, no one in the upper cave and no one on the summit of the cliff, but in the soft soil of the trail through the chaparral he made a startling discovery.

Overlaying his own footprints was a line of very much larger ones. Someone *had* followed him from Knossos; only one person there possessed feet of such a gargantuan size. It was—

II

He found Ione in the courtyard, by the fountain which the alchemy of sunlight had converted into a splash of dancing gold. She stood slimly erect in her chocolate-brown slacks and yellow sweater, a yellow scarf tied peasant-fashion to cover her black silky curls. The birds she was feeding rested on her head and fought for places on her palms; they fluttered about her shoulders like the white doves of Astarte.

"I have rarely seen them so tame," Westborough observed. She turned her head and smiled.

"You should see those at San Juan Capistrano! But pigeons seem to belong, somehow, to old Spanish missions."

"To religious edifices of any nature," he amplified. "They were associated with temples long before written history. Doves were sacred to Aphrodite at the celebrated shrine of Paphos, to Astarte at the Syrian Hierapolis, and to the much older Cretan goddess whose image your father—"

"Spare me the Cretan goddess," she laughed, flinging the last of the grain to her avian flock. "And please tell me what you want me to do for you."

The girl's mind was mobile as quicksilver.

"How," he sparred, "did you know that I came to you with an ulterior purpose?"

She reached for a pack of cigarettes lying upon the stone bench.

"Among other things, I noticed the respect with which you were treated by that hard-boiled police captain."

"Dear me!" he exclaimed in alarm, shielding a match flame for her with his hand. "Did anyone else notice, do you think?"

"I can't say." Her low-pitched voice was dramatically sober. "Aren't you playing a rather dangerous game, Mr. Westborough?"

"Admittedly," he sighed. Her luminous eyes rested for a moment on his slight elderly figure.

"You don't look like the type."

"Dear me, no!" he agreed. "No one could be less the type than I am. Fate, however, has thrust me into the ill-suited role."

"Fate or Captain Cranston?" she inquired.

He wiped the perspiration from his triangular face and wished that he had not been so unlucky as to lose his only hat. The afternoon sun was glaring like a maleficent eye from a Mediterranean-blue firmament. As solace, however, their words were drowned by the splashing fountain and would not be audible over twenty feet away. No one could approach that closely to them without detection, he reflected thankfully.

"Please do not speak of it to anyone," he requested in a very quiet voice.

"You may trust me," she said promptly. "I owe you something in the way of good turns, I believe."

"You owe me nothing at all," he denied. "However, if you wish to do me two favors, I—"

Catching his arm, she drew him quickly to the other side of the fountain.

"Do you know that Russ is watching us from an upstairs window?" she whispered.

"He has watched me all day," Westborough lamented. "That is one favor of which I spoke. It is a little troublesome to be followed wherever I go. Dear me, yes, most inconvenient."

"I'll take Russ off your hands for the rest of the afternoon. You may count on that."

"I shall be deeply grateful."

"And the other favor?"

"A matter of great importance. Mr. Starr has just departed to Ynez on his daily trip for the mail. I may not be able to meet him when he returns, and I am expecting to receive an important letter, perhaps even two." He hushed his voice to its softest tones. "It would be fatal to have either intercepted by the wrong hands."

She nodded comprehendingly. "I'll wait on the pier for Tom, and if your letter comes I'll hold it for you."

"Be very careful, my dear, that no one learns the nature of the document. For your own safety. On second thought, I do not believe that I have the right to ask you to assume so grave a risk."

"I can take care of myself," she returned. "Is there anything else?"

"Thank you, no. But you are very generous."

Her glance fixed on the entrance to the passageway, where the figure of the fresco painter could just be glimpsed at work on his second mural.

"Denis doesn't think so. Oh well! What does it matter what he thinks?"

But it did matter, Westborough reflected as he hurried away. It mattered a very great deal to her!

He took the familiar trail to poor Marc's deserted camp, pausing for a few minutes on the bluff overlooking the sea. He leaned against the railing, thoughtfully regarding the water which lapped the bluff's jagged base in a deep green pool thirty feet below. The tranquillity was in startling contrast to the booming surf of the western shore. The island was a coin with two sides—strife and peace!

It would be in a ravine, he pondered, a ravine that dipped to the sea to provide a sheltering cove. But the island had many such; its terrain was a network of dingles and ridges, paralleling and intersecting in baffling complexity. He had no choice but to explore them all, fighting the merciless pressure of encroaching time.

However, he was extremely lucky. The second arroyo was the right gulch. He followed its dry bed to the shore. The boat had been dragged clear of the water and partially covered by armfuls of brush; it would have been completely invisible from the sea. Westborough lifted the outboard motor—it seemed very heavy to him—and carried it to a spit of rock jutting well out into the ocean. He dropped the motor into the deep water, where it vanished with a wholly gratifying splash. A clumsy expedient, doubtless, but he was a poor mechanic and knew of no other sure method of putting the craft out of commission. The oars he carried inland for a considerable distance, in order to thrust them, finally, into the thick of a coppice of spiny buckthorn, a coppice very nearly impenetrable. Smiling in satisfaction, he returned to Knossos.

Ione was on the pier, chatting animatedly with Russell Stoner, held captive against his will, and Tom Starr was just swinging the *Ariadne* into port. He had brought mail, but no letters for Westborough. Constable Stebbins, Starr informed the historian in response to a carefully guarded inquiry, had been summoned to Los Angeles to testify in a land case and was not expected to return to Ynez until late that afternoon.

Westborough withdrew a little distance from the others, ostensibly to watch the white triangles that were yachts skirting the purple outline of the eastern mainland. Staring aimlessly across the 20-mile moat, he was conscious for the first time of the full extent of his isolation.

III

Gently opening the door, without the preliminary formality of knocking, Westborough peered cautiously inside. Double axes, a Minoan symbol of authority a millennium older than the Roman fasces, alternated with 8-shaped shields in a deep brown frieze circuiting the walls of a room as vast as a royal bedchamber. The lord of all this magnificence, however, splashed unseen beyond; a rendition of the "Volga Boatmen" informed the intent listener that Alexis Paphlagloss was addicted, even as lesser men, to bathroom concerts.

"Volga, Volga, Volga, Volga!" As long as that lusty melody continued, all would be well. Westborough stole quietly across the room to where his host's white flannels were draped over the back of a chair; he inserted his hand into his host's pocket and deftly withdrew a keycase.

He removed a flat brass key of peculiar shape and restored the keycase to the pocket. A succession of booming "Volga's" masked the slight noise of his retreat. He closed the door swiftly behind him. It seemed incredible that his burglary had been accomplished so easily. The return of the key, to be sure, might offer more difficulties, but "sufficient unto the day is the evil thereof." He descended the main staircase.

Russell Stoner was standing on the landing in speechless contemplation of a mammoth urn. Westborough nodded briefly and passed on. The athlete's interest in pottery was a comparatively recent development, and so, doubtless, had not yet been able to take on deep roots. The historian was not in the least surprised to hear the young man's tread echoing on the stairs behind him. It was, however, slightly annoying.

Glendon, in the front passageway, had completed his day's stint on the panel and was now cleansing his brushes in the careful manner of a conscientious craftsman. Westborough stopped to regard the mural; in the courtyard, at the entrance to the passageway, Russell Stoner stopped also.

The second fresco was a much easier task than the complicated amphitheater scene on the opposite wall. Seated on a celestial throne, in a luminous blue ether, the great Minoan goddess watched with compassionate interest the souls of a young man and a young woman, who had just been ushered by griffin-headed females into a hall of the somber brown underworld. While the judge of the Dead, a winged griffin, deliberated his verdict from a high stool, the girl stood proudly beside the young man, her hand clasped in his. It was odd how in a few deft lines the artist had contrived to suggest the face and carriage of Ione Paphlagloss. Glancing momentarily from the painting, Westborough saw that the watchful Mr. Stoner was still waiting for him.

Taking a deep breath, the historian let himself go. He had been confident that a modicum of information on the Minoan conception of immortality would suffice to bore his shadow into withdrawal, but he had vastly underestimated the athlete's staying powers. It was rather a pity, Westborough thought, that he had selected a subject on which he was so woefully ignorant. However, what he could do, he did.

He began with the obvious comparison between the Minoan beliefs and the contemporary Egyptian, referring for illustration of the latter to the Papyrus of Ani. He related to his luckless listeners how the soul of this scribe, who had died in the eighteenth dynasty, had been forced to pass in turn before each of forty-two assessors in the Hall of Osiris, while the jackal-headed Anubis weighed the man's heart against the feather of Truth, and Thoth, the ibis-headed, recorded with his reed the results of the weighings. Not being an Egyptologist, unfortunately, Westborough could only discuss the Egyptian afterworld superficially. He passed to Greek mythology, where he stood on slightly firmer ground.

He pointed out that the doggish creature which Glendon had depicted at the foot of the griffin inquisitor was doubtless the precursor of the three-headed canine Cerberus. He stressed that the Elysian fields were essentially non-Hellenic in concept and might well have been derived from the vastly older Minoan religion. He contended that Elysium differed materially from the gloomy Hades, where the shade of godlike Achilles had wandered so forlornly. Achilles was a very happy inspiration! He thought at once of the well-known passage in the *Odyssey* telling of the son of Thetis among the gibbering ghosts. He quoted several lines of Greek. That turned the trick at last; the noble language of Homer was too much for Russell Stoner. Screwing his handsome features into an expression of supreme ennui, the watcher strolled away a bare few seconds before Westborough's Greek and his breath had both become exhausted.

"WHE-E-e-e-w!" Glendon exclaimed admiringly. "How do you do it?"

"My knowledge of the topic is really quite negligible," Westborough answered modestly and sauntered slowly down the passageway toward the room holding the shrine of the Cretan goddess. As soon as the fresco painter had departed, he ventured an entrance.

He had hoped to safeguard himself, to some extent, by locking the door behind him, but the door, unluckily, had no key in its lock. Closing it noiselessly behind him, Westborough walked to the glass-walled parallelepiped on the pillar-carved base.

Restored to her black velvet throne, the little ivory lady smiled a winsome welcome. Despite the gold serpents on her forearms, she seemed to be a friendly goddess. Before thrusting his sacrilegious hand into her tiny domain, Westborough studied for some little time the curious assortment of objects by which she was surrounded. These, he realized, were symbols dating from one of the oldest religions of which the world has record—a religion which might well have been that of Plato's legendary Atlantis. The paint-streaked seashells interested him the most, but, he reflected, it was rather a pity that there should be so many of them.

However, he must take things as he found them and be thankful to the Lady of Crete for the favors she had already vouchsafed. Inserting the unorthodoxly borrowed key, he pushed open the sliding door and commenced methodically to lift the painted relics. "The oddest shell game in the world," he thought, in one of his occasional flashes of irrelevancy. "Perhaps also the oldest."

The fifth shell he raised yielded concrete results. There wasn't a pea under it, but he did find a small button—like that of a doorbell, but on a reduced scale. He depressed it with his thumbnail. One of the wooden panels on which the shrine rested slid automatically aside.

Bending his head, he saw that a hinged section of the concrete flooring had also been mysteriously lifted, revealing to his gaze a steep narrow stairway. Though he had been prepared for some such legerdemain of electrically operated mechanism, the Arabian Nights suddenness of the trick fairly took away his breath. Time was too valuable, however, to lose in wonderment.

He stooped to squeeze through the opened panel below the glass case, and descended the stairs. Beneath the floor level, he found a quite modern wall switch. He pressed it; the chamber under his feet was flooded with light, and he caught a glimpse of what appeared to be an extremely efficient-looking bank vault.

He was not, however, given opportunity to make detailed examination. A soft click, sounding above his head, caused him to scramble back up the steep stairs in a moment of near panic. The click could only be caused by the turning of a doorknob—the hall door which he had not been able to lock. Someone had walked down the passageway, someone was opening the door of the room above. Only a miracle could avert a complete disaster!

He prayed silently to the Cretan goddess, but that fickle divinity was no longer on his side. Stepping from beneath her shrine, Westborough found himself face to face with Alexis Paphlagloss.

IV

The purple-black Greek wine, which should have held the sunshine-stored essence of the grape itself, had lost its flavor, like milk turning sour during a thunderstorm. The old fable wasn't such an inapt simile, Glendon reflected, sipping moodily at the tasteless beverage. Tensions had been accumulating all day, like static electricity in a Leyden jar, and sooner or later a violent discharge would be inevitable.

There were two vacant places at the miserable dinner. Mrs. Paphlagloss, prostrate with her grief, naturally made no effort to come down, and Mr. Westborough was also missing. That was rather odd—ordinarily the little man was the soul of punctuality—but nobody thought to inquire about him. Nobody talked much at all except Ione, determinedly gay with the powerful blond animal who would undoubtedly be her future husband. And what of it? Glendon drained his wine in a single gulp. He loved her, he was in her debt against his will, and on top of everything else he'd made a fool of himself. Hell, what did it matter? He'd get over it, wouldn't he? Even over a face which sketched itself on his mind during every minute of the dream-filled night.

Well, faces were his profession. He knew them as doctors know liver ailments, lawyers musty precedents, and priests the endless ramifications of the human heart! He knew them in hope and dread, pain and passion, pleasure and anguish, but the twisted Doré caricatures sitting at the table with him tonight weren't faces. They were masks—the strained and ghastly masks of the condemned!

See how pointlessly the fated puppets employed their pitiful last moments! Nielsen nervously concocted witless professorial jokes, which Ione acknowledged with unnatural laughter and Russell Stoner echoed in risqué sallies. But the elder Stoner and Alexis Paphlagloss made no jokes, either witless or risqué. They exchanged the dour glances of men who sought to conceal hatred—the unconcealable hatred of criminals whose shameful secrets are known to each other, the limitless hate of fear . . . God, he was getting into an even worse state than the rest of them! Glendon forced himself to speak.

He didn't care what he said. Any subject, he thought, would serve to break the explosive glumness. So he spoke on the first thing that came to his mind. He asked what had happened to little Mr. Westborough. Alexis Paphlagloss took a deep draught of resinated wine. Glendon was sure his host had heard the inquiry. But Paphlagloss answered only with a warning frown.

The cockney watchfully refilled his master's glass, and Paphlagloss lifted it again to his lips. There must be something abnormal about a man who could relish such turpentined filth. Glendon repeated his question, and Paphlagloss continued to drink as if he hadn't heard. The fact that the man was a multimillionaire and the autocratic ruler of an island kingdom was not sufficient excuse for such deliberate discourtesy. Glendon's blood, none too cool at any time, boiled at the insult. He determined to make an issue of the trivial, inconsequential matter.

"I asked, Mr. Paphlagloss, why Mr. Westborough didn't come down to dinner."

His voice was loud enough for everyone at the table to hear him; in fact, a great deal louder. The Minos couldn't ignore him any longer.

"Indisposed," he returned briefly.

"What's the matter with him?" Glendon persisted. They were looking at him and he didn't care. At that moment he hated them one and all, hated them like Samuel Hall in the song. He had seen Westborough just before dinner, he remembered. And at that time Westborough had been anything but a sick man.

"I don't know," Paphlagloss said curtly, rising from the table to lead the way into the living room.

Glendon found his progress blocked by the bulky figure of Russell Stoner. "If I were you, Bud," Stoner stressed significantly, "I'd leave well enough alone."

"What do you know about it?" the painter snapped.

"Nerves!" Stoner exclaimed, with no particular malice. "Relax, fellow, relax, as the coach used to tell us just before a tough game. Do you know you were staring a hole through me all during dinner?"

"What do you know about Westborough?" Glendon retorted.

Stoner grinned slyly. "Me? I don't know anything. But why did he"—his gesture might have indicated any of the three men ahead of them—"send Starr to Ynez?"

Ione, suddenly coming between them, laid her hand on Glendon's arm and piloted him deftly to a brilliantly colored landscape of the Mojave Desert. "What's your opinion of this canvas, Denis?"

Her glowingly dark eyes asked another question, and he nodded silent assent. Faces were his profession. He could read hers very well.

"A blob of oils," he answered bluntly, hoping that Paphlagloss, who had bought the monstrous thing, was in earshot. But Paphlagloss was too deep in conversation with "H.C." to hear the voice of a minor guest. Ione seated herself at the cream-white piano. She could play well when she wanted to, but she seldom finished her aimless snatches of melodies. A woman at a piano, however, draws men as honey draws ants. Glendon slipped away, unnoticed, and went upstairs to knock on the door of Westborough's bedroom.

Westborough didn't answer his knock, and Glendon went inside. Westborough wasn't there. He wasn't on the terrace, he wasn't in the court downstairs and he wasn't in anyone else's bedroom. Glendon visited them all but that of Mrs. Paphlagloss. He had many reasons not to be fond of Mrs. Paphlagloss, but he had an ingrained respect for the abstract quality termed "grief," and so did not bother her.

Glendon began to grow more than anxious. He was not so ungrateful as to forget that Westborough had extricated him from what might have been a nasty jam a few days ago. Besides, he liked the little historian. You couldn't help but like such a mild cheerful personality.

And in this damned house anything could happen. The artist recalled that just before he had gone upstairs to get ready for dinner, Westborough had appeared to deliver a learned discussion on ancient religious beliefs. He had left the little man standing by the frescoes, which were only a short distance from the strange room, without windows, containing the shrine of the Cretan goddess. Westborough, he remembered, had been markedly interested in that room. Ergo, the best logic seemed to be to go there at once.

The door was locked, however, and there was something more than peculiar about that. Ordinarily, Glendon knew, there wasn't any key in that lock. However, it was certainly secured now. Locked on the inside or the outside? He probed the keyhole with the shaft of his smallest brush and learned the answer immediately. Whoever had produced the mysterious key had used it and carried it away again. Was Westborough a prisoner within?

Glendon rapped softly and waited a decent interval. He rapped normally, waited and rapped again. He rapped moderately loudly, then loudly, then very noisily, and the answer to all of these knocks was a profound and disturbing silence. He applied his eye in the immemorial manner of the keyhole spy, but the room was unilluminated, and he learned nothing. He tried his ear at the keyhole; he fancied he could hear a faint breathing on the other side of the door, but he wasn't quite sure, and while he was intent on listening, a hand was laid heavily on his shoulder.

"Glendon! What does this mean?"

It was the hand of Alexis Paphlagloss, whose face was very nearly the purple shade of his wine. Glendon, who had been caught red-handed in the despicable act of spying on his host and employer, should by all traditions have been ashamed and humiliated. Somehow, he was neither.

"What's your own game?" he demanded, his voice nearly as angry as the other's. "Did you lock this door?"

"Naturally I did."

"I want to know who's in here."

Paphlagloss was definitely of the generation which says, "Don't be impudent," and he said it now, plucking furiously at his grizzled mustache. For good measure, he added two more of like vintage: "You're discharged!" and, "Get out of my house!"

It was the first time Glendon had found himself in the midst of what is popularly called a situation, and he rather enjoyed the drama of it.

"Open that door," he insisted. "And open it damn quick!"

"Give orders to me, will you?" Paphlagloss choked angrily. "I'll—"

But Glendon never learned just what his employer had intended. Before he could finish his threat, the Minos, gasping as if an invisible hand were clutching at his throat, had collapsed weakly to the floor.

V

Glendon sank to his knees, forgetful of Westborough, of the locked door, of everything except that Ione's father had just collapsed in an apoplectic fit. Ione's father, with whom he had quarreled. If Mr. Paphlagloss died, he, Denis Glendon, would be personally responsible. But Paphlagloss was still alive, muttering to himself in a delirious undertone! His face had become a strange dark crimson, and his sloe-black eyes glistened in unnatural brightness.

Slipping an arm under his employer's shoulder, Glendon assisted him to his feet. Paphlagloss swayed sideways like a drunkard; he could not, obviously, stand unaided. Glendon supported him with his arm and tried to coax him to walk. Paphlagloss complied—he was now as blindly obedient to instructions as a small child. They marched through the court and into the hall leading to the main staircase. Here Glendon spied a tall carved chair and plumped the Minos unceremoniously into it, while he debated what to do next. The island's ruler sat docilely, engrossed in an idiotic game with his fingers; his face had grown dull, stupid, the face of an unwitting clod. From time to time he burst into hysterical laughter over futile attempts to catch one hand with another. But he was not drunk. The condition was vastly more serious than any form of alcoholic stupor.

Leaving the helpless man temporarily in the chair, Glendon dashed into the living room. The three men were grouped in cheerful fellowship about an open fire, while Ione's brown fingers rippled lightly over the piano keys. Tidings of death or madness, brought while a girl played "Liebestraum"!

The elder Stoner, strutting before the fireplace like a cigar-smoking Napoleon, delivered a great deal of pompously worded advice and remained where he was. It was Russell who, scorning offers of assistance, carried the bulky Paphlagloss across his shoulder like a limp sack of flour. As soon as her father had been laid on his canopied bed in the vast bedroom of the shields and double axes, it was Ione who removed his tie and loosed the collar from his thick red neck. But it was Arne Nielsen, crustily competent, who thought of taking the invalid's pulse; Nielsen who issued gruff orders to all of the others.

"Open the windows, someone. Give him air! Stand back from the bed, all of you! Let the man breathe!"

Paphlagloss moaned a delirious agreement. His hands were flushed; his face rubescent. His eyelids were swollen horribly; the jet-black pupils had engulfed all of his eyes but a narrow ring of iris. Abruptly, Nielsen dropped the wrist he had been holding and shook his head dolorously.

"It's thready and very rapid. Bad, bad! Let's see if—"

He slashed swiftly at the air, only two or three inches away from those monstrous black disks of eyes. A normal man would have blinked involuntarily, but the Greek's rigid stare remained unaltered.

"Insensible to light," Nielsen informed them brusquely. "He's lost the power of sight."

There was a moment of awful silence. "Do you know what to do for him?" Ione demanded. She looked unconsciously to Nielsen.

"Yes, get a doctor right away."

"There's one at Ynez."

"Ynez!" Nielsen snorted acridly. "Twenty miles by boat and no telephone! This place is made to order for murder!"

Ione was cool and unflustered. "I'll send Tom over right away."

Nielsen sputtered, like a fizzing fuse, "Do you know your father's been poisoned?"

"Poisoned!" both Glendon and Stoner echoed.

"I know a little about medicine," Nielsen exclaimed tartly. "Not much, it's true, but enough to recognize the symptoms of poisoning by belladonna."

"His resinated wine!" Glendon cried in a sudden flash of illumination. "He was the only one who drank from that bottle. The stuff must have been put in there."

"Probably," Nielsen snapped.

Ione bent pliantly over the bed, her tanned face appreciably whiter. She asked in a strained voice, "Do you know the treatment to give him, Doctor Nielsen?"

"Get it out of his system, first." Nielsen's goatee was bobbing below his lower lip like a furious hairy manikin. "Is there a stomach pump here?"

Ione shook her head in a dismal negative.

"No stomach pump!" Nielsen fumed. "Well, why are you all standing here like a pack of fools? We have to have a doctor, and he won't come until someone goes to fetch him."

"I'll go tell Tom," Ione volunteered meekly.

"No, stay with your father," Glendon hurriedly commanded. "I'll run down to the boathouse. Coming with me, Russ?"

Though it was the first time the fresco painter had used the nickname, he didn't realize now he had done so. Stoner nodded assent, and they started from the room together.

"Have to give an emetic," Nielsen grumbled. "Miss Paphlagloss, be good enough to bring me a jug of hot water, a pan, a spoon, a glass and a package of dried mustard. Also, while you're downstairs, tell your cook to brew some fresh coffee. It's got to be black and strong."

"Didn't you say Paphlagloss had already sent Starr to Ynez?" Glendon whispered, as he and his companion were sprinting out of earshot down the hall.

"Right, Denny. He did just that thing."

Glendon did not think to ask why. "Don't let Ione know that," he muttered in dismay. "The boathouse will be locked, and Starr keeps the key. We're in a sweet jam!"

"Jam, hell!" Stoner retorted. "We'll smash the damn door down."

As a man of action Russ had his points, Glendon conceded, warming to the big blond fellow for the first time in their acquaintance. They found an ax ordinarily used to split kindling. Stoner swung it over his shoulder, and they raced for the boathouse. Russ handled the ax; the blade bit with telling precision into the heavy timbers, and they were soon crashing through the shattered door.

An electric lantern hung on a nail beside the entrance. Glendon lifted it to examine the hulls, showing as dim black shapes in the meager light. One of the speedboats, the *Ariadne*, was gone; but the *Ariadne's* twin, the *Britomartis*, was there and so were the broad-beamed *Velchanos* and the glass-bottomed *Diktynna*. Unfortunately, however, the ignition systems of the three vessels were locked. All of the keys were in the possession of the fleet's admiral, and not a motor could be turned. "Sunk!" the artist groaned despairingly.

Stoner, however, refused to admit defeat. "I can short-circuit the ignition, maybe." One of the advantages of being a rich man's son, Glendon owned grudgingly, was the opportunity to learn the workings of such expensive toys as speedboats. He didn't know much about them himself, or motors of any kind, for that matter. "Gimme a pair of pliers," Russ ordered tersely. He had pried open a hatch at the bow of the *Britomartis* and was peering inside, like some queer headless monster.

The artist smashed the wooden tool kit without compunction and handed the requisitioned instrument to his companion. "I can't make head or tail of this crate's wiring job," Stoner mumbled disgustedly.

While the other was wrestling with his bête noire, Glendon dashed up the ladder stairway to Starr's living quarters. It didn't take long to give them a thorough combing, but Starr, apparently, was farsighted enough to carry all keys on his person. It was maddening! A man was dying, and because of that man's own orders their chances of bringing aid to him grew progressively slimmer. But perhaps— Glendon rushed hurriedly down the stairs to the water level.

"Any luck yet, Russ?"

"Hell, no! It's going to take time to straighten out this tangle."

"Maybe Paphlagloss has a duplicate key in his room. I'll run up to the house and have a look for it."

"Swell flash," grunted the headless mechanic. "Run like hell, Denny!"

Glendon clumped out of the boathouse and down the pier; he hurled his wiry body like a projectile at the long dark flight of stairs. He was nearly at the top when he heard a shrill penetrating scream. It came from the second floor—a woman's voice. God! Something had happened to Ione!

He saw a latticework for climbing roses and leaped up it with the agility of a monkey. He scarcely felt the thorns which pricked his hands as he shinnied for the terrace. Thorns didn't matter if he could save a few precious seconds! A second scream sounded, then a third. He reached the terrace; he spurted breathlessly down the hall to his host's bedroom. If he could only reach Ione in time!

But it wasn't Ione who was screaming; it was the golden-haired Mrs. Paphlagloss. She was wringing her small hands helplessly above a man stretched on the floor, while her husband cackled deliriously on his bed, blissfully ignorant that the one man on the island whose skill and knowledge might save his life had just been struck down.

The stone with which that man had been felled lay broken on the floor, a long thin stone—an Indian pestle! In the same way as the others, they had got Arne Nielsen!

PART EIGHT: THEY FIND THE MINOTAUR

(Thursday, July 14)

I

THE MURMUR OF ARGUMENT in the passageway died abruptly as a snuffed candle flame. In the darkened Indian room, Westborough was left alone with the bitter thoughts of self-reproach.

Doubtless, Russell Stoner had been his immediate nemesis. The athlete must have spied him emerging from his host's bedroom, and, after following his quarry as far as the frescoes, gone directly to Paphlagloss with the news of the felonious entry. The thought was scant comfort now.

The curiosity with which his nature was cursed had been his doom, Westborough pronounced censoriously. The scheme was being carried onward to its successful conclusion—the carefully planned crime in which murders were merely by-products—while he sat here, helplessly and hopelessly, as inoperative as a fizzled firecracker. Dolt! He should have taken precautions before recklessly essaying the descent of the concealed staircase. Blunderer! True, when he had realized his predicament, he had done his futile best to rectify the situation, but it had then been too late. A very watchful person had succeeded in stifling his outcries before he could voice an intelligible sentence. Chucklehead! He strained despairingly at his bonds.

However, he had been working at them for at least two hours without the slightest sign of success. The ropes were most securely knotted. He couldn't move his arms an inch from the sides of the chair to which they were pinioned. He couldn't move his legs. The cloth stuffed in his mouth prevented any appreciable sound of his from reaching the outside world, and while he could twist his head from side to side, the accomplishment wasn't of the slightest service to him or to anybody else. He was—to use Mr. Glendon's favored word—*sunk.* Sink, sank, sunk!

Truly an expressive verb . . . After an interminable interval of fretful waiting, the door clicked open and a man entered. He turned on the light and locked the door quietly behind him.

"Still with us, my fine-feathered friend? Glad to see my knots held. I was afraid they wouldn't; Boy Scout tricks aren't my line."

Westborough made no reply. The only sound he was able to achieve was an inarticulate "Gurk," and that scarcely seemed adequate to the situation.

"The gag was my own idea," his tormentor continued. "He would have been satisfied with locking you in here, but I talked him into believing you were really dangerous. You were, brother; dangerous to me. But I gotta hurry before Old Gabbo can ferry over the skullbusters."

Using a key to open the sliding door to the shrine, he pressed the button controlling its electric mechanism and stepped out of sight through the aperture in the wooden panels. With him he carried a large satchel, concerning which Westborough was very sure: (1) that the satchel was at present empty and (2) that it would no longer be so when its owner reascended. The historian strained his lungs to capacity in an attempt to cry for aid.

"Gurk! Gurk! Gurk!"

The miserable sounds died stillborn. Those puny noises, he reflected in lamentation, wouldn't carry even as far as the outside passageway. Presently the man with the satchel reappeared below the shrine. Not stopping to operate the mechanism closing the panel, he walked rapidly to the door.

"Success!" he exclaimed gloatingly. "It should be a quarter of a million. I didn't stop to count it, but that's the amount he drew out of the bank a few months ago—the bank where I was working. The question now before the house is, what's to be done with you?"

Westborough said nothing. "Gurk," wasn't a very helpful suggestion to contribute.

"I could slough you like the rest, but what's the use? It's been curtains for too many lugs here already, and you can't do any damage now. So long, my fine-feathered friend!" he called jauntily as he took his departure. Three or four minutes later the door opened again, and an excited trio rushed into the room. Glendon, the senior Stoner and Ione! All three of them, Westborough saw, were armed with high-powered rifles used for boar shooting.

"Told you he was here!" Glendon exclaimed. "Trussed like a turkey! Where's something to cut him loose?"

Ione remembered there was a knife in the desk which had once been poor Bayard's and deftly slashed the historian's bonds. "Dear me!" the little man exclaimed, smiling his gratitude. "I am very glad to see all of you. Yes, dear me!" He made an attempt to rise, and found he couldn't use his feet because the circulation had been cut off for so long. Glendon assisted him back to his chair, murmuring soothingly. "Take it easy, old-timer! Just tell us who's behind this deviltry."

The two men noticed the yawning panel below the shrine at about the same time. They looked to Ione, but her tanned face showed a puzzlement the equal of theirs. The secret, Westborough mused, had probably been confined to the original four builders. Two of these were dead, one was now on the high sea and the fourth—unless the historian was vastly mistaken—had been stricken tonight with a mysterious malady. It would display many of the symptoms of poisoning by belladonna, but wasn't that dangerous, thank goodness!

Since the blood coursing back to his feet and ankles no longer caused such sharp pain, Westborough made a second and more successful attempt to stand. "The first Knossos had its treasure vaults," he observed, experimentally taking a few strides. "Hence, it shouldn't be surprising to learn that the second also has a strong room. Thanks to Mr. Paphlagloss' illogical mistrust of banks, and his groundless, I hope, fears of the next depression, the coffers were well plenished. But the treasury, I regret to inform you, was looted a bare few minutes ago."

"Well, what are we waiting here for?" Stoner demanded gruffly, leading the way to the door. Westborough tottered hurriedly after his rescuers.

"Not quite so fast, please. I should like to go with you, friends, and haste, while desirable, is not imperative. The looter, I am happy to say, is unable to leave the island."

II

They halted on the bluff where Westborough had stood that afternoon. It was as good a place as any to set their trap.

"How do you know he can't escape?" Stoner broke the silence. "Why are you sure he's coming back this way?"

"He cannot escape," Westborough explained patiently, "because his craft is at present motorless and oarless. I have been lamentably stupid in other matters, but I did not neglect those necessary precautions. He will return, because when he discovers that he has been—is there not .such a word as 'bilked'?—his only chance of leaving the island is to force an entry into the boathouse."

"What if we've already missed him?" Stoner demanded.

"Russ is in there, tinkering with one of the boats," Glendon added tensely. "Alone! He hasn't a gun. If—"

"I'm going to my son," Stoner broke in. He brushed past them all, his rifle held grimly in the crook of his arm. Westborough, able to sympathize with paternal feelings, made no protest, though he wondered if it were strategically wise to split forces at the crucial instant.

"We'd better all go," Ione suggested, expressing a continuation of the historian's own thoughts.

"No!" Glendon whispered. "He's coming now. Keep quiet and duck into the brush!"

Stoner, already pounding pell-mell back to the boathouse, failed to hear the hoarsely muttered injunction. There were only three left to lay the ambush—one unarmed, and one a girl. Something like these thoughts must have flitted through Denis Glendon's mind.

"I'll handle him," he said quietly. "Both of you stay under cover."

"Don't be foolish," Ione cried. "Do you think I'm going to let you be shot just for Alexis?"

Westborough's hand closed with relief on a dry piece of manzanita wood. Though tortuous as the path to heaven, it was of iron hardness, and the historian was confident he would be able to deliver a telling blow with the cudgel, should the need arise to do so. For perhaps a dozen heartbeats, they waited in breathless silence.

Twenty paces away, a man entered their line of vision. Westborough pointed a flashlight; the others, springing from the ground at the same instant, pointed deadlier weapons. "Stay where you are!" Glendon shouted with wholehearted gusto. "Drop that grip! Put up your hands!"

The obedience average to the three commands was .000. With a single startled squawk, their prey vaulted the guardrail and plunged into the ocean, thirty feet below. Immediately Glendon dropped his rifle and whisked off his coat.

"No, Denis, no!" Ione exclaimed, dashing toward him. Glendon poised like a statue on top of the railing. "You can't see to clear the rocks!" the girl screamed. "Don't! It's too—"

But Glendon had already dived. He hit the water with a quick clean splash, and then the sea swallowed him.

Tugging frantically at Westborough's arm, Ione led him down a path that a goat might have found precarious in the daytime. That night, however, it didn't seem exceptionally difficult to either of them. They waited an infinity of seconds before hearing the sound they had been straining their ears to catch—the spatter of a man paddling toward them. It was Glendon, swimming clumsily with one hand and pushing a satchel before him.

"I was lucky!" the artist gasped, scrambling to land. "I missed the rocks, but he didn't. Maybe this overbalanced him. Anyway, he's dead!"

Westborough took possession of the satchel, and Ione took possession of Glendon. After a decent interval had elapsed, the historian ventured a discreet cough.

"Are you sure, Mr. Glendon, that he is dead?"

"I'm sure," Glendon answered soberly. "Split his skull on a rock, poor devil! I pulled him out of the water, but his heart had stopped beating."

"Handleburger?" Westborough inquired. The painter nodded confirmation.

III

Stopping at the boathouse, they found Russell Stoner still toiling vainly on the *Britomartis*, while his father stood guard with a loaded rifle. The speedboat wasn't urgently necessary, Westborough hastened to say. Starr would doubtless return in a few minutes, and Paphlagloss, the historian was able to assure them, could not be in a critically serious condition. He had been drugged, yes, but the drug was one which, while extremely startling in its effects, was rarely fatal unless given in large doses. But too large a dose, Westborough insisted, would have defeated the purpose for which it had been administered.

While Russell washed the black splotches of grease from his sunburned face and Denis changed his dripping clothing, Westborough, Ione and Harvey Stoner restored the treasure to the looted vaults of Knossos. "Amazing!" Stoner exclaimed, giving the dial a brisk twirl. "To think of opening a safe like this without explosives and without the combination!"

"Not without the combination," Westborough corrected, while they were reascending the concealed stairs.

"That thieving butler knew the combination? Impossible!"

Westborough pressed the button which closed the trapdoor and the panel below the shrine. "Before pilfering the safe, it was necessary to pilfer the mind of Doctor Paphlagloss." To this cryptic remark he added nothing more until Denis and Russell had rejoined them in the Indian room.

Arne Nielsen, head bandaged like the figure in the Spirit of '76, came with them, leaning heavily on the two young men. "I am delighted that you are on this side of the grave," Westborough said, bringing a chair. Nielsen grinned sardonically.

"Luckily for me, my skull is a good tough one." He sat down and pressed both hands to his forehead. "I write about stones, and I'm felled by one. Justice, perhaps, but no fun. Lord, how my head aches!"

"I am sorry. If it is any comfort, however, the man who hit you has met retribution."

"He landed on me like the U.S. Navy!" Nielsen complained. "Do you know what this is all about?"

"I am very nearly sure that I do. The resinated wine which Mr. Paphlagloss alone drank concealed the taste of a bitter drug—one very peculiar in its effects. To be specific, an extract of the dried root of a plant native to this island, designated scientifically as *Datura meteloides.*

"The genus Datura has long been known to both hemispheres," Westborough continued, conscious that every eye in the room was now fixed rigidly upon him. "Thugs of the East Indies employed the powdered seeds as a stupefacient. *'Coatlxoxouhqui,'* as the Aztecs termed it, was worshiped as a sacred herb. Priests of various California Indian tribes used the plant as a hypnotic and an intoxicant, and it was through delving into this lore that the late Mr. Bayard learned of the plant's astonishing properties. I can guess for what purpose he brewed his potion—there is a hint in the words of Padre Sahagan, the Mexican chronicler, 'Those who eat it have visions of terrible things'—but we must not be too censorious. A man, as Mr. Bayard himself expressed it, should not be held responsible for every mad thought that enters his brain, and I do not believe Marc ever seriously intended to give it to his enemy. Let us save all of our blame for the other person, far less scrupulous, who found in poor Bayard's mental distress a priceless opportunity."

"What opportunity?" one of the Stoners asked.

"The active principle of datura is a mixture of hyoscine, atropine and hyoscyamine," Westborough answered. "Hyoscine, or scopolamine, more popularly known as the 'truth drug,' has, as I need scarcely remind you, the weird power of submerging areas of the brain controlling volition, while leaving unimpaired the victim's memory, hearing and ability to speak. Plunged by the drug into that queer borderline state between consciousness and unconsciousness, helpless to control his own responses, Mr. Paphlagloss readily yielded the combination of his hidden safe in reply to a simple question."

"It's impossible!" Harvey Stoner objected gruffly. "Mere fantasy!"

"Fantastic, yes, but not impossible. Let me quote briefly from Christoval Acosta's *Tractado de las Drogas y Medicinas de las Indias Orientales.* Acosta, I might say, studied most thoroughly the employment of datura in the East Indies and gave the first account of its properties in 1578. 'He who partakes of it is deprived of his reason . . . often times talking and replying; so that at times he appears to be in his right mind, but really being out of it and not knowing the person to whom he is speaking nor remembering what has happened after his alienation has passed . . . . Truly, if I were to tell stories of what I have heard or seen relating to this matter, and the different ways I have seen people act when under the influence of the drug, I would fill many sheets of paper.' Acosta," Westborough concluded, "adds that he had never seen anyone die from the effects, so I have little doubt but that Mr. Paphlagloss will soon—"

Men trod heavily in the front passageway; men broke into the room with the swiftness of an invading squadron. Captain Cranston was in the van and behind crowded two of his assistants, Constable Stebbins and the weather-beaten Starr. Seldom had Westborough been so delighted as he was with the appearance of this party. The responsibility for the solo investigation had been a heavy burden on his sloping shoulders.

"That's him!" Starr cried, immediately pointing to the historian. "That's the fellow who the boss caught trying to rob him. We think he—"

"We've got some airmail letters for him," Cranston said jovially.

"Letters! Aren't you—"

"Now listen here, Tom. You did us a swell turn when you found us floating in Stebbins' boat with a broken timing gear and brought us over here, but just the same I'm going to handle the thing in my own way. Look over your letters, Professor, and we'll get down to business."

"Have you read them?" Westborough inquired.

Cranston nodded. "Elmer read 'em to me over the phone. They came into Ynez on the afternoon mail, and Mrs. Stebbins held 'em for Elmer to look over, as we'd arranged. We'd have been here long before this, but Elmer was late getting home from Los Angeles, then he had trouble reaching me on the phone, and when we finally did start out for the island in his boat, the engine conked. We'd be drifting in the Pacific yet, if Starr hadn't cruised around to look for us on his return trip. Good thing he—"

But Westborough, deep in the perusal of his two letters,* scarcely heard the long chronicle of difficulty. His conclusions had been justified, he realized a little sorrowfully. He could act, at last, without the fear of doing an irreparable wrong.

He took an accusing step forward..

"You," he said sternly, "killed Charles because he detected you emerging from beneath the shrine. You killed Mr. Bayard, either to steal the datura extract from him or because he suspected you. You schemed for months on a method of securing access to Knossos; you took incredible care in perfecting yourself for your role. But you are an impostor, Mr. Pringar, a notorious criminal! The real Arne Nielsen is spending his summer holidays in Crete!"

PORTION OF STATEMENT OF JEREMY PRINGAR

(Made to Captain Albert Cranston, Bureau of Investigation, Sheriff's Department, Los Angeles County, in connection with the Charles Danville and Marcus Bayard murder cases. Taken in shorthand and transcribed for signature of Mr. Pringar by Investigator Ernest Miller on Thursday night, July 14, at island residence of Alexis Paphlagloss near Ynez, California, in presence of Captain Albert Cranston and Investigator Gerald Brown of the Bureau of Investigation, Sheriff's Department, Elmer Stebbins, Township Constable at Ynez, and T.L. Westborough, an associate in the cases.)

CAPTAIN CRANSTON: It is my duty to warn you that anything you say may be used against you. We promise nothing if you talk, and threaten nothing if you don't. Under those circumstances, will you confess to the murders of Charles Danville and Marc Bayard?

PRINGAR: Under those circumstances—or any circumstances I'm

*NOTE: The reader, if he has carefully followed the clues already given, should have no difficulty in deducing the senders of Westborough's letters and the contents of the two missives.— C.B.C.

not such a fool as to confess to anything.

CAPTAIN CRANSTON: Come now, Pringar, we've got you dead to rights. Westborough sent a sheet of paper containing your fingerprints to Washington, and we've just got your record, airmail, from the Division of Investigation. It's a long sad story, but we'll skip most of it. You're wanted in Baltimore for payroll jobs. Slickly planned! A pal, who was probably this fellow Handleburger, worked in a bank where he could give you the inside dope on deliveries, and you supplied the brainwork and the strong-arm stuff. When Baltimore got too hot to hold you, you skipped. Uncle Sam doesn't know where, but we do. You came to Los Angeles and laid low for the time being. Handleburger got another bank job, and he tipped you off that Paphlagloss had drawn a quarter of a million from his account for nobody knew what reason. A quarter of a million is worth taking some trouble for. You studied Paphlagloss like a book, and then went after him. That's the way we dope it out.

PRINGAR: It's interesting to learn how your mind works.

CAPTAIN CRANSTON: You were sure that Paphlagloss had the cash hidden somewhere on this island, holding it in reserve for the next depression, but the trick was to get yourself invited here. A picture of his Cretan goddess, with some dope about her, was run in the rotogravure section of a local newspaper, and that gave you your starting point. Reach a man through his hobbies! Dale Carnegie gives sound advice there! You traveled all the way back to Pennsylvania so you could write to Paphlagloss from an address in the real Nielsen's home town, and you boned up like a fiend on this Minoan culture business. You even went to the extent of actually writing a book about it. Not a bad job, either, as far as you got. At least, Westborough says it isn't. I wouldn't know.

WESTBOROUGH: Indeed, it is a most creditable piece of work. It is a pity that Mr. Pringar possesses his propensities for criminal activities. Undoubtedly, he would have made a brilliant scholar.

CAPTAIN CRANSTON: Paphlagloss lent you the key to his shrine so you could examine the Cretan figurine, and you stumbled accidentally on the button controlling the electrical mechanism. You sneaked down at night to see where that led to, and the butler caught you coming up while he was making his regular 2 to 3 A.M. prowl of the house. You killed him before he could squawk. Didn't you?

PRINGAR: You're doing very well without my assistance.

CAPTAIN CRANSTON: You'd found the safe, but you couldn't open it, and the butler's murder raised a fuss that damn near blew you into the ocean. In the middle of all your troubles, your old sidekick showed up to make sure you didn't cheat him out of his split. He'd put on an act as a cockney butler, contacted Paphlagloss at the inquest and talked him into hiring him. Figured, probably, that by the time P. got around to checking his forged English references, you'd have the coin and be headed for parts unknown. Handleburger was about as welcome to you as a boil, but you hit on a way to make him earn his keep. He was given the job of doping his boss's wine. Got that idea from Bayard, didn't you? He talked to you freely because you'd shown an interest in his Indian stuff.

WESTBOROUGH: One of the most amazing facets of this remarkable man's character is that, apparently, he does possess a genuine love of knowledge.

CAPTAIN CRANSTON: You killed Bayard, took the datura extract and planted false clues all over the place. The empty tubes that had held the Greek cigarettes were pretty obvious, but the pillar-and-horns business was a good stroke. You got the idea when you found you'd lost a page of your manuscript. You had described the thing there, and you saw a beautiful chance to send Westborough down a blind alley a mile long.

WESTBOROUGH: Which I would have undoubtedly traveled had it not been I, myself, who had stolen the page of your manuscript.

PRINGAR: You stole it?

WESTBOROUGH: I trust you will forgive the theft. It was necessary to send a paper bearing your fingerprints to the National Division of Identification in Washington.

CAPTAIN CRANSTON: Westborough played his hand very well. You thought you had him buffaloed, but he's suspected you for days. The only reason we didn't act before was because he didn't want to involve you in a nasty scandal until he was sure you weren't the real Arne Nielsen.

PRINGAR: I am the real Arne Nielsen.

CAPTAIN CRANSTON: That gag's worn thinner than the seat of a bookkeeper's pants. Here's an airmail letter from the dean of Prescott University. He says that Doctor Arne Nielsen is now in Crete, gathering data for a new book to succeed his *Minoan Culture.* We've got you, Pringar, every way you step. You might as well come clean.

PRINGAR: Indeed? Did I also give myself this severe head injury in order to throw you gentlemen—if I may apply the term loosely—still further from the track?

CAPTAIN CRANSTON: I'll say you didn't! That was the work of your pal, Handleburger, who trusted you just about as far as he'd trust a rattlesnake. As soon as Paphlagloss had piped up with the combination, he knocked you cold and ran downstairs to pull the job by himself. He didn't hit you hard enough to kill—he's squeamish about murder—but he didn't mind leaving you here to take the rap for the whole thing. Nice friends you've got, Pringar!

PRINGAR: Where's Handleburger now?

CAPTAIN CRANSTON: Why do you want to know?

PRINGAR: Natural curiosity.

CAPTAIN CRANSTON: You're afraid he's squawked.

PRINGAR: There's simply no use talking to a man laboring under such delusions.

CAPTAIN CRANSTON: Do you still claim you're the real Arne Nielsen?

PRINGAR: I not only claim it, I submit as evidence my manuscript, not yet completed unfortunately, "The Derivation of the Asiatic Mother Goddess from the Baetylic Cult of Neolithic Crete." Without bragging unnecessarily, I contend that only the real Arne Nielsen could write this work.

CAPTAIN CRANSTON: Tell him where he slipped up, Westborough.

WESTBOROUGH: Doctor Nielsen has written a volume entitled *The Greece of Homeric Ages,* has he not?

PRINGAR: I wrote such a volume.

WESTBOROUGH: Then you will not mind if I test your knowledge of Homer by quoting one or two selections? Here is the first: "And Phaedra and Procris I saw, and fair-haired Ariadne, daughter of the baleful Minos, whom Theseus bore from Crete to the hill of sacred Athens, yet gat no joy of her." The second is of approximately the same length. "The glorious lame god did devise a dancing-floor like that which in broad Knossos Daidalos wrought for Ariadne of the fair tresses." One quotation is from the *Iliad,* the other from the *Odyssey.* Will you be kind enough to tell me which is which?

PRINGAR: The first is from the *Iliad* and the second from the *Odyssey.*

WESTBOROUGH: Your memory is most excellent, Mr. Pringar; that is exactly what I informed you last Sunday morning. The first passage, however, is from the *Odyssey;* obviously, since Ariadne was certainly dead at the time of the Trojan War, a mention of the visit to Hades. The second passage is from the *Iliad*; the dancing-floor devised by "the glorious lame god" can refer only to the Shield of Achilles. My mistakes of last Sunday were made purposely. I knew that the author of *The Greece of Homeric Ages* would correct such egregrious blunders at once, but you failed to mention them. Hence, I was reasonably certain that you were only a very clever impostor. Scholarship, Mr. Pringar, goes more than skin-deep.

EPILOGUE

WESTBOROUGH'S OVERTAXED HEART, collapsing after the release of the tension, compelled the historian to spend the next two days in bed. During the period, Denis Glendon completed his mural in a burst of fevered activity, so the two were ready to leave the island at the same time. The painter waited at the *Ariadne* while Westborough paused on the shore end of the pier for a few final words with his host, now fully recovered from the strange effects of the datura-doctored vintage.

"Isn't there one little thing I can do in return?" Paphlagloss asked gruffly.

"Yes, if you please." Westborough had been planning all forenoon the best manner of broaching the delicate subject. "Mr. Glendon risked his life to recover your property from the ocean. If you—"

"All taken care of." The Minos twirled his mustache in jovial condescension. "When he unpacks, he'll find an unexpected bonus. I slipped it into his bag this morning."

But no amount of money, the historian pondered, is adequate compensation for broken dreams. "Dear, dear, dear!" he thought. "It seemed so right the other evening, but it has all gone wrong. I am sorry for them both, but dear me. What can one do?"

He blew his nose self-consciously.

"I meant something for yourself," the Minos specified.

"Be kind to your daughter," Westborough said gently. "She is—a very lovely person."

The Minos stiffened immediately. It is useless to expect people to change, Westborough reflected tristfully. Trees bowed by the wind resume their original erectness directly the storm is over. Only in story books are permanent reformations possible.

"Russell will make her a good husband. I must say that I am pleased with the boy. Very pleased! From what I hear, he came through the other night with flying colors."

"Yes," Westborough agreed. He liked Russell Stoner better than he had—a great deal better, in fact—but still . . .

"Shall we go?" he said aloud.

They strolled to the end of the pier, where Glendon paced restlessly. Though good-bys had already been said at the house, the three men shook hands all over again, anticlimactically waiting the arrival of the *Ariadne's* pilot.

Until Tom Starr descended the long flight of stairs from the gleaming portals of Knossos, the Minos was ruddy, genial and hearty—in all respects the ideal host wishing Godspeed to the ideal guests. But when he saw his caretaker bowed beneath the weight of a great quantity of matched luggage his expression changed at once. For Westborough's battered bags and Glendon's cheap suitcases were already within the *Ariadne's* hold, and this luggage was new, expensive and unmistakably feminine. Grinning sheepishly, Starr opened a hatch and began the task of stowing it in the speedboat's stern.

Paphlagloss glowered at the baggage-loader and followed that up by glowering at each separate piece of impedimenta. Being of the generation which says, "What does this mean?" he spoke those words now, and glowered—most fiercely of all—at his tall daughter.

"Simply that I've made up my mind, Alexis," Ione explained quietly. She was dressed in a dark green traveling outfit which suited her perfectly.

"Your *mind?*" her father fumed. "*Your* mind? What mind?"

"I don't intend to found a dynasty, and I don't intend to mother a litter of department stores. I'm marrying Denis!"

The purple splotch, which had already formed on the Minos' thick neck, suffused the whole of his face. "You won't get a thing from me," he informed her in a choked voice.

She jumped lightly into a leather-upholstered seat. "We're young, healthy, and we love each other," she called up to him. "Who cares about the rest? I've learned, Alexis, that you can't have it all, so I'm choosing what I want most, and that's Denis."

"Darling!" Glendon exclaimed, springing into the boat beside her. He began to say the foolish things young men think of when they are in love. Paphlagloss cuttingly turned his back.

Westborough clambered into the front seat, Starr took the wheel, the motor roared into noisy animation, and the *Ariadne* leaped like a live thing through the myriad dancing sparkles. Spray encrusted Westborough's gold-rimmed bifocals. When he had restored them to a fit state for vision, only the tops of the ridges were visible above the silver girdle that veiled the Island of Minos.

But the historian did not notice; he was thinking of the island's ruler as he had last stood on the pier—aloof, lonely, implacable. Westborough was just a little sorry for Alexis Paphlagloss.

And presently even the mottled hills faded away.

THE END

BIBLIOGRAPHY

Sources used by the author for *Murder Gone Minoan*

BAIKIE, THE REVEREND JAMES
Life of the Ancient East, The—1923
Sea-Kings of Crete, The—1926
BELL, EDWARD
Prehellenic Architecture in the Aegean—1926
BREASTED, JAMES HENRY
Ancient Times—A History of the Early World—1916
BURN, A. R.
Minoans, Philistines, and Greeks—1930
ENCYCLOPAEDIA BRITANNICA
EVANS, ARTHUR, J., SIR
Palace of Minos, The (4 volumes)—1921-1936
Prehistoric Tombs of Knossos, The—1906
FORSDYKE, E. J.
Minoan Art—1929
FRAZER, JAMES GEORGE, SIR
Golden Bough, The (Volumes IV, V, VI)—1919
FULTZ, FRANCIS M.
Elfin-Forest of California, The—1923
GARDNER, HELEN
Art Through the Ages—1916
GLASGOW, GEORGE
Minoans, The—1923
GLOTZ, GUSTAVE
Aegean Civilization, The—1925
HAMMERTON, J. A.
Wonders of the Past (Volumes I and II)—1923
HAWES, CHARLES H. and HARRIET BOYD
Crete, the Forerunner of Greece—1922
HOLDER, CHARLES FREDERICK
Channel Islands of California, The—1910
KROEBER, A. L.
Handbook of the Indians of California—1925
LOOMIS, ALFRED F.
Hotspur's Cruise in the Aegean—1931
MAGOFFIN, R. V. D. and DAVIS, EMILY C.
Magic Spades—1929
MOSSO, ANGELO
Palaces of Crete and Their Builders, The—1907
ROGERS, DAVID BANKS
Prehistoric Man of the Santa Barbara Coast—1929

SAFFORD, WILLIAM E.
Daturas of the Old World and New: An Account of Their Narcotic Properties and Their Use in Oracular and Initiatory Ceremonies (Annual Report of the Board of Regents of the Smithsonian Institution—1920)
ST. HUBERT, R. LA MONTAGNE
Art of Fresco Painting, The—1924
WALKER, EDWIN F.
Indians of Southern California—1937
WEBSTER, HUTTON
Ancient Civilization—1931

About The Rue Morgue Press

The Man from Tibet (0-915230-17-8), an earlier case featuring Professor Westborough, is also available from the Rue Morgue Press, which specializes in reprinting vintage mysteries from the 1930s to the 1950s. To suggest titles or to obtain a catalog of their publications, write: The Rue Morgue Press, P.O. Box 4119, Boulder, CO 80306.